Praise for Lenora Worth and her novels

"*Secret Agent Minister*, by Lenora Worth,
is a fun- and danger-filled treat,
with love blossoming along the way."
—*RT Book Reviews*

"This second in the Texas Ranger Justice
series solves one mystery as it
skillfully advances the ongoing one."
—*RT Book Reviews* on *Body of Evidence*,
a *New York Times* bestseller

"This is a suspenseful and exciting story
about love in all its forms."
—*RT Book Reviews* on *Heart of the Night*

"[P]lenty of action and a nicely done reunion between
two people in love who were unavoidably parted."
—*RT Book Reviews* on *Risky Reunion*

SO...
MEMORIAL LIBRARY
14680 DIX-TOLEDO ROAD
SOUTHGATE, MI 48195

D0830490

LENORA WORTH
Secret Agent Minister

❦

Deadly Texas Rose

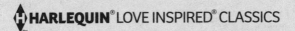

♦ HARLEQUIN® LOVE INSPIRED® CLASSICS

If you purchased this book without a cover you should be aware that this book is stolen property. It was reported as "unsold and destroyed" to the publisher, and neither the author nor the publisher has received any payment for this "stripped book."

Recycling programs
for this product may
not exist in your area.

™ LOVE INSPIRED BOOKS

ISBN-13: 978-0-373-65161-0

SECRET AGENT MINISTER AND DEADLY TEXAS ROSE
Copyright © 2013 by Harlequin Books S.A.

The publisher acknowledges the copyright holder
of the individual works as follows:

SECRET AGENT MINISTER
Copyright © 2007 by Lenora H. Nazworth

DEADLY TEXAS ROSE
Copyright © 2008 by Lenora H. Nazworth

All rights reserved. Except for use in any review, the reproduction or utilization of this work in whole or in part in any form by any electronic, mechanical or other means, now known or hereafter invented, including xerography, photocopying and recording, or in any information storage or retrieval system, is forbidden without the written permission of the editorial office, Love Inspired Books, 233 Broadway, New York, NY 10279 U.S.A.

This is a work of fiction. Names, characters, places and incidents are either the product of the author's imagination or are used fictitiously, and any resemblance to actual persons, living or dead, business establishments, events or locales is entirely coincidental.

This edition published by arrangement with Love Inspired Books.

® and ™ are trademarks of Love Inspired Books, used under license. Trademarks indicated with ® are registered in the United States Patent and Trademark Office, the Canadian Trade Marks Office and in other countries.

www.LoveInspiredBooks.com

Printed in U.S.A.

CONTENTS

Books by Lenora Worth

LENORA WORTH

has written more than forty books for three different publishers. Her career with Love Inspired Books spans close to fifteen years. In February 2011 her Love Inspired Suspense novel *Body of Evidence* made the *New York Times* bestseller list. Her very first Love Inspired title, *The Wedding Quilt*, won *Affaire de Coeur*'s Best Inspirational for 1997, and *Logan's Child* won an *RT Book Reviews* Best Love Inspired for 1998. With millions of books in print, Lenora continues to write for the Love Inspired and Love Inspired Suspense lines. Lenora also wrote a weekly opinion column for the local paper and worked freelance for years with a local magazine. She has now turned to full-time fiction writing and enjoying adventures with her retired husband, Don. Married for thirty-six years, they have two grown children. Lenora enjoys writing, reading and shopping…especially shoe shopping.

SECRET AGENT MINISTER

Do they not go astray who devise evil? But mercy and truth belong to those who devise good.

—*Proverbs* 14:22

To Merline Lovelace and the participants
of her workshop Four Steps to Perfect Plots
at the 2006 Written In The Stars NOLA STARS
(North Louisiana Storytellers and Authors)
conference. Thanks to all of you for
giving me this story idea!
And special thanks and acknowledgment to
paratroop and skydiving instructor Jim Bates at
aero.com for his help on how to "let go of a plane."
Any mistakes were my own!

ONE

Someone was going to have to explain about the dead body in the bathtub. *Really.* That thought kept running through Lydia Cantrell's head as she looked from the grotesque body of a wide-eyed dead man wearing a bloody suit to the shock-filled stare of the surprised and *very alive* man standing in front of her.

Then her practical mind went into overdrive. She would probably have to explain how she'd wound up in Pastor Dev's hotel room late at night, only to find him wearing a bright red action-figure T-shirt and old, faded jeans, while staring at the body in the tub, his expression filled with shock and something else Lydia couldn't quite figure out, something that looked like anger and resolve. Since she'd never seen Pastor Dev angry, she couldn't grasp what was happening or the strange look she saw in his deep blue eyes.

And she certainly couldn't grasp his attire. Lydia rarely saw Pastor Devon Malone dressed in anything other than a nice suit and interesting tie, so she was a bit taken aback, seeing him in jeans and a T-shirt and realizing that the man was built like a regular weight lifter and football jock all rolled into one mighty good-looking package. That, and the body in the tub, really set Lydia into a tizzy.

But she *had* come here for a reason. A very legitimate reason. They were supposed to go over Pastor Dev's notes for his speech the next day. They were attending a statewide religious conference in Atlanta, Georgia. That's why Lydia was in his hotel room tonight—to help him go over his notes and make sure his speech was tip-top.

Pastor Dev was funny that way. He was thorough and very detail oriented. He liked to do things the right way. Some implied he was a perfectionist, but Lydia called that just plain hardworking and dedicated. That's why the man was such a good minister. His speech, entitled "Pastoral—Finding Inner Peace in a Troubled World" would, of course, be excellent. Everything about Pastor Dev was excellent, in Lydia's mind, at least. Which was why she refused to believe there was a dead man in the room, or that Pastor Dev had anything whatsoever to do with it.

Closing her eyes to the image of the dead man, Lydia thought about how people would react to a young, impressionable girl of twenty-five visiting a single man's hotel room late at night, but she kept telling herself this was all beyond reproach—if you didn't count murder, of course. This was Pastor Dev, after all. Even the church matrons who'd ridden the bus up to Atlanta with them had given this meeting their blessings. Because they knew Lydia and the pastor had work to do—God's work. And because Pastor Dev was always a perfect gentleman. Everyone knew that.

And there had been a chaperone present—Pastor Dev's roommate. Except his roommate and mentor, Pastor Charles Pierson from Savannah, was in no shape to chaperone, since he was the dead man in the bathtub.

Lydia thought about all the people who had put their trust in Pastor Dev and her. This certainly wouldn't sit well with the church members back home in Dixon, Georgia. It was where Pastor Dev preached and Lydia worked as his secretary ever since she'd come back with a business degree from the University of Georgia.

And she'd worked hard to get the job at the First Church of Dixon, because she had decided instead of building a career in some big company with stock options and a great 401K plan, she wanted to work for Pastor Dev. She'd fallen in love with him one Christmas during her senior year at UGA, when she'd met him at her parents' annual Christmas Eve open house. He was the new preacher, single and just a few years older than Lydia. And he was so good and sweet and kind, she knew immediately that he was the man she wanted to spend the rest of her life with.

Only, he still didn't know that. Because, though

Lydia made goo-goo eyes at him all the time and twirled her long, dark blond hair each time he came to stand by her desk back in the church office, he'd never once noticed a thing about her or her feelings. He was always too preoccupied with taking care of church members—he was so very dedicated that way.

Lydia felt safe with Pastor Dev. He was such a mild-mannered, quiet man, and she just knew she was perfectly safe with him even now, with that horrible body staring up at them.

But she had to admit things looked mighty suspicious with Pastor Dev standing there all shocked and surprised and looking from the body back to her with a kind of dread.

Finally, Lydia managed to speak. "I know you didn't kill that man, Pastor Dev. Please tell me you didn't kill your roommate?"

"Of course I didn't do this, Lydia," he replied, a soft plea in his words. Then he just stared at the body, that strange look on his face.

While she waited for an explanation, Lydia reminded herself that Pastor Dev was so quiet and focused, so kind and polite, so good and solid, that he could never lift a hand in brutality or violence toward another human being. The man was a walking example of what being a true Christian was all about. Period. End of discussion.

So, Lydia asked another question. "If you didn't kill your friend, then who did?"

* * *

Devon Malone heard the doubt in Lydia's appeal. And because he couldn't explain things, he repeated his words. "Lydia, I didn't do this. You have to believe me."

Lydia Cantrell, of the South Georgia we-pioneers-settled-this-town-with-wagons-and-mules Cantrells, apparently wanted to believe him. She bobbed her head. "I do believe you. I do, Pastor Dev. But—"

He grabbed her by the hand, hauling her into the room as he shut the door. Which really threw him and her both, since he had never tried to touch her, not even so much as touch a strand of her hair or press his fingers along her arm as he opened a door for her. He'd always followed proper decorum when it came to his relationship with Lydia. But now, he had her by the arm, tugging her along with him as he grabbed equipment and weapons out of a steel briefcase. A briefcase he'd hoped never to use again.

Lydia looked at him in surprise. "What's with all those fancy gadgets?" When he didn't respond, she said, "You don't even carry a cell phone like most normal human beings."

It was true. He rarely bothered to use the computer they'd had installed two years ago at the church office. He mostly devoted his time to reading the Word and taking care of members' needs and visitation. Dev was a stickler about visitation—always going out amongst his flock, sharing their good and bad times. Graduations—even from kindergarten—

weddings, births, medical emergencies, cataract surgeries, deaths, anniversaries, christenings, baseball games, soccer matches, birthdays and retirements. You name it, Pastor Dev was there to celebrate it. The rest of the time, he worked on preaching the word of the Lord. And while he preached and tried to forget the past, Lydia sat in her same pew each and every Sunday, as devoted as ever. She was like a guiding light out in the congregation. A guiding light he refused to lose, ever. And now, she'd been exposed to the ugly side of his life. The secret life. This could get very messy, very fast.

As Lydia watched Pastor Dev gather strange little gadgets involving beepers and bullets, they heard a commotion at the hotel room door.

"Don't open it," he said, his fingers working at loading weapons and clicking against a slick cell phone. His whole expression had changed. He looked dangerous.

Lydia watched, awe and fear overcoming her. "What's going on?"

He grabbed her again. "Lydia, do you trust me?"

She didn't even have to think about that. "Of course I do, Pastor Dev."

"Then you need to listen to me and follow my instructions, do you understand?"

She bobbed her head. "Yes. But—"

He hushed her with a finger to his lips. "No questions now. No time to explain. We have to get out of here."

"Excuse me?"

"I have to take you with me. They must be watching. They probably saw you come into the room. You're in danger."

"Oh, okay."

Lydia was completely baffled now. Why was she in danger and where was he taking her? And why on earth was Pastor Dev talking to her in that *Mission: Impossible* kind of voice, so intense and husky and brusque, so very different from his regular soft-spoken drawl?

"What's happening?" she managed to squeak out, even as they heard the banging on the door again. "Is this some sort of joke? I know how you and your buddies like to pull jokes on each other."

"No joke, Lydia," Pastor Dev said, guiding her to the adjoining room. And he now had a big gun in his hand. A sleek-looking gun with a long, thin barrel. It reminded her of something out of a spy movie. And she had no idea where it had been before. Probably inside that steel case he had hidden inside his real suitcase. Good thing they'd taken the bus to Atlanta. He never would have made it onto an airplane with all those gadgets or that gun.

Because Lydia stood frozen, staring at the gun, Dev shook her gently. "Lydia, I need you to be alert. Stay focused, okay?"

"Uh-huh."

"We have to get out of here."

"Uh-huh."

"Lydia, honey, are you with me?"

He moved close enough to see the solid fear in her pretty eyes. "Lydia?"

"I'm with you," she whispered, slowly moving her head again. "But I sure would like to know why we're getting out of here. I mean, we can't just leave your friend in the bathtub. We should call the police. We should—"

"No police," he said, his tone firm. "I'll explain everything later, I promise," he added in a soft whisper, his fingers brushing through her bangs.

She nodded and said, "Okay."

Then Dev reminded himself that she was probably in shock. Things had taken a distinctively different swing from the original plans. And getting Lydia involved in a life he'd tried to put behind him was definitely not in the plans. But he couldn't change that right now. He could only try to protect her.

"Let's go," he said, throwing a dark shirt toward her. "Put this on to camouflage yourself."

Lydia put on the shirt. "This smells like your laundry detergent," she said as he tugged at her sleeves. "I know which brand you use. I saw it on your to-do list one day. Not that I'd ever snoop."

Dev ignored her chatter. Let her chat. Lydia was a talker, especially when she got nervous. Right now, he had to focus; he had to get her out of here. "Button up," he ordered, keeping his tone firm.

She hurriedly buttoned the big shirt over her demure summer sweater, a dazed expression on her face.

"Ready?" he asked, his no-nonsense gaze focused on her as he looked directly into her hazel eyes. Dev wondered if she knew how much she meant to him. He'd have to tell her one day.

She nodded and held tight to her tote bag. "I think so."

Dev worked quickly to get them through the locked door to the empty room adjoining theirs. Putting a finger to his lips, he motioned for Lydia to stay quiet as he waited for the right moment. They managed to sneak down the hall just as the intruders came bursting into the other room.

"We're going to take the stairs down to the street," he explained, his voice back to normal now. Almost too normal. He stayed calm and in control, for Lydia's sake, but taking fourteen flights down to the street wasn't exactly a leisurely stroll. And leaving a room with his dead best friend in it wasn't too good, either. But he'd deal with that later. Much later.

"Okay," Lydia said. What else could she say, since she couldn't take her chances on the elevator and meet up with those Very Bad Guys? Her mama and daddy didn't raise a complete idiot, after all.

So down the stairs they went, flying so fast Lydia wondered if her sensible black Easy Spirit pumps were even touching the steps. But she was glad they were durable enough for someone on the run. She was amazed she didn't even get a blister. And she was also amazed that they didn't get shot. Lydia could hear the Very Bad Guys clunking down the stairs above them, the sound echoing like a death knell each time they rounded another floor. Then just as they reached the seventh floor, she felt the whiz and ping of a bullet ricocheting off the stairwell, very close to her head.

Screaming, Lydia put a hand up, as if that would stop a bullet from killing her. The look in Pastor Dev's eyes told her the same thing. For once, the man looked scared. Scared for her, since he grabbed her and held her tight.

"Keep running, Lydia," Pastor Dev said to her, pushing her in front of him. Of course, he would be the gentleman, even in such a desperate life-or-death situation, so he naturally put himself in harm's way between her and the VBGs. That was a relief, until she started worrying that he'd get shot and then he'd be dead and she'd never grow old with him, or have his babies or be able to be the pastor's wife like she'd dreamed about for the last few years. Not to mention, the VBGs would still be after her. And she'd be all alone, wondering how she'd somehow wound up in Pastor Dev's hotel room with a dead body in the bathtub. Not to mention, having to explain all of that to the entire congregation.

But, she thought as she ran ahead of him, hadn't Pastor Dev asked her to trust him? Knowing that there was much more to this story, Lydia put her trust in God, praying to Him to help them out of this situation. Right now she only knew three things for sure. She was still in love with Pastor Dev, the Very Bad Guys were still chasing them and they were both in a whole lot of trouble.

TWO

So now they were on MARTA—the Metro Atlanta Rapid Transit System—heading north. Lydia was riding through the city on a commuter train at a very fast speed, sitting by a man she thought she knew. But, she realized as she watched Pastor Dev jab at a sleek black PDA, she didn't really know this man at all. Since when had he owned a BlackBerry, for goodness' sake? Her mama would laugh out loud at that notion.

Thinking of her mama and daddy back in Dixon, Lydia felt hot tears pricking at her eyes. She normally was a stand-up kind of girl, good in a pinch, solid in a crisis. But she had to admit, this was a bit much even for someone with her strong constitution. She didn't know what to do, so she clutched at her loaded tote bag, glad, at least, that she had her own supply of obsessive-compulsive ammunition tucked into the many pockets and packets inside. She had a cell phone—that might come in handy. She had Tylenol and Advil and a little bit of touch-up makeup.

Okay, that was maybe a bit vain, but Lydia liked to look her best around Pastor Dev. Which meant she also had some of those travel toothpaste samples. And sample sizes of everything from deodorant to hair spray—all bought with her hard-earned money at the big discount store out on Highway 19 back in Dixon. And boy, had she earned her salary tonight, she thought, her feet hurting from all that pounding and running all over Atlanta.

And she also had a combination diary and day-book, which she was itching to record in right now. She'd always kept a diary, since she'd been old enough to form letters, as her mama liked to tell it. This mess tonight was gonna be a doozy of a story, she decided. But she wasn't at all sure how it was going to end.

By this time, it was very late and she was so tired she could barely hold her eyes open, so she missed the blur of skyscrapers that turned into suburbs as they headed out away from the city. She missed the ancient old oaks and the tall pines whizzing by. She didn't even notice the constant stream of traffic along Interstate 75. All she could see was her own shocked reflection in the dark window of the train. That and the image of Pastor Pierson's bloody body. She wanted to cry about that, but she couldn't find the tears. Yet. So she prayed for the dead minister, and for the evil person who had killed him.

Lydia had never felt so alone and frightened, even

if Pastor Dev did seem like he could handle this situation.

Then it hit her—she could at least call her parents and let them know she was all right. She started digging in her tote, then proudly pulled out the little silver picture phone she'd bought at the big mall in Albany.

Dev watched her, knowing what he was about to do would only confuse her even more. He grabbed her hand, then gently took her phone away. "Don't do that, Lydia."

"I need to call my parents," she said, giving him a hurt look.

Dev figured she was wondering why he seemed so distant and businesslike. But he had to think; he had to figure out a way to get her out of this mess.

Lydia's hurt soon changed into frustration. Just a tad irritated, she said, "Give me my phone back, please."

"Not just yet," he said, pulling out his own top-of-the-line, state-of-the-art, shiny black Treo. "We have to wait for further instructions."

Further instructions?

"Oh, okay." She gave him a wide-eyed look after he pocketed her plain little phone.

Dev hated to treat her this way, but if she called home, they could easily pinpoint the signal. "I know you think I'm crazy," he said, a twist of a smile playing at his lips, "but it's very important that you do not make contact with anyone. It's too dangerous, not just for you but for your family, too. Do you understand?"

"Too dangerous?" She stared over at him, her shock evident, her disbelief shimmering in her eyes. "Oh, okay," she said, not looking okay at all. "Honestly, you sound so condescending. I'm not some child about to have a tantrum." Before he could respond, she gave him a no-nonsense look. "You know what? I've had about enough of this game. You need to tell me what on earth is going on. Because I'm tired, I'm hungry and I'm getting mighty cranky. And that won't be good for either of us."

Now she had Dev's complete attention. Apparently, he wasn't the only one who could change from mild mannered to dead serious in the blink of an eye. Thinking he'd better do something quick to calm her bad mood and make up for his rudeness, and because he didn't have time for theatrics, he gave her a long once-over look, then pulled her against him and said, "Rest."

"Huh?"

Not a very sophisticated response, Dev thought, but she had been fighting mad, so now she probably felt a bit off-kilter and befuddled by his quick mood change.

"Rest, Lydia," he said again, reaching around to tug her head against his shoulder. She felt like a small, fragile doll in his arms. "Just rest and then I'll explain everything. You don't deserve any of this, but you do deserve some answers."

"I sure do," she said into his T-shirt, causing him to become very much aware of her nearness. Then she mumbled, "Where'd you get this shirt, anyway? You never wear T-shirts, except during basketball camp and volleyball games."

Dev decided he could at least talk about that, hoping it would make her forgive him for dragging her all over Atlanta. "My nephew, Scotty, gave it to me. To keep me safe."

Something about that confession must have tugged at Lydia's heart. Her next words were all husky with a little catch of emotion. "That is so sweet." Then she glanced up at him, her pretty face angled close to his. "I didn't even know you have a nephew."

"He's six." He felt the rumble of surprise moving through her. He didn't talk about Scotty much. "My sister's kid. They live up north. I don't get to see them much, but at least he's safe. Last time I visited, he was having an anxiety attack about starting first grade. I gave him a little pep talk and told him he was my hero. I knew he would be strong and courageous, for his mother's sake."

Dev heard her let out a sigh, then he held his breath as she snuggled deeper in his arms. He'd never realized how fresh her shampoo smelled—like apples and cinnamon.

"Now Scotty loves school. He told his mom I helped him to be strong. He wanted me to feel safe, too, so he sent me this shirt for my birthday. I promised him I'd always carry it with me whenever I travel. I just slipped it on tonight, because, well, because I miss him and I had him on my mind."

He wanted Lydia to understand that Scotty's safety was important to him. Just as her safety was important to him, too. So maybe she could forgive him for being so brusque with her before. "I'm sorry, Lydia."

"For what?"

"For snapping at you. I have to protect you. I'm responsible for you."

"It's okay," she said, her words sounding sleepy. "That must be a very special shirt."

"It is. Scotty told me he said a prayer for me when he helped his mother wrap it."

"Now that just makes me want to cry," she whispered.

Dev prayed she didn't do that. But her voice sounded shaky. "I'm glad your shirt is so blessed." Then she wiggled closer and drifted off to sleep, the rattle and hum of the fast-moving train seeming to soothe her frazzled nerves.

Dev closed his eyes, too, then he kissed the top of her head while he held her there in his arms, against his blessed shirt.

Lydia woke with a start, trying to remember where she was. When she looked up to find Pastor Dev staring down at her, and looked down to find herself settled nicely into the crook of his strong arm, she gasped and sat straight up. "What—"

"The train's stopping. End of the line. We get off here," Pastor Dev explained. A little old lady across the aisle smiled over at them.

And as usual Lydia said, "Oh, okay." Until she remembered everything that had happened—dead body, bad guys, strange gadgets, a memory of a gentle kiss on her hair—she'd have to get back to that one. "Where are we?"

"Somewhere north of Atlanta," he replied as he tugged her to her feet. "Near Roswell, I believe." But he wasn't looking at her. Instead, he glanced all around, his dark eyes on full-alert mode. But he was kind enough to let that little old blue-haired lady pass first. He checked the front of the passenger car, and the back, again and again. He gave other passengers a hard, daring stare which seemed to make all of them quake in their boots. Except the grandma. She simply smiled her sweet, wrinkled smile and held on to her sensible black purse as she slowly ambled her way toward the train doors.

Pastor Dev did one more search. "I think we're safe. Let's go."

So they got off MARTA along with a few other people—probably night workers coming home from the city. It was very late, actually early morning, the wee hours, as Lydia's mama would say. She'd never stayed out this late in her life, even in all her sorority days at UGA. But then, she reminded herself, things on this night were not at all what they seemed.

And neither was the man pulling her away from the cluster of passengers heading to their parked cars or waiting rides. She worried about the old woman. Did she have a ride home? Was she all alone in the world?

But Pastor Dev didn't give Lydia time to visit with the old woman. Lydia watched as the spry woman shuffled off in another direction.

"What now?" she asked, breathless from being tugged at a fast-footed pace across the cracked commuter parking lot.

Pastor Dev stopped underneath a large oak tree. As if right on cue, his fancy phone beeped. "Yes?" he said into the phone. Then he said something really odd. "Have we put out a search for any lost sheep?"

She had to blink at that one. But she'd figured out not to ask questions, not when he was in that instruction mode, anyway. So she just listened. That's how she'd learned so much in school. She was a good listener.

"Copy," he said into the phone. Then, "Where is the way to the dwelling of light?"

If Lydia hadn't known better, she would have thought he was quoting scripture. Job, if she remembered correctly. She had always been good at memorizing Bible passages back in Sunday school.

But then he said, "Yes, I understand." And that was that.

"We have to go," he told her after he put the tiny phone away. "I have to get you to a safe place."

She looked around. The train was gone. The carpoolers and night-shift workers were gone. They were all alone at a train station somewhere in North Georgia. She glanced around, seeing the lights of the city miles away. "How are we going to get out of here?"

"We walk," he said, as if this was the most normal thing in the world. Then he kept right on talking in that calm, normal voice. "It's not seemly—you and I running off together. I have to consider your reputation. I need to get you to a safe house where there are highly trained chaperones who can help me watch over you. Before I leave."

That got her dander up. "What did you say?" she asked, stopping and digging her heels into the asphalt. It still felt warm from the spring day. Or maybe that heat was coming from the steam rising inside of her.

He turned, let out a sigh. "Lydia, you shouldn't be here. I would never forgive myself if something happened to you."

And because that kind of sounded as if he cared about her just a tiny bit, she cut him some slack. But she still needed answers. "Nothing will happen to me if you'll just tell me the truth."

He stood there, his eyes touching on her face before he glanced off into the darkness. "We need to find a vehicle."

"No, you need to tell me the truth." She skipped two beats, giving him ample time to chime right in, then she let him have it good and proper. "Look, Pastor Dev, I've known you for close to three years now and…well, never in those three years have you ever so much as raised your voice at me. But tonight, tonight, something changed. I mean, besides the dead man in your bathtub and that big, scary gun and those goons chasing us. *You* changed right in front of my eyes. And I do believe that means you owe me some kind of explanation." Then she took off, her pumps pounding pavement. "You can talk while we walk."

He caught up with her right away, reaching for her swinging arm. "Okay, all right. But the less you know, the safer you'll be."

"I can't be safe if I don't know what I'm fighting."

He considered that for a minute. "You're right. And you're a very smart woman."

"Well, at least you've noticed that about me."

That comment made him frown in that kind of confused way men do when they don't understand the underlying meaning. But she let it slide. As much as she'd like to have had a real heart-to-heart with the man, what she needed more was concrete information.

"Go on," she said, coaxing him like a teacher coaxing a kindergartner.

"You're right about me. I'm not what I seem."

"I got that right after you pulled out that big gun," she snapped back. "Not to mention the dead man."

He frowned again, a new respect for her in his eyes. "Before I came to Dixon, I was…something besides a preacher."

"Uh-huh. What?"

He let out a breath. "After I got out of seminary school, I was approached by a very elite organization and asked if I'd like to join their ranks." He shrugged. "I fit the profile exactly. Athletic, excellent grades, exemplary conduct. Single and young. And very devoted to the Lord."

"You do fit all those qualifications," she blurted out. Then she put a hand over her big mouth. "Keep talking."

He gave her another strange look, but continued, "This organization is so top secret that I couldn't even tell my immediate family what I would be doing. I had to use a cover."

"A cover?" Lydia shot a glance over at him. He looked completely sincere. "You mean, like a spy?"

"Yes, something like that. But more like a Christian operative."

"A Christian operative?"

"Yes. I'm like a soldier, only I don't work for the government. I work for the church."

"You're a soldier? For the church?"

She knew she sounded stupid, but Pastor Dev didn't look at her as if she were stupid. Instead, he looked at her as if he were hoping she'd understand. Which she didn't.

"I know it sounds like something out of a science fiction novel, but I'm telling you the truth. And before I go any further, you have to promise you will not divulge anything I'm telling you. It could mean your life."

She stopped on the side of the road. "Well, when you put it that way—"

He whirled her around so fast she felt as though she was back on that train. "I'm serious, Lydia. This is not a game. We are in a very dangerous situation."

The way he looked at her gave her hope, even while his words scared her silly. He looked as though he really cared about her. "Okay," she said in a tiny voice. "I'm sorry."

Then he touched a hand to her hair, sending nice little shivers down her backbone. "No, I'm the one who's sorry. I shouldn't have gotten you involved in this."

"I'm here now," she said, her practical nature taking over. "Might as well spill the rest, so I can be prepared."

He smiled then. "That's what I like about you. You are so organized and sensible."

Wow, that kind of remark could sure go to a girl's head, right? Now Lydia was even more anxious to find out what he'd gotten her involved in. "Just tell me, Pastor Dev. So I can help you."

He stood back, then started walking again, his

eyes ever alert to the shadows along the highway and the forest noises off along the fence line. "For ten years now, I've belonged to an organization called CHAIM. That's Hebrew for 'life.'"

"Nice," she said, suddenly caught up in what he was saying. "What does this organization do, exactly?"

He stopped again, and put his arms on hers. "We save people."

Lydia's heart thumped against her rib cage. "As in?"

"This is the secretive part, Lydia. My parents thought I was off doing missionary work, but I wasn't—at least not in the usual way. CHAIM stands for Christians for Amnesty, Intervention and Ministry. We go into other countries and rescue Christians who are in danger."

Lydia let that soak in, then put a hand to her mouth. "You mean, you're some sort of special-ops agent?"

He nodded. "Yes, I was for seven years before I came to Dixon. I had to retire from the force. We've saved hostages, we've helped stranded Christian missionaries out of volatile situations, and we've rescued good, honest people who've found themselves in the wrong place at the wrong time. Because we don't work for the government, we have our own set of rules. We try not to do any harm—we just get in, get out, and save lives on both sides."

"So you're not violent and mercenary?"

He looked away, a darkness settling in his eyes. "Only if we have to defend ourselves or the people we're helping."

That thump in her heart was at full throttle now. "How? Why? I don't understand."

"I know it's hard, seeing me in such a different way. But you're safe as long as you're with me. You have my word on that."

"But if you're retired—"

He glanced around. "Someone wants me permanently retired. Whoever killed Charles Pierson obviously thought they had me."

Lydia's heart sputtered. She couldn't breathe. Hadn't she figured this out already, since she'd been chased and shot at? But hearing him say it out loud made it so real. "You mean, you might have been the one—"

His voice went low. "I gave Charles a key to my room, and told him to meet me there. I had to talk to another colleague before our meeting to discuss my speech. Charles went up ahead of me. They must have ambushed him. It should have been me."

She stared up at him, flabbergasted at what he was telling her. "You could have been killed tonight?"

He nodded. "Yes. I'm out of CHAIM and no one, not even the other operatives, knows where I've been assigned. But someone has breached the security of the entire organization. Just to have me killed. And I'm pretty sure I know who that someone is."

Lydia's whole body was shaking now. She couldn't

breathe, she couldn't think beyond the fact that Pastor Dev might have been killed tonight. Up until now, she'd wanted to believe it had all been some sort of mistake, that they weren't the target. She looked back up at him, tears brimming in her eyes. And then she started shaking so badly, she felt sick to her stomach. With a rush, everything that had happened came at her, causing her to grow weak. "You could have been killed."

He touched his thumb to her chin. "I might still be killed, Lydia. And you right along with me, if they find us. That's what I've been trying to tell you."

He caught her in his arms just before she passed out.

THREE

Dev hated to bring Lydia out of the relative peace of her little fainting spell. But he had to, so he carried her to a big stone bench. "Lydia, wake up." He held her in his arms, scoping the spot just as the little old lady they'd seen on the train came charging around the corner.

Obviously trying to focus, Lydia lifted her head and spotted the woman. And in her usual Lydia way, said, "How nice. She's worried about us." While Dev went into combat mode, Lydia sent the woman a reassuring smile. Then asked, "How long has that nice little lady been tailing us, anyway?"

"She's not so very nice, and she really isn't a lady at all," Dev whispered. There she stood, glaring at Lydia and Dev through her bifocals. And she was packing more than just antacid and Advil.

Even in her stupor of confusion, Lydia seemed to figure things out. "That woman's gun is much bigger than yours, Pastor Dev."

"You can say that again."

The woman aimed the gun right at Lydia and Dev. Then she spoke. "'Will your riches, or all the mighty forces, keep you from distress?'"

"Job again," Lydia murmured, her shock obviously bone deep. And it was about to get worse, Dev thought.

Everything after that was in fast-forward. Dev pushed Lydia down into the leaves and grass behind the bench, his hand on her back. "Stay down," he hissed.

Since Lydia seemed paralyzed with fear, staying down wasn't a problem. She cringed low as Dev managed to position himself behind the concrete back of the bench, trying to protect her with his body. But her head came up in spite of his best effort as she strained to peek at their assailant.

Then she gasped. Probably because she saw what Dev had already figured out. The old lady wasn't actually a woman. She was a *he*. A wiry young man dressed like an old lady. And that man was trying to kill them. Shots clinked and pinged all around them, but Dev didn't let that bother him. He kept Lydia's head down, his body protecting hers, and kept himself out of the line of fire. While he waited for his chance.

Amazed and paralyzed with fear, Lydia watched him—but it was like a slow-motion dance of some sort, surreal and bizarre. He stood, then crouched forward, all the while firing that big-barreled gun at the enemy. One of the shots hit its mark. But Pastor Dev didn't kill the VEP—the Very Bad Guys had been elevated in Lydia's mind to Very Evil People. Pastor Dev shot the man in the leg, causing him to drop his weapon and roll around in agony. The wound must have hurt something awful from the way the man was screaming.

"Don't worry, I just maimed him," Pastor Dev explained, in a tone he might use to say, "Don't you just love long walks in the woods, Lydia?"

"What if he tells someone about us?" Lydia asked as Pastor Dev sank back behind the bench.

"He won't. Because then he'd have to explain his presence here. And he was never here. Neither were we."

"Part of the cover?"

"Yes."

Lydia put her hands over her head and closed her eyes, thinking of her nice little garage apartment back in Dixon. She loved that tiny apartment. It sat right over an old train depot that had been converted into a thriving antiques and collectibles minimall, complete with a country diner, both run by Lydia's Aunt Mabel. She thought of the wonderful view of downtown Dixon—which encompassed about one square block. She thought of the great old live oak right outside her window, and the Carnegie Library and the Dixon Pharmacy and Soda Shoppe, safe, secure places with ready supplies of books, ice cream, hair spray and flavored lattes. What more could a girl ask for?

Right then, Lydia could have used a white chocolate mocha latte. She wanted so badly to be back in her four-poster bed with the frilly magnolia-embossed comforter and sheets, reading a good novel from the library, her beloved portrait of Clark Gable and Vivian Leigh in *Gone With The Wind* hanging on the long wall opposite her bed. Her cat Rhett would be curled up beside her on the bed, his one black patched eye contrasting sharply with his white face. Oh, how she wished to hold Rhett.

"Lydia, are you all right?"

She heard Pastor Dev's words echoing across her mind, tugging her away from that peaceful, normal scene and back to the dark, scary, not-so-normal woods. "I'm just dandy. Where's that strange old woman?"

"She—he's over there in the bushes, moaning."

"Should we help him?"

"No. He won't die. He's trained to stop the bleeding."

"That sure makes me feel better. What now? Will he try to follow us?"

"No. He's injured. He'll have to report back to his superiors that his mission has failed."

"And just who does he work for? Surely not CHAIM?"

"That's the question, isn't it? And that's what our

mission is all about. We have to find out who's behind this and who sent him."

"Do you have an idea?"

"I have a theory. But I have to get to a secure place before I can figure this out."

They heard more moans, but Lydia didn't feel as much empathy now for the old woman—possible killer.

"Not my problem," she said, getting up to brush off her clothes. "Let's get out of here."

"Good idea." Pastor Dev looked around, probably thinking there were others lurking in the shadows. Or maybe Lydia was the only one thinking about that possibility.

"We'll cut through the woods until we reach the river," Pastor Dev whispered. "Then we'll find a way to get to our next destination."

Lydia didn't even know they were near a river, but a few miles later, sure enough she could hear a soft gurgling off in the distance. The Chattahoochee? Or maybe all that gurgling was coming from the bleeding man in the granny wig who was probably hobbling along after them.

"What will be our next destination?" she asked, afraid to hear the answer.

"New Orleans," Pastor Dev said as he shoved her into the shadowy oaks and pines.

She gave him just enough time to get them hidden, then stopped. "I can't go to New Orleans. My parents would have a royal hissy fit about that."

"I'll be with you," Pastor Dev said in that condescending, I-know-best voice. "You'll be safe."

"Not in that city. My grandmother says the French Quarter's a regular den of iniquity."

Taking her by the hand, he stalked through the woods as if he knew exactly where he was going. "Not all of New Orleans is like that, Lydia, and besides, you don't have any choice. Those are my instructions."

"To get us to New Orleans?"

"Yes. We need to get out of Georgia."

"Is the dwelling of light there—in New Orleans?"

He shook his head, then let out a sigh. "You are so smart."

She refused to let flattery stop her. "Just answer me."

"Yes—that's a code for a safe house. Can you trust me?"

"You said I don't have any choice."

He gave her a long, steady look. One of his commando looks. "I'm sorry about that. Do you trust me?"

"I'm trying, Pastor Dev. But you have to admit this is all a bit new for me. You might need to give me a few minutes to adjust."

"Okay. Take all the time you need. But remember, you have to listen to me and trust my decisions."

"Okay."

They walked along in silence for a few minutes. Lydia used the time to pout. She liked to be in control of any and all situations and right now she felt completely out of control. "Can I at least call my parents now?"

"They have been apprised of the situation."

Lydia stopped again, then glanced over at him. "They have? Who did the apprising?"

"We have operatives everywhere. The situation has been explained in detail. Your parents know you're safe and with me."

"Somehow, that doesn't make me feel any better."

In a lightning move, he tugged her close. Which, in spite of her pouting, did make her feel better. "You shouldn't be here, Lydia," he said, his gaze moving over her face.

That soft-spoken, regret-filled statement didn't sit well with Lydia, since she had always dreamed of being in his arms. But she understood what he meant. Actually, neither of them should be here—technically speaking.

Lydia shrugged. "I'm here now. No use crying over spilled milk."

Then he started laughing. That didn't help Lydia's mood. She backed away from him, pushing her hands through her tangled hair. "You think that's funny?"

"Yes. I mean, no." He pulled her back into his arms.

"It's just that…Lydia, you amaze me. You are so practical and pragmatic. *Spilled milk*."

"Well, this is a big old puddle of a mess, don't you agree?"

He probably could tell she was getting all worked up. He didn't try to hug her again. Instead, he stopped laughing and let out a sigh. "That is correct. A big mess that I've somehow managed to get a nice girl like you involved in. Not only that, but one of the best men I know died tonight. Because of me."

What could she say to that? She'd been so scared and confused that she hadn't even stopped to think about his friend. She couldn't resort to bickering and sarcasm after hearing the anguish in his words. Especially his next statement.

"This is all my fault."

Since Pastor Dev walked on ahead, she had to follow him or risk getting left out in the Georgia woods with all the varmints and bugs and men in wigs. She caught up with him, but remained silent, sending up prayers for the soul of his friend. Lydia's mother had always told her silence was golden. Since the woods were so dark and quiet, with only the moonlight and stars to guide them, she decided it was a good time to go to God in prayer about this whole bizarre situation.

Lydia worried as she prayed, not only about herself and her life, but also about Pastor Dev. He was right. He'd lost one of his best friends back in that hotel room. Now she reckoned he was grieving in a kind of delayed reaction way. And what about Reverend Pierson's family? How was anyone going to explain this to them? What about the authorities back in Atlanta? Would they be hushed up, or would Lydia's and Pastor Dev's names and pictures be plastered all over the news? How would they ever get out of this?

She asked God all of these questions as they walked along, then she asked Him to show them the way. Lydia knew in her heart that Pastor Dev had to be telling her the truth, but she wondered how in the world such a good and decent man had become involved with killers and thugs. Then she reminded herself CHAIM was supposedly a Christian organization, meant to help those in need. And that would mean sometimes having to deal with dangerous, unscrupulous people.

He's one of the good guys, Lydia, she reminded herself as she chanced a glance over at him. *Remember that.* Then she tried to imagine all the places he'd been, the horrible things he'd seen in his operative days. And he'd said he had to retire? What did that mean? Not, *I retired,* but *I had to retire.* There was a big difference in that particular wording. And just who wanted him dead?

He'd said he thought he knew who.

So she asked him. "Who's behind this?"

"I can't tell you."

"But you think you know, right?"

"I'm pretty sure, yes."

"Did you do something bad, for someone to want you dead?"

Dev didn't speak for a while. Their feet crunched on leaves and twigs, each sound causing Lydia to walk closer to him. He grabbed her hand to keep her from tripping against his feet, since she was like a shadow right at his heels.

"I didn't do anything bad," he finally said. "I did do something that made some people very angry at me. But I had my reasons."

"Such as?"

"I can't explain it right now, Lydia. I've got people investigating things. It's very complicated." That was an understatement. He didn't know where to begin.

"Yeah, well, it would have been nice to be fore-warned about…your past life. I've known you for a while now, and I never would have guessed—"

"That's how CHAIM wants things. We're trained to fit right in, wherever we go. Sometimes, we fit in too well."

"You can say that again. Are you even a real preacher?"

He looked over at her, masking the piercing hurt her doubt brought. "Of course I am. I attended seminary in New Orleans. I trained to be a minister. I just got sidetracked for a while." Then he shook his head. "No, that's not exactly correct. Being in CHAIM taught me more about being a Christian than anything else, even preaching."

"I guess so, what with all the deception and intrigue. I'm sure that comes in handy each Sunday when you're quoting the Gospels to all the good, decent folks back in Dixon."

"I know you're confused and angry," he said, taking her hand again. "But my experiences in CHAIM have helped me with my messages each Sunday. My past life has taught me compassion and understanding and unconditional love." Then he squeezed her hand tight. "Lydia, I can't bear you being angry at me. But I certainly don't blame you." He let out a long sigh, his hands dropping to his side. This wasn't going to be easy, not with Lydia. She was too innocent for this. "If I've lost *your* respect, then I truly am lost."

That comment shut her up, good and proper. But she glowed in her silence, and she didn't exactly feel like pouting anymore. He wanted her respect above all else? Did that even hint at any type of feelings he might have for her, other than those of friend and coworker and fellow Christian?

Lydia swallowed hard, prayed for guidance, then said, "You *did* have my respect, and you still do. I just wish I'd had your trust so you could have told me about all of this."

He pushed a hand over his face. "It's not a matter of trust. CHAIM doesn't allow us to give out information. We tell no one. We don't share the details of our jobs. That would put too many people in danger. And I think someone has done exactly that— given our identities and our locations away. There are people all over the world who'd like to see all of the CHAIM operatives dead."

"Starting with you?"

"It looks that way, yes."

"But now that I know about CHAIM, can't you give me a few more hints? I need to be prepared for the worst."

He heaved them both up an embankment, then stopped to take in the lay of the land while Lydia stopped to marvel at his strength—not just his outer physical strength, but an inner core that now radiated around him and made him seem powerful and heroic in her eyes. And made her wonder, yet again, just how many secrets he was carrying.

Too tired to figure all that out, Lydia concentrated on their surroundings. The woods were shrouded in a blanket of gray moonlight; the river glistened like a silver necklace. She could hear the rustling of forest creatures off in the distance. At least, she hoped it was forest creatures and not humans dressed in disguise, coming for them.

Since he just stood there like a good-looking block of stone, she reminded Pastor Dev again, "I need to understand. I like details, I like to be organized and prepared. So I need to know everything, just in case."

He got moving then, his boots stomping through the underbrush. "No, you don't. You just need to do exactly as I say, for your own protection and safety."

She hurried to catch him, then stopped to stare at his retreating back. "Will you ever tell me all of it? I mean, why we're really being chased and what you did to cause this?"

"Probably not. You're better off not knowing."

And that's the only answer she got. He refused to give her the details—for her own protection, of course. Lydia was getting mighty tired of being kept in the dark for her own protection. But then, what choice did she have? Right now, she could only follow the man she loved as they marched blindly along.

So she stomped after him in her sensible pumps, so very glad that he at least thought she was amazing, practical and pragmatic. The compliments couldn't get much better. The man might be able to leap tall buildings in a single bound, but he didn't have a clue as to a woman's heart. Not one clue.

Lydia didn't know where she was going to wind up after this. Right now, she just had to find a way to survive New Orleans. If they ever got there. But after what happened when they did get there, Lydia would have rather stayed hidden in the woods of North Georgia.

FOUR

"Why New Orleans?" Lydia asked an hour later as they drove over the Alabama state line, heading for Mississippi and eventually, Louisiana.

Pastor Dev shifted the gears of the beat-up Chevy truck he'd managed to "buy" off a kid near Marietta, his eyes straight ahead on the back road they were taking to the Interstate. Lydia didn't try to figure out how he'd arranged to buy the truck, but then, finagling a truck from a teenager in the middle of the night was only one of his many talents, she imagined.

"I told you, there's a safe house there. It's the least likely place anyone would look for us."

"Now, that makes sense," she replied, tilting her head back on the rough fabric of the seat. Then she glanced over at him again. "Are you sure about my parents? I don't want them to worry."

"They know you're safe."

He wasn't much for giving out unnecessary information. And now that Lydia thought about it, he'd always been that way. Not a big talker—about himself.

But he could talk a bobcat through a pack of bull-dogs, faithwise. Was that the mark of a good minis-ter? Or the cover of a man full of secrets?

Tired of all the questions running amok inside her head, she decided to try a different tack. "What happens in New Orleans? I mean, do we just sit and wait?"

He shook his head. "No, you rest and I work."

"Work? What kind of work?"

"I have to locate my superiors, let them know I'm okay. I'll need to give a thorough report, then wait for further instructions."

Lydia was getting mighty tired of this "further instructions" business. She didn't like being under-cover, not one little bit. But she didn't want to ruffle Commando Dev's already riled feathers, so she tried to sound excited. "That should be interesting." Then she closed her eyes. "What about Pastor Pierson?"

He didn't speak for a full minute. Lydia slanted her eyes to watch him for signs of wear and tear. "Are you okay?"

Pastor Dev tapped the steering wheel in a soft gentle cadence, then glanced at the NASCAR-emblazoned key chain that dangled like a necklace around the truck's rearview mirror. "Arrangements are being made. The official report—a break-in and robbery."

"What about us? What's the official report on us?"

"We were in a different room. We were never there."

"They switched your room?"

"Yes. To protect you. And to keep my cover. The official report will be that we had to leave the conference suddenly. After a few days, the official report will be that we're on a working retreat."

Lydia felt her dander rising, but she held back. "Y'all like to stretch the truth to the limits with all this undercover stuff, don't you?"

"It's for our safety and protection."

"Yeah, there is that."

He didn't answer, and Lydia felt small and petty for being so snippy. But then, it was late and she was tired and still suffering from shell shock. And since she hadn't been through the school of special-ops etiquette, she thought she was doing a fairly good job of winging it.

"So Pastor Pierson's family thinks he was attacked and robbed? And that's it?"

"That has to be it. And that is the truth. He was attacked."

But Lydia could tell by the way he stated the obvious, that wasn't all of it. One of his best friends was dead, and she could see the weight of that pulling at Pastor Dev's strong shoulders. "I'm sorry about your friend."

"Me, too. Get some rest, Lydia. We have a long way to go."

Then he went completely blank, effectively shutting her out. Lydia felt the burn of tears in her eyes, but she stubbornly refused to give in to the need to cry herself a little river. So she prayed, her eyes closed, her mind emptying of all the questions and the unpleasant images. She put an image of the Lord front and center in her head and held on to that image as she asked Him to protect them. And while she prayed, she wondered if might made right. If the need for the better good of all made up for the small sins of omission. If the end justified the means. Was this all in the name of God? Or was this man's way of misinterpreting God's word?

Either way, Lydia was in the thick of it now. There was no turning back. She needed her faith now more than ever. And so did Pastor Dev.

Dev exited off the interstate at a little roadside rest area just past Montgomery, making sure they were in a secluded, hidden spot. Glancing over at Lydia, he was relieved to see that she was sleeping, her head pressed against the window, her hands crossed in her lap. Good. She needed her rest. The poor woman had never been through anything like this night, he was sure. He knew this simply because he knew Lydia. She was a good girl. Everyone loved Lydia. *Everyone.*

Dev opened his door and deftly hopped out of the souped-up truck, careful not to wake Lydia. He needed to breathe. He needed to think. He needed to pray.

So he went to an old stone picnic table, which sat in clear view of the truck, his mind alert to the sounds from both the highway and the hills behind them. He'd forgotten how tense this work could make a man. He'd forgotten how complacent he'd become, living in Dixon, preaching God's word. But he hadn't forgotten all the years of being in CHAIM. How could a man ever forget that?

God's word? *What is that now?* he wondered as he placed his head in his hands and tried to gather his thoughts.

Someone had breached very tight-knit security. Someone had taken a mighty big risk.

"Do you want me dead so much?"

Had he said that out loud? Dev looked around at the moonlit little roadside park, a discarded soda bottle winking at him in the dark while he wished his former friend and colleague could answer that question for him. So much water underneath the bridge; so much pain held captive in his friend's lonely heart. "Are you the one, Eli?"

To keep his mind sane, Dev once again checked his Treo. No messages. He half expected to find one from his rogue associate, telling him exactly where the next hit would be—just because Eli was that kind of guy—precise and brilliant and apparently past the breaking point. But there was nothing. No messages from his superiors, or his wayward friend, or from the Lord, either. So he sat in the dark and pondered and prayed as he thought of dear, sweet Lydia, so trusting, so innocent, so…Lydia. He went over everything inside his head, wondering if he still had it in him to do this kind of work. He was rusty, softened by the kind folks of Dixon, softened by the kind eyes of the woman sleeping in the truck. He'd actually believed it was all over and behind him, all this secretiveness and espionage, all this creeping into darkness. He'd hoped—

He glanced back at the truck and thought of Lydia. What must she think of him now? What happened to his hopes and dreams now?

He felt completely hopeless, completely alone in the dark. He wanted to cry out, he wanted to revolt, to run. But he couldn't do any of those things. So he just sat there, staring at the truck, his mind centered on the woman inside. As he sat, he relived the horrible moment he'd found his hotel room door open and saw his friend's body slumped over in the bathtub. And somehow, he'd known that his safe, blessed life in Dixon was about to change. If only he'd had time to warn Lydia, to save her from all of this.

He'd never forget the look on her face when she'd walked into that room. Her fear and revulsion still shocked Dev to his core. How he wanted to protect her, to keep her safe. But what if he failed?

Dev did what he'd always done in tough situations. He turned to God. "'With my whole heart have I sought thee,'" he quoted from Psalms. "'O let me not wander from thy commandments.'"

And then he wept.

Lydia thought she heard weeping. Coming awake with a gasp, she followed that with a groan. Her neck felt as if someone had twisted it into a French braid and her head didn't feel much better. It pounded and tightened as if someone were truly pulling her hair and twisting it without mercy. She couldn't remember where she was. Then, as memory pushed through her disorientation, fear replaced all of those concerns.

She was alone in the truck.

"Pastor Dev?" she croaked, her eyes adjusting to the still, dark countryside. She sat straight up, pushing at her hair, her gaze moving over the moon-dappled woods. A tattered white plastic grocery bag hung like a flag of surrender off a moss-draped live oak, and the moon lounged with a smirk right up there in the night sky. An unfamiliar fear gripped Lydia, making her take in several rushed breaths. She wanted away from this place. But where was Pastor Dev?

And then she saw him.

He was sitting on a picnic table a few feet from the truck, a dark, somber silhouette with his head in his hands. At first, he looked so still and unmoving, Lydia thought she was just imagining him there. But then, she saw the slight shaking of his shoulders and heard the intake of a long, shuddering sob.

Lydia's fear dissipated like a cloud parting for the moon. Her heart lurched as she went into overdrive, opening the truck door to make a straight run toward him, her pumps echoing across the asphalt with a clip-clop cadence.

"Pastor Dev?" she said, not stopping to think of her actions as she grabbed his hands. They were wet with tears.

He looked up at her, his eyes dark with torment before they became fully alert and clear. Then he tried to push her away. "No."

"Yes," Lydia said, determination and love bringing out her fiercely protective instincts. She might not be highly trained in undercover maneuvers, but she was extremely skilled in the compassion department. "Yes." She pulled him into her arms, her whispers filled with her own tears. "Let me help you. Lean on me. Let me help you, please."

He stared at her long and hard, an armor of pain and confusion shining in his eyes, then he pulled her into his arms and held her while he cried, rocking back and forth against her, his head on her shoulder, his big hands clutching at her back, until her shirt was as wet as his own.

Lydia cried, too, because it tore her heart apart to see this strong, solid man in such bad shape. She knew he was just having a delayed reaction to seeing his friend murdered, and to whatever forces had pulled him back into that other life. What man could handle that? Not even one as strong and sure as this one, Lydia thought, as she held him and stroked a hand through his hair. "I'm so sorry," she whispered. "So sorry."

He pulled away to look up at her, his eyes so soft and misty and full of a dark longing, Lydia wondered if she *were* dreaming. For a single heartbeat of a second, she thought he might kiss her. But instead, he pushed at her, then jumped away from the table as if the solid stone was on fire.

"We need to get back on the road," he said, wiping his eyes with a swat of his hand.

"Okay."

Lydia's heart fell apart with a shattering like little fractured bits of stained glass falling from a window. She stared after him, then she followed him back to the dark truck. She wanted to wake up safe in Dixon. She wanted to get up and drink her two cups of coffee and get dressed and walk down the street to the church, where she'd find various volunteers waiting to help her with her duties there. And she wanted to find Pastor Dev sitting at his desk eating a banana muffin from Aunt Mabel's diner. He would offer her a bite. She would decline, but she'd bring him an extra cup of coffee to wash it down. She *wanted* that so much.

She wanted normal back.

And she wanted Pastor Dev back.

They drove over Lake Pontchartrain as the sun was rising behind them. A fine mist of fog rose off the lake, rays of newborn sky filtering through to wash the dawn in bright white-pink light.

"We'll be safe here," Pastor Dev said, his voice weak and hoarse from not speaking. Not since his meltdown at the roadside park, at least.

Lydia had honored his need to remain silent. She'd had some thinking of her own to do. Now she could tell he was trying to reassure her.

"I'm a burden to you, aren't I?" she asked now. "You're stuck with me—with protecting me."

His smile was rusty. "I don't mind that burden."

Something inside Lydia deepened and widened at that simple statement. He was that kind of man. He'd gladly carry the burdens of those he loved.

Does he love me? she wondered now, wishing, hoping and praying. Then she told herself to shut up. Don't be selfish. Please get us out of this, Lord. Keep him safe. That would be enough for a lifetime, Lydia decided.

"I'm sorry you have to watch out for me."

He looked over at her as they came across the Mississippi River into New Orleans. "Don't apologize, Lydia. None of this is your fault."

"It's not yours, either," she replied, watching for signs of distress.

But he was back to being Commando Dev now, all business with brusque, curt replies. "Yes, it is. But I don't have time to explain that right now. I need to brief you."

Brief her? Lydia accepted that things were probably about to get dicey again. "Go ahead."

"The safe house—it won't be all white picket fences and magnolias in a garden."

She let that soak in, her mind reeling with images

of dark, smoke-filled alleyways and double-locked doors. "Keep talking."

"It's called Kissie's Korner. It's in the Quarter."

"My mama—"

"Would want you safe," he finished before she could voice her mother's disapproval.

"Not in a place like that. It sounds so—"

"Decadent?" he asked with that tight little smile. She didn't dare look at him. "Yes."

"It's a blues club. Some of the best blues and jazz musicians in the world have passed through Kissie's place. But that's just a cover."

"Uh-huh. So you're telling me that even though this place sounds like the devil's playground, it's really as squeaky clean as a church pew?"

He actually chuckled. "Ah, Lydia, I'm almost glad you're with me on this."

That caused her heart to glow just like the dawn all around them, bright and full of hope. "Thanks, I think," she said to hide that glow. She had to keep reminding herself she did not want to be here. "But you didn't answer my question."

"Kissie's Korner is a very clean place, faithwise. Kissie takes in troubled teens, turns them toward the Lord and sets them on their way. She's probably saved more teens in her thirty-five years of being an operative than anyone else on the planet."

"That is mighty respectable."

"Kissie is a good-hearted woman. She loves the

Lord and serves only Him. She doesn't put up with any bunk, I can tell you."

"Drunken, rowdy blues players constitute bunk in my book."

"Kissie doesn't allow for any of that kind of stuff. Her place is a coffee bar."

Lydia's mouth fell open. "Nothing stronger than caffeine? I don't get it."

"Neither do the ones who try to pull anything. She boots them out, but they usually come back, begging for redemption. Kissie is that good."

"Wow."

"Wow is right," he said as he steered the truck down a narrow street just on the fringes of the French Quarter near Louis Armstrong Park. Then he parked and glanced around, his eyes doing a recon roll. "We're here."

Lydia looked up at the massive house in front of them, a soft gasp of shock shuddering through her body. It looked so old and dilapidated she had to wonder if it had been here since the beginning of time, or at least since the beginning of New Orleans. Two-storied and painted a sweet baby blue, the house leaned so far to the left, a lush hot-pink bougainvillea vine actually floated out and away from it. The house reminded Lydia of an old woman holding a lacy handkerchief. The tall, narrow windows were surrounded with ancient gray-painted hurricane shutters. Antique wrought-iron tables and chairs filled the lacy balconies and porches. Petunias in various clay pots bloomed with wild abandonment all around the tottering, listing porch, while a magenta-colored hibiscus flared out like a belle's skirt right by the steps. And a white-lettered sign over the front porch stated Kissie's in curled, spiraling letters that matched the curling, spiraling mood of the house.

"This is a safe house?"

"Completely safe." Pastor Dev came around the truck to help Lydia out. "Trust me."

"Trust you?"

"You will, won't you, Lydia?"

The way he looked at her, the way he asked that one simple question, made Lydia feel as sideways and unstable as this old house, while the look in his eyes made her want to stand tall and believe in him with all her heart.

"I guess I have to, now, don't I?"

His smile was as brittle as the peeling paint on the house. "Yes, I'm afraid you do. Because, I have to warn you, this is only the beginning."

"Oh, great," Lydia said, using humor to hide her apprehension. "You mean, there's more ahead?"

"Lots more before it's over," he said. "They won't stop until they find us."

And this time, he wasn't smiling.

FIVE

"Get yourself on in here, man, and give Kissie a good and proper hug."

The tall, big-boned woman stood at the door of the leaning house, the colorful beads on her long dreadlocks bouncing against her ample arms and shoulders. She wore a brightly patterned silk caftan that swished each time she chuckled and smiled. And she smelled like vanilla and spice.

That was Lydia's first impression of Kissie Pierre, code name, Woman at the Well. Lydia watched as the voluptuous Kissie grabbed Pastor Dev and hugged him so tightly he nearly lost his breath. But he didn't seem to mind. He returned Kissie's exuberant hug with one of his own, a gentle smile on his face as he winked at Lydia over Kissie's cocoa-colored shoulder.

"It's good to see you," Pastor Dev said as he came up for air. Then he turned to Lydia. "Lydia Cantrell, meet Kissie Pierre."

"Mercy me," Kissie said, grabbing Lydia by her

arm, her big dark eyes widening with glee, her gold bangles slipping down her arm. "You sure are a pretty little thing."

"Thank you," Lydia said, the heat of that praise causing her to blush. "And thank you for...helping us."

Kissie cluck-clucked that notion away. "Part of my job, honey pie. That's why I'm here. Now y'all come on back to the kitchen and let me get some decent food and strong coffee in you."

Pastor Dev guided Lydia through the long, cluttered "club" part of the establishment. Lydia cast her gaze about, feeling as if she were in a forbidden zone. She saw reds and burgundies on the walls and in the furniture, plush Victorian sofas and dramatic Tiffany-style lamps, tassels and fringe in gold and bronze, and a huge white grand piano that sat in a prominent place by the floor-to-ceiling window in the front parlor. Across the squeaking, creaking, worn wooden floor of the wide hallway, another room was filled with bistro tables and chairs and a gleaming mahogany bar along one wall. A huge sign running the length of the bar stated "Commit your work to the Lord, and your thoughts will be established." —Proverbs 16:3.

"I just don't get it," Lydia whispered, the paradox of this seemingly decadent place running amok in her pristine mind. "I don't see any alcohol behind that bar."

"That's the point," Pastor Dev said into her ear.

"It's a cover, remember. The coffee bar works just fine. But Kissie makes it pretty clear that if you enter this establishment, it won't be to drink liquor and carry on. She offers tea, lemonade and a full range of coffees, as well as all kinds of sweet treats. It's more of a coffeehouse than a real bar, and her patrons know that."

"But Kissie has her faith right out there for all to see, right along with her dreadlocks and her coffee and chicory," Lydia retorted. "How can she get away with that and still run a blues club?"

"Kissie can be very persuasive. She's like a preacher and a party girl all rolled into one neat package. Since she also lets wayward teens live here, she won't allow any shenanigans. And that's what makes everyone love her so much," he said with a little grin. "Trust me."

There was that request again. Lydia thought about that, thought about Kissie and wondered how many strange people she was going to have to trust before this was all over. Her notion of a proper Christian included a church dress and a set of pearls—not a bright orange-and-brown silk caftan, shiny gold hoop earrings and two gold teeth to match.

But then, maybe her notions were just a bit narrow-minded and preconceived. Kissie did have a brilliant, loving smile and she had helped lots of people to the Lord, according to Pastor Dev.

Plus, her coffee smelled divine and those cinnamon rolls she slapped onto gold-edged china did look too good to pass up. When she added two slices of crisp bacon, Lydia decided Kissie was her new best friend.

"Thank you," Lydia said as Kissie handed her a cup of coffee and passed the cream. "I'm starving."

"'Course you are, child." Kissie glanced from Lydia to Pastor Dev, a serene smile on her face. Then she motioned for the teenage girl she'd called Jacqueline to leave the kitchen. Jacqueline gave them a blank look, but walked out of the room. Kissie waited a couple of seconds. "I've been briefed." Then she shrugged toward Lydia. "SOP."

"Standard operating procedure," Pastor Dev clarified.

"With a special urgency, of course," Kissie added, her voice low.

Lydia glanced up, amazed that the woman's laid-back tone had changed to all business now. Watching Pastor Dev and Kissie, she could tell things were about to get serious.

So she took a long drink of her coffee and let out a sigh of relief. For some strange reason, she did feel safe here in Kissie's Korner.

For now, at least.

A couple of hours later, Dev peeked in on Lydia. She was sleeping in one of the dark-shaded upstairs bedrooms, her skin pale against the purple floral sheets and lavender satin comforter, her hair fanning out like golden-brown wheat against the shimmering pillow. Dev watched and listened, glad to hear her steady, peaceful breathing. Maybe she would get the rest she needed so much.

But there would be no rest for him.

So he headed downstairs to the room in the back that served as Kissie's office. The room with all the computers and monitors and cameras. The official CHAIM room.

"How's our baby girl?" Kissie asked as Dev entered the long, dark area that had once been a sleeping porch. Neither the sun nor the moon reached this place now. The area had been completely sealed off, a secret place hidden from most that frequented this establishment. There were no windows, and a small door was hidden behind a kitchen cabinet. Anyone who might notice would just think it was a storage room. Not even Lydia would see this dark corner.

"She's fast asleep."

Kissie nodded, causing her long braids to fall against her plump shoulder like fringe falling from an afghan. "Poor baby. This ain't easy."

"No," Dev said, closing his eyes to his own fatigue. "I'm sure the food and the hot shower helped."

"She'll be okay. I got a man posted nearby, watching. The whole system is on high alert, of course."

"Good. What's the word from upstairs?"

Kissie smiled at his reference. It was a little joke amongst the CHAIM team, and a gentle reminder that none of them was really in charge. God was their main boss.

"Well, the higher-ups are not happy. They believe one of their own has turned rogue. There's the law, and then there's the law of CHAIM, you understand?"

"Only too well," Dev replied, remembering his days as a full-time operative. One did not mess with the system. But apparently someone had.

"So do I have new orders?"

"To sit tight right now," Kissie replied over her shoulder as she hit buttons and flipped switches. "You'll receive word soon. But not here. The message will be posted at a different location. Probably somewhere else in the city." She sat down in front of a flickering computer monitor. "So, let's see the latest. We'll look for any unusual activity out there."

Dev watched as numbers and codes flashed by. "What if it's Eli, Kissie?"

"Of course it's Eli, honey," Kissie replied. "No one else would dare break the CHAIM brotherhood. But Eli always was a bit of a renegade, even after he turned his life over to the Lord. It makes sense that he'd be the one."

Dev ran a hand over his shower-damp hair. "Eli was one of us, one of the best. And because of me, he's out there on his own now. I can't decide if he's truly gone insane, or if he's just trying to get my attention."

"Murder could indicate both."

Dev stared at Kissie, the pain in her eyes matching what he felt in his heart. "I can't believe he'd deliberately murder someone—even me. It just doesn't add up. Whoever did this got the wrong man. That's not like Eli. He's more thorough. He wouldn't kill another person just to get to me. He'd just kill me and get it over with. But Eli was—is—a good man. Or at least he was until I blew the whistle on his extracurricular activities and ruined his life."

"It wasn't all your fault, Dev. Eli always had a dark streak a mile wide. We had to rein him in many a time, and you did the right thing by reporting him to our superiors. He was a walking time bomb."

"But look what it caused. I failed him. I wanted to get him some help, not turn him against all of us. I never dreamed it would lead to murder."

Kissie turned in her chair. "Are we talking about the current murder, Devon? Or the…other?"

"Both," Dev said, rubbing the back of his neck with his hand. "And they are both my fault."

"But you don't believe Eli actually committed *this* crime?"

Dev thought about that. "It's just a gut reaction. Eli is hurt and angry, and he's grieving. But he has the heart of a warrior—a Christian warrior. He wouldn't do something like this, but I believe his actions might have triggered it, somehow." He tapped his fingers on the sleek black desk. "And I believe something went wrong. Now Eli's on the run. He's either after me—and my hunch is wrong—or he wants to seek my help. Either way, he's going to be in big trouble when we find him." The tapping stopped. "And as we both know, CHAIM has its own system of justice."

Kissie's bright red-painted nails hit the keys with precision. "I'll see what I can find out."

Dev watched as she typed,

Pastoral, looking for a lost sheep. Please respond ASAP.

"That's obvious," Dev said, shaking his head. "He knows I'll be looking for him."

Then she wrote,

Judgment and justice take hold of you.

Dev understood the code. It was Kissie's way of saying, "Don't take your own form of justice." And they both knew that was exactly what Eli special-ized in. Even after rigorous training, Eli still had a vigilante streak.

Then she wrote,

Do not walk with wicked men.

Dev knew that Job was CHAIM's special book of the Bible, the one the organization used to talk in code. Would Eli, known as The Disciple, see the codes embedded in their main website and know Dev was trying to reach out to him? Or would this bring Eli right to Kissie's door? Eli was smart enough to break through the encryptions and find the exact location of the router. He would be here within hours if that happened. Maybe that needed to happen, and if Lydia wasn't here with him, Dev would almost welcome that confrontation. Once and for all.

Dev thought about the woman sleeping upstairs and vowed he couldn't let that happen just yet. Not until Lydia was safe. "What now?" he asked after Kissie keyed in a few more carefully worded messages.

"We wait," she said, her dark eyes giving him a sharp look. "And you try to get some sleep." When he looked doubtful, she added, "Don't worry. I rerouted everything and it's all encrypted. It will only reach those who might be looking for it, and those who know where to look. I believe Eli is good at that sort of thing, but if he's smart, he won't come near New Orleans right now." Then she got up, pushing him toward the door. "Rest."

"I can't sleep," Dev replied. "I have to watch."

"And pray," Kissie added with a soft smile.

"Who's on the agenda for tonight?" he asked, hoping for a diversion.

"The Gospel According to Pauly."

He nodded, flexed the tight muscles in his back. "I love that band. Perfect harmony of all the oldies but goodies."

"Good solid gospel and soul," Kissie said, getting up to shuffle some printouts. "Can't go wrong with that mix."

"I need a good mix to get us out of this mess," Dev said as they exited the room. "Of course, Lydia and I might have to miss the show."

"We'll see, once we receive your next orders."

After they'd safely secured the secret entranceway, Kissie turned to face him. "Pastoral, you did everything in your power to keep Eli on the straight and narrow. The Disciple has strayed on his own. He didn't seek help. In fact, he refused any help...after the South America incident."

"But he went through his own form of grief and repentance," Dev said, his voice low. "He went into seclusion, but it was at CHAIM's demand. It was the best thing he could do, but Eli would have chafed under that sentence. And he would have plotted."

"Well, now he's out," Kissie said with a pragmatic shrug. "And apparently, his time to reflect *didn't* help him. He's not well, Devon."

Dev's palm hit the granite counter. "That's because the man is heartbroken, Kissie. We destroyed—"

"Destroyed what?"

Dev turned to see Lydia standing at the arched doorway to the kitchen, her hair cascading around her pale face. "What did you destroy, Pastor Dev? Or is that information classified?"

Everything around here was classified, Lydia decided later. Pastor Dev had refused to clue her in, for her own protection, of course. So she'd spent most of the afternoon either napping underneath one of the many ceiling fans around the big house, or reading one of the many interesting books and magazines Kissie kept stashed in her upstairs living quarters. The woman had everything from *O* magazine to the *Wall Street Journal* and *People* magazine, not to mention various forms of Christian fiction and nonfiction.

Lydia had read an entire *O* from cover to cover—some of those life lessons in there were pretty good. Then she'd skimmed all the celebrity rags—her daddy wouldn't approve of that—and read a short inspirational romance that had a nice, sweet, happily-ever-after ending.

And wondered if she'd ever have the same.

Then she'd visited with the two girls living here under Kissie's supervision. Jacqueline was moody and resentful. She hated the foster home system. Amy was sweet and unassuming. She loved being safe here with Kissie. Both had been caught up in bad situations. Jacqueline, alcohol and boys; Amy, in an abusive, drug-infested home. They'd been careful not to reveal too much to Lydia, but they'd plied her with curious questions about everything from her favorite songs to what type of perfume and makeup she liked. Careful to be honest but not too forthcoming, Lydia had indulged in a little girl talk until Jacqueline had gone upstairs to clean and Amy had left to run an errand.

Afterward, bored and looking for something to

distract her from all her worries, Lydia had explored the old house and found all sorts of nooks and crannies. This place was one-part history, one-part cabaret and one-part haven.

"Lord, I hope You have a sense of humor," Lydia said to herself now as she slowly made her way down the long staircase. Determined to question Pastor Dev again, she decided to look for him. Both he and Kissie could get gone faster than humanly possible, but Lydia reckoned that was a CHAIM trait. She also knew that even though the two were as thick as thieves and up to their elbows in espionage, they had others stationed here and there, watching out for Lydia. Or as she'd heard Pastor Dev whispering to Kissie, "Keeping visuals." She had to be in someone's line of sight at all times, apparently.

That would explain the tiny cameras hidden everywhere. She'd found them in lamps and in pictures, in plants and in the intricate crown molding on some of the walls.

Not only was this whole house equipped with more cameras than the Pentagon, but Kissie also employed a lot of hardworking, very observant people.

A petite little maid here, dusting and watching.

A nice elderly gardener there, clipping hedges and waiting.

A cable repairman on the roof, realigning the satellite dish while he did a little recon work on the entire neighborhood.

"I didn't just fall off the turnip truck," Lydia said

out loud, then instantly wished she hadn't when she spotted Pastor Dev at the bottom of the stairs, smiling up at her.

"Well, if you did, that must have been one pretty turnip crop."

Lydia tried not to blush. "You shouldn't sneak up on a girl that way."

The smile faded away. "Sorry, old habits die hard."

That was sure the truth. Come to think of it, Lydia and the church staff had all been amazed at how quietly this man could enter a room. Now she understood why, at least.

She met him at the bottom of the stairs, then plopped down "I don't like being idle. Idleness is the devil's workshop."

He tilted his head and gave her a sideways glance. "The devil would have his hands full with you, Lydia."

"I'd give him a run for his money, that's for sure."

She liked the way he smiled at her. His smile made him look so young and carefree, the way he used to look before all of this, back when she thought he was just a kindly minister. "You seem in a better mood."

He sat down beside her, then stretched his jean-clad legs out over the stairs. "This place makes me feel safe."

"Me, too," she admitted. "How long have you known Kissie?"

"Since I attended seminary here in New Orleans. She was one of our special instructors."

"Get out? What did she teach you—the history of blues?"

He laughed at that. "Kissie is a computer whiz. That's her specialty. But you wouldn't know it to look at her."

Lydia grinned at that. "Not your average professor type."

"No, not at all. She was one of the first people I met when I was…introduced into CHAIM."

Lydia was dying to hear the whole, long, drawn-out story, but she didn't want to break the gentle truce of this quiet summer afternoon. Sitting here, she could almost believe they were just visiting New Orleans on vacation. But she did ask one burning question. "What if you'd said no to CHAIM? Would they have burned you at the stake or something?"

"You have a vivid imagination."

"Just curious."

"No, nothing so bad. They would have let me get on with my life. And it would been as if—"

"As if you'd never heard of them, right?"

He touched his arm to hers, poking at her, a grin on his face. "You're learning."

Lydia felt the burn of that playful touch all the way to her toes. It made her edgy and antsy, so she got up. "I need something to do. And don't tell me there isn't anything to do. I see all these people pretending to work around here, that is, while they keep watching me. It's getting on my last nerve."

As if on cue, Kissie came bustling around the corner. "I got something for you to do, child."

"Great," Lydia said, pushing her hair back behind her ears. "I can sort mail, make some calls, file some papers—"

"No, no, honey," Kissie said with a grin. "This is a special project. We're gonna give you a good and proper makeover."

Lydia glanced from Kissie's expectant face to Pastor Dev's blank one. "I don't want a makeover."

"You need a cover," Kissie explained. "They know what you look like now, honey."

"How do you know that?"

Pastor Dev got up, let out a sigh as if to say, Break time is over now. "We've received reports. CHAIM now has a dossier on you. And that means so do the bad guys, probably. We can't take any chances."

Lydia slapped a hand against the newel post. "Well, that's just lovely. How exciting for CHAIM— and the bad guys." She'd have to record all of this in her diary immediately so she'd have her own report. "So, what now?"

"Now," Kissie said, a firm hand on Lydia's arm, "we change your looks. Amy just got back with our ammunition."

Lydia held to the post. "I don't want to change my looks. I like me the way I am, thank you. And I don't need any ammunition."

Dev took her other arm. "Lydia, do this, please. For me. We have to blend in and look the part."

"What part?"

"That of a very wealthy, happily married couple."

Lydia's knees seemed to turn to mush. Holding tightly to the newel post, she glanced from Kissie to Pastor Dev. "You and me, you mean?"

"You and me," he said, a soft smile creaking across his face. "I need you to cooperate, please."

She could see the no-arguing look in his eyes, and she could certainly hear the commando mode in his words, but how could she resist the opportunity to pretend to be his wife, just for one night? Hiding her secret glee behind a show of agitation, she said, "I guess I don't have much of a choice, do I? Just like I didn't have a choice in coming here, or a choice in being in that room at the wrong time, right?"

"I'm sorry," he said, the apology darkening his eyes. "We have to protect you."

That caused her glee to dissipate. "But I thought I was safe here."

"You are, for now," Pastor Dev explained. "But we can't stay here forever. And later tonight we have to go out and do some…research. That's why we need to dress you up, so to speak."

"So it's like I'm playing a spy part or something?"

"Something," Pastor Dev said, nodding. "At first, I thought I'd just leave you in a safe place. But I've reconsidered that. I don't want you out of my sight.

You have to be by my side at all times so I can protect you. Tonight, we have to look like a couple."

"Is that an order?"

"It's a request."

Lydia didn't know whether to laugh or cry. She'd always dreamed of being by his side at all times. But never like this. His *request* sure put her in a pickle. "I see," she said, not really seeing at all. "So who do I get to be? Lois Lane, Catwoman, Mary Poppins, maybe?"

Kissie let out a hoot of laughter. "She's a live wire, this one. Pastoral, you may have just met your match."

Lydia looked over at Pastor Dev, their eyes meeting in the brilliance of the golden dusk that filtered its way throughout the house. The look he gave her sent shards of hope and longing through Lydia's heart. He looked sweet and unsure. But Lydia was very sure she was the woman who would love him and stay by his side at all times, for the rest of their lives, however long that might turn out to be.

"Let's get this over with," she said to break the spell of his powerful gaze. "I don't have all day, after all."

Kissie laughed again, then shook her head. "You gonna be just fine, honey pie. Just fine. We'll get you all fixed up and pretty for this high-society party tonight."

Lydia shot Pastor Dev a questioning look. He didn't seem as confident as Kissie. He looked downright worried. But Lydia couldn't be sure if it was because someone was trying to do him in, or because he'd just realized Kissie might be right. Maybe he had finally met his match.

SIX

Dev waited, pacing at the bottom of the stairs, for Lydia and Kissie to come down. It was almost dark now; the New Orleans dusk was alive with the sounds and scents of nature. Jasmine and magnolias competed with honeysuckle and hibiscus, their sweet, cloying fragrances merging into a sultry perfume. Blue jays and sparrows made swishing sounds in the big live oak by the back gate, while squirrels chased each other in the banana fronds near the water garden in the courtyard. And somewhere a mockingbird lifted its voice to the sky.

He wished he could let these things distract him. But his mind was on this mission and the woman he had to protect. And from the sounds of feminine giggles and gasps upstairs, that woman had just undergone an amazing transformation.

Which was why he was now pacing and sweating in the hall, while the gospel group set up in the big coffee bar.

Devon Malone had scaled ten-foot walls to save

human lives; he'd walked through fire to rescue trapped missionaries from rebels and drug lords. He'd swum through alligator-infested swamps to get to another person in need. He'd been shot at, attacked, taken hostage, stabbed, robbed, beaten and left for dead.

But none of that had ever prepared him for Lydia Cantrell.

Her very innocence and sweetness took his breath away.

And now, because of him, she was about to change. She would not be so innocent from now on. Who knew what this journey would do to her delicate, sweet nature. Or to his own frazzled, confused mind. He'd always considered Lydia a dear friend and a wonderful office assistant. He'd taken her for granted for so long now, he automatically kept her front and center in his thoughts all day long.

Only now, she was invading his nighttime thoughts, too. That was certainly understandable, under the circumstances. He had to protect her. He'd done this kind of operation a hundred times over. He'd been assigned to escort important people before, had played bodyguard to ministers' wives and children all over the world. But he'd never actually cared too deeply about those people, other than an abiding Christian love for his fellow man, and because of the pledge he'd made to protect human life when he'd joined CHAIM.

But Lydia was…well, she was Lydia. Solid and sure, pragmatic and practical, cute and lovely, pretty and so very sweet. Lydia was the girl next door, the good and proper young lady, the person he considered not only a friend but also a valuable member of his church and his staff.

So when had he starting noticing things like her pretty, pouting lips and her soft, shimmering blond-brown hair? And those big hazel eyes, always changing colors like a kaleidoscope, so bright and trusting, so confused and questioning. When had he started wanting to get to know her on a more intimate level—all things Lydia, all things about her life and her hopes? How had he not seen the radiance of her smile before? And why did that smile tug at his heart so much now?

It's because you have to protect her, he told himself as he paced over the soft, faded fleur-de-lis-patterned wool rug that covered the downstairs entryway, the sound of a saxophone warming up drifting around him. After all, close proximity always brought out feelings of protection, didn't it? Being with another person so many hours of the day caused one to discover the most interesting things about that person.

Such as that cute little mole on her right cheek. And her endearing dimples. And the way she lifted her dark eyebrows each time she doubted him.

Which seemed to be a lot lately.

Devon had to rein in all the emotions rushing through his system. Of course, he cared about Lydia.

She was one of his flock. She was a dear friend. She was—

"Beautiful." The word came out of his mouth as he glanced up to find Lydia standing at the top of the stairs, a hesitant, scared look on her face.

Her very different face.

Her hair was now highlighted with soft hues of blond. Kissie had trimmed it into a long shag of some sort. Little wisps fell around Lydia's face and across her brow. Her eyebrows, lifting now in another kind of doubt, had been shaped and trimmed to make them even more alluring and intriguing. She wore makeup, something Lydia rarely did. But it wasn't too fussy or heavy. Just a little shimmer of glitter here, a bit of gloss there. The smoky hues around her vivid eyes made them look the color of rich bronze. Her whole look had changed to the point that not even he could have recognized her out on the street. That would serve their purposes, but Dev almost regretted this change.

Except for the dress. Though modestly cut, the dress was over the top, even for Kissie. And it looked great on Lydia.

"I can't leave the house wearing this," Lydia said as she traipsed down the stairs on her new high-heeled sandals. "If my daddy saw me—"

"Your daddy's not here," Dev said in a husky voice, wishing he hadn't even thought that. He had to turn around, take a breath. Pushing a hand through his hair, he struggled for control. Then he felt a hand on his shoulder. He whirled, ready to do battle. Then he let out a sigh. Kissie had managed to sneak up on him.

"You're losing it," she whispered. "Get yourself together."

He nodded, turned to face Lydia, who was now on the bottom step of the stairs. She was getting as good at this stealth business as the rest of them.

"I look awful, don't I?" she said, tears welling in her eyes. "I'm not…this is not me…I don't know if I can—"

Dev glanced over at Kissie and saw the warning look in her eyes. He needed to say exactly the right thing. "Lydia," he began, his words sounding shaky but growing firm with each syllable, "you look… amazing. The dress is very attractive and necessary. Now be a good girl, and just go with it."

Lydia came down the last step to glare at him, so close now he could smell the scent of lily of the valley. Kissie sure did like floral perfumes. "Go with it? I look like a floozy and you know it."

"No, you don't," he said, meaning it. "You could never look that way. You look like you, only different. I like the hair. You look like a proper society lady."

"But this dress…" She looked down at the shimmering, slinking fabric that fell straight and fitted to just below her knees. "I tried another one, but it was way too short. At least this one is a decent length. But this red, beaded stuff…it's just not me."

Dev whirled on Kissie. "Is that the only dress you could find?"

"In her size, yes, sir," Kissie replied, all business. "It's this or nothing. And we have to remember, she has to be dressed to the nines to fit the part. And so do you, so you're next. Upstairs, now."

Dev focused on the assignment, tearing his eyes away from Lydia. "What…what am I wearing tonight?" he managed to ask, gazing at Lydia's pretty eyes, accentuated by her hair.

"A tux," Kissie said. "Y'all are set to attend a masquerade party in the Garden District. Some big shot is throwing it for a group of important out-of-town visitors, if you get my drift. Your presence has been requested."

Dev understood. He would meet one of his superiors at this party and receive further instructions. CHAIM had operatives in all sorts of places—governments, churches, businesses, university systems, hospitals—you name it. It gave new meaning to the term "never alone."

"I'll just go get ready," he said, giving Lydia one last glance. Then he touched a hand to her arm. "Lydia, you look beautiful. I promise."

Lydia didn't look convinced. "Is it too…risqué?"

"Not on you," he replied, smiling for the first time since she'd come down the stairs. "It just looks… good."

"And you get to carry a feathered mask, too,"

Kissie added. "I'll give that to you when you get ready to leave."

She finally let out a sigh of relief. "I guess I can pull this off. I'm just not used to fancy threads and too much makeup."

"It becomes you," Dev said again, to reassure her. "If you feel uncomfortable, just keep your mask over your face."

"Hiding behind a mask—that just about sums this up," Lydia said, resolve coloring her expression. "Go on and get ready. I'll be okay."

Her tentative smile captivated him, so he tried again to reassure her. "I'll make sure of that, I promise."

But as he hurried up the stairs, he knew this wasn't about reassurance. Lydia Cantrell might have been plain and simple before all of this, and that had been just fine with him. But now, she was a knockout, a beautiful, attractive woman.

And that wasn't just fine with him. Because it was causing him to be careless. And CHAIM didn't allow for carelessness. He had to stay focused on the mission, on protecting Lydia.

And that meant he couldn't think about things that were inappropriate and risky, such as kissing her, or holding her close, or taking her out for a real romantic dinner. So he turned at the top of the stairs and looked down on her as she stood in the middle of the hallway, taking once last glimpse at her—just to get her out of his mind.

In the coffee bar, the gospel singers started a rendition of "Softly and Tenderly." The old hymn was all about Jesus calling all sinners to come home. But for Dev, the terms softly and tenderly also described how he felt about Lydia. He never wanted to see her hurt, or worse, dead. Which was why he had to remain distant and professional. Until he could have her safely home.

Her gaze caught his, held him there, held him captive with sweetness and temptation. He gripped the old oak banister in order to control his emotions. And his longings. Then, reminding himself he had a job to do, he hurried away and slammed the door to his room.

Lydia turned to Kissie, her heart pounding with uncertainty. "This is so embarrassing. He doesn't approve. He's not used to seeing me like this."

"You can sure say that again," Kissie replied, a wry twinkle in her eyes.

Amy came downstairs, her smile sweet and shy. "I'm done straightening Lydia's room now, Miss Kissie."

"Thanks, honey. Go on in the kitchen and get you some supper."

Amy, all pale and blond and wearing baggy khakis and a worn T-shirt, glanced over at Lydia. "You look great."

"Thank you," Lydia said, "and thanks for all your help." Amy had helped with her makeup and had even suggested she put on some perfume. Deciding earlier to use lotion instead of the heavy spray concentrate, Lydia now hoped the lily scent didn't provoke her allergies.

Amy nodded, then strolled toward the back of the house. But she turned at the door to the kitchen, her blue eyes going wide. "Take care, Lydia."

Kissie added an "amen" to that.

"I need to change," Lydia said, moving toward the stairs. The high-heeled, glittery sandals were not so easy to move around in. "I can't do this. I just can't."

"Child, stop right there," Kissie said, grabbing her by the arm with a mighty firm hold. "You gonna be fine. That man more than approves of the way you look. He's just having to get used to the new you, on top of all his other problems. And we don't need you adding to that load."

"I'm not planning on staying this way," Lydia declared, determination making her voice rise. "And I'm trying very hard *not* to *be* a problem. Why can't I just stay here, safe and sound? I'd stay out of the way. I could read a good book and go to bed early. I'll write in my journal and read my Bible. I'm behind on my devotionals anyway."

Kissie shook her head. "Can't let you. Devon wants you with him at all times. He knows it's his responsibility to protect you."

"But why do I have to be someone I'm not?"

"Part of the game, honey. Our contact can't just show up here at my door, so we have to send you to this party, partly to throw them off, and partly to keep our operatives secret. An exchange will be made, information given over. If they're watching, which we're pretty sure they are, they won't recognize Devon and you—or they won't expect you to show up at this party. The element of surprise and all that. It's important to blend in with the crowd and look as if you belong, and they won't expect a sweet thing like you to look like that, trust me."

"I don't plan on staying like this, and I mean it," Lydia repeated, crossing her arms in a stubborn stance.

"Nobody said you have to stay this way," Kissie replied in a calm, serene voice. "In fact, this is probably just the first of many disguises. But the haircut is cute. And the makeup does play up your pretty eyes. And the dress...well, that's just for show and just for tonight. You do not look like a floozy, okay? Kissie don't do floozy, all right?"

"I didn't mean to insult you," Lydia said, embarrassment causing her skin to heat up. "I've just never worn anything so fancy and so...clingy."

"I'm not offended," Kissie said. "I'm having a good time. Haven't seen this many fireworks since Christmas down on the river."

"Fireworks?" Lydia looked around, confused as usual.

"Girl, you don't see it, do you?" Kissie chuckled then started toward the coffee bar. "I got to get ready for the gospel crowd. They're already pouring in."

She waved a hand toward the coffee bar. "We should have a full house tonight."

Lydia followed her, just to keep busy. "I'll help."

"Not in that, you won't."

"What did you mean, that I don't see it?"

Kissie turned at the long counter. "That man up there. He…he's got a clear thing for you, honey."

Lydia's heart bounced and lifted like a string of beads being tossed through the air, then righted itself. "He…we're…coworkers and fellow Christians, so yes, I'm sure he cares about me through the love of Christ."

Kissie grinned. "Yeah, right. Baby, there is the love of Christ, and then there is the love of a man for a woman. Maybe you're both blind to it."

Lydia knew how *she* felt, but it had never occurred to her that Pastor Dev might have even the tiniest bit of an inkling of returning those feelings. "Are you saying—"

Kissie held up a jewel-bedecked hand. "I'm just saying something's brewing in this place besides the coffee, understand?"

Lydia smiled then, gaining a new confidence. "I think I just might."

Kissie gave her a long, intense look. "Good, then. 'Cause the better you understand Devon Malone, the more able you'll be when the time comes for him to reach out to you. He's gonna need someone strong when this is all over. You just might be the one."

Lydia let the echo of that prediction reverberate throughout her system. Then she remembered last night and how he'd cried in her arms. How he'd looked into her eyes as if he were a drowning man. A woman didn't forget a look like that. A woman didn't forget a man like Pastor Dev.

"I'll be here, always," she told Kissie. "You have my word on that."

"I never doubted it," Kissie said with a soft smile.

Lydia took a seat on one of the plush settees and waited for Pastor Dev, her thoughts going from a working relationship to something more meaningful and deep. Closing her eyes, she let the soothing praise music coming from the next room help to calm her frazzled nerves.

Could it be so, Lord? she asked, prayed, hoped. Did the man she love also love her back? Well, he was going through a whole heap of trouble to protect her. And he did have about a million burdens on his mind. Maybe it was simply being thrown together. That alone was enough to make him more protective and considerate.

Lydia thought about that angle, and decided instead of whining and fighting him at every turn, she would try really hard to be more cooperative. She wouldn't be any trouble at all. She'd do everything he said so that they could get back home to Dixon and the work of the church.

And then, once all of this was behind them and they were back on a routine, she'd see if Pastor Devon

Malone still looked at her the way he'd looked at her tonight. And she'd find out if it mattered whether she was wearing a red dress or not.

SEVEN

Lydia realized two things as she looked through the eye slits of her red-sequined feathered mask at the formal parlor of the elegant Garden District antebellum mansion. One, she was way out of her league with all these rich folks wearing real diamonds and fake smiles. And two, Pastor Dev sure looked good in a tuxedo and a black satin mask.

The big white-columned two-storied house had to be well over one hundred years old. The furnishings were all priceless antiques. And Lydia knew antiques from living over her Aunt Mabel's Antique Depot. The names Hepplewhite, Chippendale, Windsor and Duncan Phyfe floated through her mind as she admired the huge sideboards and buffets loaded with food and the gleaming secretary sitting in one corner, a crystal bowl of floating magnolia blossoms its only adornment. She was pretty sure the ornate burgundy-and-gold strung rug in the parlor was an aged Aubusson. And the artwork and knickknacks indicated an eclectic taste, with a mixture of old-world style and modern abstracts vying for the attention of the dressy crowd.

The French doors on every side of the long square house were thrown open to the mild summer night, while ancient ceiling fans hummed and swirled, bringing down refreshing breezes from the high, ornately scrolled ceilings. Classical music wafted out over the wind, courtesy of a string quartet centered on one of the long verandas.

Lydia tried to concentrate on her surroundings and not on the man who'd gone to find them some fresh lemonade. But Pastor Dev was back, right at her side. In fact, he'd somehow managed to keep his gaze on her as he'd crossed the dining room to the huge punch bowl centered on the long Queen Anne table. She'd watched him, their eyes meeting in spite of the masks they both wore.

"Here you go," he said, handing her a dainty crystal cup of the chilled lemonade concoction. Then he reached his other hand around. "I found some brownies, too. I know you love brownies."

Lydia could have kissed the man, but then that probably wasn't such a good idea, considering all the erratic thoughts moving with the same whirl as the ceiling fans through her mind. "Thank you." She took a bite of a moist chocolate square and closed her eyes. "You know, I have to say that the eating on this particular little adventure has been fine so far. I'm not starving."

"No, you're not," he said, his eyes sweeping over her face for reassurance. "You look fit as a fiddle."

Lydia laughed at that, and then flushed. "Nothing wrong with my appetite."

"Sorry." He gulped his own lemonade, as he looked around. "I would have thought we'd make contact by now."

Lydia smiled at the way he looked all flustered and embarrassed, and the way he had quickly changed from flirtatious to commando in order to hide his own discomfort. That was rather endearing. But then she remembered the circumstances. Best not to flirt. Best to concentrate on staying alive.

"This mask is making my face itch," she said after she'd swallowed the last of her brownie. "Can't we find a corner so we can take these things off for a minute or two?"

"Not until after our contact approaches us."

"Any idea who we're looking for?"

"No. That's how things go with CHAIM. It's so secretive and undercover that I might not even see the operative. But I'll get the message. A word here, a gesture there."

"Well, that should be easy."

He laughed at her smirk. "No, the easy part is spending time with you. You look right at home here, Lydia."

She rolled her eyes, even though she wasn't sure if he noticed. "Yeah, right. I am not to the manor born, Pastor Dev, as you well know."

He shook his head. "You could be, though."

"Thank you," Lydia said, deciding to just accept his compliment. She finished off another brownie. "Wow, I must have eaten that too fast. I feel a little funny." She touched a finger to the scratchy stitching and feathers at her temple. "My face feels so warm."

Pastor Dev immediately became concerned. "Maybe it's the heat."

"I'm not hot," she replied. She felt chills sweeping through her body even as she said the words. She'd felt chilled earlier, but just figured it was because of the cross ventilation from the open doors and the competent ceiling fans. "Maybe I just need to sit down."

He took her cup and set it on a nearby tray. "Let's go out on the veranda."

Lydia nodded. She didn't want to alarm him, but her skin did feel all clammy and hot now. She went from chills to what felt like fever, back and forth. She wondered if she'd eaten too much sugar. She did have a big sweet tooth.

"Sit here," he told her as he urged her down onto a lacy white bistro chair in one corner of the planked porch, away from the crowd at the big double-entry doors. "There's a nice breeze here by this big magnolia tree."

"Thank you." Lydia sat down, careful to pull her dress around her knees. She breathed in the fragrant lemony scent of the magnolias, then swallowed back the nausea in her stomach. "I'll be fine. Just got a bit too stuffy in there."

"Here, get this thing off your face," he said, tugging at her disguise. Slipping it over her head, he stared straight into her eyes. "You don't look so good."

Lydia waved a hand, trying to make a joke. "Not what I expected when I revealed my identity to you at last, kind sir."

Pastor Dev shook his head, smiling slightly, then he looked around, a frown replacing his smile. "I'm going to try and make contact so we can get out of here and get you home to rest." Then he put his hands on his hips as he gave her a once-over. "But I don't want to leave you."

"I'm fine, really," Lydia said. "It's nice out here, and now that I've removed all those feathers away from my face, I don't feel so scratchy."

"I still can't leave you alone." He stood over her, protective and hovering. Then in frustration, he yanked off his own simple black mask. In spite of the situation, that made her smile. Then she glanced across the porch and saw a tall, distinguished-looking man staring at her through an elaborate swirled-silver domino. Lydia smiled at him. He smiled back. Then he started toward them. Maybe Pastor Dev wouldn't have to leave her.

"Pastor Dev," Lydia said under her breath, "we might have company."

Dev glanced around, his actions carefully controlled. "Okay. Let's see what happens." Then he leaned close and slipped his mask back on, then handed Lydia hers. "We have to pretend we don't see him. Don't be obvious." After she grudgingly put her domino back on, he whispered into her ear. "Look at me."

Lydia did as he asked, glad to have the excuse. "Did I tell you that you look nice in that tux?"

"No, you didn't. But thanks." He touched a finger to a stray wisp of hair near her temple. "Is he still coming toward us?"

Lydia made a quick scan of the veranda, her shivers now coming from Pastor Dev's touch. She quickly reminded herself that this was just playacting. The man moved right past them and didn't even bother looking back. But Lydia felt the brush of air as he casually walked by, then strolled down the steps into the big front yard.

"He was right there, but I don't see him anymore." Then she looked back up at Pastor Dev, blinking because she was suddenly seeing two of him.

Dev turned again, discreetly showing her a folded note. "He left us his calling card right here in the potted plant."

Lydia giggled. "You people actually do that— leave things in the potted plants?"

"I know—it's so cliché, but it worked. Neither of us even saw him do it, but I certainly saw the note lying there when I turned."

"Glad you're the one who found it." She swallowed the ache in her throat and croaked, "What does it say?"

He read it to her in a soft whisper. "'The eagle dwells on the rock. Go to the eagle.'"

"I guess that's from Job, too, more or less? What does that mean?"

He leaned close, so the casual observer would think he was filling her ear with sweet talk. "It means we're going to be traveling again. I know where we need to go now, to keep you safe."

"How—" Lydia tried to form the words, but her heart rate accelerated too fast, causing her to feel faint. "Oh, boy," she said, grabbing for his arm.

"Lydia?"

She heard Pastor Dev's voice, but she couldn't seem to focus on his words. She tried to stand. "I don't feel so good."

He caught her to him. "Lydia, are you sick?"

She tried to nod. Her skin felt as if it was on fire. "Hot." Then she pushed at him as shivers moved up and down her arms. "Cold."

Pastor Dev grabbed her by the waist. "Lean on me."

She tried to do that, but everything was becoming murky. She couldn't focus. "Hot...cold." The chills and fever seemed to be warring with her skin, raking her with heat followed by ice. The fire of it hissed over her arms, her neck, her face. "Must be having an allergic reaction."

Another man came to them. Lydia vaguely recognized him as the distinguished gentleman who'd just brushed past with the note. Their contact? Or the enemy? Had he been watching after he left the note?

"Come with me," he said over her head to Dev.

"I don't think—"

"You'd better listen," the man told Dev. "Come with me now. I just got a message from the Lady at the Well. She was afraid to call your line."

Dev nodded. "Lydia, can you walk?"

"I think so." She wanted to sit back down and rub this fire off her skin. "Hot. Fire."

Dev spoke into her ear. "Just hang on, honey. You're having some sort of reaction. We'll take care of you, but we have to be very discreet."

Lydia knew the drill. He didn't want to bring any more attention to them. Even in her frenzied state of mind, she could sense his anxiety. So she managed a smile. "Let me go," she whispered to both of the men. "I can get through that side door over there around the corner. No one will notice."

Dev shot a glance toward the back of the wrap-around veranda, where a French door stood open. "She's right. No one is looking at us and no one is roaming back there. If we take her through the front, everyone will notice."

The gray-haired man nodded, his eyes calm and sure through the slits of his mask. "I agree. Okay, let's smile and laugh, just in case."

Lydia did laugh. She laughed because her skin felt as if a million fire ants were crawling over her.

She laughed because she knew she was in serious trouble and that something had gone terribly wrong somewhere between the limo ride and the lemonade. She even laughed at the note in the potted plant. Another good one for her journal.

Then she stopped laughing, the heat of the big, bright blue bedroom they'd stumbled into causing her to want to throw up. "Did I do something wrong?" she asked Pastor Dev, her eyes brimming with frustrated tears. "I did something wrong." She tugged her mask off and threw it on the floor.

He sat her down in a blue brocade wing chair, his hand touching on the pulse at her wrist. "No, sweetheart, you did everything just right."

She gulped back a sob. "You called me sweetheart."

He tossed his mask down next to hers. "Yes, I sure did."

She lifted her gaze to his face, but he was staring over at the other man. "Her pulse is erratic. What did Kissie report?"

Distinguished Gentleman shook his head, which made him look like a gargoyle with that creepy mask shimmering in gray and silver. "It seems we've been compromised. She wouldn't tell me. You need to call her."

"I'll secure the line." Pastor Dev got out his trusty phone, punching codes while his gaze and one hand stayed on Lydia. "Hold on, honey."

He was being awfully sweet, Lydia thought, her

hands scraping at her burning skin. "I need... I'm hot, so hot." She tried to speak, but her throat seemed to be closing up.

"Kissie?"

Pastor Dev listened, then hissed a breath. "I'm on it." He hung up, stared across at the other man. "I need a bathroom."

Lydia started giggling. "Me, too, come to think of it. Too much lemonade."

"It's not the lemonade," Dev said. "It's the perfume. She's wearing lily of the valley." He was speaking to Distinguished Gentleman, Lydia noted, but she heard him loud and clear. "Amy poisoned the perfume—Kissie thinks it was pesticide. We have to get her washed down."

Lydia's head came up. "Me? You have to wash *me* down?"

Pastor Dev helped her up as the other man motioned toward a bathroom just off the bedroom, then headed off in that direction. "Yes, Lydia. You've absorbed some sort of bug spray through your perfume—pesticides. That's what's making you sick."

She registered that, then added, "Amy? But Amy was the nice one. She was so sweet."

"Not that sweet," Pastor Dev said through gritted teeth. "She's high now. She traded information for drugs, apparently. Then she agreed to poison you, probably for even more drugs. But Kissie managed to get the truth out of her."

"Oh, no. The VEPs got to Amy. Poor Amy."

Distinguished Gentleman looked confused. "Who—"

"Very Evil People," she said to him over her shoulder as Pastor Dev gathered her up. He lifted her into his arms, then headed toward the bathroom, but Lydia couldn't enjoy his touch—it hurt her skin to be touched. Then she heard water being turned on, but that didn't bother her half as much as the white-hot pokers branding her skin and the fact that Pastor Dev had her in his arms and drat, she couldn't even enjoy it.

"Ugh, pesticides?" she said, her fingers scratching at her burning, itching skin. "I'm allergic to things like that. Hives. I told Amy—I told Amy I couldn't wear strong perfume. I used the lotion, because the perfume made me sneeze. I only used the lotion. I get the hives if it's too strong."

"This will be more than hives if we don't hurry," Distinguished Gentleman said. "Most common pesticides don't cause an immediate reaction, but we don't know how much she's been exposed to or for how long, especially if the girl put it in the lotion. And we don't have much time before they find out where you two are. This might help temporarily, but she will still need medical help."

"Do we have people posted?" Dev asked.

"Yes. I'll alert them immediately." Then the man nodded toward Lydia. "You take care of her."

Pastor Dev put one hand on her chin. "I'm sorry to have to do this, Lydia. Please forgive me."

And then Lydia felt the warm wash of water hitting her in the face, along with Pastor Dev's hands on her shoulders, holding her under the shower spray.

"Let me go," she cried out, the lukewarm water merging with the agony racing down her body. Her skin was raw with pain and heat, tears were streaming down her face and she wanted to be somewhere else. Somewhere safe. So she tried to pound that thought into him as she hit against his chest. "Let me go."

But he didn't let her go.

Instead, he got inside the open shower with her, both of them fully clothed, and held her so tightly that soon they were both completely soaked, too.

Lydia looked at him, sobs moving throughout her body, the sensation of being burned alive clawing at her flesh. "What's wrong with me? What did they do to me?"

He held her face in his hands, his eyes focused on hers. "Listen to me. You're going to be all right, Lydia. I promise. I promise."

"You always promise so much," she said, angry now. Angry with him, and with CHAIM, and with the world in general. "You always promise, but…I'm hurting. I'm hurting." She realized she was screaming now, but she didn't care. "So don't make me any more promises, all right?"

"All right," he said, his voice low and calm, even though his eyes blazed with the same tears and frustrations she felt. And the same rage. "All right. No more promises."

And then he kissed her.

EIGHT

He'd had no other choice, Dev kept telling himself as he kissed Lydia, and he kept right on kissing her long after she'd stopped pounding her tiny fists into his chest. Long after she'd slumped against him and settled into his embrace. He probably would have continued, since her lips had gone warm and tender, if they hadn't been interrupted by their gray-haired friend.

"You must leave. Now!"

That urgent command brought Dev back to full alert. And made him realize that once again, he'd been distracted enough to put Lydia in even more danger. But she had been near hysterics, so what else could he have done? He wouldn't strike a woman. Kissing her quiet had seemed the best plan at the time. But now...

Their helper turned off the water and tossed a big towel at Lydia. "Get her out of there."

"What's going on?" Lydia asked, her eyes dazed, her skin flushed. Chill bumps dotted her arms.

Dev pulled her out onto the tiled floor and tugged the big pink towel around her ruined dress. "C'mon, Lydia. We have to get you some medical help."

"I'm all wet."

"We'll take care of that later. How do you feel?"

"I'm better. I think."

Her big eyes sent him a look that said they'd have to talk about things later. Much later. She was shaken by that kiss. And shocked, no doubt. It hadn't been the most proper thing to do—kiss his secretary. Or his administrative assistant, as Lydia liked to be called.

"Hurry," the gray-haired man said, urging them toward the door.

"How many?" Dev asked, glancing out the tiny bathroom window, his hands guiding Lydia forward.

"Four. They pulled up in a dark BMW, then fanned out."

"Did you recognize any of them?"

"No, dear boy, I'm afraid I didn't. If they're associated with CHAIM in any way, it's news to me. But they didn't stop for an introduction."

"Let's go," Dev said, giving his friend a nod that he was ready. "Lydia, hold on to my back and don't let go."

Lydia grasped his ruined jacket with a weak grip, as if she didn't have the strength to hold on. "Don't let go," he told her. He had to know she was right behind him at all times. "Got it?"

She nodded, her hands clutching the wet black wool, her eyes big with fear and fatigue.

"This way," the man said, guiding them out yet another door to a hallway. "This leads to the kitchen and then the yard beyond. Follow the hedge and stay in the shadows. There is a delivery truck waiting at the back entrance, right past the service gate. Get in it. I have people in place to hold them off, but only for a brief time."

"Who are you?" Lydia asked, lifting her head toward the man as Dev dragged her down the narrow hallway.

The man leading them smiled behind his mask. "Me? They call me The Peacemaker." He shot a glance at Dev. "I'm sure you've heard of me."

Dev nodded. He'd heard all right. They'd sent in a big gun to help him out of this mess. That could either be good or bad, depending on the outcome of this operation. And right now, that outcome didn't bode well for any of them.

"'Blessed be the peacemakers,'" Lydia said, her voice monotone and quiet. "'For they shall be called sons of God.'"

Dev prayed she wasn't going into shock. "I have to get her to a poison control center."

"You will have the proper help waiting in the truck," The Peacemaker assured him. "Kissie did her research and found an antidote to the pesticide, then she sent the truck to fetch you. The antidote is with the driver. Just get it into her system as quickly as you can."

They'd reached the butler's pantry leading into the long, modern kitchen. The Peacemaker checked to make sure no one was around. "I've distracted the caterers. You have just enough time to make a run for it." He opened the back door, then motioned them through.

Dev turned on the porch. "Who's really behind this?"

The Peacemaker looked down at the floor. "We're still not sure. But we're beginning to think it has something to do with the South American rescue that went bad a few years ago."

Dev let out a sigh. "The one Eli Trudeau—The Disciple—was involved in?"

"Yes. And we both know how that ended."

"But we still don't know if it's Eli, or someone else trying to get to me? We made a lot of enemies down there."

"Yes, we did. We'll keep searching until we have an answer, but everything we've found so far indicates The Disciple. We won't make a move until we're sure, of course. Meantime, you have your orders. I suggest you follow them to the letter."

Dev tugged Lydia close. "Eagle Rock."

"Hurry."

Dev looked back. "What about you?"

"Me? My dear boy, I was never here."

With that, The Peacemaker jumped off the porch and disappeared into the New Orleans night.

Lydia clung to Dev, then looked toward the shadowy path. "He never even took off his mask."

Dev didn't bother waving goodbye to The Peacemaker. They'd meet again before this was over, he was sure. He pulled Lydia away from the muted light coming from the crowded house. When he glanced back, he thought he saw something move just beyond the corner of the house.

"Lydia," he whispered close, "if I say run, you take off and don't look back."

"Will I turn into stone?" she quipped, but her voice sounded weak and shaky.

"Just don't look back. I mean it. Someone is following us."

Lydia moaned, but she kept moving. "What are you going to do?"

"I'm going to stop whoever it is. I want you near, but not harmed. If things go bad, you have to get to the truck and hope our man is inside. The code word is Eagle Rock. Do you understand?"

"Yes."

"Okay, here goes," Dev said, shoving her into a clump of hydrangea bushes, his body shielding hers. He waited, watching as the dark form crept along the shrubbery line. He had to take out the weapon first. With a practiced ease that surprised him since he'd been out of CHAIM for so long, Dev positioned himself in the shadows, then pounced hard, his foot lifting into a powerful kick toward the sleek hand-gun in the stranger's grasp.

The gun flew out into the air. The assailant grabbed his arm, then went into fight mode. Dev was ready with a second swift kick to the man's mid-section, followed by a focused chop to his neck. The dark stranger fell into a clump by Dev's feet.

"Go," Dev whispered to Lydia, pushing her ahead of him. He glanced back once to make sure no other assailants were behind them. But The Peacemaker should have had a way of stopping assailants, and Dev figured his superior had taken care of the others by now.

Once they reached the dark alley, Dev turned to check on Lydia. "How are you?"

"Cold and wet," she said, pushing damp strands of hair off her face. "And I guess my makeup is ruined, huh?"

"You look fine," he told her. "But you're not out of the woods yet. We have to make sure the pesticides didn't get too far into your system."

"I'm not itching nearly as much now. But it's still hard to breathe."

"We'll take care of that." He gave her a quick hug, then turned to look up and down the alley for the truck. "There's our ride," he said, tugging Lydia by the arm. She had to hold on to the big towel to keep from tripping over it.

"I wish I had my Easy Spirits," she said. "These shoes are not made for quick getaways."

Glad her wry sense of humor was back, Dev looked down at her wet strappy high heels. "Just a few more steps. Once we get settled, we'll find dry clothes." He almost said "I promise" but then he remembered Lydia's heated words to him earlier.

And his to her. *No more promises.*

He wouldn't promise her anything beyond each moment he could keep her alive. He'd just silently ask God to help him make that happen. *Please, Lord, help me. Keep her safe. Give her the promise of Your protection. Please.*

As they approached the big truck from behind, Dev held a finger to his lips, warning Lydia to stay quiet. He stood her beside the truck, then swiftly opened the driver's side door. "Where does the eagle dwell?" he asked the man he now had by the throat.

"It dwells on the rock," said the frightened man, "and resides on the crag of the rock and the stronghold."

"How do we get to the eagle?"

"Eagle's Rock, sir."

"We need to get out of here," Dev replied. Then he let the man go. "I'm The Pastoral."

"I've heard of you, sir," the young driver said. "I'm David. Nice to finally meet you."

"I wish we had time to chat," Dev replied, shaking the younger man's hand. Then he made a quick sweep of the shadows. "But I have to get this woman to safety."

"I understand. Climb into the back."

Dev nodded, then turned to Lydia. "Here, I'll help you up."

"Why the back?" she asked as he lifted her over the open flatbed with wooden, slit panes on each side. "Wouldn't it be much nicer to ride inside with the driver?"

"Perhaps, but it would be much more dangerous."

Looking resigned, Lydia held her towel and dress and quickly climbed up onto the truck.

Dev hopped in after her, then glanced around. "Hay. Wonderful."

"And watermelons," Lydia said, the big towel held tightly around her. "I hope I don't start sneezing."

"You're allergic to watermelons?" he asked, hoping to at least lighten the moment a bit.

"No, silly. Hay." She grinned, then looked sad all over again.

Because of him, Dev thought. Because he'd brought her to this point.

"The hay and watermelons help to shield us from bullets," he explained. "We can hide back here much better than sitting up front. But if you're feeling worse—"

"I'll be all right," she said, her head down, her breath coming hard in spite of her efforts to be calm.

Dev hated the way she seemed to be slipping into defeat. He couldn't let Lydia give up. He hadn't. Not yet.

They sank into a corner near the cab of the big

vehicle. Dev tugged her down, made sure she was covered, then knocked on the window.

The driver opened the panel. "Yes, sir?"

"Antidotes? Do you have any antidotes or a first-aid kit? I was told we'd have help for the poison in Miss Cantrell's system."

"Yes, sir," the young man said. He shoved a small package through the window. "We ran a research based on the information from Miss Kissic. There's an injection inside this pack."

"A shot?" Lydia said, sitting straight up against the wood-paneled truck. "I hate shots."

"I have to do this, Lydia," Dev told her. "To make you well."

"But I feel better now."

He hated the fear in her eyes. "But we have to be sure."

David cut his gaze toward the house. "And we need to hurry."

Dev quickly prepared the syringe, then looked over at Lydia. "I'll try to make it as painless as possible."

"Famous last words." But she held out her arm like a soldier about to be executed.

"I have to give it to you in your thigh," Dev explained, trying to sound calm.

Lydia let out a breath, then extended one of her legs. "Just get it over with, please."

Dev worked quickly and efficiently, thankful for the hours of training and fieldwork he'd had to school him for this. Lydia closed her eyes and let out a little groan as the needle penetrated her skin.

"How was that?" he asked as he pulled the damp towel back over her leg.

"I hardly felt a thing." But her eyes were still squeezed shut.

"You might become drowsy, but you'll be able to breathe much better soon." Dev tapped the window. "Let's get out of here."

David cranked the truck and they were off. The jostling caused Dev to fall toward Lydia, but as he tried to right himself, she reached out to grab his arm. "Stay close," she said. "Please?"

Her soft words were filled with a vulnerability that tore at his heart, and again, Dev felt the guilt of her fears washing over him. He had to take care of her, get her to a safe place. Then he'd find whoever was chasing them and take care of matters himself, if need be.

The way Eli did?

That question shot through his head like the glare of a rocket. Because of Lydia, Dev would have to be very careful to do things by the book.

So he scooted over to the corner and pulled her into his arms, holding her and making sure the damp towel had her covered for now. "Rest," he said into her ear. "Just rest."

He remembered telling her that the very first night they'd been on the run. Had that really been only a couple of days ago? As he held her, cushioning her with each bounce and shift of the big truck, he thought about how their relationship had gone from employee and employer to friends, and now to something much more intimate and intense.

Now they were two people on the run, forced together under extreme circumstances. And Dev had once again become the protector, because Lydia was dear to him and someone was trying to kill her. He'd keep running in order to save her.

Now he'd breached all decorum and protocol and broken all the rules. He'd kissed her. And he wanted to kiss her again. But that couldn't happen.

He'd hurt her too many times already.

And how would Lydia feel when they reached the end of the line? Would she still be his friend—his treasured friend—or would she hate him forever?

I'm hurting. How could he ever forget her angry face, the pain in her beautiful eyes, or those words she'd hurled at him? He never would forget. And he certainly couldn't forget that kiss they'd shared.

I'm hurting, too, Lydia, he thought now as he pulled her head down onto his chest. *I'm hurting for you, and for what might have been...for us.*

Lydia woke with a start, the smell of diesel fuel permeating her nose. Glancing around, she looked up into bright sunshine and Pastor Dev's haggard but handsome face. "Hello."

"Hello," he said, helping her to sit up. They were still in the back of the watermelon truck.

"Where are we?" she asked, squinting into the sun. The road was busy and multilaned, an interstate. Then she saw signs for Austin. "We're in Texas?"

"Yes, and we'll be at our destination soon." As if on cue, the truck turned off the interstate and headed down a long and winding county road. He gave her an appraising look. "How are you?"

Lydia knew she must look hideous with her smeared makeup and ratty hair. "I don't know. I need a mirror before I answer that question."

"You look better this morning. No rash or hives, and your pulse and breathing are both back to normal. I think the antidote did its job."

"I look like a drowned rat, and you know it."

He touched a hand to her temple in a gesture she was beginning to both love and hate. "You look beautiful to me, because you're not sick anymore." The fatigue in his eyes told her he'd kept vigil over her all night.

Feeling petty and contrite, she lowered her gaze. "Thank you for saving my life."

He shrugged. "Part of the job."

That felt like a slap in the face, and just because she was weak and sore and dehydrated and hungry, she retorted. "And I guess that kiss was just part of the job, too, right?"

He had the good grace to look away. "That shouldn't have happened."

Her heart held the leftover fire of last night's rage. "Right."

"But…I had to calm you down."

"Well, that certainly did the trick, didn't it?"

"Lydia—"

"Don't," she said, holding up a hand and blinking back tears. "Don't try to explain or justify things. We're in deep trouble and…I know things are not as they seem. Even between us. Being chased, running for our lives, being thrown into such a chaotic situation, makes us do things we'd never do on a normal, routine day. Things such as kissing each other. Bad idea. So you need to understand, if…when we get out of this, I don't expect anything from you. Not one thing, except my old job back, of course. I do have bills to pay."

He actually managed a smile then, his eyes sweeping over her with regret and what looked a whole lot like longing. "We will get back to our old routine, Lydia. Somehow. And then, the worst thing we'll have to run from will be Mrs. Gordon's prune cake."

Lydia thought of ornery eighty-year-old Mrs. Gordon, bringing prune cake to each and every church function. Then she started giggling. Pastor Dev did, too. They both laughed so hard tears were streaming down their faces when the truck came to an abrupt halt.

Lydia wiped at the tears, and wondered if they really were from laughing, or from a deep need to just sit and cry her eyes out. Maybe she was just too tired to think straight, but she thought the tears in Pastor Dev's eyes weren't from humor, either.

They both missed the life they'd left behind. Lydia's heart ached with all that had happened, all that he'd tried to save her from seeing. Not only did he have the burden of his friend's death back in Atlanta, but he had the burden of protecting her. And the memories of a past he'd tried to leave behind.

She couldn't stay mad at him. He was still a good man, still her hero, even if he did regret kissing her. She reminded herself that she wasn't supposed to complain, and she certainly wasn't supposed to take one little kiss seriously. One little, heart-changing, mind-altering kiss.

He gave her a long look filled with a dark intensity that scared her. She sent him a hopeful smile as a counteraction. "I'm okay. And right now, I'm so hungry, I'd even be willing to eat prune cake."

His eyes grew bright again, then he looked away at the rich green pastures of the Texas hillside while he swiped at his face with his dirty jacket sleeve. And when he looked back, his eyes were dry. And blank.

NINE

Lydia relaxed in a luxurious robe, her face slathered in a mud mask, wondering how she'd gone from a drowned rat to reclining diva in a matter of minutes.

It was those women. The three with the big hair and the even bigger diamonds. Wishing she had her journal—which, along with Pastor Dev's trusty briefcase full of gadgets, had been left behind at Kissie's place—Lydia thought back over this morning's events, trying very hard *not* to think about that kiss that had started them on yet another grand adventure.

At least they were safe here in this country-club retreat deep in the Texas hill country. After they'd gotten off the watermelon truck—and Lydia felt as if she'd fallen off the watermelon truck—Pastor Dev had turned her over to some of the richest matrons in Texas—or at least from the way they talked and acted, Lydia had surmised that. Then after telling her he'd see her later, he'd promptly disappeared to give a "briefing" to someone.

Lydia herself had been briefed on what to expect, but this briefing was more of a flutter of chatter and chuckles coming from her three matrons as they each introduced themselves and gave her a little bit of background.

"Hello, darlin', bless your heart." This from Lulu Anderson. Lulu had old oil money to burn, from everything Lydia could glean. And she had the bouffant blond hair and expensively altered skin to back it. "You just come with us, suga'. We're gonna get you all cleaned up and polished like a new set of pearls."

Lydia could only nod as she was ushered into a big, sprawling Spanish-style ranch house. The interior was light and open, with cool terra-cotta tiles and soft leather furniture everywhere. Out back, a large pool bubbled and flowed in never-ending serenity in front of a beautiful view of the distant hills and vistas. Servants hurried here and there, following Lulu's clipped, cultured instructions.

"We're putting Miss Lydia in the French suite," Lulu told an aging butler. "Hurry now, Alexandre."

"Don't worry about a thing, honey," Sally Mae Barton said, her black hair shimmering in its chignon. "We know how to handle these situations." Sally Mae reminded Lydia of an aging Scarlett O'Hara. And she seemed just as formidable.

"Are you all members of CHAIM?" Lydia, shocked and fatigued, asked.

"No, sweetie pie, not anymore. Now we're just married to men who are."

That caused Lydia's mind to venture into a territory she probably shouldn't be exploring at all. "So, CHAIM members are allowed to have families?"

"Sure, honey. Not only is it allowed, but it makes for a good cover." The third woman wrapped a plump arm around Lydia's shoulder. "I'm Rita Simpson. I'm an executive director with Mary Kay. You need a mask. Immediately."

"Of course she needs a mask, and a long nap, too," Lulu said, rolling her heavily lined blue eyes. "She'll get all of that, and yes, Rita, you can give her a makeover and some complimentary samples." She giggled. "Suga', this woman has made a fortune with Mary Kay. She's legendary around these parts."

"Do you drive a pink Cadillac?" Lydia asked, fascinated with these prim, overdressed, overperfumed women. Rita looked young in spite of her shimmering white, precisely clipped hair.

"Of course," Rita said with a dismissive shrug. "I'm on about my tenth one, I believe."

Remembering her first foray into being a diva in New Orleans, Lydia held up a hand. "I don't want anything too over the top. I just want to be clean and natural."

"We can do clean and natural," Rita said, her bright green eyes twinkling. "In fact, we have a whole line of products that'll give you the natural look."

Lydia wondered why she had to put on makeup to look natural, but she didn't argue. She was too dirty and tired to refuse the kindness of strangers, after all.

They stood Lydia in front of a massive, intricately carved door. Lulu gave the other two a wink, then said, "Now, Miss Lydia, this is your room. You're safe here. My husband, Alfred, hired the best security firm in Texas to make sure we are always safe here. If you open the door out onto the porch, an alarm will sound. So don't do that just yet, unless you have to escape right quick like. The Pastoral gave us strict orders to keep you inside unless he himself can escort you out for some fresh air. No one else. Just him. He wants to protect you. Do you understand, darlin'?"

Lydia did understand. She nodded, but couldn't manage to speak. She was just too tired to be mad at Pastor Dev's commando mode right now. "Thank you," she said.

"Let's pray," Lulu suggested, grabbing Lydia's hands in hers. The other women gathered in a protective circle around Lydia, then closed their eyes. Lydia stood silent as each one prayed for her safety.

"Lord, help our men find the ones behind this horrible situation. Bring them to a swift and fitting justice."

"And Lord, help this poor girl find some rest here in one of Your safe pavilions. Protect our CHAIM warriors."

"Also, Lord, help us to help Lydia understand… about CHAIM and about…masks…and about men, too, I reckon."

"Amen." Lulu looked across at Rita. "Was that mask part really necessary?"

"I figured it couldn't hurt. A girl has to know how to look her best in any situation—and she is undercover."

With that, Lulu gave Lydia a quick hug. "Go on in. You'll be safe and you'll have complete privacy."

After the women brought her the softest robe she'd ever felt, Rita slapped something white and scented on her face, telling her to let it set for about ten minutes, then to rinse and pat her face gently.

"We'll send in some coffee and muffins for now, then we'll come back after your nap to get you up and ready for an early dinner out on the back patio."

"When will I see Pastor Dev again?" Lydia asked, wondering if she would ever see him. Had he abandoned her here, locked in a big, sprawling house with these matronly "What Not To Wear" experts?

Lulu glanced over to Sally Mae and Rita, her carefully etched eyebrows lifting. "You'll see him soon, honey. Meantime, we three might need to sit you down and explain what being in love with a CHAIM man involves."

Mortified, Lydia tried to hide her embarrassment. "But—"

Sally Mae patted her arm. "No buts about it, honey. We know love when we see it. After all, we've each been there. It's not easy to love a warrior, but it can be done."

"Does it show that much?" Lydia asked.

"Only when you take a breath," Rita replied, her eyes full of understanding.

Then the ladies had fluttered out like three butterflies, with waving hands and soft sighs and whispers.

So now here Lydia sat, on a brocade chaise lounge, with a mask drying over her features, wondering if Pastor Dev had a clue that she loved him. If everyone else could see it, why shouldn't he? Or maybe he did, and he was just ignoring it right now. But he'd kissed her as if he knew exactly how she felt.

"What am I to do, Lord?" she prayed out loud, her words echoing out over the high ceiling of the fancy gold-and-cream bathroom. "I've tried so hard to hide my feelings, but being on the run is getting to me. I love him so much, but I was in love with the man I knew. Now I don't even know him at all, and I still love him."

But, Lydia thought as she leaned her head back on the soft, scented pillow, her heart knew a real kiss from a necessary-for-the-circumstances kiss. And that kiss back in New Orleans had turned from necessary to much needed before it had ended. He'd needed her. She'd felt it in the way his lips had touched on hers, in the way he'd held her close. In the way he'd taken care of her and held her all night in the watermelon truck.

A kiss in the shower, a ride in a watermelon truck. It was all too unbelievable, even for Lydia's romantic mind.

"He must think I'm a regular twit, a loose woman

who'd throw herself at anyone, including her own boss and minister. What have I done, Lord? Why did I act so wanton and careless?"

Because you love him, came the reply. But Lydia knew the reply hadn't come from God. That would be hers alone. Because she did love Pastor Dev. And she wished with all her heart he could return that love.

Sinking down into the fluffy pillows, she waited for an answer from above. But she heard only the silence of her gold-encased prison. And the beating of her own treacherous heart.

Dev stared across the table at the three men who'd brought him to Eagle Rock. Three distinguished, retired soldiers from CHAIM, men he'd admired and served with over the years. Men who now wanted the same answers he needed.

"I've told you everything I know," he said, worry and weariness causing him to sound harsh. "I know I was brought here for a reason. After all, it's not every day that a man gets invited to Eagle Rock."

Eagle Rock meant even more big guns had become involved.

Alfred Anderson leaned forward, his craggy face etched in a frown. In a deep Texas drawl, he said, "Pastoral, we know it's been hard, being thrown back into the thick of things. But we can't keep holding them off, and you can't keep running—it's like squatting with your spurs on. We gotta find out who's behind these attacks and end this thing, once and for all."

Dev knew what that meant. "But we've never attacked one of our own. And we still don't have proof that The Disciple is behind this."

Gerald Barton got up to pour himself another glass of iced tea, then he stood, tall and big chested, his crystal glass in his hand. "But all indications lead to him. He swore he'd get even with all of us whenever he got out of the retreat."

"The prison, you mean," Dev countered. "We sent him to a locked, carefully watched facility. Eli knew what we were doing. Call it a spiritual retreat, but we locked the man away."

"We had no other choice," John Simpson said, anger coloring his words to match his ruddy complexion. "Eli was getting too bold, too careless. And we still don't have all the clear details of what happened in South America. For all we know, his actions were what caused this tragedy."

Dev hit a hand on the marble-topped table centered in the dark-paneled library. "I turned the man in, John. I was the whistle-blower who caused Eli to lose his family. And for that, I can never forgive myself. I don't really blame him for coming after me. I deserve whatever he wants to do to me."

"You don't deserve to die," Alfred retorted, "and that young woman certainly doesn't deserve any of this."

Dev sank back in the oxblood leather chair. "No,

Lydia is an innocent victim. And she's the only reason I haven't taken matters into my own hands."

"Don't be foolish, son," Alfred said, a hand up. "You know what going off on a vigilante quest did to Eli. You're too good a man to let that happen to you."

"But I can't bear it if Lydia becomes collateral damage. If..." He closed his eyes to the fatigue draining him. "I just couldn't bear that."

"Then there's only one thing to do," John said. "We have to draw Eli out, get the truth out of him. Whatever it takes, you need to meet with him face-to-face."

"How can we make that happen?"

Gerald leaned forward. "Let's review the situation, then go from there. We have to be sure. CHAIM is not in the mercenary business. We try to save people, not take them out. Harm none. That's why we brought you here. To give you time to think clearly."

Dev got the meaning of that statement. He was being ordered to chill out. "I'm clear on everything, gentlemen. Especially the fact that someone is out to get me. As angry as Eli was and probably still is, he was...he is my friend. I can't believe he'd do this to me, to this organization. It just doesn't add up."

"But Eli has possibly compromised our entire operation," John replied, frowning. "You yourself said he blames you for turning him in before he could go after those people down in South America. It might come down to you or him, Devon."

"I won't kill him," Dev said, his tone brooking no

argument. He'd die himself before he'd take another human being's life. Especially that of his friend and fellow team member.

"Did your assailant in Atlanta leave any clues at all?" Gerald asked, turning to Dev.

"Nothing that I know of," Dev replied. He lifted a thick file from the table. "We've all read over the official CHAIM report. Our operative in the Atlanta police department was careful to make sure we received a detailed CSI report. It was a clean crime. No prints, no weapons found. They used a silencer and they got out quickly."

"Then they realized their mistake," John added. "And that's why someone is still out there, trying to kill you."

"Eli wouldn't do that. He wouldn't send someone else."

"He's changed, Dev." Gerald shrugged. "It happens. Eli was a good man in training, but his faith was always shaky. He might not pull the trigger, but he could order it done."

Alfred nodded. "He only joined CHAIM to please his father. I don't think his heart was ever in it."

Dev nodded. No one knew who Eli's father was, and Eli refused to ever talk about him. But the man had been a high-ranking official in the CHAIM link until he'd been killed many years ago, somewhere in Africa. That had been the saving grace in Eli's enforced seclusion and recovery. Out of respect for his father, and his loss, their superiors had been lenient and forgiving with Eli.

"Maybe Eli joined for all the wrong reasons, but then he lost his wife and unborn child, because of us," Dev reminded them. "Because of me."

"Or because of his own hotheaded carelessness," John countered. "We just don't know."

Dev ran a hand down his unshaven face. "My gut tells me that there's something more to this. And I can't help but think it still involves the cartel we infiltrated in South America. It stands to reason that if Eli is out, the cartel leaders might be after him. And maybe they came to Atlanta hoping to send us a warning."

"By killing you?" Gerald shook his head. "I doubt that. Why wouldn't they just find Eli and end it once and for all?"

"Because Eli knows how to hide," Dev said. "What better way to bring him out of hiding than by killing a team member and a friend—a former friend whom he now considers to be an enemy?"

"You have a point," John said. "If Eli thought you'd been killed, he might go after the cartel again. Either to avenge your death and that of his family, or to join up with them as a reward."

"And the glaring problem is," Alfred added, "we don't know which way Eli has turned. He might be back in the fold, or he might be lost to us forever."

Dev got up and walked to the big window that gave a stunning view of the hill country surrounding the secluded hideaway. "Then we have to keep searching. We need to put out more encryptions, see if we get anyone's attention. If Eli is in danger and if he wants our help, he'll answer us."

Alfred turned to the command system set up on his antique teakwood desk. "Then let's get to it." He keyed in a message, then turned to face the others. "Each guest room here is equipped with laptops—cleared for use by CHAIM members only. Check yours when you retire to your rooms. All we can do for now is watch and wait."

"And pray," Gerald replied.

Dev stayed by the window, his thoughts on Lydia. Her safety was his main concern right now. If Eli had turned rogue, he wouldn't stop at just getting even. He might kill Lydia just to get to Dev. But if Eli was in trouble, if someone from South America was after the entire CHAIM team, then they would do worse damage, far worse damage, than Eli ever thought about. Because these men were the very essence of evil.

And he shuddered to think what they would do to an innocent young woman.

Lydia woke to late-afternoon sunshine streaming into her room. Rubbing her eyes, she longed for her own bed back in Dixon. Even though this white-wood, elegant sleigh bed with the beautiful peach silk comforter and sheets was lovely, Lydia felt strange being encased in so much luxury.

"My mama would flip her lid," Lydia said to herself, her voice sounding scratchy and husky.

She got up, determined to try and salvage what little decency she had left. She felt so out of sorts, dressing up in fancy evening clothes, kissing a man in the shower, sleeping the day away. This wasn't Lydia's style. She was used to hard work and a strong moral fiber. Not silk sheets and sparkly dresses.

But everyone she'd met on this strange trip had been kind and devoted. All believers, even if they did march to the beat of a different drummer.

"Are You trying to teach me something, Lord?" she asked as she hurried to the big wardrobe across the room. Rita had told her she'd find clothes inside. "Are You showing little sheltered, protected, narrowminded Lydia Cantrell that the world is made up of all kinds of Christians?"

The silence of the still summer day echoed out over her head. "Okay, maybe You've just abandoned me altogether."

She instantly regretted thinking that way and said a quick prayer for forgiveness. God had not abandoned her. He'd been right there, helping Pastor Dev to protect her. And being alive on this nice summer day was proof of that.

"I'm going to shut up and get dressed," Lydia told herself and God. She found a nice floral T-shirt and some denim capris in her size, wondering how everyone knew how to dress her. At least she was learning important wardrobe tips, if nothing else.

She'd just started combing her hair when she heard a knock at the door. "Who is it?"

"It's Alexandre, ma'am. I'm to bring you to the dining room. Casual dress is fine."

"I'll be right there," Lydia replied to the butler, thinking casual was more to her liking. Looking in the bottom of the wardrobe, she found some pink leather flip-flops. They matched the flowers in her shirt, so she put them on and found they fit. "Close enough."

But before she could reach the door, it swung open. In pranced Rita and Sally Mae, all smiles and floral scents.

"You can't possibly go to dinner without proper makeup," Rita said, slapping her Mary Kay case down on the bed. "We sent Alexandre away. Honestly, that man is the most uppity butler I've ever seen. He didn't want to let us in. Sit down over here, honey, and let us work on you a little bit."

"I don't want much makeup," Lydia replied. But she sank down on the soft cream-colored stool in front of the elaborate French provincial vanity. "I just need a little blush and gloss. You know, Kissie fixed me up in New Orleans and it was just a tad too much."

"We understand," Sally Mae said, smiling at Lydia's reflection in the mirror. "You don't want to paint the barn door too red, right?"

Lydia nodded, confused. "Right." Then she pivoted. "Is Kissie okay?"

"She's fine. The girl who tattled has been taken care of—sent to a rehab center."

Lydia sighed. "I'm glad Kissie is all right. I liked her, even if she did dress me in slinky red."

"We won't overdo it, but you don't want to look like you've been rode hard and put up wet," Rita said, then grinned at Lydia's shocked expression. "Like an old mare that's been on a long gallop."

"Oh." Lydia shook her head. "I don't want to look like an old mare, that's for sure."

"You will look just right," Rita said, one diamond-heavy finger posed on her face as she analyzed Lydia's skin. "Nice complexion. So creamy and with just a touch of cute freckles. And that hair—it's to die for."

"Well, someone has been trying to kill me," Lydia quipped.

"She has the right attitude," Sally Mae said, her diamond tennis bracelet winking at Lydia. "When you love a CHAIM man, you have to have a sense of humor."

"How did y'all do it?" Lydia asked, curious and hoping to gain some pointers. "How'd y'all meet your husbands?"

Rita chuckled as she plucked Lydia's eyebrows. "I sold Mary Kay to John's mother and sisters. They set us up, but of course, he balked. CHAIM men have a definite commitment problem, being as they are always out saving the world and all that." She shrugged. "But I didn't give up. I just bided my time and waited for him to come home. Then I pounced on the man and told him I loved him and wanted to spend the rest of my life with him. He was so overwhelmed that he said yes right away. That was thirty-five years and three children ago. I've prayed many a night for him to come home safe. Now he's retired and I'm as tickled as a pig in a mud puddle."

Lydia laughed, then turned to Sally Mae. "Your turn."

"I was a CHAIM operative," Sally Mae explained, grinning. "Met Gerald in London. It was during the late seventies and we were in place to watch some really aggressive cult members who'd snatched a young American girl. I posed as a free-spirited girl and infiltrated this rather nasty cult. He was my contact person on the outside. It wasn't love at first sight. He had to chase me until I let him catch me. Been letting him chase me for over thirty years now."

Lydia was amazed that petite, spry Sally Mae with the long, perfectly manicured pink fingernails and matching toes had been an undercover operative. "That must have been some adventure."

"It was. We saved a lot of Christians from terrible things. And CHAIM still does that."

"These are hard times," Rita added, her fingers buffing and blending Lydia's eyes and face. "World terror, countries in chaos and the innocents who get caught in the fray. Our men are very special to us, but when called to duty, they have to go."

"For the greater good," Lydia said, her eyes going wide as she stared at them in the mirror.

"For the greater good," Sally Mae repeated. "I see you've heard some of the rules already."

"More than I ever wanted to know," Lydia said.

"It's all about serving the Lord," Rita said, her hand holding Lydia by the chin while she painted gloss on Lydia's lips. "These men are trained to help Christians the world over. But sometimes it's all about loving your man so much it hurts."

"I do," Lydia admitted, the pain of that admission searing her heart. "I loved him when I didn't know about any of this, and I think I love him even more now. But I don't think he's even aware of it. He was barely aware I was even alive until someone tried to kill both of us."

"Oh, he's aware, all right."

They all turned as Lulu came clicking into the room, a soft smile on her face. "In fact, I feel pretty sure that if we don't get you out there to dinner soon, the man will come charging in here and throw you over his shoulder, the way Alfred did me when I refused to elope with him thirty-six years ago. I was a debutante and sorority girl and he was a hard-edged wildcatter, but mercy, I didn't want to admit that I loved him. So he kinda took matters into his own hands."

Stunned, Lydia said, "Oh, Pastor Dev would never—"

Just then, there was a pounding on the door. "Lydia, are you in there? Is everything all right?"

It was Pastor Dev.

"I'm coming," Lydia called. "I'm fine, just running a little behind."

"Well, hurry up. I was worried sick."

"I rest my case," Lulu said, a knowing smile on her face. "Now, suga', let's get out there and have a nice evening with our menfolks."

"But…I need to know how to do that," Lydia whispered. "I mean, I need to know how to love such a complicated man."

Rita finished, then rubbed her hands together. "Oh, that's easy, honey. Just keep smiling and praying. No matter how much your poor heart is breaking."

"For the greater good?"

"For that, and your own sanity."

TEN

Lydia woke with a start.

Someone was in her room. She couldn't make out any human shapes since it was raining heavily and there was no moonlight. But she could feel the presence in the big wide bedroom.

And she could hear her own fast breathing.

She pulled the covers up to ward off her fears. "Who's there?"

Nothing.

The rain fell in a continuous drone, muffling any noise that might seem different. When had the storm approached? And how had she slept through that and someone entering her room? Maybe she'd just been dreaming.

Just to be safe, Lydia searched for the phone on the bedside table. There was a red button for emergencies. Lulu had shown it to her and stressed that she should touch it if she felt in danger.

She reached for the button, but a strong arm pushed her hand away. Her breath caught and a cold wave of fear rushed through her system. She tried to speak, but no words would come.

"I wouldn't call anyone just yet."

"Alexandre?" She recognized the cultured voice of the butler. She almost wanted to giggle—they could actually say the butler did it. But she couldn't muster even a scared chuckle. She swallowed, prayed, tried to think. Tried to stall him. "Alexandre, is everything all right?"

"No," the man holding her said. "Everything is not all right. You're a very pretty woman, but you know too much. You've seen too much. I hate to do this… but beware the wolf in sheep's clothing."

Lydia watched as he raised a pillow in the air, and she knew right then that she would die if she didn't do something quick to help herself. If she could just make it to the French doors and then the porch, she could trip the alarm system. She had to do something, right now.

In his room across the hall, Dev sat skimming his e-mails. He couldn't sleep, so he'd decided to give it one last shot. Blurry eyed, he blinked as the screen flashed white and alive before him. Then he saw it—an instant message popped up on the screen.

The black sheep has no shepherd. He has no master. He is scattered on the mountain.

Dev sat up in his chair, his mind humming, his heart racing. Eli?

The Disciple had a mountain retreat in Colorado, and he'd always joked that he was the black sheep of their particular team. Was Eli trying to tell Dev something?

Dev typed,

'What do you understand that is not us?'

Eli would know to look to Job. He'd know the verse and understand the code. What do you know?

The answer came quickly.

'Both the gray haired and the aged are among us.' Hide anything received.

Not "Do not hide" like the original verse from Job. But "hide." Eli wanted Dev to withhold information? That could be a trick, or it could be a warning. Did Eli know something that would help them both?

His pulse pounding, Dev typed,

'What shall I answer you?'

The response came back. The black sheep has no shepherd. Then no more codes, but an outright denial.

I didn't do it, Pastoral. It's a setup. Beware the gray-haired man. Don't walk with the wicked men.

Then Eli was gone, leaving Dev to stare at the words frozen on the screen. Eli had broken procedure to speak bluntly, which meant he, too, was on the run. Dev could only hope no one else had intercepted the message. But who? What was Eli saying? He'd repeated part of the message Kissie had sent earlier, so Dev knew Eli was keeping tabs on them. But what was he trying to say?

Dev thought back—what gray-haired man? Did Eli mean the man dressed as a granny back in Atlanta? Or the three men who were now helping Dev? They all had a tinge of gray in their hair. But even that description could be some sort of coded warning. Who else had helped Lydia and him? Kissie? No one in her charge had gray hair.

Then it hit him as though doused by the rain outside.

The Peacemaker. He certainly was a distinguished-looking, gray-haired man. And because of the mask, Dev had never actually seen his face.

Was Eli trying to warn him that The Peacemaker was behind this? But that didn't make sense. The Peacemaker had purposely helped Dev and Lydia in New Orleans. Thinking back over it, Dev realized The Peacemaker had been the one to send him here to Eagle Rock. He'd also been the one to give Dev a message from Kissie. And that message had saved

Lydia's life. So how could he be involved, other than trying to help?

But…Dev hadn't confirmed that message. He hadn't spoken to Kissie again since coming here. He'd only talked to her about the poisoning and how to stop it. Grabbing his Treo, he immediately dialed Kissie's private number.

She didn't answer. And he didn't dare leave a message.

Dev got up and ran a hand through his hair. The rain picked up, the wind howling around the long, rambling house. He heard something bang, then he heard what sounded like a scream. The next thing he heard was the alarm.

Lydia!

Dev dashed across the hall to Lydia's room, his fists banging hard against the door. "Lydia?" The door was locked, so he quickly stepped back, aiming his entire body against the heavy wood. The door-jamb shattered even as his shoulder throbbed with a white-hot pain, but he was inside and running before he even registered that.

"Lydia?" He called her name over and over as he raced to hit the light switch. When he turned on the overhead light, he saw the crumpled form of Alexandre near the night table, a shattered lamp pedestal lying nearby, and the patio doors wide open. Then he saw Lydia standing out in the middle of the yard, rain washing over her.

And she was screaming.

* * *

Lydia hadn't known what else to do. She'd received an e-mail long ago with self-defense tips for women. She'd memorized it. And boy, had those tips come in handy tonight.

First, she'd managed to use her own trapped arm for leverage, yanking with all her might so she could land a kick in his midsection. That had caused Alexandre, the so-called butler, to scream out in pain. Then she'd used her free elbow to jab him in the face and her fingers to poke at his eyes. He crumpled away from her. Since his only weapon was a pillow, Lydia could only imagine that he'd planned to smother her, asleep or awake. She wasn't about to let that happen.

While Alexandre held his hands to his eyes, Lydia, working on pure adrenaline, hit him over the head with the crystal lamp on the side table, and ran for the doors, opening them wide, welcoming the blaring sound of the security alarm.

The rain felt good on her fevered skin, the wind cold on her heated face. She remembered to scream as loud as she could. And she was still screaming when Pastor Dev grabbed her up in his arms and pulled her back to the long porch.

"Lydia," he said, his hands on her hair. "Lydia, are you all right?"

She stopped screaming, her breath coming in big gulps now. "I'm fine. Just mad, is all. The butler tried to kill me. How stupid is that?"

The look in his eyes—part terror, part admiration—told her that he did care about her. And that gave her a sense of calm. Gulping a deep breath, she said, "I'm all right, really."

"Thank You, God," Pastor Dev said, lifting up the prayer to the heavens. Then he pulled Lydia into his arms and held her close. "I'm so sorry. I was supposed to be watching out for you."

"I'm all right," Lydia kept telling him. "I…I remembered…somehow I remembered my self-defense tips."

He pulled back to stare down at her. "You sure did. Alexandre looks pretty beat up."

"He made me mad," she retorted. "I'm just so tired of people trying to kill me. They act nice, then they turn nasty. It's just not right."

Pastor Dev planted a kiss on her wet forehead. "Let's get you inside."

"Do you know that every time you kiss me, I'm all wet?" Lydia asked. "It's not very romantic." Then she held a hand to her mouth. "Oh, never mind. I mean…forget I said that. You were just being kind."

He didn't answer. Instead he just stood there looking at her, his dark eyes as bright and shimmering as the rainwater falling off the tiled roof. "Lydia, I—"

They were interrupted by a herd of Eagle Rock dwellers coming out onto the porch. Lulu had on a white satin robe, her hair still just as big and perfect as it had been all day. "Mercy, what in the world happened in there?"

Alfred was right behind her, the few hairs he had on his head standing straight up. "Alexandre is hurt."

"Alexandre tried to harm Lydia," Pastor Dev replied. "I hope he's more than hurt. Don't let him get away."

Alfred shouted back into the room. "Detain the butler."

"My Alexandre?" Lulu asked, her hands on her hips. "But…that just doesn't make sense."

"Nothing does right now, darlin'," her husband said. "This is worse than a bee after a bull. We can't trust anyone."

"Alexandre?" Sally Mae stood just inside the open doors, her hair down now and hanging in waves to her waist. "I can't believe it. We did a thorough background check on that man."

"He's only worked for us a few months," Lulu pointed out. Then she gasped. "He was planted here, wasn't he, Alfred?"

"Apparently," Alfred said, his gaze sweeping over the others. "We have to be more careful. I'll have to have a meeting with the other employees and explain what happens when someone is disloyal."

Lydia didn't dare ask about that. She tried to remember that CHAIM didn't want to do harm, but anyone would do harm to protect their loved ones, wouldn't they? Even this Disciple person everyone was talking about.

That made her remember something Alexandre had said while he held her down. "Alexandre told me to beware the wolf in sheep's clothing. Do you think he was talking about The Disciple?"

Pastor Dev looked at John and Alfred. "I've had a message from The Disciple."

Alfred nodded, his expression taut. "Why don't we get you two dry, then meet in the kitchen. You can fill us in."

"I won't meet without Lydia. I'm not leaving her alone again."

John nodded. "Lydia can be trusted."

Lydia beamed in spite of being so scared. She'd rather be in the thick of things than resting comfortably in a room where she'd almost been smothered. "I'll go get changed."

Lulu guided her back inside. "You remembered to open the doors to set the alarm off. Smart, honey, real smart."

"I can take care of myself," Lydia replied. But she gave the still-moaning Alexandre, who was being held down by Gerald and the very strong-armed Rita—who looked stunning even without all her Mary Kay—a very wide berth. Lydia did not want to have to kick Alexandre back down. But she would. She'd had just about enough.

Everyone left, Gerald dragging Alexandre out. Pastor Dev turned at the door, facing Lydia and Lulu. "I'll wait right outside."

"I'll get her dressed," Lulu said, patting his arm. "I'll make sure—"

Pastor Dev didn't let her finish. Pushing back inside, he asked, "Are you sure you're all right, Lydia?"

Lydia nodded. "I'm okay. I'm fine. I'm not going into shock and I'm not going to fall apart. I just want this to be over."

Lulu shot a worried look at Pastor Dev. "Maybe I should give the two of you some privacy."

"Good idea," Pastor Dev said, his eyes on Lydia.

Lulu nodded. "Coffee. We need coffee. And I don't need a butler to make that." Then she added, "You have five minutes before I come back." She left, but not before giving them a long, meaningful glance over her shoulder.

Lydia waited while Pastor Dev stood in the open doorway. Not wanting to add to his burdens, she said, "I'll be fine, honestly." Then she saw him wince and grab his right shoulder. Unable to stop herself, she touched her fingers to his mighty biceps. "You're hurt!"

"It's nothing," he said, eyeing the splintered door frame. "I ran into the door."

"You broke the door down," Lydia said, observation style.

"I broke the door down," he replied, commando style.

"You did that, for me?"

"I…was afraid—"

"I told you, I'm fine."

"Lydia," he began. Then he stopped, let out a frustrated sigh and pulled her into his arms. This time, he didn't kiss her to calm her down, or to shut her up. This time, Lydia had no doubt that he was kissing her because he wanted to.

So she kissed him back, wanting this, too.

The room was quiet, the only sound the rain now coming soft and gentle outside the house. That and Lydia's contented sigh as the man she loved showed her with tenderness what he couldn't say with words.

He loved her, too. A little bit at least.

Dev stared across the table, trying to look anywhere but into Lydia's big, questioning eyes. It had been so hard, earlier, to let her go, to stop holding her, to stop kissing her. But he'd somehow managed to pull away, to push her back into her room and urge her to change out of her wet pajamas.

He couldn't allow his feelings for Lydia to sidetrack him. Someone was out to do him in and he was beginning to think that *someone* was much closer than he had imagined. His gut told him to believe Eli's warning.

Which meant he had to keep Lydia close, but he also had to keep her at arm's length. He had hoped to leave her at Eagle Rock, safe and sound, while he finished this job. But now he couldn't do that. Now he had to take her with him. Just until this was over. And he could only wonder what their lives would be like if and when this were ever truly over.

"Here, Pastoral, drink this." Lulu handed him a

large glass of orange juice and two pain pills. "You look like you need it. Your arm is bruised."

He didn't miss the meaning in her eyes. Her expression held the same warning look Kissie had given him in New Orleans the night he'd first seen Lydia in the red dress. Lulu Anderson was a wise woman. She knew more than just his arm was bruised.

He had to hold it all together. "Thanks," he said, taking the juice from Lulu. He tossed back the pills, then drank the juice, his eyes closed. When he opened them, Lydia was still staring over at him.

They were all up now and Lulu was cooking an early-morning breakfast of blueberry pancakes and bacon. The aroma of the sweet pancakes merged with the tantalizing smell of crisp bacon. Dev wasn't hungry.

Gerald leaned forward, drumming his fingers on the long cypress-planked breakfast table. "What do you think Eli's message means?"

Dev hadn't given them the complete message, so he looked down at his hands. "I think he's trying to warn me. He said he didn't do it. I believe him."

"But…who then?" John asked, glancing around the full table. "Eli could be trying to throw you off, Devon."

Alfred poured himself another cup of coffee and sat down by Lydia. "Alexandre isn't talking…yet. But he has implied that he's been in contact with The Disciple. Maybe that's who he got his orders from, too."

That caught Dev's attention. "What did he say?"

"He would only tell us that The Disciple is out there and he's after the people who wronged him."

"And how does Alexandre know this?" John asked, his expression skeptical.

"Well, he did mention a wolf in sheep's clothing," Gerald reminded Dev. "That certainly sounds like Eli."

"Or maybe Alexandre was just trying to finger Eli," Dev retorted, trying to gauge the body language around the table. Were they all evading him? Did John's fisted hand mean he was preparing for a fight? Why wouldn't Gerald look Dev in the eye? And Alfred was as fidgety as a mad rooster. Did they all know something Dev needed to know?

Dev had never had any doubts about trusting the other CHAIM operatives. But now, he had to wonder if one or all of the men at this table were behind this whole sordid affair. Was someone inside CHAIM somehow connected to the drug cartel they'd busted up a few years ago? Had that same someone ordered the executions of Eli's wife and unborn child?

It couldn't be possible.

And what about The Peacemaker? Dev had never worked with the legendary agent, but the man was well-known in the secret CHAIM brotherhood. Well-known, but not really accessible. No one even knew the man's real name. He was that elusive, that deep undercover. And yet many successful rescue and recover missions had come under the leadership of The Peacemaker. Was he the wolf in sheep's clothing?

Gerald's words brought Dev out of his musings. "Alexandre pledges that he only wanted to scare Lydia, that he was ordered by someone very high up to scare the girl so that Dev would take her and leave."

Dev got up, then looked around the table. "Well, that's exactly what I'm going to do. I am going to take Lydia and leave. Only this time, I'm not telling anyone where we're going."

"You can't do that, son," Gerald retorted, shocked. "You know the rules. Operatives have to report in on a daily basis."

"I'm changing the rules," Dev told them. "And you'd all be wise to stay out of it. I don't want any of you blamed for a decision I'm making on my own."

"Why are you doing this?" Lulu asked, her hand on his arm.

"Because every time I think Lydia's safe, someone else comes along to put her in danger. She wasn't safe in New Orleans and she isn't safe here. The fewer people involved, the better. I won't put any of you in jeopardy."

Alfred nodded, then held up a hand when the others sat up to protest. "He has a point, gentlemen. Sometimes, in the thick of things, we have to make tough decisions. We've all been there. And right now, Devon is thinking he can't entirely trust us. Am I right, Pastoral?"

Dev didn't even blink. Let them sweat. "You are,

sir. So I hope you'll understand why I have to do my job. I have to protect Lydia."

Sally Mae nodded, then patted her chignon. "I certainly remember those days—having to do what we knew was right. The Pastoral can give a thorough report when this is settled and over."

"It's the VEPs," Lydia said, her quiet voice echoing out over the room.

"Excuse me?" Lulu asked, frowning.

"Very Evil People," Lydia replied. "Someone very evil is behind this. And none of y'all look evil." She shrugged. "But I've been wrong before."

"Oh, like VIPs, but different," Sally Mae said, nodding. "It's not us, honey. I stand by that." She looked around as if to verify her words.

"I'd like to believe that," Lydia replied. She looked shaken, but she held up her chin. "Pastor Dev will find them, whoever they are. I know that."

"Then we should do everything in our power to make that happen," Alfred said, nodding toward Dev. "But going off on your own—that dog don't hunt, Devon. We need to work together."

"Yes, together," the others echoed, their sincerity reeking of a setup in Dev's paranoid mind.

They all agreed so easily, Dev noted, watching for any signs of deception. But it was hard to see anything. These men were old pros, which made it nearly impossible to access their real motives. Even their wives wore blank expressions that revealed nothing.

"Why was I summoned here?" Dev asked, giving each of them a direct look. "I need to know that before I go anywhere, or before I agree to anything else."

Alfred let out a sigh. "Pastoral, we've been behind you since you left Atlanta. You did the right thing, going to Kissie. She got the message out to The Disciple and now he's responded."

"Yes, that's the good news," Dev said. "But how in the world did someone get to that girl in New Orleans? How did we allow Lydia to be contaminated with a dangerous pesticide?"

"Someone is watching and working from the inside," John said, his expression open and sincere. "We just have to find out who the mole is. There are many who want us to fail. Someone is passing on inside information, hoping to bring down this organization."

"And that information brought danger right to our door again," Dev said. "I thought this was a safe haven for Lydia. But the butler? It even sounds cliché to me and I've seen it all."

"We brought you both here because we thought we could protect you and help you find our enemies, and we needed to stall you for a while," Alfred said. "This place is a stronghold. Alexandre was a blunder. Someone set him up with the best of credentials, knowing that a lot of our agents pass through here."

"How did that someone know to do that? How did that someone know I'd wind up at Eagle Rock?"

John hit a hand on the table. "Because it's standard procedure to bring an agent in trouble here," he said, his eyes going wide. "You know that, Devon. We brought Eli here when he…when things went bad for him. This is the resting place for agents who need a time-out."

"So Alexandre just happened to be in the right place at the right time?" Dev asked as he leaned forward. "Exactly when I was brought here for a… time-out."

"I'm afraid so," Alfred replied. "Good help is hard to find."

"We're sorry we let you down, son," John said. "We're still trying to locate The Disciple and we're still investigating all of these actions, but you're free to go—as long as you do things by the book. We'll get to the bottom of this. In the meantime, how can we help you?"

Dev glanced at Lydia, then motioned for her to get up. "Well, you can loan me a means of transportation."

"Of course," Gerald said. "We have all sorts of vehicles."

"I don't need a vehicle," Dev said. "I need a plane. Lydia and I are going to fly out of here. And none of you will know where we're going."

"You can't—"

"I can and I will," Dev shot back, his glaring gaze stopping Gerald in midsentence. "Don't make me do this the hard way. Just let us leave."

"What about the pilot?" John asked. "He'll need a flight plan."

"I'll be the pilot," Dev replied. "And let's just say, I'm going to fly under the radar."

"I don't like this, not one little bit," Alfred said, getting up to stare across the table at Dev. "Son, you need to think this through."

"I have thought it through," Dev replied, his hand on Lydia's arm. "Since I can't trust anyone right now, I have to do things my way. And that means getting out of here."

"We'll have to report this," John said, his expression grim.

"I'd expect no less," Dev replied. "And I'll accept responsibility for my actions."

Sally Mae looked around the room, then she sent her husband a pleading look. "Let them go, John. We have to trust Dev's decision and his instincts."

Dev nodded. "Good point. But I'm only worried about one person's opinion right now." He looked at Lydia. "Do *you* trust me?"

She stood silent, her eyes speaking volumes as they went from bright and luminous to frightened and unsure. But behind her ever-changing gaze, Dev saw the spirit and spunk he'd come to admire. Lydia was one of the bravest women he'd ever known.

She gave him a slight nod. Then she stood closer to him, smiled at everyone in the room, looked back over at him and said, "When do we leave?"

ELEVEN

Pastor Dev turned to Lydia. "All buckled in?"

She nodded, then glanced at what looked like television screens in front of them on the instrument panel. "Are you really going to fly this plane?"

"I'm trained to fly this plane."

She was still in awe. People with power sure could get things done in a real hurry. "I can't believe they let you go so easily—and gave you a private Cessna to boot."

He was in full commando mode again, checking the controls with the precision of an astronaut. "Oh, that was just a front, sweetheart. They'll send someone to monitor us—no doubt on that." Then he grinned. "If they can find us, that is. But this isn't just any old Cessna. This is a sweet Skyhawk SP, top-of-the-line. A very intelligent plane. This instrument panel is cutting edge—a G1000—"

"I'm glad you're so happy with our new ride," Lydia interrupted. "But I'm a wee bit concerned that we might be shot down in midair."

contrite, Lydia dropped her hands in her lap. "No, I'm the one who should be sorry. I'm not usually so sarcastic and catty."

She looked out the cockpit window, staring out into the night. The stars twinkled like a box of jewels set against velvet. Lydia felt as if she'd aged a hundred years in a few short days. But this wasn't over yet. She'd agreed to do this. She'd agreed to get in a plane with Pastor Devon Malone, in spite of all those superior warnings they'd been given back at Eagle Rock.

"I said I trusted you," she told him, her hand reaching out to touch his arm. "I meant it."

"I know," he replied, his gaze straight ahead. "And I appreciate you. So much."

He *appreciated* her. Not a mention of love or hope or kisses. He appreciated her. Well, wasn't that so very special. Lydia bit back the impulse to retort in kind. Instead, she said, "Well, I'm trying to work with you. I'm trying very hard to follow the commands and go with the flow. I'm sorry I got all snappy."

"You have every reason to be snappy," he said, lifting his gaze to her, his eyes holding hers with a blue as bright and flashing as the instrument panel. "Every reason in the world."

Lydia remembered Kissie's words to her, about how Pastor Dev would need someone there with him when all of this was over.

I'll be there, Lord, she silently promised. No mat-

He sent her a reassuring glance, then nodded toward the little flat screens. "I'm not worried about that, not with this high-tech setup. Great situational, real-time awareness with both this PDF and MFD— that's primary flight display and multifunction display in laymen's terms. Even if they come after us, this baby will make a clean getaway. This is a go-fast plane as long as we fly her under 14,000. She gets a little antsy in dense altitude." He actually winked at her, then gave her a Bogart kind of smile. "Sweetheart."

Lydia let his uncharacteristic excitement and technotalk roll right over her, noting that this was the most the man had ever spoken to her, outside of preaching a sermon, of course. She thought about mentioning that he'd been calling her *sweetheart* an awful lot lately, but she refrained from that. Why spoil a perfectly good getaway moment with mushy stuff?

"So they let you go just to save face?"

"Something like that. As I've told you, CHAIM is not a violent organization. More like passive persuasion."

"Oh, right. VEPs use the old-fashioned, killing kinds of persuasion, but y'all are just ever so friendly and accommodating. Do you really expect me to believe that?"

"We only resort to brute force when necessary. Like when the man at the train station tried to gun us down—he was carrying a lethal weapon. I had to maim him to stop him from killing you. The same with Alexandre. He's being taken care of—but he won't be harmed. He'll just live to regret what he did."

A shudder went down Lydia's spine as she imagined Alexandre stuck in a padded room, having to learn the books of the Bible...or else. Of course, that would serve him right for trying to put a pillow over her face. "You say that with such ease. Doesn't all this trickery and double-crossing stuff get to you after a while?"

He stopped fidgeting with the instrument panel, his hands going still on the controls. His expression told her that after enjoying a brief reprieve with the distraction of this sleek cockpit, he was now back to reality. "It did get to me. That's why I retired. That's why I wish you weren't involved."

Lydia could see the torment in his eyes. Wishing she could take back her question, she asked him another one instead. "Why do they call you The Pastoral?"

He gave her a wry smile. "I got that name in training school. Eli and some of the others said I had this look of serenity about me, always calm and quiet, like a perfect picture. The name stuck—even if it didn't make much sense to the outside world."

"But it makes perfect sense when you're talking in code, right?"

"Right."

"You know what I wish?" she asked, hoping he'd understand. "I wish you and I could have a real conversation, no codes, no deciphering or trying to or interpret Bible passages, just a real conversation."

She saw the blank wall falling across his face, a shutter slapping against a window. "Lydia, I know this is hard on you. You're away from everything you know and love. But—"

"But when this is all over, things will go back to normal for us? I don't think so. I'm not sure I'll ever be normal again." She touched one of the cool black joysticks in front of her. "I mean, I'm sitting in a Cessna, about to take off for parts unknown. I've gone from my first MARTA ride to my first private plane ride. Not to mention my first masked black-tie party, my first and only pair of stilettos, and my first ride on a watermelon truck. Oh, and I left out being shot at, being poisoned and almost being smothered. I don't think there is such a thing as normal anymore."

"Okay, I get it." He went back to his work, a frown furrowing his forehead. "Look, I have to get this plane in the air before they change their minds and call in reinforcements. Just be aware that they'll put a tail on us. People will be watching, waiting. It could get dicey."

"And what's it been up until now, a picnic?"

He let out a long sigh. "I'm sorry. I don't know what else to say."

She hated the way his broad shoulders slumped in defeat while his eyes filled with regret. Feeling ter the outcome. "I'll try to be more appreciative myself," she told Pastor Dev, her words quiet and level now.

"Okay."

He went in complete shutdown mode, just as he'd done the night after she'd held him while he cried in the roadside park. The man sure didn't like emotional encounters. He concentrated on getting the plane going, his every action precise and determined. And noncommunicative. Lydia felt so alone, sitting there by his side in the plane, the lights from the control panel illuminating them as they started off into the summer night.

She thought about her parents back home. She could picture her dad puttering around in his vegetable garden, gathering fresh cucumbers and tomatoes for all the neighbors. She could see her mother standing at the stove, frying up chicken for Sunday dinner, stirring the fresh cream peas she would have picked and shelled herself. There would be biscuits in the oven, sweet tea sweating in the refrigerator and a pound cake with fresh peaches waiting on the buffet in the dining room. Her whole family would be there right after church.

Did they miss her and wonder what in the world had happened to her? Lydia pushed the bittersweet images out of her mind, her prayers as silent and glowing as this still night. *I want to go home, Lord. I just want to go home. But before that can happen, I need You to help me. I have to be strong. I have to get through this with Your help. And I have to remember that Pastor Dev is a good man.*

Stubborn, hardheaded, determined, noble, fearless and downright aggravating. But he was still a good man.

Telling herself all these things, her prayers echoing over and over in her mind, Lydia took a deep breath and waited, bracing herself for whatever might happen next.

After Pastor Dev had been officially cleared for takeoff—they were on the Eagle Rock private airstrip and so they got whatever they needed, per CHAIM of course—he sat silently watching the monitors, his hands resting on the twin control sticks in front of him.

The screens displayed weather conditions, upcoming terrain and just about anything else they wanted to see. Lydia couldn't decipher much, but she saw what looked like a map on one of the screens.

"Where are we going?" she finally asked after her stomach had settled down. She hated flying, and being this up close and personal during a flight had left her a bit shaky and disoriented. But then, she reasoned, she ought to be used to getting shaky and disoriented by now.

He didn't speak for a minute, then he said, "I'm only telling you this because I don't want you to be surprised or alarmed. We're going to Colorado."

"Colorado?" She was certainly surprised and alarmed anyway. "Why?"

"Because The Disciple has a cabin there. And I think he wants me to come there. At least, that's the impression I got from his cryptic message."

"And what if he doesn't show up? What if—"

"He'll show. If he's truly in trouble and trying to find a way out, he'll know to come there. It's his secret place. Not many know about it, so he'll head there first. Either that, or he'll at least know we're safe."

"How can you be sure? I mean, what if it's another setup?"

She saw the flash of irritation in his eyes. "I *can't* be sure, so I'm going on instinct. I know Eli. I know how he operates. He wouldn't have risked everything by sending me that message if he didn't feel it was absolutely necessary."

"Okay, then. I guess I finally get to meet this notorious Disciple person."

"I think so. Either way, you'll be safe in Colorado."

"Famous last words," she retorted. Then she added on what she hoped was a more positive note, "I've always wanted to see the Continental Divide."

Dev hoped he'd managed to throw them off the trail. It hadn't been easy. After making a nocturnal stop on an "unofficial" airfield to refuel halfway through the flight, he'd been able to get them to Colorado and find the secluded landing strip that Eli had shown him years ago. And somehow, he'd handled landing the expensive plane in the deep valley between two jutting mountain ranges. That was a relief.

Now, convincing Lydia that they had to trek up the side of a remote mountain would be the next challenge. But if everything went according to plan, this would be their last trek, their last stop on this long journey to find the truth.

The truth. Dev let out a sigh, then started shutting down the plane. He had to wonder what the truth really was. For most of his adult life, he'd followed the dictates of CHAIM, because he had believed in everything the top-secret organization represented, everything it had taught him—Christianity, amnesty, intervention and ministry. But now, he had to wonder if all of that was just a cover-up for a much more glaring and dangerous operation. What if someone high up in CHAIM had forgotten that mission statement? What if someone with unlimited power had taken that power and used it to his or her own advantage, without regard for the safety of Christians or God's word?

That would explain Eli's defection. That would explain Dev's gut feeling that something wasn't quite right. And that certainly would explain why someone was trying to kill him. Someone wanted his team to stay quiet. Starting with him. And maybe ending with Eli.

Because there was one glaring fact, one truth that

Dev knew with all of his heart. If Eli Trudeau wanted him dead, Eli would have killed him by now. Eli wouldn't send others to do the job.

"We're here," Lydia said on a rush of breath, bringing Dev out of his thoughts. "I can't believe it. We're back on solid ground. I just might kiss the dirt."

Wishing he could take away her worries, Dev said, "Did my landing scare you that much?"

"Oh, not that much," she said, her tone light in spite of her wide-eyed expression. "Not any more than those fancy dips you did, or the fact that we traveled at nearly warp speed or how we had to constantly check for fighter jets scrambling to escort us to the nearest federal facility. I'm getting accustomed to flying beneath the radar, so to speak." Then she took another breath. "I just kept telling myself that God is my copilot."

He smiled at that. "At least you're still sure of the One in charge."

"Aren't you?" she asked, genuine concern etching her expression.

Lydia would fight all the hounds of darkness if she thought Dev was having doubts about his faith. That was one of the things he loved about her. He was beginning to think he loved a lot of things about her, but he had to block that realization out of his mind for now.

"I know God is in charge," he said to reassure her.

"But right now, I don't know who in CHAIM is in charge. Someone is certainly trying to play God."

"Or someone is giving a very good impression of being one of the sons of God," she replied.

Dev felt a shiver of awareness go down his spine, an elusive memory just within his reach. "Say that again."

She frowned. "You know—the Beatitudes— 'Blessed are the peacemakers, for they shall be called the sons of God.'"

Dev felt the shiver turn into full-blown comprehension. He hit the steering control with such force, Lydia jumped.

"What's wrong?" she asked, grabbing his fisted hand.

"I think I just figured out who's behind all of this." He turned to face her. "Remember back in New Orleans when we met The Peacemaker?"

She nodded, then gasped. "I quoted that passage to him, didn't I?"

"You do remember," he replied. "You were kind of out of it, but you remember?"

"I remember a lot about that night," she retorted, her eyes holding his.

Putting their first kiss out of his mind, Dev nodded. "I do, too, but…Lydia, I think you summed this entire situation up when you quoted that passage to The Peacemaker."

She put a hand to her mouth. "You don't mean that kind old man is the one—"

He sent her a reassuring glance, then nodded toward the little flat screens. "I'm not worried about that, not with this high-tech setup. Great situational, real-time awareness with both this PDF and MFD—that's primary flight display and multifunction display in laymen's terms. Even if they come after us, this baby will make a clean getaway. This is a go-fast plane as long as we fly her under 14,000. She gets a little antsy in dense altitude." He actually winked at her, then gave her a Bogart kind of smile. "Sweetheart."

Lydia let his uncharacteristic excitement and technotalk roll right over her, noting that this was the most the man had ever spoken to her, outside of preaching a sermon, of course. She thought about mentioning that he'd been calling her *sweetheart* an awful lot lately, but she refrained from that. Why spoil a perfectly good getaway moment with mushy stuff?

"So they let you go just to save face?"

"Something like that. As I've told you, CHAIM is not a violent organization. More like passive persuasion."

"Oh, right. VEPs use the old-fashioned, killing kinds of persuasion, but y'all are just ever so friendly and accommodating. Do you really expect me to believe that?"

"We only resort to brute force when necessary. Like when the man at the train station tried to gun us down—he was carrying a lethal weapon. I had to maim him to stop him from killing you. The same with Alexandre. He's being taken care of—but he won't be harmed. He'll just live to regret what he did."

A shudder went down Lydia's spine as she imagined Alexandre stuck in a padded room, having to learn the books of the Bible…or else. Of course, that would serve him right for trying to put a pillow over her face. "You say that with such ease. Doesn't all this trickery and double-crossing stuff get to you after a while?"

He stopped fidgeting with the instrument panel, his hands going still on the controls. His expression told her that after enjoying a brief reprieve with the distraction of this sleek cockpit, he was now back to reality. "It did get to me. That's why I retired. That's why I wish you weren't involved."

Lydia could see the torment in his eyes. Wishing she could take back her question, she asked him another one instead. "Why do they call you The Pastoral?"

He gave her a wry smile. "I got that name in training school. Eli and some of the others said I had this look of serenity about me, always calm and quiet, like a perfect picture. The name stuck—even if it didn't make much sense to the outside world."

"But it makes perfect sense when you're talking in code, right?"

"Right."

"You know what I wish?" she asked, hoping he'd

understand. "I wish you and I could have a real conversation, no codes, no deciphering or trying to twist or interpret Bible passages, just a real conversation."

She saw the blank wall falling across his face like a shutter slapping against a window. "Lydia, I know this is hard on you. You're away from everything you know and love. But—"

"But when this is all over, things will go back to normal for us? I don't think so. I'm not sure I'll ever be normal again." She touched one of the cool black joysticks in front of her. "I mean, I'm sitting in a Cessna, about to take off for parts unknown. I've gone from my first MARTA ride to my first private plane ride. Not to mention my first masked black-tie party, my first and only pair of stilettos, and my first ride on a watermelon truck. Oh, and I left out being shot at, being poisoned and almost being smothered. I don't think there is such a thing as normal anymore."

"Okay, I get it." He went back to his work, a frown furrowing his forehead. "Look, I have to get this plane in the air before they change their minds and call in reinforcements. Just be aware that they'll put a tail on us. People will be watching, waiting. It could get dicey."

"And what's it been up until now, a picnic?"

He let out a long sigh. "I'm sorry. I don't know what else to say."

She hated the way his broad shoulders slumped in defeat while his eyes filled with regret. Feeling contrite, Lydia dropped her hands in her lap. "No, I'm the one who should be sorry. I'm not usually so sarcastic and catty."

She looked out the cockpit window, staring out into the night. The stars twinkled like a box of jewels set against velvet. Lydia felt as if she'd aged a hundred years in a few short days. But this wasn't over yet. She'd agreed to do this. She'd agreed to get in a plane with Pastor Devon Malone, in spite of all those superior warnings they'd been given back at Eagle Rock.

"I said I trusted you," she told him, her hand reaching out to touch his arm. "I meant it."

"I know," he replied, his gaze straight ahead. "And I appreciate you. So much."

He *appreciated* her. Not a mention of love or hope or kisses. He appreciated her. Well, wasn't that so very special. Lydia bit back the impulse to retort in kind. Instead, she said, "Well, I'm trying to work with you. I'm trying very hard to follow the commands and go with the flow. I'm sorry I got all snappy."

"You have every reason to be snappy," he said, lifting his gaze to her, his eyes holding hers with a blue as bright and flashing as the instrument panel. "Every reason in the world."

Lydia remembered Kissie's words to her, about how Pastor Dev would need someone there with him when all of this was over.

I'll be there, Lord, she silently promised. No mat-

ter the outcome. "I'll try to be more appreciative myself," she told Pastor Dev, her words quiet and level now.

"Okay."

He went in complete shutdown mode, just as he'd done the night after she'd held him while he cried in the roadside park. The man sure didn't like emotional encounters. He concentrated on getting the plane going, his every action precise and determined. And noncommunicative. Lydia felt so alone, sitting there by his side in the plane, the lights from the control panel illuminating them as they started off into the summer night.

She thought about her parents back home. She could picture her dad puttering around in his vegetable garden, gathering fresh cucumbers and tomatoes for all the neighbors. She could see her mother standing at the stove, frying up chicken for Sunday dinner, stirring the fresh cream peas she would have picked and shelled herself. There would be biscuits in the oven, sweet tea sweating in the refrigerator and a pound cake with fresh peaches waiting on the buffet in the dining room. Her whole family would be there right after church.

Did they miss her and wonder what in the world had happened to her? Lydia pushed the bittersweet images out of her mind, her prayers as silent and glowing as this still night. *I want to go home, Lord. I just want to go home. But before that can happen, I need You to help me. I have to be strong. I have to*

get through this with Your help. And I have to re-
member that Pastor Dev is a good man.

Stubborn, hardheaded, determined, noble, fearless and downright aggravating. But he was still a
good man.

Telling herself all these things, her prayers echoing over and over in her mind, Lydia took a deep
breath and waited, bracing herself for whatever
might happen next.

After Pastor Dev had been officially cleared for
takeoff—they were on the Eagle Rock private airstrip and so they got whatever they needed, per
CHAIM of course—he sat silently watching the
monitors, his hands resting on the twin control sticks
in front of him.

The screens displayed weather conditions, upcoming terrain and just about anything else they wanted
to see. Lydia couldn't decipher much, but she saw
what looked like a map on one of the screens.

"Where are we going?" she finally asked after
her stomach had settled down. She hated flying, and
being this up close and personal during a flight had
left her a bit shaky and disoriented. But then, she
reasoned, she ought to be used to getting shaky and
disoriented by now.

He didn't speak for a minute, then he said, "I'm
only telling you this because I don't want you to
be surprised or alarmed. We're going to Colorado."

"Colorado?" She was certainly surprised and alarmed anyway. "Why?"

"Because The Disciple has a cabin there. And I think he wants me to come there. At least, that's the impression I got from his cryptic message."

"And what if he doesn't show up? What if—"

"He'll show. If he's truly in trouble and trying to find a way out, he'll know to come there. It's his secret place. Not many know about it, so he'll head there first. Either that, or he'll at least know we're safe."

"How can you be sure? I mean, what if it's another setup?"

She saw the flash of irritation in his eyes. "I *can't* be sure, so I'm going on instinct. I know Eli. I know how he operates. He wouldn't have risked everything by sending me that message if he didn't feel it was absolutely necessary."

"Okay, then. I guess I finally get to meet this notorious Disciple person."

"I think so. Either way, you'll be safe in Colorado."

"Famous last words," she retorted. Then she added on what she hoped was a more positive note, "I've always wanted to see the Continental Divide."

Dev hoped he'd managed to throw them off the trail. It hadn't been easy. After making a nocturnal stop on an "unofficial" airfield to refuel halfway through the flight, he'd been able to get them to Colo-

rado and find the secluded landing strip that Eli had shown him years ago. And somehow, he'd handled landing the expensive plane in the deep valley between two jutting mountain ranges. That was a relief.

Now, convincing Lydia that they had to trek up the side of a remote mountain would be the next challenge. But if everything went according to plan, this would be their last trek, their last stop on this long journey to find the truth.

The truth. Dev let out a sigh, then started shutting down the plane. He had to wonder what the truth really was. For most of his adult life, he'd followed the dictates of CHAIM, because he had believed in everything the top-secret organization represented, everything it had taught him—Christianity, amnesty, intervention and ministry. But now, he had to wonder if all of that was just a cover-up for a much more glaring and dangerous operation. What if someone high up in CHAIM had forgotten that mission statement? What if someone with unlimited power had taken that power and used it to his or her own advantage, without regard for the safety of Christians or God's word?

That would explain Eli's defection. That would explain Dev's gut feeling that something wasn't quite right. And that certainly would explain why someone was trying to kill him. Someone wanted his team to stay quiet. Starting with him. And maybe ending with Eli.

Because there was one glaring fact, one truth that

Dev knew with all of his heart. If Eli Trudeau wanted him dead, Eli would have killed him by now. Eli wouldn't send others to do the job.

"We're here," Lydia said on a rush of breath, bringing Dev out of his thoughts. "I can't believe it. We're back on solid ground. I just might kiss the dirt."

Wishing he could take away her worries, Dev said, "Did my landing scare you that much?"

"Oh, not that much," she said, her tone light in spite of her wide-eyed expression. "Not any more than those fancy dips you did, or the fact that we traveled at nearly warp speed or how we had to constantly check for fighter jets scrambling to escort us to the nearest federal facility. I'm getting accustomed to flying beneath the radar, so to speak." Then she took another breath. "I just kept telling myself that God is my copilot."

He smiled at that. "At least you're still sure of the One in charge."

"Aren't you?" she asked, genuine concern etching her expression.

Lydia would fight all the hounds of darkness if she thought Dev was having doubts about his faith. That was one of the things he loved about her. He was beginning to think he loved a lot of things about her, but he had to block that realization out of his mind for now.

"I know God is in charge," he said to reassure her.

"But right now, I don't know who in CHAIM is in charge. Someone is certainly trying to play God."

"Or someone is giving a very good impression of being one of the sons of God," she replied.

Dev felt a shiver of awareness go down his spine, an elusive memory just within his reach. "Say that again."

She frowned. "You know—the Beatitudes—'Blessed are the peacemakers, for they shall be called the sons of God.'"

Dev felt the shiver turn into full-blown comprehension. He hit the steering control with such force, Lydia jumped.

"What's wrong?" she asked, grabbing his fisted hand.

"I think I just figured out who's behind all of this." He turned to face her. "Remember back in New Orleans when we met The Peacemaker?"

She nodded, then gasped. "I quoted that passage to him, didn't I?"

"You do remember," he replied. "You were kind of out of it, but you remember?"

"I remember a lot about that night," she retorted, her eyes holding his.

Putting their first kiss out of his mind, Dev nodded. "I do, too, but…Lydia, I think you summed this entire situation up when you quoted that passage to The Peacemaker."

She put a hand to her mouth. "You don't mean that kind old man is the one—"

"Eli told me to beware of the gray-haired man," Dev said, knowing he could trust her with this information. "I didn't tell the others because—"

"Because they were all gray haired, more or less," she interrupted. "But the Peacemaker—" Lydia's eyes got even wider "—he was definitely gray haired. And so helpful. Why would he help us if he's the one trying to kill us?"

"I'm not sure," Dev said. "It could be that he felt the heat and decided to steer us away—so no one would connect him to trying to do us in. It might be that Kissie's call alerted him—he had to play the part of friend and protector to hide his real motives."

"Why did Kissie call him instead of you?" Lydia asked.

"That's the question. She would have tried my phone first. She knows to do that, but The Peacemaker implied she was afraid my phone wasn't clear."

"Are we sure Kissie is all right?"

"Last time I dared try, she didn't answer her phone, which is not like her at all."

"Try again," Lydia said, shaking his arm. "I don't want anything to happen to Kissie."

"Good idea." He unbuckled his seat belt. "Let's get out of this plane. It's got a big target on its back. And unfortunately, I left my Ruger back in New Orleans."

"I don't like guns," Lydia said. "And I especially don't like having a target on my back."

He hopped down, his mind racing as he ran around to help Lydia. Taking her into his arms, he became very aware of her clean fresh scent, of the way her hair fell in soft layers around her shoulders. She was still dressed in her cute capri pants and floral blouse, but she had been practical enough to exchange the flat sandals for a good pair of walking shoes, at least.

Because they'd be doing a lot of walking.

Lydia took his mind off both her prettiness and the road ahead. "Call Kissie."

Dev guided them away from the plane to a clump of bushes near the deserted strip, then pulled out his Treo. "I've got a weak signal, but I'll try." She answered on the third ring.

"Valarie, how ya doing, baby girl?"

Dev frowned into the phone. "It's me, Kissie. Are you all right?"

"I am, but we have a bad connection."

"Is someone there with you?"

"You could say that, yes. The house is rocking tonight."

"Just tell me if you're safe."

"For now, yes. We could do lunch soon maybe. We have a lot to catch up on. I want to hear all about your vacation down south."

"South America?" Dev asked, his eyes connecting with Lydia's questioning gaze.

"That's right. Sand and sun, tropical flora and

fauna. The works. I want to hear everything about that nice cruise. But, honey, right now, I have to go."

"I got you," Dev said, dread coloring his words. Kissie was trying to give him the rest of the story. "Stay safe," he said. "I'll be in touch."

"Right, Valarie," Kissie said into the phone, her tone light. "Remember, trouble and anguish make us afraid—"

The line went dead.

"Kissie?" Dev stared at his phone, then looked at Lydia. "I think she's in trouble. She was trying to warn us about something."

"What?" Lydia came close, her hands on his arm. "What did she say?"

"She called me Valarie. That's her daughter. Valarie. Why would she call me Valarie?"

"Maybe it was a clue," Lydia said. "Where does Valarie live?"

"In Florida." He thought back over the conversation. "She wanted me to figure out South America, so that means this *is* tied to that, just as I suspected."

"What else?"

"A cruise. She mentioned a cruise."

"Valarie, Florida and a cruise in South America," Lydia said. "They must all add up."

Dev closed his eyes and thought back. So much had happened down there and he'd tried to block most of it. "It's been a while. We were in a place called Rio Branco. It's the capital village of Acre, deep in the jungles of Brazil. It's a university town

full of college students. We went down there to rescue a young woman from a religious cult that uses
hallucinogenic vines to induce visions. Her wealthy
parents wanted her home. We hired a boat guide, a
trader, to take us up the river to a large *fazendeiros*—
an estate, very large and lavish. That has to be what
Kissie is talking about. The girl was being held on
that estate. We never did find out who owned the
plantation house."

He stopped, wondering how much more he should
tell Lydia. "That's when everything went bad. She's
confirming what I'd already figured out." But who
was there with Kissie?

Lydia held his arm, steadying him. "Does this
bad stuff have to do with The Disciple getting into
trouble?"

"Yes." Dev looked up at the night sky and the
mountains all around them. Telling Lydia this final
truth would be just like climbing a mountain. "Let's
get out of here and then I'll explain everything to
you."

She let go of his arm. "Maybe she just called you
Valarie off the top of her head. And Florida is tropical, like the jungle. She was grasping at ways to
communicate."

"Yes, but the boat ride firms things up in my
mind." He tugged her back toward the plane. "Let's
get our backpacks," he said. "We'll need our supplies. We can talk on the way."

"Where is this cabin?" she asked as she slung the pack he handed her over her shoulder.

"Up there," Dev said, pointing.

In the newborn peaches-and-cream dawn, Lydia squinted up at the mountain face in front of them, then back to him. "You're kidding, right?"

"Afraid not," Dev told her. "We have to climb that piece of rock to get to the cabin."

Lydia looked back up at the craggy rock dotted with evergreens and shrubs as far as the eye could see. "This had better be worth it."

He took her by the hand. "We can go over everything we've put together, to take your mind off hiking."

She gave him a mock smile. "You are so very clever, but that's not funny." Then she squinted toward the east. "But that is certainly a beautiful sunrise."

Dev's phone rang, echoing eerily out over the trees and rocks.

"Hello?" His heart started pumping a hard beat. "Kissie? Are you clear?"

"As clear as can be expected, considering I just had a nice visit with The Disciple. He was here, Devon. And he's very upset."

"What did he say?"

"Pretty much that he'd been set up. That what happened in South America was not your fault. He's not trying to kill you, Pastoral. He's trying to save you."

"Why me?" Dev asked, glancing around. They were exposed out here. And the woods could be full of secret watchers.

"Because…when you reported him as being too shaky to continue the operation down there, you apparently ruffled some big feathers. Whoever is in on this thinks you know something you shouldn't know. And they think you'll blow the whistle on the whole enchilada."

"But I don't have any information. I only know that after I told the truth, Eli lost everything dear to him."

"They did that as a revenge tactic, because he was too close to the truth and your trying to help him only confirmed their suspicions. Apparently, they're after him, too. And they think he told you something. Something that could ruin CHAIM for good."

"I don't understand—Kissie, it's been years and I don't know anything. Why now?" He stared over at Lydia. She was still and questioning. "I have to get Lydia somewhere safe. We're sitting ducks out here in the open."

"I have more," Kissie replied. "Eli said to stay at the hideaway until he can find you. His exact words to me were 'Tell The Pastoral to lie low.'"

"I plan on doing just that, but I need to talk to Eli."

"He doesn't want to be found, but he thinks they'll come there looking for him and you. He said he'd catch up with you very soon."

"Why didn't he just tell me this himself? Why didn't you put him on the phone earlier?"

"He wasn't the one with me earlier," Kissie said, her voice low. "I was stalling so Eli could get away."

"Someone else was there with you?"

"Yes."

"The Peacemaker?"

"He didn't identify himself. Tall, gray haired. Implied he was my superior. But I'm pretty sure he's the man Eli told me to call the night of the Garden District party."

Dev let out a breath. "Eli called you and told you to call someone else instead of warning me?"

"Yes. He was rushed, but he made me promise to call a certain number. He said your life depended on it. I didn't ask questions. I called the number and got this man. Very cultured Southern voice. Very polite. He said he'd help."

"That's him," Dev confirmed. "The Peacemaker."

"I don't even want to know the rest," Kissie said. "Just get to wherever you think you should be. I've got to go. Things are very tense down here."

"Okay. Thanks. I'll figure something out."

"Oh, one more thing," Kissie said on a rush of breath. "The Disciple said to tell you—he has something you might want."

"What is that?" Dev asked, his whole being alert to the sounds of the morning. It was a quiet dawn. Still and uncertain, like a rattlesnake about to spring.

"He has Lydia's diary," Kissie said. "And he's

reading it page by page. It's very detailed, from what he implied."

"Lydia has a diary?" Dev looked at Lydia and saw her go pale. *A diary?* "You have a diary?"

She bobbed her head. "I keep a journal, yes. I left it at Kissie's."

"I gotta go," Kissie said. Then the call ended.

Dev stared at his phone, then let out a frustrated sigh as he looked sideways at Lydia. "What exactly was in your diary, Lydia?"

She shrugged, ran a hand through her hair. "A lot of things." She blushed. "Personal stuff." She waved her hands in the air. "I might have mentioned a few other things. You know, about us being on the run from the VEPs and…things like that. Right up until we left for the fancy party." Then she lowered her head and whispered, "Is that bad? Did I do something wrong?"

Dev didn't have the heart to voice the angry thoughts coursing through his head. "No, sweetheart, you didn't do anything wrong."

"Except put us in even more danger, right?" she asked, tears beginning to form in her eyes.

"Except that," Dev answered, his dread now at full throttle. "But, hey, you keeping detailed records of our *every move* is just a minor point in the overall scheme of things."

He shouldn't have raised his voice. But he was tired and angry. And, too late, he could see that same fatigue and anger in the misty reflection from Lydia's amber-flecked eyes.

Just before she threw her backpack down and took off in the other direction.

TWELVE

"Lydia, come back here."

"No." She kept walking, stomping toward the mountain. "Why don't you just go on and finish the job? I'll find a way out of here by myself."

"That's impossible. You'd never survive."

And he'd die before he allowed that to happen.

She lifted an arm in the air, waving him away. "That's just it. Poor little Lydia. So helpless and such a problem for everyone involved in this sordid operation. And apparently, I'm too stupid to live since I just happen to write in a journal—because, mercy, I wouldn't want to burden you with all my problems. I understand. I get it. I don't need to be here, and you don't need to be worried about me. So just let me go."

He looked down at the barren ground. "I can't do that. You know I can't do that. Lydia, I'm sorry. I didn't mean to imply—"

She turned then, her fury and pain piercing him like a golden lance as her eyes met his. "You didn't mean to imply that I've really messed up, but I saw it there in your eyes. I saw everything. And I understand everything. Your having to babysit me. If I wasn't in the way, you could do your job and get it over with. You could keep your secrets and your regrets close, without anyone else being the wiser, right? But I'm here and I left my diary in New Orleans because I couldn't bring it to that fancy party anyway, and then I was poisoned and we had to get out of there quick and now we don't know who's read it. I've put us in even more danger."

She brought her arms up, wrapping them around herself at midwaist, as if that action would protect her from all she'd seen and done. "I just want this to be over. Just tell me—when will this be over?"

Dev stood there, a few feet separating them, his heart going from hard and uncompromising to soft and yielding. He could yield everything for this woman. He would walk through fire to save her, to get to her. But right now, there was a big gap between his feelings and his duty.

"I honestly don't know how to answer that," he said. Then he couldn't stop looking at her, his heart warring with his head. "Lydia, please don't walk away from me. It's not safe. It's…"

He gave up with words. Instead he stomped toward her, and from the startled expression registering in her misty eyes, he must have looked like Sherman marching into Georgia. She didn't move, but he could tell she was holding her breath. When he got within inches of her, he grabbed her with one hand sliding around her waist. Then he pulled her close and put his arms around her.

Closing his eyes, he held her there, the scent of her floral shampoo washing over him like a cleansing breeze. "Lydia," he said on a whispered plea, "don't you know what you mean to me?"

She raised her head, drawing back to stare up at him, her eyes as shimmering and bronze as the sunrise glinting off the mountains. "No, I don't. Why don't you tell me?"

That simple request hit Dev square in the face, the dare in her words heating him with guilt and remorse. He couldn't tell her anything about his feelings. Not yet. Not now.

So instead of sparring with words, he went into action. He pushed his hands through her hair and kissed her. Not to calm her, not to stall her, not even to convince her.

He kissed her because he wanted to kiss her. And…he realized he wanted her by his side, not just to protect her and get her safely back home. But always and forever.

But first, he had to keep her alive.

Lydia felt so alive, so aware, so alert. They were standing in a deep valley between two twin mountains, and the man she loved with all of her heart was kissing her. As their lips touched, she realized two things. Pastor Dev cared about her, and he also had a job to do. He wanted to keep her safe, but not just out of duty. Now there was so much more at stake between them.

Now there was a chance for that always and forever she'd dreamed about.

If she'd just behave long enough to let him do what he had to do. He had every right to be mad about the diary. And she shouldn't have gotten so bent out of shape.

She drew back, a blush heating her skin. "I'm sorry," she said. "I should have told you about my diary."

He leaned his forehead against hers, his hands still caught in her hair. He stayed there a moment, then said, "It's okay. Even if Eli is enjoying all your private thoughts, he won't pass that information on to anyone else. And by telling us he has the diary, he's also telling us we can trust him. As long as he has it, no one else will ever get their hands on it."

Her blush went deeper. "I'd rather he *didn't* have it. It *is* very personal. And technically, it's a journal. A diary makes me sound like a high schooler."

He smiled at that, his words low and husky. "Did you write anything about me in there?"

Lydia was sweating now. She could feel a little trickle of dampness moving between her shoulder blades. "I'd rather not say."

The look he gave her made her fidgety. His eyes were a soft, sweet blue, as wide-open and all encompassing as the sky. "You did, didn't you?"

Wincing, she thought about the intimate passages

of glowing, detailed adulation and love she'd professed there in her private ramblings. She might as well be an adolescent girl. It probably sounded that way. "Just a little. Will that compromise this mission?"

He laughed then, some of the tension leaving his face. "You're beginning to sound like an operative, sweetheart."

Like a real pro, Lydia tried to distract him from wanting to know more about her diary…uh, journal. "What can be done about the situation?"

"Very smooth." He took her by the hand. "Let's concentrate on one worry at a time. Right now, we need to get up this mountain."

"What about The Disciple?"

"Kissie says he'll find us here later. Eli will come whenever Eli is ready. He'll want to make sure he's not being tailed. And he'll want to have all his facts straight."

"So who do we trust, The Disciple or The Peacemaker? Or should we be wary of both of them, and everybody else, too?"

"Good question, and probably a good observation—trust no one." He tugged her along over the rocks and shrubs. "Right now, however, I'm liking The Peacemaker for being thc troublemaker."

"That nice old man gets a new name."

"Yeah, know any good scripture quotes for that one?"

"You reap what you sow," she shot back.

"You do know your Bible."

She was working on a retort when the first shot rang out.

"Get down!"

Dev didn't wait for Lydia to do his bidding. Instead, he pushed her behind an outcropping of rocks, their bodies crushing the delicate lavender columbines blooming nearby.

Holding her down, he scanned the distant trees and formations. When another shot rang out, he ducked down again, this time behind a sturdy shrub oak.

"It's coming from that copse of trees over there just beyond that ridge." He pointed to a spot about one hundred yards away from the plane where an outcropping of junipers and birch trees hung off the nearby hillside. "We need to get back to the plane."

"Why?" Lydia asked, her breath coming in huffs. "I mean, won't they see us?"

"Yes, but it's the fastest way out of here," he explained. "I'm not sure what they're shooting with, but if we head up the mountain, we'll be easy targets. And there might be more of them behind us, just waiting."

"Can't we just hide behind the rocks and trees?"

"They might have air support. They obviously tracked our flight." Which made him wonder if all the gray-haired men were in on this. He'd figured the CHAIM head honchos would put a tail on them, but he'd never figured they'd actually try to kill him.

Lydia grunted into the weeds. "Oh, right. Why didn't I think about air support!"

Glad she was back to her feisty self, Dev held her down. "Listen to me, Lydia. We're going to follow these rocks until we can come around to the other side of the plane."

"Sure we are."

Another shot pierced the air. Dev held Lydia's head down. "They probably have rifles with scopes. It'll be easy for them to spot us. And there might be more than one shooter."

She huffed a breath. "Just like when we take the youth paintballing."

"I'm serious, Lydia. You have to stay down. We're going to crawl along the rock bed. Do you understand?"

"I'm not deaf or daft," she said, frustration coloring her words. "And I sure don't want to be shot. I've got it. Stay low and hurry up."

"And don't raise your head unless I give you the all clear."

"Got it. I'd like to keep my brain intact."

"Okay, then you have to stay right behind me, so I can keep you out of the line of fire. Promise me you'll do that? And you have to stay low to the ground."

"I will. But…how are we going to get to the plane?"

"We'll figure that out once we get to the other

side. I'm hoping the plane and that sun coming up over the mountains will shield us until we can get inside. And I'm praying whoever is up there isn't a very good shot."

"What if they shoot the plane down?"

"They'll try. But I'm going to get us out of here."

She didn't respond to that. Dev knew what she was thinking. *How in the world was he going to do that?*

Since he didn't have a clue, he could only act on instinct and years of training. "We'll be all right. Just follow me," he told Lydia, his breath winded. "Stay to my right."

She did as he asked, crawling along beside him. Dev dug his elbows into the dry rocks and sand, the grime of dirt, weeds and wildflowers sending up a cloud of dust. He glanced over at Lydia and saw her grimace each time they took a slow slide toward the next rock.

"I hope we have bandages in that plane," she hissed, the pain etched on her face causing her to draw in a long breath. "I'm going to be scraped to pieces."

"Just keep moving, sweetheart," he told her. "We're almost there."

Two more rapid-fire shots rang out, and this time Dev felt the whiz of a bullet as it passed right over their heads. "Lydia?"

"I'm here. That was so close, I think it split the hairs on my head."

"But it missed, right?"

"Yes. I'm right behind you."

They made it to where the plane sat at the end of the haphazard runway. Dev had tried to hide it near a group of aspen trees, just in case. Now that the "just in case" was here and they were being attacked, he turned to lie on his back, sweat and dirt merging on his face. "Okay, here's the tricky part."

Lydia let out a snort. "And here I thought we'd gotten past the tricky part."

He reached out a hand to her. She lay on her stomach staring over at him, then she glanced down at their joined hands. "I'm listening."

He saw the trust in her eyes and the little bits of columbine blossoms in her hair, and fell in love with her completely as they lay there in the dirt and flowers, with shots being fired all around them. Lydia never faltered, never gave up, even when she was fighting him tooth and nail. She might get weary, but she was still willing to fight the good fight. For God. And for him.

Because he saw the love in her eyes now, he could acknowledge that same love in his heart. Maybe it had been there all along, but now it shined brightly against the blue of the Colorado sky. So brightly it almost blinded him with its hope and longing. He would not lose her now. He had to get her out of this mess.

"Are you ready?"

"As ready as I'll ever be. But, before we go—let's go over our list of options again."

He let out a sigh. "We don't have any options. If we go up that mountain, they'll track us and shoot us."

"We could just stay here until dark."

"And let them get in even closer? Not a good idea."

She glanced up toward the plane. "What's next then?"

"We're going to run to the plane, but you need to stay low to the ground. When we get there, squat down beside the back pilot's side wheelbase, okay? It's not much, but if you crouch there, you'll be shielded. Hopefully the rising sun and the thickness of those aspens will both work in our favor."

"Hopefully."

"I'm going to open the door on the pilot's side and I want you to get in as fast as you can."

"What about you?"

"I'll be right behind you." *Trying to keep from getting shot myself.*

"And then, you'll just crank her up and we'll take off?"

He didn't want to mention just yet that they didn't have much fuel. "Something like that."

"I hope that plane is bulletproof."

"If I know Alfred Anderson, it is."

He gave her hand a squeeze, then he leaned in to kiss her forehead. "Ready?"

"Absolutely." It was feeble and weak, but her eyes still held that look of trust and resolve. "Let's go."

Dev rolled over. It was too quiet out there, which could mean the shooters had given up, or that they were moving in. "On the count of three—" He ticked off the numbers, ticking off prayers inside his head while he said the words.

They rocketed out from behind the brush and shrubs, the sound of gunfire, closer now, rising to follow their paths. Dev prayed while he ran beside Lydia, his hand reaching to shield her and to try and keep her down as she moved. Bullets hit rocks behind them and bounced off the plane in front of them, but Dev kept pushing Lydia forward. "The wheel," he called to her. "Get behind that wheel."

Lydia dived toward the plane's tiny covered wheel, grabbing at the mushroom-shaped white metal covering, her body curling up in a tight little ball, her head down.

Dev scrambled toward the nose, then hopped around the plane to grab the door. Another shot rang out, then he heard Lydia's cry of pain.

And saw blood running down her arm.

Intense agony poured over Lydia as a scalding pain caused her arm to go numb. She looked down at the blood spilling against her hand, then glanced up in time to see Pastor Dev's hand snaking out toward her. She tried to reach him, but she felt sick, the waves of nausea rolling over her with the precision of a fast-moving waterfall. She was going to pass out.

"Lydia!"

She heard his voice coming through the roar of the blood pounding inside her temples.

"Lydia, take my hand."

The flare of more shots brought her head up. She blinked, lifted her good hand, now covered in blood, toward him. Then suddenly she was propelled through the air and into the cockpit of the plane. Pastor Dev shoved her over the controls, causing her to cry out in pain.

"I'm sorry," he said on a winded breath. "I've got to get us moving."

"They finally got me," she said, her words weak and low, her eyes shut to the sight of blood. "Finally got me."

"You'll be okay," he said. "It's not that bad. Just a flesh wound. Thankfully, whoever's out there isn't a very good shot."

Or they'd both be dead right now. Lydia got that unspoken message loud and clear. Through the hum of pain rumbling inside her brain, she could hear the roar of the plane's engine coming to life.

Briefly, she felt his hand on her arm. "Try to put some pressure on the wound with your other hand, to stop the bleeding."

She grimaced, gritted her teeth and did as he said. "It hurts," she told him, her eyes tightly shut.

"I know it does, sweetheart, but you're going to

be fine, Lydia. Do you hear me? I won't let anything happen to you."

"You don't sound convincing," she replied, thinking she liked him better when he was in his confident, commando mode. He sounded scared. She didn't like scared. But she knew he wasn't a coward. He was worried about her, scared for her sake. That brought a little bit of warmth and comfort to the pain coursing through her system.

She reluctantly opened her eyes, watching as he turned the plane on a quick tailspin and got it lined up on the haphazard runway. The sound of bullets hitting the fuselage didn't help her mood.

"They're still shooting."

"I can see them now," Pastor Dev said, his hands moving over buttons and controls. "Two of them. They're on foot and they're lousy shots, so we have the advantage."

"What advantage would that be?" she asked, one eye open toward him.

He leaned back and looked straight ahead. "This."

The plane picked up speed, and then in a matter of seconds, they were lifting off into the air, the roar inside Lydia's head now a steady match for the roar of the big engines. She felt sick all over again, but she swallowed back the queasiness and tried to pray her way back to being coherent.

Until she looked up and saw the mountain straight ahead of them.

"This isn't good," she said on a moan. "Not good at all. Do you see that big rock?"

"I see the mountain, but we're not going to hit it. It's farther away than it looks." Pastor Dev's gaze met hers. He started hitting buttons, his eyes going back to the screen. "And we don't have enough fuel to get very far."

"What?" Lydia sat up, dizziness clouding her vision. On the instrument panel, the lights were fading like fireflies, one by one. And the mountain which he'd just assured her was far away loomed straight ahead. Panic rising in her stomach, she tried to focus. Then she screamed, "What do we do now?"

Pastor Dev reached behind them, scrambling around until his hand hit what he'd been looking for. "We jump."

THIRTEEN

Lydia looked at the mountains around them, and then fixed her gaze on Pastor Dev. "Jump?" she shouted at him over the roar of the plane. "Did you say jump?"

He didn't answer. Instead, he hit some buttons and switches before climbing into the back of the plane, then turned and grasped her waist, lifting her up after him. He flipped her around and forced a harness over her head and down around her shoulders.

"This is gonna hurt," he said as he lifted her arms.

It did. She screamed out in pain as her wound throbbed in protest, then tried to push his hands away. "Let go of me."

"I can't," he said close to her ear, his hands working on shutting and snapping and arranging. "We have about a minute before we have to let go of this plane."

He was actually hooking them together, her harness connecting to the one he'd somehow managed to get around his own body. And she didn't dare look too long at the contraption attached to all of the harnesses and belts.

"Let go of the plane?" She shook her head, her gaze glued to the ever-approaching mountains all around them. "I don't want to let go of the plane. I want the plane to land again, with me inside."

She could hear him adjusting and fitting clunky things around them. He leaned in close, his voice coming in her left ear. "The plane is going to crash, Lydia. But we're going to bail out before that happens. It's the only way."

Lydia swallowed the fear and nausea roiling up from her insides like a giant tidal wave. "I can't do that."

"Yes, you can." He had his hands over hers now. "We're going to jump—it's called a tandem jump, actually more like a Mr. Bill jump. You'll be with me—hooked to me. All you have to do is wrap your arms and legs around me like a pretzel and hang on. I'll do the rest. But first, we have to get this door open and ourselves into the exit position. Piece of cake."

Lydia pushed his hands away. "You expect me to believe that?"

"I expect you to be brave and to stay quiet and to do exactly as I tell you." He dragged them both toward the exit door as he kept talking. "Don't worry, I've been trained in every kind of jump possible. I've got my jump wings, been through HALO and HAHO jumps. All part of the job."

His commando mode.

He was really going to throw them both out of this plane. Lydia prayed his HALO or HAHO or whatever it was he'd learned would be enough. "I'm praying," she said, her breath heaving. "I'm just going to pray."

"That would be appreciated, sweetheart."

While he hooked and connected and checked and rechecked, Lydia looked at the mountains, looked around the plane, then squinted at him. "Is this our only option?"

"I'm afraid so," he said, kissing the top of her head. "And since this plane is going to tilt when we shift our weight, we have about twenty seconds to get ready."

Lydia let out a groan of fear and frustration. "I can't do this."

"You can do this," he told her, his voice calm and gentle and firm as he looked into her eyes. "We can do this, Lydia. Just look at me the whole time. I'll be right here."

She figured she had two choices on how she would die—in a plane that would surely crash into a mountain, or in the air as she plummeted to the rocky ground. She knew she wanted to go attached to the man she loved.

"Okay," she said, sniffing back tears. "Okay. But…Pastor Dev…promise me you'll hold on to me. Promise you won't let go."

"I won't let go," he said, his lips grazing her

cheek, his head pressing against her temple. "I won't let go, Lydia. Ever."

She nodded, closed her eyes as she prayed for courage and strength. *No matter where I land, dear God, please let us be together. I just want this to be over and I want to find peace in Your loving arms. And I want Pastor Dev to be right there with me.*

He started shifting them both toward the plane's door, explaining how they had to perch on the jump step, but Lydia refused to open her eyes. She kept praying, mixing the Lord's Prayer with the Twenty-third Psalm, just for good measure. "The Lord is my shepherd...I will fear no evil...thy will be done...on earth...forgive us our sins...the valley of the shadow of death...I will fear no evil...comfort me...the power, the glory...forever and ever...amen."

Did God hear frantic, half-worded, sheer-out-of-terror prayers? She believed He was listening.

"Here we go," Pastor Dev shouted. "We're at around seven thousand feet in elevation. Time to go."

Lydia's heart seemed to stop beating then. Her whole body went rigid. She heard the door groaning, felt the tug as he helped her find a foothold. She felt the rush of a hard wind surrounding them, blasting on her skin, on her face. She couldn't, wouldn't open her eyes.

"Lydia, come on, sweetheart. We have to move close."

Somehow, she opened her eyes and did as he said,

shifting her body along with his as they perched in the open door. "I can't—"

"You can. You have to. I won't let you die in this plane. I don't intend to let you die at all."

He explained their position and how he would free fall through the air. "I'll push us out," he told her. "We'll somersault and then…it'll be easy from there."

She nodded, her eyes shutting again. She couldn't breathe, couldn't speak. She just kept praying, her mind centered on her family and her world back home. Her safe, protected, sunny, wonderful world where fear and pain and evil didn't exist. She thought of the crape myrtles blooming along the streets of Dixon, thought of the giant magnolia tree in her parents' front yard, the ancient palm trees lining the city park. She could almost smell the gardenias blooming so bright white and sweet in her mother's garden. She could taste the sweet tea and the coconut cream pie her mother would have waiting for her when she got home. Then she thought of heaven and wondered if she'd be able to find Pastor Dev when they got there.

Heaven.

I won't be afraid, she told herself. *I refuse to be afraid. I can do all things through Christ, who strengthens me. I can. I can. I will. I will.*

"I love you," she said out loud, her eyes lifting open, her only thought that she had to tell him this before they both died.

He didn't answer. Instead, he looked straight into

her eyes, then pushed them out into thin air. And all Lydia could feel after that was a strange weightlessness and a rush of pure adrenaline. Closing her eyes again, she felt the warmth of the sun, felt the brightness of the blue sky surrounding her, felt the warmth and strength of the man holding her and guiding her back down to earth.

She opened her eyes just as he pulled the rip cord.

And suddenly, they were floating, slowly and surely, as if they were dancers on a cloud.

Lydia felt his head over hers, felt the quick touch of his face to her hair. He managed a feathery soft kiss somewhere near her neck.

The rush of wind subsided as they neared the earth, and, oh, my, what a view.

The mountains, some high and distant and still tinged with long-lasting spots of stubborn snow, sparkled in lavender and rose all around them, the rich greens of the aspen trees mingled with the lavenders, whites and yellows of the wildflowers covering the colorful valley beneath. A turquoise-colored lake came into view, bright and shimmering with waterfalls, its fresh blue waters making Lydia hold her head up as she breathed deeply.

"Is this heaven?" she said, relief and awe in her words as she gazed over at him. "Or are we still alive?"

"Not heaven yet, sweetheart," he replied, his eyes sparkling with hope and relief. "We're alive."

Then they heard it. The boom of the plane as it hit a far mountain and exploded.

The flare of the fire blinded Lydia, but the explosion was too far away now to hurt them. Floating here in Pastor Dev's arms, she felt as they were too far away for anything to hurt them. Ever again.

But she knew she'd have to come back down to earth very soon.

And then it would begin all over again.

She'd told him she loved him.

Had Dev imagined her words or had she really said that to him? Of course she'd said it. Lydia loved him. He knew that now.

He could have answered with the truth, telling her that he loved her, too. More than he could have imagined, more than he had ever dreamed of loving a woman.

He loved her.

But unlike Lydia, he didn't have the guts to say that yet. Not yet. Not when he'd tried to hold back on his promises. Not when someone was determined to end both their lives. He had to make sure she was safe and back home in Dixon where she belonged. Only then would he feel that he had the right to tell her the same.

Right now, he had to land this chute and get her to a warm, safe place.

"Hold on," he told her as they came gliding down

to the meadow. "Just lean into me and I'll catch us when we hit."

She did as he asked, and in the next few minutes Dev felt the thud of the earth meeting his body as the chute dropped and dragged them. Steadying himself, he gripped the suspension lines and tugged at the now-deflated chute as he fell toward the ground. His body took the brunt of the landing to protect Lydia.

"Let's get out of this thing," he said, hurrying to release the harness. After helping her out and up, he tugged free of the chute, then turned to her. "How you doing?"

"I've been better," she said, running a hand through her mussed hair. "No, strike that. I'm great. I'm fine. I'm alive." She grabbed him by the shoulders, tears shining thorough her smile. "We're alive."

"We are," he said, grinning down at her. "That was quite a ride."

"You can say that again. It was so…beautiful."

"Once you got past the thought of being hurled out of a plane, right?"

"Right." She stood staring up at him, her heart revealed in the rich coppers and soft greens of her shimmering eyes. "Right."

Then she turned to look around, but not before he saw the pain in those sweet eyes. She wanted to hear the words he couldn't voice.

"Where are we?" she asked, one hand grasping her hurt arm. She was covered in dirt and grime and blood, but she'd never looked more beautiful to Dev.

He wanted to pull her close and kiss her again. But that might only lead to a confession. He had a feeling if he held her again, he'd never want to let go. And he had to let go so they could get their lives back. So they could have a life together—without the shadow of danger hanging over their heads.

Pushing on, he tugged the chute up, working to pack it. They might need the material to make a tent later. "We're in Glenwood Canyon, somewhere just east of Hanging Lake. If I have my bearings, I-70 and the Colorado River are off to the west. But we need to head east."

She nodded, breathing deep. "It's so fresh and clean, so quiet."

"We could use some quiet," he said, taking her by the hand. "But first, I need to look at that arm."

He sat her down on a nearby rock, then held her arm out to inspect the wound. "Looks like the bleeding has eased up. How does it feel?"

"It hurts like all get out," she admitted, wincing as he poked at the ugly gash just above her elbow. "But you were right. I think it just got grazed."

Dev thanked God for that. Things had happened so fast back there, he hadn't been sure if she'd been nicked or mortally wounded. He released a deep breath he hadn't even realized he'd been holding. All he could see in his memory was her face and the blood running down her arm. But she was going to be all right now. He'd make sure of that.

"We'll find some water and wash it out, at least.

Then we'll cover it with some of the material from the chute."

She sat silently, letting him examine her. Then she halted his hand on her arm. Dev looked up to find her staring at him, her big eyes wide. "Where are we going now?"

He looked around, toward the east. "Well, I think I can find Eli's cabin. I remember once we hiked to Hanging Lake in a day and stayed to camp overnight, but it's been a while."

"And you think you can just take us straight there, through mountain and valleys and rivers and lakes?"

He nodded, smiled. "I do." Then he grinned. "I just took us through an almost impossible bailout, kiddo. You don't think I can accomplish getting us over another mountain?"

"I do believe you can," she said, returning his smile. "At least, I sure hope so." Then she quit smiling. "Will we be safe there?"

Dev prayed they would. "Well, since it's remote and extremely well hidden and since Eli and I are about the only two people on earth who even know it exists, I'm banking on that."

"But…people are after us," she reminded him. "Those shooters—"

"Don't know that we survived the plane crash," he explained. "They probably think we're dead."

"Oh, and I guess that's to our advantage, right?"

He grinned at her businesslike words. "I would hope so, yes. At least it will give us some time."

"And what do we do when we get to this cabin? Just wait it out?"

That was a very good question. "I don't know, exactly. I have my Treo. If the battery works and if I can get a signal, we just might be able to do some behind-the-scenes work. But with the area being so far away from anything, I doubt that will happen. So we might just have to lie low for a few days, then hike out."

"Or we could pick wildflowers and frolic on the mountain."

He looked up at her then, and saw the hope in her eyes. "We could do that, yes. We deserve a little R & R."

"But…we'll be all alone."

Dev understood what she was saying, the reassurance she needed. "Yes, we will. But you're safe with me, Lydia. I would never do anything to compromise you…or embarrass you. You have to know that."

"Am I? Safe with you, I mean?"

The tight, clipped question took his breath away. "You don't think—"

She waved her good arm in the air. "I know you are a perfect gentleman. I know I can trust you. But what I'm asking, what I need to know and understand is…if my heart is safe with you."

"Your heart?" He hated to play dumb, but she was so direct and so beguiling and so cute and so hopeful, he had to stall just to find the right tactic.

"My heart," she replied, getting up to pace and

stomp through the wildflowers. "You've rescued me, saved me, kissed me, pushed me out of a plane and done just about everything in your power to keep me safe and alive. But you have yet to sit me down and have a real heart-to-heart talk with me—about us, I mean. About what's happening between us."

He turned away. She pulled him back around. "Don't go all commando on me, either. Don't shut me out. I just need to know. I trust you with my life, but can I trust you with my heart? Because I don't want to keep climbing mountains with you if I can't."

FOURTEEN

Here she was, traipsing up the mountain with him.

And he had yet to answer the burning question. The one about her heart.

Lydia huffed out a breath, then turned to take in the spectacular vistas surrounding them. They were moving away from the stark orange-and-red canyon walls as they headed southeast. But there were plenty of hills and rocks ahead of them, literally and metaphorically. Lydia tried to concentrate on putting one foot in front of the other, instead of worrying about what was going on inside the head of the infuriating man beside her.

"You should know you can trust me," he'd said, just like that. "You have to know by now...."

Then he'd simply grabbed her and turned her toward the foothills. "Let's find some water."

Lydia had been so shocked, so flabbergasted, that she wondered now how her head had managed to stay on. She wanted to scream, really loud. But that wouldn't accomplish anything, except making her look childish and petty. Here she was, wanting a declaration of undying love from him, in the midst of running for their lives.

I am beyond help, she thought, her gaze tracing the lone flight of what looked like a hawk up above them. Wishing, for a moment, *she* could just fly away, she remembered their emergency parachute jump and decided she'd had enough of flying for a while.

"This way," he said, dragging her up a rock cluster.

Commando Dev. Intense, focused, confident, cool.

And scared to death of facing what his heart knew to be true. How could he not know? She'd told him she loved him. And she knew deep inside her own heart that he loved her back. She could see it in his eyes, in the way he protected her and watched over her. In the way he'd touched a kiss to her neck as they drifted to earth.

How am I supposed to convince him that his heart is safe with me, Lord?

Lydia didn't have the answers to that question. She'd just have to tough it out. But once this was over—

He stopped, causing her to lose her footing. Pastor Dev caught her against him, straightening her as he pointed ahead. "See that little stream just beyond the ridge?"

Lydia pushed her hands through her hair, then

took a calming breath. "Yes, I could use some of that water."

"We're headed there right now."

"Thanks for the update," she retorted, fuming with a smile on her face.

He kept straight on. "I want to get that wound washed."

"I want to get a bath."

"That might be hard to do. We need to keep moving."

"I was just wishing out loud."

He wouldn't look at her. He stared ahead as if his life depended on it, and Lydia reckoned it probably did. His love life anyway.

She didn't get it. This man was fearless in the face of mortal danger, deliberate and thorough in preaching the word of God, but he was a real wimp when it came to baring his own soul and telling her the truth. Didn't he know she'd take care of that part of things, that she'd nurture him, cherish him and love him enough to protect all of his carefully controlled defenses?

Apparently not.

"How much longer?" she asked, wondering if he'd get the hidden meaning of that question.

He didn't. "Not too far now. We'll stop and rest up at the stream, then one more ridge or two and I think we'll be near Eli's property. We should be somewhere between Four Mile Canyon and Dry Hollow. Eli's place is way off the beaten path, but I think we're on the right track."

"That's good." He was *so* off the right track for getting in touch with his emotions, she thought. Maybe she should just tell him that, get him good and mad and talking. Talking in real words instead of tried-and-true clichés.

Off the beaten path. On the right track. "Whatever," she said, then realized she'd actually spoken that word out loud.

He finally chanced a look at her. Lydia hoped her smirk would get him riled, but it didn't. He just tugged her toward that welcoming body of cool water.

"Sit," he ordered, nodding toward a fallen tree on the water's edge.

Lydia sat, but not because he'd ordered her to do so. She was tired and thirsty and her arm was throbbing as if a woodpecker had chosen her arm instead of a tree. She pushed at her hair, wiped at the grime on her face then took another deep breath.

"Here." He pulled her around. "Can you reach the water for a drink?"

Lydia fell to her knees, then cupped her hands in the clean water, grabbing a handful of the glistening liquid to bring it to her dry lips. She took a long gulp, then another, letting the extra stream down her face. "That is so good."

Pastor Dev did the same, then washed his face

and ran his wet hands over his hair. "Okay, let's get your arm cleaned."

Lydia didn't argue. She sat still as he gently splashed water over the deep gash. The water burned its way down into the ugly injury. "I'll have a scar," she said, looking up at him as the wound was washed clean.

He stopped, his fingers tracing the pink welt of the deep nick. He didn't speak. He just held his fingers there as if to heal her with the strength of his emotions.

And Lydia could feel the heat of those emotions, the warmth of his touch, pouring through her wound. She reached out a hand to his hair, pushing the short, damp strands back from his forehead. "It feels better."

He looked up at her then, his blue eyes blinding her with a need that mirrored her own, his words low and rough. "I think you'll have more than this one scar, Lydia."

He moved away from her to sink back in the grass and dirt, his wet hands moving over the five-o'clock shadow on his face. "How could I let this happen?"

Lydia felt a tug in her heart. Was he gearing up for some soul-searching? She sank back beside him. "It wasn't your fault."

He looked at her wound again. "Yes, it is my fault."

"You sure do seem bent on taking all the blame for everything. Why is that?"

He glanced away, out toward the mountains in the distance. A gentle breeze played around them, and he held his face up to the wind. "Because all of this is my fault, from the very beginning. Isn't it amazing, how one act can cause a whole ripple effect on so many people's lives?"

Lydia wanted to know what that one act had been. He'd hinted enough. Maybe he was ready to confess what he thought was his greatest sin.

"Are you going to hold it all inside? Or can you talk to me about it?"

He dropped his hands over his bent knees, shaking his head. "You know, I need to practice what I preach. I need to remember that I, too, sometimes need spiritual counseling."

Lydia glanced around. "Well, since I'm the only one available, you can talk to me. I'm not a trained counselor, but I am a good listener."

He looked into her eyes then, branding her with a sweet longing. "Yes, you are, that's for sure. You've always been my good listener. All those years we worked together, side by side—I can see it so clearly now. You were always the one I turned to, for advice, for guidance. You were my quiet strength, Lydia. My rock. I took you for granted, but no more. Never again." He shrugged, looked down at his hands. "But this…it's just so hard. I've held my secrets so close, for so long now—"

"We're in this together, Pastor Dev."

He touched a finger to the ugly tear in her arm. "Lydia, why don't you just call me Dev?"

Lydia should have been thrilled that she'd managed to jump over another hurdle, or in this case, get up another hill. But his request only made her want to cry. Her words trembled and tripped over her lips. "You'll always be Pastor Dev to me."

"No," he said, shaking his head. "No, things have changed. I'm no longer that man. And you've changed, too. It'll hit you once we get home. You'll be going along, everything fine, your life back to normal…and then you'll remember the gunshots, or the reaction you had to the pesticides in New Orleans, or how you almost died several times over and you'll know that things will never be the same. You were right about normal, Lydia. There is no normal." He got up to stare down at her, his finger hitting his chest. "And I did that to you."

Not one to back off, Lydia lifted up toward him, grabbing him by the arms. "But you also did this to me."

She kissed him, her efforts gentle and sweet, her aim to show him that he hadn't ruined her innocence completely. He'd given her the strength to show him how much she wanted to love him. She kissed the lone tear that streaked down his face. She kissed the dirt smears on his jaw. She kissed the scrapes and scratches on his cheek and across his nose. Then she looked into his eyes, closed her own eyes and kissed him on the lips.

He resisted at first, but after a still, silent struggle she could feel with the intake of his breath, he finally gave in and returned her kiss. And for a brief moment, all the ugliness and bitterness was washed away, gone, forgotten. Forgiven.

Lydia pulled back to stare up at him, her hands cupping his face. "You did that, for me. You made me stronger. You made me follow my heart. And it brought me to you."

He backed away, gulped air. "Don't count on that."

Lydia felt tears piercing her eyes, but she held them back. "Oh, but I am counting on that. I'm depending on you to do the right thing. Or rather to do the thing that you know is right—for both of us."

He turned to stare at the mountains, his hands on his hips. "We need to go."

Because she was bone tired and highly alert to his denial, Lydia prepared to dig in her heels. "So you'll just turn away, shut down, refuse to let me help you the way you've helped me. Why is that…Dev?"

He pivoted to face her, his expression full of torment. "You don't need to know everything. I don't want to tell you everything. I'd like to keep part of you the way you were."

She didn't doubt that. He wanted to keep her as meek, mild-mannered, plain little Lydia. He wanted to keep her at arm's length when they both knew she belonged in his arms. And he needed to be in her arms, too.

"Too late," she retorted. "Way too late."

That angered him. He stalked closer, his hand swinging through the air, slicing, chopping away at his frustrations. "You want to know and understand the real Devon Malone, Lydia? Well, here it is—the short version. I've betrayed my best friend to protect someone else I love. Eli was losing it down in South America. It had been a long, grueling mission, trying to find this girl who didn't want to be found and bring her home safely to her worried parents. Eli wanted to get home to his wife. She was eight months pregnant with their first child. I became concerned about him—he talked about getting things done his way. Eli always was a hothead, always impatient and hard to restrain, but he was so worried about his wife and child he became careless. He was about to compromise the whole mission by just going in with guns blazing. So I discussed it with some of our superiors. They tried to take him off the mission, and he blamed me for that."

She held up a hand, shocked and confused, but determined to keep him talking. "What happened down there?"

"Too much happened," he shouted, his words echoing off the nearby mountains. "Too much. Before I brought things to a halt, Eli had been undercover on his own, trying to get in with the powerful cult members. So instead of heeding my warnings and the orders from CHAIM to take a time-out, he went out on his own to keep things moving.

"We had to be so careful, we could only sit and

wait. But Eli showed up again with the information we needed to go in and get the girl. We had to be very careful after that and wait until we could find her. These people—they were part of a large drug cartel and they got suspicious. We think somebody tipped them off with the wrong information, because they thought we were undercover DEA.

"They followed us onto the river and ambushed the boat as we were bringing the girl out. The girl was killed. Eli and I got away, but he knew he was in trouble. And he blamed me for turning on him. He said some things—claimed I'd messed things up with my delays and worries. So now, he had our superiors on his case and these unscrupulous drug lords chasing him and threatening his family."

He stopped, leaned down, his hands on his knees as he sucked in a deep breath. "When Eli got home to Louisiana, his wife was gone."

Lydia gasped, her knees going weak. Sinking down on the fallen log, she looked across at him. "Dead?"

"Not at first. They took her, held her. We couldn't find her for a long time. Eli went berserk and disappeared, trying to find her, searching all over Louisiana and then down in South America. But…in the end, it was too late, we thought, for Eli and for his family." He stood then, tears streaming down his face. "We *thought* it was too late. We couldn't find Eli, but we finally found her. We tried to save her."

Lydia's heart was thumping so loud she could hear it racing like distant thunder. "What do you mean?"

"His wife was in a coma for weeks. Weeks. But he didn't know. He never knew."

"You mean...you never told him?"

"We couldn't locate him. He was distraught and half mad with grief. It was so bad that by the time CHAIM got to him...he had to be hospitalized. He was a threat to everyone, too dangerous and distraught to be out on his own. We had to get him some help, for his own sake. We sent him to a safe place to heal."

"The retreat?" she asked, swiping at her tears. "And that's why he blames you? Because you started this whole thing by trying to help him?"

Dev lifted his head. "In his mind, the time it took to delay the situation in South America, time used to control him and keep him from finishing the job, caused the problem. We could have been in and out, but I had to make sure he was up to it. So I held him back a few days, based on advice from CHAIM, and that gave this cartel time to get suspicious. Then we were compromised and we had to rush in after this girl and...everything just went crazy."

Lydia tried to state it in terms he could understand. "You failed at your mission."

"Yes, but worse, I failed my friend. I've failed him."

Which would stay with him a lot longer, gnawing at his soul, Lydia thought. "It wasn't your fault."

"Yes, it was. I could have waited until we were home, until we knew we were clear and safe. I could have made him take a rest, get some counseling. Retire maybe. I could have saved all of them, Lydia. Don't you see, I could have saved Eli and his family? All of them. But instead, I had to be self-righteous and sanctimonious, for the greater good. For the sake of CHAIM. I had to make a tough decision, and it was the wrong decision."

Lydia wanted to hold him, to help him. But she didn't dare touch him, not now when he was so caught up in his own misery. He'd only push her away again. "You did the best you could." Even that reassurance sounded lame and inadequate in the face of his pain.

He turned away again. "Well, my best wasn't good enough."

And suddenly, standing there in a wildflower meadow with the purple mountains' majesty all around them, Lydia understood why he couldn't tell her he loved her.

Because his best might not be good enough.

Because in his mind, he might fail. Again.

FIFTEEN

They found the cabin just before sundown.

Dev lay on a narrow ridge, his hand holding Lydia's, as he scoped the woods and trees. He had to be sure no one else had beaten them here. And without a weapon, he could only protect Lydia with his fists and his wits, both of which were not working at full capacity right now.

Protecting Lydia. That was his goal. But he was trying to protect her from so much more than the people who were after them, so much more.

He hadn't told her the end to the story.

And he probably never would. Too many people could get hurt, or worse.

"Let's take the back way in," he said now, pushing the dark thoughts out of his mind as he focused on staying alert. "I want to be sure no one else is here."

"We didn't invite anyone else," she said, back to her quick quips and wry retorts again.

Dev hated the way she'd gone all quiet and reflective after he'd bared his soul to her earlier. She'd stopped asking, stopped pushing, and now he had to wonder if she was so full of disgust and loathing for him, in spite of her reassurances, that she couldn't bear to hear any more details of his past. He couldn't blame her for that, not at all.

But, oh, how he wanted Lydia's respect again. And now he ached, wanting her love, too. She loved him; he knew that without a doubt. But love was a very fragile thing. It could quickly change to hate and resentment. He'd witnessed that with Eli. He couldn't bear that with Lydia. No, better to let her think the worst of him. Because whatever she was thinking now couldn't compare to how she'd feel if he told her the whole truth.

Determined not to let that happen, he guided her in a low crouch through the thick foliage around the perimeter of the square cabin, his eyes scanning the open pasture and winding stream that bordered the property. Then he glanced up toward the hills and ridges behind the cabin.

"A lot of hiding places around here," he whispered to her. "But maybe we won't get any company tonight. This place is so off the map, even CHAIM operatives shouldn't be able to find it."

"It's a beautiful place," Lydia replied. "Probably very peaceful and soothing in most cases."

But this wasn't like most cases, Dev reasoned. This was not a vacation. This was survival. "Eli always came here to find his center, to get his head together," he said. "I think he probably came here after South America."

Only Dev never had found Eli here when his wife lay in a coma, when she needed her husband by her side. Of course, Eli would have been on full alert back then. He'd probably left long before Dev even made it over the last ridge. Eli Trudeau had been raised in the swamps of Louisiana, so the man knew how to disappear.

He also knew how to reappear without warning.

And for all Dev could see, Eli could be out there right now, watching them, waiting to seek his own brand of vengeance. Dev would almost welcome that, if not for Lydia.

Taking her with him, he did a quick scan of the back of the house, where a tiny deck reached out toward the mountains. He didn't like entering a place cold, without benefit of equipment or weapons, but Lydia needed to rest and this was his last chance, his last hope.

Maybe Eli would come and they could get to the bottom of this once and for all, or at least try to make things even.

"Okay, let's go inside and see how things are," he told Lydia. "Stay close."

"Like I'd run out into these mountains on my own," she retorted.

Dev didn't need to remind her that early this morning she'd almost done that very thing. They both knew this had been the longest day—trekking through the mountains was hard work on a good day—but they were dragging a lot of excess emotional baggage. Or at least, Dev knew he was.

They crept quietly up onto the porch, then Dev kicked at the door, opening it wide. "No need for locks out here," he whispered. "At least never before."

He did a quick scan of the dim room, enough natural light left to allow him a clear view of the drab fixtures. It was a small kitchen. "No electricity," he whispered over his shoulder. "But I think I can remember where he keeps matches and flint. And there should be some oil lamps around here somewhere."

"What about food?" Lydia asked. "I'm so hungry."

"We might find some rations somewhere in here. There's an old well for water and washing, and he used to keep potable water on hand."

Dev held her behind him, protecting her with his body as they slowly entered the quiet, empty room. Then the hair on the back of his neck stood up.

Turning to Lydia, he put a finger to his mouth to silence any words. Pulling her close, he backed toward the door. What had it been? A sound, a soft creaking of wood? Maybe some nocturnal creatures scurrying away? But something wasn't right.

Something wasn't right.

At the door, he turned her around. "I think—"

"You thought right, bro."

Dev heard the familiar Cajun accent coming from deep inside the dark cabin. *Eli.*

"C'mon on back in, Pastoral. You're always welcome in my home, *mon ami*."

Lydia gasped, stared at Dev with a questioning look.

Dev sent her a warning message to stay silent. "Eli, is that you?"

"Stupid question. This is my cabin, after all. Why wouldn't it be me?"

Dev held tightly to Lydia, willing her to stay quiet. "I thought you were going to take the long way back here."

Then they heard footsteps moving through the tiny cabin. And suddenly, Eli's body formed a dark silhouette in the middle of the kitchen.

"Hello, Pastoral. It's been a while." He bent his head, his expression full of caution and warning as he lifted his gaze toward Dev. "I tried to meander, you understand. Tried to get rid of the hound dogs on my trail, but—" He shrugged, winked, tilted his head to the left.

Dev tried to read Eli, careful to keep Lydia behind him. "But what? Are you ready to get things settled between us?"

Eli shrugged again, grinning, but Dev didn't miss the warning in his friend's coal-black eyes. "Me, I've got a lot of things that need settling." Then Eli cut his gaze away toward the left again.

That action brought another person into view.

Eli nodded toward the other man. "But him, he has even more at stake in this little game, *oui*."

Dev felt Lydia stiffen behind him, felt the fast-moving current of adrenaline flowing through his system as he stared at the man moving toward Eli.

"Hello, old boy. So good to see you again."

The Peacemaker was standing beside Eli. And he had a Colt .45 aimed at Eli's head.

Eli smiled, but the look in his dark eyes was deadly. "I told you it wasn't me, Pastoral."

Dev registered that, his gaze centered on the tall, gray-haired man holding Eli by the arm. "Why?"

The Peacemaker didn't respond at first. He just stood there staring at them. Then he said, "I don't have to explain my actions. I don't need to explain anything to you."

Dev glared at him, hating the smug, condescending expression on the man's face. His mind raced with ways to get Lydia out of this situation. He moved a fraction, holding her behind him.

"Don't do anything you'll regret, Pastoral," The Peacemaker said, his gaze slipping over Lydia. "She is such a pretty woman, isn't she? And so very hard to kill."

"You—" Dev rushed forward, and found the gun aimed at him.

Lydia screamed, moving forward, too. "What's going on?" she said. "I mean, why are you so determined to kill both of us? I don't know anything. I just want to go home."

Dev settled back, his arm pressed behind him to

keep Lydia from rushing in with her own brand of justice.

The old man pushed Eli toward them, then turned the gun on all three of them. Eli sent Dev a look that said "How are you going to get us out of this one?" Dev wondered the same thing.

The Peacemaker shook his head, still glaring at Lydia. "But, my dear, you do know things. You now know all about CHAIM. Such a sanctimonious organization, don't you think? Taking the law into its own hands, so to speak. Seeking the ultimate justice where others have failed. You know our secrets now, dear, and you know my face. I can't allow that."

Dev noticed how Eli had moved closer, helping him to shield Lydia. A plan formed in his head. He knew he could count on Eli to get Lydia out of this cabin and keep her alive out there. He'd just have to distract this madman so they could make a run for it.

"Let her go," he told the other man, his hand slicing through the air. "She got caught up in this when you had my friend murdered in Atlanta."

"Didn't she, though?" The Peacemaker said. "And you, being so very noble, took her on the run with you."

"I had to protect her," Dev retorted. "I'm going to protect her." He sent a brief look toward Eli. "No matter what."

"Not if you're all dead," the older man said, his smile serene. "I had to abort my plan down in New Orleans, but I'm getting tired of chasing you all over the country." Then he nodded toward Eli. "But this one, he brought me right to you. Once I nabbed him, he was more than willing to help me out, just to save that crazy Kissie."

Dev looked toward Eli, giving him an expression of gratitude. Then he hoped his friend would see the signals in his eyes. *I need your help.*

Eli let out a snort, but nodded briefly at Dev. *Message received.* Then he made a big show, sighing, shifting, his expression serene and misleading as he cut his gaze toward The Peacemaker. "Now, tell me again exactly why you need to eliminate all of us?"

The Peacemaker kept his gun trained on them. "It's a long story, really. Let's just say you both stirred up a hornet's nest down in Rio Branco. Your actions have jeopardized my operations there. You were trespassing on my estate, you see."

Eli grunted, then lifted his dark eyebrows. "You're a drug lord, *oui?*"

The older man laughed, held the gun higher. "That's such a derogatory way of describing it, don't you think? I provide a service to people. I have my own religion, my own way of teaching the word of God." He shrugged, shook the gun at them. "It's that simple."

"Why?" Dev asked again, needing to know how a supposedly good, faithful man could go so terribly wrong. But then, he reasoned, there was evil all over the place and some couldn't overcome the temptation.

The Peacemaker gave him a simmering smile. "It was just so…easy. The money, the power, the ability to control something. I had the perfect cover."

Dev nodded. "You used your CHAIM position and your connections. How could you do that?"

"Easy. I took what was offered."

Eli stopped smiling, and Dev recognized the deadly calm of his friend's whole countenance. "And you got rid of anyone standing in your way, right?"

"Unfortunate, but necessary. You two rushed in to save that silly girl, and, well, that brought too much attention to my little community."

Dev saw Eli's expression change, a darkness settling like a shadow on a mountain over his haggard features. "You killed my wife."

The Peacemaker didn't respond. He just stood there, a blank look on his face. Quiet came over the room as Dev watched Eli wrestling for control. Dev prayed Eli would stay centered and do what needed to be done to bring this man to justice.

"Did you kill my wife and my unborn child?" Eli asked, his fists clenched tightly at his side, his eyes as wild and dark as a forest creature's.

"I'm so sorry," The Peacemaker said, his voice filled with a false inflection of pain. "If Devon here hadn't reported your extracurricular activities, that might not have been necessary. But when he brought your noble mission to a halt and you went off snooping on your own…well, things just got too hot. I couldn't take that risk. I mean, how would it look if one of your CHAIM superiors was accused of being the head of such a mighty cartel? Not good at all. Especially considering that poor girl also knew too much about me. I couldn't let you rescue her and return her home. I'm very sorry, truly I am."

Dev felt sick inside, seeing the deranged gleam in the man's eyes. This man, so high up and such a legend within the ranks of CHAIM, had turned into an evildoer of the worst kind. Murder, drug trafficking, illegal activities, all beneath the guise of helping Christians. Dev felt such shame washing over him. It was he who had brought them all to this moment.

Then he heard a voice as clearly as if someone were standing right beside him. "Not you. But him."

Dev felt a new courage pouring over him. He looked toward Eli, saw the rage and torment there in his friend's dark eyes. But he also saw something else. Eli's eyes shone with a new understanding, a new hope and a forgiveness that had not been there since the awful events of that day.

Dev knew what he had to do. He had to make this up to Eli and he had to save Lydia. He could almost read Eli's thoughts. *Now, bro.*

Steeling himself, Dev said a quick prayer. Then he stopped thinking and went on adrenaline and impulse. "You will not get away with this," he said, just before he lunged toward the man holding the gun.

The gun went off and the fight was on.

* * *

Lydia screamed, her mind going numb as Pastor Dev moved like lightning toward the other man. She heard the gunshot, saw the two men engaging in an all-out battle. But before she could see if Pastor Dev had been hit, she was dragged away.

By him. By Eli Trudeau.

"Let me go," she shouted, kicking and screaming as he lifted her up and stumbled out the back door. Lydia's efforts were fruitless. The man was solid muscle, as tightly built as an iron freight train.

"Let me go," she cried, glued to the open door, tuned to the noises coming from within. She could hear crashes, shouts, grunts. "I have to get back to him."

A big hand came over her mouth as Eli set her on her feet behind a jagged rock. "Shut up," he said into her ear, his tone almost conversational. He wasn't even out of breath. "If you behave, I'll take my hand away. Don't make me have to gag that cute mouth of yours."

Lydia tried to reason that this man was on their side. Or so Pastor Dev wanted to believe. But what if this were a setup to get her away from Pastor Dev?

She decided in order to keep herself alive, she would pretend to be docile. For now. So she slumped down, nodding toward the man holding her as she slanted her head around.

"That's better." Eli pulled his hand away, then hissed in her ear. "Don't make a sound."

Lydia didn't dare breathe. She waited, listening for more gunshots. All she could hear now was her own unsteady breathing. And a long sigh from the man behind her.

"We're sure up the creek without a paddle, *chère,*" he said. "I need you to listen to me."

Lydia sure knew this drill, but she was so worried about Pastor Dev she couldn't think straight. "But what about—"

"Devon knows how to take care of things in there," he retorted before she could even form the words. "He'll be okay."

"Not if he's wounded." She squirmed around to face her captor. Then stood silent as she got her first good, long look at the notorious Eli Trudeau, aka The Disciple.

He was just a tad taller than Pastor Dev. He was dark, bronzed and baked like a golden statue. His hair was so dark it shimmered almost black in the growing dusk. His eyes were the same way—dark, intense, brilliant with secrets. She was both intrigued and terrified.

"Hello," he said, glancing back toward the silence coming from the house. "I'm Eli."

"I know who you are."

"*Oui,* and I know who you are. Your journal was very detailed."

She wanted to smack him. "Where is my journal?"

"In a safe place."

Lydia didn't have time to dwell on that. "Are you just going to stand there or are you going to help him?"

"I am helping him, by keeping you out of the fray."

She pushed away from him. "I can't do this. I can't let him die just so I can live."

"He would want it that way."

"I *don't* want it that way."

He shrugged, held a hand up to block her way. "I can't let you go back in there. I have to honor Dev's wishes."

"How do you know this is his wish? And how do I know you're not in on this? You could easily let him die, then kill me."

"I could do that, very easily," he answered with another eloquent shrug. "But not today, love. Not today. Today I have to keep you safe while Dev finishes up in there."

"So we're just going to stand here all night and let him do battle with that evil man?"

He shook his head, his long hair falling around his grizzly face. "*Non,* I didn't say that, now did I?"

Lydia saw the glint in his dark eyes. "I hope you're the man Pastor Dev says you are. I need you to prove that to me."

He grunted, pushed a hand through his hair. "I don't need to prove anything to anybody, but I do owe my friend in there."

"Which one?"

"You don't trust—that's a good thing."

"I don't trust. You're right on that."

"Well, then we have a little problem. Because I can't do my job if you don't behave."

"And what exactly is your job right now?"

"To get you as far away from this cabin as possible." He took her by the arm. "So c'mon."

"No." She pulled and tugged, but it was as if an iron vise had her arm in its grip. Then she tried pleading. "Please, don't leave him in there. He'll die."

"He won't die. But he will get us out of this. You have to count on that."

"I can't," Lydia said, tears spilling down her face as he shoved her up the mountain. "I can't leave him."

Eli didn't respond. She saw the unyielding gleam in his eyes, though. This man wouldn't relent. So she'd just have to find a way to get back to Dev herself. And she'd just have to be the one to save them all.

SIXTEEN

He was alive.

That at least made Dev feel triumphant.

He was also tied up and in intense pain from the gunshot wound in his left leg. The bullet had passed through, but its path still throbbed and pulsed in protest. But that pain didn't bother him as much as the relief of knowing Lydia was still alive, too. For now.

In the muted light from a single kerosene lamp, the other fellow didn't look so good, either. The Peacemaker had fought valiantly, the force of evil propelling him with an almost superhuman strength. If Dev hadn't been wounded, he might have been able to take the older man. But he *was* wounded and that slight distraction had cost him his freedom.

And given Lydia hers.

He prayed Eli would know what needed to be done. He hoped Eli would get her to safety, then disappear for his own sake. But if Dev knew Eli, and he probably knew the man better than most, then Eli would be back here very soon to end this thing one way or another. Especially since Eli now knew this man was responsible for the death of his family.

But Dev wasn't going to sit idle while that scenario stewed. He had a plan. He always had a plan.

"You've worn me out," The Peacemaker said from his place across the floor. He was leaning in front of the empty, silent fireplace, winded and wounded, his gun at rest beside him. "I do believe you cracked a couple of my ribs."

"I'd like to do more," Dev countered, hatred and loathing filling his soul. "You've caused the people I care about a lot of pain. And all for drug money."

"Not to mention a nice estate in South America, cars, planes, boats and beautiful women."

"You don't have a conscience, do you?" Dev asked, amazed at how calm the other man seemed to be. "Don't you know you won't get away with this?"

The Peacemaker laughed and shook his head, streams of dirty sweat pouring down his face. "But I have, for years now. And once I eliminate you and those other two out there, my life will go back to being wonderful."

"You might get rid of me, but you will have to answer to a higher source for your sins."

The Peacemaker held up a hand. "Spare me, please. I don't need a sermon on my eternal soul."

"No, you don't need it, but you're sure going to get one when you go to meet your maker."

"I think I'll be just fine," The Peacemaker replied, his whole demeanor one of calm assurance. "All of this getting through the narrow gates stuff is rather silly, don't you think?"

Dev couldn't say what he was thinking, but it didn't have anything to do with the narrow gates. "When did you switch over to the dark side?"

He looked away at that. Dev watched him carefully, saw the change come over his demeanor. The Peacemaker went from being hostile and angry to quiet and reflective. "When I lost my son to CHAIM."

That brought Dev's head up. He was still a minister and a counselor, after all. "Want to talk about it?"

"I do not. Let's just say that I didn't appreciate how he gave his life for what is supposed to be such a fine, Christian organization."

"We all take that risk when we sign up," Dev pointed out, hoping to get to the heart of this matter.

"Do we? Or are we brainwashed and persuaded into doing someone else's bidding in the name of God?"

"Do you feel that way?"

He looked back at Dev then, his eyes feral in the yellow lamplight. "I didn't at first. But…you see, Pastoral, I was the one who convinced my only son to join up with our legions. He did something in his youth that I found scandalous, so I thought he might learn a valuable lesson from being amongst our ranks. I never dreamed he'd be killed at such a young age."

"So you're blaming yourself right along with blaming God?"

Anger unfolded like aged parchment paper over his wrinkled face. "I blame God for making me think we were all invincible. I blame God for taking my son. After he died, I died inside. I didn't care anymore." He gave Dev a long, hard stare. "There is nothing noble left in me, you see."

Which meant he had nothing to lose, Dev reasoned. He could almost sympathize with this tired old man. Except that this tired old man had killed people in order to appease his own torment and guilt. Why hadn't he turned to God, instead of away from Him?

Dev thought back over his own career in CHAIM, wondering to whom this man was referring. "Can you tell me his name? Your son, I mean?"

"He died years ago, before you were ever in the organization. You don't need to know that."

"I can find out on my own."

"Not if you're dead."

Trying to keep the man talking, Dev said, "If you want me dead, why didn't you kill me when you had a chance? Why did you wait for five years?"

The other man brought a knee up, then placed a hand across it. "I did think along those very lines myself at first. I almost came after both of you right after you left South America. But my operation had been compromised and it was too dangerous. I had to bide my time and stay the course in CHAIM. So

I waited until The Disciple was released, then put my plan into action—killing you to set him up, thus eliminating him from CHAIM forever. But of course, that plan went awry in Atlanta. I became so angry after that failure, I wanted to see you suffer just as I had suffered. So I decided to eliminate the girl, then you. I thought by killing someone you cared so deeply about, I'd have my revenge."

Dev didn't flinch, but that image gave him cause to push on. "Well, why didn't you do that?"

"You foiled that plan, over and over. In Atlanta, in New Orleans, even at that fortress at Eagle Rock. It became so very tedious, sending incompetent people to do the job."

"So you weren't in all of those places?"

"No, I sent underlings and new hires to do my work. They are always so willing to please, but they are also very inexperienced and stupid. When I realized things were going wrong in New Orleans, I directed you and the woman toward Eagle Rock, this delicious sense of justice in my mind. You know, kill the woman, distract the agent, all the while looking like the concerned superior I'm supposed to be, that sort of thing. Alexandre let me down on all accounts, however."

"Thank goodness," Dev said, meaning it. He couldn't think past what would have happened if Lydia had died there. He surely would have wound up like Eli—at some remote retreat trying to get over an unimaginable grief. Which is obviously what this man had wanted.

"I had to take matters into my own hands," The Peacemaker explained. "I had to track The Disciple down. I knew he'd lead me to you. He might be bitter, but his heart is still weak. I had to keep tabs on him and use him."

"Ah, because you'd so carefully set it up to make him look like the guilty one."

"A perfect solution. That man has always been a thorn in the side of CHAIM." He waved a hand in the air. "And now, here we are."

"So…get it over with," Dev goaded. "Kill me."

"I can't do that just yet, old boy. I have to wait for the girl to come back."

Dev's heart lurched at that remark, said in such a conversational voice. He didn't want to think about that scenario, and he couldn't let it distract him now. "She won't be coming back."

"Oh, but she most certainly will. She's in love with you. And we both know love is a very powerful tool in this business. Even The Disciple with all his muscle won't be able to hold her back." He laughed low in his throat. "That's the only reason I'm not out there tracking them down. I can rest here and know she will find a way to return to you. And that you, in turn, will die for her."

Dev sat staring at the other man, thinking no truer words had ever been spoken. He loved Lydia; he was willing to die to save her. This man, whoever he was, had loved his son, and he was willing to turn to evil in order to appease that love. A thin line...a very thin line.

And Dev could see that line drawn very clearly between his kind of love and the kind this man had tried to justify.

But sitting here, he also knew that God understood all motives and all suffering, and all forms of love, good and bad. So he prayed for Lydia and Eli and himself.

And he prayed for The Peacemaker, too.

She was praying.

It was full dark now. The Disciple had her up on a ridge, in a spot where he had a clear view of the cabin below. They were hidden here, but Lydia felt completely exposed.

Because he was watching her like a hawk.

She had to figure out a way to sneak past him and get back to that cabin. Maybe if she got him talking.

"You sure are a man of few words," she said, her voice calm in spite of her shaking hands.

"Not much to say at this point, *chère*."

"Tell me about yourself, your life."

"No."

"I'd like to understand you better."

"No one can understand me *better*. I'm beyond all understanding."

"Pastor Dev understands you. He tried to help you."

He went so still that she wondered if he'd turned into rock. "*Oui,* he certainly did. But he should have stayed out of it. He didn't know what he was getting involved in."

"You can't blame him for what happened. All of this is that man's fault. That man down there who's holding your best friend—he's the one to blame."

He whirled, fists clenched. "You talk too much."

Lydia glared up at him. "I want to go back and help Pastor Dev."

He got up, moved around the makeshift camp he'd erected. All in all, he wasn't a bad host. He'd found them water on the way up the mountain, and he'd offered her some sunflower seeds he'd managed to smuggle into the big pocket of his frayed cargo pants.

But Lydia could tell this man did not like sitting still. He moved around like a caged panther, ready to strike at any time. Lydia didn't know how she was going to get away from such a fierce warrior.

But she was going to, somehow.

She watched him pace, saw him glance back toward the cabin. Maybe he had a plan, too. While Lydia was waiting for him to reveal that plan, she found one of her own. There was a big branch from a fallen tree near her feet. She could yield that as a weapon. She wouldn't kill him; she'd just knock him down long enough to make a run for the hills and then on to the cabin.

And she'd be carrying that big stick with her when she got there.

* * *

Dev woke with a start. He hadn't meant to doze off, but his leg was throbbing with all the precision of a marching band, beating at his fatigue, dragging him down. He so wanted to sleep for a good week, at least. But he had to stay alert.

"Don't worry, old boy. I'm not going to fall over in a slump," The Peacemaker said, his gaze centered on Dev. "Unlike you, I can't sleep. I'm watching for the lovely Lydia. She'll be here soon. I can feel it. The night is so still. Not a breeze stirring. This canyon is waiting for something to happen."

Dev imagined Lydia was doing the same. And Eli, too, he hoped. He hoped Eli was making sure Lydia was far away from here and safe. And reinforcements would be coming soon.

But then, Dev couldn't be completely sure of Eli's motives, either. Surely he wouldn't hurt Lydia just to get back at Dev. But he had brought this man right to their door. Eli could have easily outsmarted The Peacemaker, so why hadn't he? Maybe he did it for Kissie's sake, or maybe that had been a convenient cover for his real motives.

An uneasy feeling settled over Dev then. He couldn't just sit here, waiting. He'd done enough waiting during this whole ordeal, thinking everyone else would help Lydia and him. That had only brought more trouble. He had to get away from The Peacemaker and find Lydia. He had to end this thing, one way or another, tonight.

* * *

Lydia bided her time. She could be very patient when she had to. She prayed, sometimes out loud.

"'Blessed are those who mourn, for they shall be comforted.'"

Eli whirled to stare down at her. "You are seriously getting on my last nerve."

"I have to stay calm. Praying and quoting scripture helps me to stay centered."

"Well, I have to think, so pray silently, okay?"

Lydia shook her head, managing to ease toward the big stick. "I thought the prayers might bring both of us some comfort."

He grunted. "I said to be quiet."

Lydia pretended she didn't hear that command. "'Blessed are the merciful, for they shall obtain mercy.'"

He kicked at a rock, then scoffed at her. "Mercy? Do you see any mercy around here, *catin?*" He bent close, wagging a finger in her face. "That old man down there shows no mercy. He is hard and mean and callous. He always was."

"You know him?" Lydia asked, slipping closer to the thick tree branch. Bending over, her hands on her knees, she managed to roll it underneath her sneakers. "How do you know The Peacemaker? I mean, you've been with him for a while now, obviously, trekking all the way to Colorado—"

"We flew here on his private jet. It was a quick trip. He did most of the talking."

Lydia could picture that. This man did not like to give up words. "Okay, then I guess you learned a few things about him, right?"

Eli threw his hands up in frustration, then bent over her again. So very close. "I didn't have to get to know him. I've known him most of my life."

That admission sent up warning flares in Lydia's mind. If The Disciple already knew The Peacemaker, then they could indeed be in on this together. "Are you holding me here so he can kill Pastor Dev? Are you in this with him, just to get revenge for whatever you think happened in South America?"

He glared down at her, his silhouette dark and forbidding in the moonlight. "What are you saying?"

"I'm saying, I don't like the way you're handling this," she told him as she carefully rose to her feet. She had the limb in one hand now and hidden behind her back, the benefits of darkness and shadows working in her favor. It felt fairly solid, even if the weight was causing her hurt arm to protest. "I'm saying you're just stalling and I don't like that. I want to know why we're just sitting here when we should be down there helping Pastor Dev."

"Because I know better than you how to deal with this situation. We wait until it's good and dark, then we make our move. But we're not going back to that cabin. I have to get you away from here. You know too much already and you don't need to see anything else. For your own good."

"Pastor Dev has been telling me the same thing

for days now," she retorted, good and mad at the lot of them now. "I'm so tired of hearing that. I can think for myself and anyone can see that you're holding me here for your own purposes. Pastor Dev—"

He stood up straight like a bear rising, smiling then, his arms crossed over his barrel of a chest as he jeered at her. Arms still crossed, he leaned down again. "That's real cute, for true, the way you call him Pastor Dev. I read all about how you love him so much—there in your journal. Sappy stuff, that. Pastor Dev this, Pastor Dev that. Oh, Pastor Dev, I love you so much. Oh, Pastor Dev, I'm praying for you. Oh, Pastor Dev, I love your superhero T-shirt."

"You shouldn't have taken my journal. That's private."

Looking down at her, he shook his head. "You are so out of your league, *catin*. If I hadn't found that book at Kissie's, we'd probably all be dead now. You wrote about—what did you call them— the VEPs. You didn't name names, but you had evidence. Strong evidence, tracking both of you from Atlanta to New Orleans. You need to learn to keep your mouth shut and your pen dry. CHAIM does not operate in a tell-all fashion. So be glad I hid that journal for you."

"After you read it, of course."

"I read it to get clues—and I thank you for that, at least. But, *oui,* I could have done without all the mushy love letters."

Lydia's anger and shame caused her to find the

strength she needed to bring the broken limb up. With a swiftness that had him lifting his eyebrows in surprise, she brought the heavy limb around and managed to land a sharp whack on his head, right above his left temple. Then she watched as he stumbled and fell down, his hands flailing in the air. He wasn't out completely, but he was rattled. He came to enough to hear her next words, though. And since she knew he'd be up and after her soon, she shouted as she was backing away at a fast sprint, "I do love him. And that's why I'm going after him."

SEVENTEEN

Everything after that happened in a blur of darkness and shadows. Lydia ran down the mountain, keeping her eyes on the single light shining from the cabin below. Thank goodness she'd memorized landmarks and rock formations on the way up, or she might have been lost in the wilderness for a very long time. But she knew God was leading her; she wouldn't lose her way. So she stayed the course, all the while aware that Eli Trudeau was right on her heels.

She heard him call out, "Don't be foolish, Lydia. You're going to get all of us killed."

Lydia kept on running. If she died tonight, well, at least she could die knowing she tried to help the man she loved. She was stronger now than she'd been a week ago. Never again would she be meek and mild Lydia. Now she would be assertive, firm Lydia, sure in her faith and even surer in her path in life.

And right now, that path was leading straight to that little mountain cabin.

* * *

Dev waited for just the right moment. He was tired, thirsty, hungry and hurting, but a rush of pure adrenaline had him on high alert right now. Something didn't feel right. Something was about to happen.

He watched as The Peacemaker paced in front of him, his gun held in place to keep Dev still and co-operative. Dev wasn't afraid he'd be shot again. But he was deathly afraid that if he made a wrong move, Lydia would die.

He still hadn't put it all together, but his analytical mind had pretty much figured most of it out. The Peacemaker had been running drugs for years now, under the guise of working for CHAIM. And somehow, Eli must have found out more than he'd let on. Then in true Eli fashion, he'd gone off by himself to fix that wrong. But why had Eli almost gone off the deep end down there? Why? Dev just hoped Eli would come clean on that angle and finally end the mystery once and for all. Whatever the case, when Dev had brought things to a halt, someone had inadvertently alerted The Peacemaker, and then everything had gone wrong.

Now they were after Dev, at first making it look as if Eli was the one seeking revenge. The Peacemaker had certainly been patient, waiting to strike exactly when Eli was released from his "retreat." But there was one missing piece to this entire puzzle. Why hadn't The Peacemaker killed Eli already, since Eli obviously had the goods on the man's illegal operations? Why had The Peacemaker let Eli live for five years, when he could have so easily had him murdered either at the retreat or now when they'd been chasing each other all over the country? And why hadn't Eli told anyone about what he'd found in South America? Why?

"You're very quiet," The Peacemaker said now, whirling to stare down at Dev. "Are you contemplating meeting your maker?"

Dev laughed and shifted his weight, grimacing as pain shot through his leg. "No, actually I'm contemplating how you managed all of this. I've pieced together most of this equation, but I have yet to understand the connection between you and Eli. There has to be one."

"Of course you'd figure that out," The Peacemaker replied, nodding. "That, my dear boy, is a rather long and sordid story."

Before he could get an answer to that burning question, a commotion from outside caused The Peacemaker to hurry to the back door, his gun at the ready as he slowly opened the door a few inches.

Which presented Dev with the opportunity he'd been waiting for. It was now or never.

Lydia cried out just as she reached the clearing leading to the cabin. She was once again being held by a set of supersized arms. Eli had caught up with her.

"Let me go," she hissed, tears of frustration falling down her face. "I have to help him. I have to—"

He held her, but his grip gentled as he leaned close, whispering into her ear, "I understand that, honey, but you need to understand something else. You can't do it alone."

Somehow, Lydia heard the sincerity and the resignation in his words. "Will you help me, then?"

She felt his nod. "*Oui,* although I keep thinking fools rush in—"

"Where angels fear to tread," she finished, gulping back a sob. "What are we going to do?"

"Well, you've foiled my attempts to keep you out of harm's way, and you made enough racket to wake up the whole mountain, so we don't have a choice except to go back in for a nice little visit. But I do have a plan. I always have a plan."

"Just like Pastor Dev," she said, tears falling from her face to land on his big hand on her arm. She could see the wetness glistening in the white wash of moonlight. "Thank you."

"Don't thank me until it's over."

"It will be over soon," she replied, her silent prayer echoing that sentiment. "So what's your plan?"

Eli pushed her away. "I'm going to surrender myself to The Peacemaker. He's really after me anyway, you see. We both know that, but he's been stalling, hoping to get in three kills with one strike, so to speak. I need you to stay right here and wait for

Dev. He'll come for you soon, because I'm about to give him a head start. I'm going to be the first kill."

With that, he took off toward the cabin, calling out in a loud voice, "Hey, old man. Go ahead on and get this over with. Take me out and let them go. The girl doesn't know anything. And Dev is a good man. Besides, I never told him anything about what I knew. And I never will. So let's end this thing now, just you and me. What do you say, *Grandpère?*"

Grandfather?

Lydia gasped as she rushed forward. At about the same time, the cabin door came crashing open as Pastor Dev pushed the old man out the back door with all his strength and body weight. In a shadowed dance, they fell together, rolling off the porch onto the ground, while Eli ran toward them.

Lydia was right behind him.

Eli shouted again, reaching them just as Pastor Dev managed to rise into a crouch, his features etched with pain, his hand holding tightly to The Peacemaker's forearm as he tried to wrestle away the gun. Lydia watched in horror as Eli flew into the fray, struggling with the older man. But in the muted moonlight, she couldn't be sure if he was trying to help or hinder Pastor Dev's efforts.

Then The Peacemaker twisted with a grimace, aiming the gun right toward Lydia, with Pastor Dev slapping and hitting at his arm to stop him while Eli stood over him, calling out for him to let go. Dev shouted at Lydia, trying to warn her, then a shot rang out. Seconds passed, then another one followed.

Lydia waited, her eyes squeezed closed, for the pain she was sure would come. The gun had been aimed right at her. But she didn't feel the pain of being shot. Instead, she watched in shock as Eli slumped to the ground.

And then the mountain went still and quiet again.

Dev saw Eli go down, but he also saw The Peacemaker slump over in defeat. Then he heard a soft moan.

"Lydia?" he called out, rushing to her, his hurt leg dragging as he met her beside Eli's still form.

Lydia fell down, her hands touching Eli's face. "He's still breathing," she said, tears streaming down her face. "He's not dead."

Another shot rang out. Dev turned to find The Peacemaker struggling toward him, his gun wobbling in his shaking hand. "I'll kill all of you. I'll kill everyone—"

Then he fell over to the ground, the gun dropping away from his hand. Dev looked down at Eli, then turned to Lydia. "Stay here."

She nodded, her hand rubbing against Eli's arm. "Don't die on me," she said, her tone pleading. "Disciple, don't die on me."

Dev went to The Peacemaker and checked his pulse. He was dead. Then Dev saw the blood streaming from his midsection. In the struggle, one of the shots had hit him.

The Peacemaker was dead, and as Dev kneeled over his lifeless body, he prayed that God would grant this bitter old man the peace he had not found on earth.

Then he rushed back to Lydia and Eli. "Eli, can you hear me? Eli?"

Eli moaned, slanted half-shut eyes toward them. "It wasn't me, bro." Then he passed out again.

"We have to do something," Lydia said, her sobs coming hard now. "He saved us, Dev. He saved our lives."

Dev dragged her close, kissing her tears, her hair. "I know, honey, I know. Eli is that kind of man. We'll try, I promise we'll try."

He went about that task, giving Eli first aid, doing what he'd been trained to do when someone went down. He worked on reviving his friend, trying to determine there in the moonlight just how bad the wound was.

"Eli, stay with us," he said over and over, his own tears coming at last. "Eli, you can't die now, do you understand? You can't die." Grasping at how to save his friend, Dev knew there was only one secret left. And he had to tell Eli that secret in order to save him.

He looked over at Lydia, praying that she'd understand why he'd never told her this. Then he grabbed Eli by both arms and held tightly to his friend. "Eli, stay with me. Stay with me, please. Eli, you have to live. You've got a very good reason to live." Then he leaned close. "Eli, you have a son. Do you hear me? You have a son."

Dev heard Lydia's gasp of surprise, saw the glaring brilliance of his secrets and his betrayal there in her confused eyes as she looked up from Eli to him.

And then, he heard the helicopter coming through the night, its lights shining like a welcome beacon in the moonlight. He heard Kissie's voice calling through the megaphone.

"Hang on down there. Help is on the way."

Reinforcements were here at last.

It wasn't too late for Eli, but Dev wondered if it was way too late for Lydia and him.

She wondered what would happen now.

Three days later, Lydia stood in her bedroom, safe back in Dixon now. Remembering how her parents had met them at the airport in Albany, she dashed at the tears that always seemed nearby these days.

"Lydia, baby," her mother had said, rushing up to touch her, hug her, then touch her again. "I can't believe you're home. We were so worried. No one would tell us—except that you were in some sort of danger and Pastor Dev had you in a safe place while the authorities searched for a killer. Honey, that doesn't make a bit of sense to me."

Her father, ever stoic and stern, had only nodded, hugged her tight, and then backed up, swallowing what surely must have been a big lump in his throat. "Girl, you gave your mama a surefire scare."

She'd tried to explain it all; she'd tried to gloss over everything, sticking to the story that Pastor Dev had suggested way back when this had begun. Yes, they'd been involved in a murder, and yes, they'd been safe. They'd been on a retreat, a quest of sorts, working hard to find the truth while the authorities found the killer. But Lydia knew no one was buying that story.

Yet even when her mother pressed her for the truth, Lydia couldn't put it all into words.

"Just pray for me, Mama," she'd told her mother last night. "Just pray for Pastor Dev and me."

At her mother's concerned expression, she'd ventured on. "Nothing happened between us. I'm still Lydia, Mama. I'm still your baby girl. And I'm so glad to be home."

Her mother's instincts had hit the nail on the head however. "Something did happen. Something big, I know. You fell in love with each other, didn't you?" Then her mother had opened her arms wide, letting Lydia cry. All of her sorrows, all of her doubts and fears were expunged in that gentle purging.

"He's a good man, Mama. The best. He saved my life. He was always putting me first. I love him."

And that had ended the questions. Even though the whole town was whispering, wondering, comparing notes, Lydia's family had somehow managed to put a shield around her.

Or maybe Pastor Dev had done that.

Right along with avoiding her like the plague.

Now she stood staring up at her poster of Rhett and Scarlett, her heart hurting with such grief that all she wanted to do was curl up with her cat and never leave the safety of this room. But she'd have to get over that notion.

"I had a life," she said as Rhett brushed up against her legs. "I will have a life again."

She'd just have to find another job. Because she couldn't work with him, not now, when her love for him hurt her in every fiber of her being.

He apparently did not love her enough to fight for her, since she hadn't seen him in three days, not since they'd left the airport in separate cars. She with her parents. He with some high-up bishop or elder from the church, and probably from CHAIM.

He had some explaining to do, no doubt.

But all Lydia had were her memories and her nightmares. Memories of his smile and his kisses, nightmares of Eli as he lay near death, and of The Peacemaker, that pitiful old man who apparently had not one ounce of love in his jaded heart, even though he'd masqueraded as a missionary down in South America.

"Forgive him, God," she said now, wishing with all her heart that someone had been able to penetrate that wicked man's soul. "And help Eli, Lord. He's suffered enough. Too much. Help all of us, Lord."

Eli Trudeau had a son. That much she knew. But Pastor Dev hadn't bothered explaining that little tidbit to her. Not on the helicopter ride to a Denver hospital, not in the long hours they'd waited as Eli went through surgery and not even after Eli had survived and they'd been cleared to come back home.

Now she had no idea where Pastor Dev was, or Eli, either. CHAIM took care of their own, one way or another.

Lydia grabbed up Rhett, holding him close as she snuggled her face into his thick fur. "I guess it's just you and me again, Rhett. Another lonely night."

Dropping the purring cat, she decided she'd make some chamomile tea and watch a sappy movie. As if she needed to cry even more. But what else could she do? The man she loved still didn't trust her or love her enough to share everything with her. Maybe he never would.

And even though she knew he loved her back, maybe a man like Pastor Devon Malone just couldn't let go of his warrior's heart long enough to show her that love.

"We'll think about that tomorrow," she said in a long, drawn-out drawl to Rhett. "Won't we, pretty boy?"

And then, the doorbell rang.

Dev stood at the door, his mind reeling with hope and need. He'd tried to stay away, tried to distance himself from Lydia's purity and goodness. He didn't want to taint her anymore. And he couldn't promise her anything else.

He'd been debriefed, analyzed, scrutinized, questioned and reprimanded. He was so tired, so very tired, that he only wanted to curl up on the couch back at his house by the church and sleep for a month. But now that he was standing here, knowing that Lydia was right behind that door, a new energy coursed through him. He had to see her. He had to tell her he loved her.

When she opened the door, her expression full of hope and regret, he took her in like a long drink of pure water. She was wearing a pretty blue floral sleeveless sundress that flared out from her waist in soft, gentle pleats. She was barefoot, her hair caught back in a ponytail, her face devoid of makeup.

She was beautiful.

"Hello," he managed, shifting as he put his hands in his jeans pockets.

"Hello," she whispered, her voice sounding raw and husky.

Her cat made a dangerous meowing sound, the animal's rich green eyes issuing a challenge that clearly spoke of terrible things happening to anyone who dared hurt his owner.

"Hi there, Rhett. Protective as ever, I see." He looked back up at Lydia. "Can I come in?"

"Sure," she said, but her eyes held so much doubt.

Dev wanted to erase that doubt. Once and for all.

"Have a seat," she said, whirling like a ballerina. "I was about to make some hot tea. Want some?"

"No, but I'd take a soda."

She put the teakettle on, then brought him a soft drink. And she sat down in a chair across from him, her body language showing him she wasn't comfortable with him being here.

Hating that, he put the unopened drink down on a rose-patterned coaster and said, "Lydia—"

"How's your wound?"

He wondered to which wound she was referring, his leg or his heart. "Just a little sore, and I walk with a limp, but the doctor said I'll be fine in a few weeks." He tried again. "Lydia—"

"Eli has a son," she interrupted, her hands folded in her lap. "I'd really like to hear all about that."

"That's what I came to tell you," he said, dreading this final admission. "It's a long story—"

"But one I need to know," she retorted, her eyes as steely and glistening as copper that had aged to a brilliant green. "It's a blessing for him, at least."

He nodded, opened his drink. Took a long swallow. "First, Eli is doing great. He's going back to Louisiana in a few days. Kissie is going to watch over him. You know, she teamed up with Sally Mae and made the CHAIM team at Eagle Rock track us down."

She nodded. "That's good to hear." Then she held up a hand. "Before you tell me this story, I need to tell you something."

Surprised, Dev said, "Okay."

"Back in Colorado, Eli…he called The Peacemaker grandfather. Do you know anything about that?"

Dev blinked, willed himself to talk. "Eli told me everything. The Peacemaker—his real name was Pierre Savoy—came from a wealthy New Orleans family. His only son, Edward, met and fell in love with Polly Trudeau. Polly got pregnant. Eli." He looked down at his hands. "They never married. Polly was poor and not suitable for Edward in Pierre's eyes, so Pierre enlisted Edward in CHAIM. She never heard from Edward after the baby was born, and Pierre never acknowledged the baby. Then Polly heard that Edward was killed, so she raised her son Eli the best she could and never married again."

He took a long breath, raised his head.

Lydia had tears in her eyes. "That's so sad."

"Yes, it is sad. Eli's mother wanted him to have a better life, so she sent him to a community college to get a decent education. That's where Pierre found him and told him about his father and CHAIM. But he sure didn't do it out of love for Eli. More as revenge against his mother and him."

Lydia got up to pace around the room, wiping at her eyes. "So that old man bullied Eli into joining up."

"Yes, and because Eli was starving for any connection to the father he'd never known, he jumped at the chance. And it seems The Peacemaker has had him in his grip off and on through the years since."

"Until South America."

Dev had always admired Lydia's sharp mind. "Yes, until then, when Eli discovered to his dismay that his very own grandfather was behind a huge drug cartel down there. He stumbled right into it—"

"And because The Peacemaker both loved and resented him, the old man decided he had to make Eli suffer."

"Yes, by trying to kill his wife."

Lydia stopped pacing, then looked down at him. "But she didn't die right away. You did tell me that."

"No, she didn't. Eli was AWOL and we had to make a quick decision. She had no other family, because she was an orphan. Eli met her when he was doing some community work at a local children's home. They got married as soon as she turned eighteen. Eli loved her so much, but he thought she was dead and we couldn't find him. So we hid her—without even CHAIM's knowledge—"

"Who is we?"

"Me," he said. "Just me and Kissie and a few other people who were concerned about Eli and about… the baby."

She nodded, held up a hand. "Let me finish this for you. While she lay in a coma, the baby was delivered?"

"Yes. It was the only way. She died shortly after the baby was taken by C-section. It was as if she were waiting for that baby to be born. I wanted to tell Eli, but we couldn't find him. So we decided to hide the baby—to save the child. Eli was so unstable once we did locate him, everyone involved decided the best thing for the child was to keep him hidden. After that, time just passed so quickly, and Scotty was so happy and safe—"

Lydia sank down on her chair, but the teakettle started whistling, causing her to jump up again. Dev got up to follow her across the open room to the kitchen. "Lydia, you have to understand—"

"I do," she said, her attention on making her tea. But Dev could see her hands shaking.

He grabbed her, stopped her with his hands on hers. "I wanted to tell you. Right from the start. But I had to protect Scotty."

She gasped, pulled away, her hands going to her mouth. "Oh, oh, now it all makes perfect sense. Your nephew? Eli's son is your nephew, Scotty?"

"Yes," he said, relief washing over him. "That's it. That's the final truth. My sister has been raising him up North. That's my big secret, the main reason I had to take you on the run with me. I was so afraid someone was trying to get to Scotty—that Eli had found out the truth and was coming after me."

He moved toward her, forcing her hands away from her face, forcing her to look at him. "I was afraid they'd kill you to make me suffer and…that's exactly what Pierre Savoy was trying to do. That's what he did to Eli. I couldn't let that happen to Scotty. That little boy means the world to me. And he's innocent. He's innocent, Lydia."

He hadn't realized he was crying until she reached

up to touch her fingers to his tears. Dev grabbed her hand, kissing her fingers, hoping against hope that she would forgive him. "I'm so sorry. For everything. Please, Lydia, I need you to understand and to forgive me. Please?"

Lydia felt the warmth of his hands on hers, felt the love shining in his eyes. "This is…incredible," she said, her heart hurting for Eli and for his child.

And for this man who'd taken on the burden of protecting both of them, and her, too. "Does Eli know now?"

Dev looked down at their joined hands. "Yes, he does. He knows everything. He's bitter and hurting, but he did thank me for saving his child." He shook his head. "He kept quoting one of the Beatitudes— 'Blessed are the merciful, for they shall obtain mercy.' He said to tell you thanks for that one."

Lydia's heart opened wide in a prayer for Eli Trudeau. He had been listening to her prayers that night up on the ridge after all. "What's he going to do now?"

Dev backed away, then rolled a hand down his face. "First, he has to get better. He's still recuperating, and it'll be a while before he can travel again."

"And when he's well?"

He turned to face her, his expression full of hope. "He'll go and find his son, I'm sure."

"Then it will truly be over?"

"I hope so. I'm done for now. I'm out of CHAIM for good."

She moved toward him, wanting to make sure he was real, needing to see his honesty. "And…no one else will come to kill us?"

"No. That's all been taken care of. The authorities in both the United States and Rio Branco are on the case now. It's truly over." He gave her a wry smile. "Things might actually get back to normal."

"Normal?" She shook her head. "Not really. I have to find another job."

"Why?"

She couldn't help but savor the solid fear in his eyes while she asked God to put forgiveness in her heart. And because she was a different person now, she decided to be a bit more assertive and bold in telling him the truth.

"Because it's not proper—what with me being in love with my boss. Rumors are already flying left and right around here."

He lowered his head as he came toward her. Then he tugged her into his arms. "I can fix the rumors, I promise."

"I've heard your promises before, remember?"

She saw the hurt passing through his eyes, but she had to know she could count on him.

He leaned his forehead against hers, then backed up to stare at her. "I know you have, and after that night in New Orleans, I decided I wouldn't make any more promises to you unless I knew I could deliver on those promises."

Lydia gazed up at him, her breath in her throat. "And can you? Deliver now, I mean?"

"I plan on it," he said as he leaned down to kiss her. "You know, I always have a plan."

Breathless and suddenly giddy with hope, she smiled. "What is your plan?"

"I plan to marry the woman I love," he said, fresh tears forming in his blue eyes. "I plan to make you my wife, and I plan to preach the word of God right here in our church, and I plan to have children with you, and grow old with you, and—"

He let out a yelp of pain. "Your cat just bit my leg."

She slapped at his shirt, grinning through her own tears. "Rhett, oh, he's just making sure you can live up to all those promises and plans."

"I can," he said. "I will." Then he gave her a serious look. "Lydia, will you forgive me for all that I've done to you? For all the things I've withheld from you, including my heart?"

"I will."

"And will you marry me?"

"I will."

His expression changed from fatigued and unsure to content and relaxed. "Thank You, God," he said, lifting his words to the heavens in a prayer. "Thank You, Father."

Then he looked back down at her. "You are so amazing, and I love you so much."

Lydia silently thanked God, too, for the words she'd always longed to hear. Then she fell into his arms, all of her doubts melting in a pool of sweet warmth. "I love you, too, Pastor Dev."

"You can call me Dev now, for sure," he said into her ear.

"You'll always be Pastor Dev to me," she replied. "Always. Even when I'm Mrs. Devon Malone and life is perfectly normal again." Then she touched a hand to his face. "Even if life is never normal again."

"I can live with that," he said. "I'm so glad God put you in my life. And…I like normal. A lot."

Then he whirled her around in his arms, and they both laughed and cried together.

While Rhett the cat watched, purring away in delight.

* * * * *

Dear Reader,

This story was a departure for me. I have this secret love of action-adventure movies and stories, so it was a thrill to write one of my own. When I was about seven, I told my mother I wanted to be a secret agent. She told me that was fine, but I might get shot. That didn't sound very good, so I just pretended to be a spy in my yard and the surrounding country. Thankfully, I changed my mind about being a secret agent when I realized I was born to write books. Maybe you have a secret dream you've never pursued. I hope you follow your heart and work toward that dream. Lydia's only dream was to marry Pastor Devon Malone. But when she discovered that the man she loved had a secret, she was both devastated and intrigued. Devon wanted the same thing as Lydia—a simple, faith-filled life away from all the pain and suffering he'd seen. But before either of them could find their dream, they had to work together to stop the bad guys.

With God's grace and guidance, we can survive and become stronger and better. I hope that you will find it in your heart to let God be your guide, no matter your dreams.

Until next time, may the angels watch over you.

Always.

Lenora Worth

Questions for Discussion

1. How did Lydia react when she realized Pastor Dev wasn't the man she believed him to be? Have you ever thought you knew someone only to find out you really didn't?

2. What was the one thing that remained the same for Lydia throughout this story? Why was her faith so important to her?

3. Why did Devon feel it was necessary to keep his past life a secret? Do you think he truly wanted to become a better man?

4. Why was Devon so torn between the past and the present? How did Lydia help him to overcome his torment?

5. Do you believe Devon was an honorable man? Do you think a person can be honorable even when that person isn't completely honest?

6. How did Devon's feelings for Lydia change? Do you believe he loved her all the time but had to see her in a different light before he could acknowledge that love?

7. How did Lydia's idea of a proper Christian change through this story? Have you ever been surprised by other Christians?

8. Why did Devon keep the final truth from Lydia? Do you believe he was protecting his friend Eli, or himself?

9. Do you believe some Christians use their faith as an excuse for being dishonest or criminal? Have you ever known someone like The Peacemaker?

10. Do you believe Eli is redeemable? Have you ever known someone who was tormented by the past but found solace in Christ?

DEADLY TEXAS ROSE

O that thou wouldest hide me in the grave, that thou
wouldest keep me secret, until thy wrath be past,
that thou wouldest appoint me a set time,
and remember me!
—*Job* 14:13

To Faye Ulmer, everyone's Nana.
I love you.

ONE

"Don't move or I'll kill her."

Deputy Sheriff Eric Butler did as he was told, since the mustached stranger standing about five feet away had the new waitress at the Courthouse Café held against her will and a revolver pointed at her head.

"We're all cool here," Eric said, nodding toward all the other customers and the three or four employees who had just minutes before been laughing and talking. "Nobody wants to get hurt today." He silently prayed, asking God to keep everyone safe.

"That's good," the dark-haired, sweating man said, his head bobbing up and down. Then he slanted his gaze around the room where he had ordered the kitchen staff to gather with the customers. In the kitchen, unattended food sizzled and burned on the griddle. "Everybody here, listen to the officer."

Acting on instinct, Eric held his hands away from his body and stared down the shaking man, wondering what kind of idiot would try to rob a restaurant right across from the courthouse in the tiny East Texas town of Wildflower. Any number of cops and sheriff's deputics ate here every day, and any smart criminal would have scoped the place out in advance to save both himself and everyone else grief.

Of course, desperate people did desperate things, and this man seemed very near the brink. Eric took in the scene and tried to decide how best to handle the situation.

Cat Murphy, the petite, no-nonsense owner of Cat's Courthouse Café, stood just to the left of the man holding waitress Julia Daniels near a wall that gave the culprit a bird's-eye view of both the entrance door and the kitchen. Cat's expression showed shock, but her eyes held a kind of resolve that didn't bode well for the grungy-looking man who'd disrupted the last minutes of the lunch hour. Cat had been married to a police officer who was killed in the line of duty. And given that Julia Daniels was related to Cat and had moved here about five months ago at Cat's request, Cat sure wasn't going to stand by and let anything bad happen to her. That made her not only dangerous but impulsive, too, Eric reasoned.

But right now he was more worried about Julia. He liked her a lot, had even thought about asking her out on a date. So that made him just a tad dangerous, too. Not impulsive like motherly Cat, yet dangerous just the same. But he had to protect Julia and everybody else in here, somehow. *Help me, Lord.*

The other diners had stopped eating to stare with

fright at the man and woman in the corner of the room. And Eric's buddy and fellow deputy Adam Dupont was sitting across from Eric, his trigger finger itching from the way the pulse was pounding in his jawline.

"Steady," Eric whispered to Adam. "He looks real serious about using that gun."

"Shut up!" The robber's fidgety, shifting gaze moved from Eric to Adam. "I mean it, *man*. You two need to take out your guns and slide them across the floor."

Eric glanced at his friend, sending Adam a silent message. Then he nodded. Best not to argue with the man holding the gun to the blonde's head. Besides, she looked as pale as a ghost, her big gold-green eyes widening each time the gun was pressed harder against her temple.

Carefully, with one hand in the air, both deputies took out their weapons. "Okay," Eric said. "I'm gonna send them both your way."

The robber nodded, then waited, watching intently as Eric did as he'd promised. The only sound in the tiny café was that of weapons hitting linoleum and fat hitting the grill as the guns flew across the black-and-white-patterned floor.

"What do you want?" Julia managed to ask the man, her tone shaky.

The man holding Julia glanced around, hesitant at first, sweat popping out on his forehead. He eyed the back of Julia's head so close to his own, then glanced around the restaurant as if he were looking for something or someone. Then his gaze skittered to the counter near the kitchen.

"I need some cash," the burly man replied, lifting his chin toward the back of the restaurant. "All of it."

Cat nodded. "I'll have to go behind the cash register. Don't hurt Julia, okay? You can have the money, but you don't need to hurt anyone."

"Shut up and get it." Then he pressed the gun closer to Julia's tousled hair a little harder. "And let me worry about *Julia*."

The robber shifted around, facing Cat as she slowly moved toward the counter in the far corner of the room, forcing Julia to turn. "And if anybody tries anything, I'll kill her."

Eric watched as Julia pivoted around with the man, her willowy frame shaking, her shoulder-length golden hair swishing over her black-and-white uniform. The woman was terrified, but she was cooperating. That showed she had common sense, at least. He just prayed she wouldn't try anything crazy, like fighting this man. He stared at her, willing her to let Adam and him do their jobs.

Her gaze met Eric's and held. She seemed to be silently screaming a message at him. He could see the plea in her eyes, could almost feel exactly what she was thinking: What about my little girl? What will happen to her if I die?

He knew from hearing Julia and Cat chattering away as they worked that Julia was Cat's cousin and she was a widow with an eight-year-old daughter named Moria. And he also knew that she was a devoted mother. He'd seen both mother and child in church last Sunday.

He wanted to see both of them there again next Sunday, too. So he held her gaze, hoping he could relay a sense of calm to her. He sat silently, his mind screaming for her to hold on. *I won't let anything happen to you, I promise.* He inclined his head just an inch, but it seemed to be enough to give her courage. She lifted her chin a notch in response.

Eric tore his gaze away, then tilted his head toward Adam. They'd worked together for the past seven years, to the point where they could almost read each other's minds. He hoped Adam was doing that very thing right now. They needed a distraction.

But they also needed to be very, very careful so no one in here would end up dead.

Especially the pretty blonde who'd only lived in Wildflower for a few months. Julia might be new to the area and new to the café, but she was already a favorite among the lunch crowd.

Eric liked Julia, even though he didn't know that much about her. He surely wasn't going to sit by and witness something horrible happening to a hard-working, quiet, pretty woman who didn't bother anyone. No, sir. That wasn't gonna happen. Not today, at least. And not before he'd had some of Cat's famous hamburger steak and mashed potatoes.

* * *

Be still and know that I am God. That verse played through Julia's head, so she stood still and decided to keep her eyes on the deputy sheriff. There was something about Eric Butler that made her feel safe. Maybe it was his quiet, controlled nature, or the way he tried to put everyone he encountered at ease. He had always been polite to Julia, in spite of his friend Adam's jokes and flirtatious nature. Eric didn't flirt. He just made small talk and asked her about Moria, his chocolate-colored eyes full of life and contentment. Eric had a secure, sure masculine presence that could fill a room. That presence, that security, such a contrast to her late husband's passive personality, was the only thing keeping Julia sane right now. She said a prayer, silently and quickly. *Please, God, help us.* She hadn't turned to God very much throughout the ordeal of her husband's death. But she sure needed Him here today. Because of Moria.

Julia kept telling herself to stay calm, to do as the skittish robber holding her body in front of his as a shield had said, to not move. But it wasn't so easy. She was worried about Moria. Her daughter was safe at school. She had to keep repeating that phrase inside her head, her heart pounding in cadence with the rapid breaths of the man holding her. Moria was safe; she had to be. Isn't that why she'd taken Cat's advice and left San Antonio to come to this nice, quiet little town all the way across Texas, near the Louisiana border? *Moria is safe. Please, Lord, keep her safe.*

Safe. Julia had brought her daughter here after her husband Alfonso had been murdered while he was working late one night. Murdered at his fancy desk in the high-rise De La Noche building in downtown San Antonio. And Moria had been there with him, hidden in the ladies' lounge down the hall, dialing Julia's number on her father's cell phone even as the murder had taken place, from what the authorities could piece together.

"Tell Mommy to come right now," Moria had repeated to Julia and the police after they'd found her sitting in a chair in the lounge, her doll Rosa clutched in one hand and the phone in the other. "Daddy said we were playing a game, like hide-and-seek. He said to talk to you and tell you to come and find me. Where's my daddy?"

Julia hadn't been able right then to tell the little girl that her daddy was dead. That had taken all of Julia's courage a few hours later at home.

Julia and the therapists still weren't sure what Moria had seen or heard that night. The little girl didn't talk about it much and the therapists couldn't agree on the validity of repressed memories. But her nightmares told the tale of horror Moria had gone through, sitting there all alone, waiting for her parents that night at the De La Noche complex.

Alfonso had worked for the Gardonez family since high school, only to end up dead.

Of the night. The La Flor De La Noche, or the flower of the night, was what had started the Gardonez family dynasty over one hundred years ago in Mexico. Night-blooming jasmine, moonflowers and the beautiful but deadly angel trumpet, started from seeds, and one woman's determination, had created a legend within the floral industry. Now the Gardonez family not only grew beautiful flowers but also farmed and marketed vegetables and fruit, too. And they had worldwide distribution, with a trucking and shipping company that was the industry standard.

But someone within their ranks, or someone who wanted to do the company harm, apparently had a secret that had killed her husband. Did her child also know that secret?

Now as Julia stood here in the bruising grip of an armed man, she had to wonder if that secret had followed her all the way across Texas. She didn't know anything for sure; she only wanted to protect her daughter. But she did know that something had been bothering Alfonso before his death. Something that had him up at night and brooding all day long. Something that had told Julia not to let him pick up Moria from school that day. It was as if he'd also known something bad might happen to him. As if he'd known he'd have to take some sort of secret to his grave.

What if this man wanted that secret? What if this man hadn't come here just to rob the café? What if he'd come for her, instead?

* * *

Eric sensed the war behind those pretty golden-green eyes. He knew that look. Julia was weighing her options. He'd seen that kind of confused, centered gaze before in the eyes of men who'd made the wrong choices and regretted them. He'd also seen it in the eyes of other victims, haunted and frightened, wondering and waiting. She was afraid, but she held her head up with a determination that caused him to admire her. The woman had so much to live for. She had a child. He only hoped that spark of spunk shining inside her eyes wouldn't get her killed.

And he hoped this nagging feeling inside his gut would just go away, that it wasn't a sign of things to come. He didn't like this at all. The man had come in through the door and zoomed right in on Julia instead of the cash register. Now, why was that? Eric wondered.

"What now?" Adam asked as he watched Cat fumbling with the cash register.

"We wait," Eric replied under his breath.

Cat started walking slowly back toward Julia and the man, her ever-present red cowboy boots clicking against the linoleum, her eyes slanting toward Eric and Adam. She knew they would stop this. She had to know. Cat trusted them, as did everyone else in this sleepy little town. Eric gave Cat a reassuring look, holding his breath as she neared the gunman.

The robber clutched at Julia and said the words no lawman ever wanted to hear. "I'm gonna have to take *her* with me. Just until I get down the road." He pushed at Julia. "Hold the money."

Adam shot Eric a look. The chances of Julia surviving this once the strung-out man took her to another location were slim to none. There was no apparent reason for this man to take a hostage. Well, except maybe that he knew the two deputy sheriffs staring him down would surely come after him. They had to do something before the culprit got Julia away from the premises, or this could go from bad to worse.

Cat shook her head, obviously thinking the same thing, her usually down-to-earth candor breaking. "You've got the money. Please, let her go."

But the man wasn't listening. He kept pushing at Julia. "Take it, so we can get out of here!"

And then everything happened at once.

One minute Cat was stretching her hand out, pressing a wad of cash toward Julia, her gaze meeting Julia's in a silent communication. Then Cat went into action, and instead of handing Julia the money, she dropped it just out of Julia's reach, all around the robber's feet. Adam took over, scraping his chair back with just enough abrasiveness to cause the robber to tear his eyes away from the fluttering money falling to the floor. The robber turned, yanking Julia around as Adam skidded his chair again, this time knocking it over and slamming his body behind it for protection.

Eric yelled, "Get down! Everyone get down!"

The frantic robber shook his gun in the air, giving Julia a split second to kick Eric's gun back toward him. Watching the gun slide across the floor, the robber grabbed at Julia, holding her tightly as he spun around to shoot at Adam and Eric. Adam ducked low, while Eric slid his body across the floor in a drop and roll, diving for the gun Julia had sent his way. It landed right on his trigger finger.

Julia watched in horror as the two deputies went into action. Then Cat's hand dug into her arm, pulling her free as the man waved his gun and dived for the fallen money all around his feet.

And then Julia heard the deputy scream again, "Get down! Everybody down!"

Julia saw Deputy Butler lift his gun and skid back toward the protection of his table at the same time the robber aimed his own gun toward the deputy.

Julia waited, her breath held, for the man to fire. Instead, he pushed Cat away and grabbed Julia again. "She's going with me. Get it?" He had the gun back at her head, but he was shaking almost as hard as Julia. Maybe because Deputy Butler now had his own weapon aimed at the robber.

Julia looked at Eric, saw the message clear in his eyes. He wasn't going to let this madman take her.

"Over my dead body," the deputy said, his determined eyes centered on the criminal holding Julia. "Now do us all a favor and drop the weapon."

Julia looked from Eric to Cat, wondering what

she could do to get away. Then she remembered the swinging door. If she twisted ever so slightly, she could use it as leverage to make the man lose his balance. Mustering all her strength, she fought against the man holding her, twisting until she could see the door in her peripheral vision. Hearing her own scream locked inside her head, or maybe she was screaming out loud, she braced herself as the robber held her tight, dragging her toward the kitchen door. "I have to take her, man. I have to. I don't want to hurt anyone, but I have to take her with me." He held the gun close. Guiding Julia backward with him, he reached the swinging door, then stood inches away.

"Don't do it," Adam called, standing up. "Just drop the gun and we'll get you some help."

The man shook his head. "Can't do that." Then in one swift motion, he grunted, tugging Julia toward the rickety old door. Julia took one last look at Eric Butler, hoping to give him a sign that she wasn't going to go willingly through that door.

But Eric was watching the man holding her. "Don't make me shoot you. Because I can bring you down before you ever pull that trigger."

"Try it," the robber goaded, stepping back, the swinging door now inches behind him.

Julia knew if they got past the swinging door, she might not live to see her daughter again. She had to do something right now. With a grunt and all the force she could muster, she pushed with one foot against the wobbly door, then grabbed the solid wood frame with both hands as she used her body to slam against the man behind her. When she felt him shifting backward, she held on to the frame so she wouldn't fall with him, steeling herself against the chance of getting shot.

Shocked to find himself moving through the open space, the man had no choice but to loosen his grip on Julia and grab for a handhold. While Julia lunged back against the robber, Cat pushed at the door, causing the confused man to let go of Julia as he went falling through the open doorway. He hollered his displeasure, then lifted his gun in the air as he lost his balance. A round of shots rang out. Then the man grunted as he went flying into the kitchen. Scrambling up, he clutched his left arm, then ran out the back door of the kitchen, leaving Julia crumpled on her knees, shaking, as she clung to the door frame. The swish of the door banging back toward Julia's slumping body echoed through the building, followed by the slamming of the metal back door. The man was gone and she was still alive.

And then silence, followed by a rush of action all around her.

"It's over, honey," Cat said, pulling Julia up to hug her close. "It's all over."

Adam jumped up, heading for the kitchen door. "I think you hit him, Eric. Everybody okay?"

People begin getting up off the floor. Julia heard women crying and saw a crowd gathered at the front door. A buzz of energy surrounded the screams still echoing inside her head. Her ears were ringing; her blood pressure was pumping inside her temple. But she was alive.

Thanks to Deputy Butler. He'd shot the man holding her. She knew because she had splatters of blood on her white shirt.

"Where's the other deputy?" she asked Cat as Adam brushed past her, her head coming up to search for Eric.

And then she saw him, lying behind an upturned table with blood covering his left shoulder. He wasn't moving.

"He needs help!" Julia shouted, pointing toward Eric. "Somebody help him."

"Eric?" Adam bolted around, then screamed, "Call 911, Cat. Eric's been shot." He headed past Julia and through the kitchen door, already talking into his radio about being in pursuit. "I'm going after him!"

The call was unnecessary. Julia could hear the sirens and the banging of the front door as the café became swamped with deputies and policemen and the lone reporter from the town newspaper, the *Wildflower Gazette*.

The first responders looked over the place and took in the grim scenario, then started moving people out of the café, which had now become a crime scene.

"He saved my life." Julia went limp against the wall, all of the strength drained out of her as the reporter's camera flashed in her face. Deputy Butler had saved her life.

And now he might be dead because of it.

TWO

Eric woke up in the emergency room, his left shoulder throbbing to beat the band.

Trying to raise his head, he called out, "What—"

A gray-haired nurse pushed him back down. "Easy, cowboy. You've been shot and you're about to go into surgery to debride the wound. We just need to clean it out a little bit, make sure everything's intact in there. You're lucky, though. Bullet went straight through without hitting any major arteries or bones."

"Bullet?" Eric lay back, trying to remember. Then it all came rushing back. Julia Daniels. An armed robbery. The man was going to take Julia as a hostage. They'd exchanged gunfire. Darkness and voices in his head. Adam telling him to hang on. Now he had vague flashes of the EMS team…someone applying pressure to his wound, asking him questions about his medical history, a needle shoved into his arm.

"The waitress?" he managed to croak over the sound of doctors rushing all around, poking him here and there and shouting out orders about X-rays and vital signs.

"That pretty little thing," the nurse said as she checked the IV drip, her expression all business. "She's just fine. Outside waiting with your family to hear how you're doing, though. She said you saved her life."

Eric managed a weak grin. "My buddy Adam did most of the hard work."

"Yeah, right. But you shot the bad guy."

Eric tried to lift up again. His bloody shirt was gone. "The robber, where…is he?"

The nurse shook her head. "From what we're hearing, he got clean away. But don't fret, now. Your buddies have put out an APB on him."

Eric tried to speak, but his fatigue, coupled with whatever medication they were pumping into him, caused drowsiness to overtake him. He went to sleep with the memory of Julia's face, front and center in his frazzled mind.

Julia paced the tiny E.R. sitting room, her sturdy, black wedge-heeled work shoes clumping with each step. Cat had insisted she go home and rest, but Julia was too keyed up to do that. After rushing to the elementary school to check on Moria—no, make that after making a scene at the school because she was so frantic to make sure her daughter was safe—and then checking Moria out and taking her to the neighbor's house just to be sure, she'd come straight here.

And she planned on being right here when Eric Butler came out of surgery.

Thank goodness Mrs. Ulmer hadn't minded watching Moria. Julia knew Moria would be safe with the Ulmers. They'd seen how upset she'd been and promised to keep Moria inside and quiet. Even though he didn't get out much these days, Mr. Ulmer had once been an avid hunter and he'd assured her he'd watch over Moria, using one of his many rifles and shotguns if need be. But there had been enough shooting for one day, Julia thought, her mind reliving how the gunman had tried to take her and how Eric had fired a shot to stop him. Then she remembered seeing Eric lying there, bleeding and unmoving.

Please don't let him die, she prayed.

She'd seen too much death lately.

And her daughter had seen enough grief and death to last her a lifetime.

That thought caused Julia's knees to go weak. Sinking down in a fabric-covered blue chair, she put her head in her hands and prayed that Moria didn't hear about this. She'd warned the Ulmers not to discuss it in front of her already-fragile daughter.

"You okay?"

Julia looked up to find Adam and Cat standing in front of her. Cat settled in the chair beside her while Adam stood with his hands in his pants pockets, looking as worried about his friend as she felt.

Down the way in another chair, Eric's father, Harlan, sat staring at the tiled floor. Julia had introduced herself to him the minute she'd come in the door, telling him how much she appreciated what Eric had done for her. But Mr. Butler had only grunted and nodded, his eyes so like his son's, blank and unyielding, in spite of their warmth.

Harlan Butler was a retired sheriff's deputy himself, who, according to Cat, now lived out on the lake in a cabin his son had apparently built right next to his own house. Eric wanted his widowed father near, which only endeared him to Julia since she'd never been close with her own parents. So now the Butler men lived on connecting lots, two bachelors enjoying their time as father and son. Mr. Butler certainly understood the risks of the job. But right now that didn't help matters. Right now they were all worried, and somehow Julia couldn't help but feel responsible for all of this.

"I'm fine," Julia said in answer to Cat's question, shaking her head as she stared at the lone man at the other end of the hall. "I couldn't go home. I had to come and see—"

"If he's gonna be all right," Cat finished, her arm going around Julia's shoulder. "We're all right here, honey, praying for him. I think the whole town is praying right now. That was mighty close." She glanced at Harlan, too. "His daddy is real worried, I can tell you." Then she lowered her voice. "Of course, a Texas lawman can't show his true emotions. It's an unwritten code." She shot Adam a pointed look. "Got to be tough as nails, every last one of 'em."

Julia closed her eyes, reliving the vivid scene trapped inside her mind. She wasn't as tough as nails. She could still feel the cold steel of that gun pressing at her temple. And she wondered for the hundredth time if that bright, stark terror was how her husband Alfonso had felt just before he died.

Was that the kind of terror her daughter experienced each time she suffered another horrible nightmare about her father?

Alfonso. She remembered sitting in another hospital room, waiting to hear the details of her husband's brutal death.

She didn't want to hear that again today. She didn't want that nice, unassuming sheriff's deputy to die. Not on her account. Not for something as stupid as a robbery that would have yielded very little money.

Trying to make sense of everything, she looked up at Adam. "Did you find the robber?"

Adam shook his head. "No. He took off like lightning. Pretty sure there was a getaway car parked around the corner, and in all the confusion we missed it." He looked as if he were taking that failure very personally. "He was bleeding, so he's wounded. I tried to find him, searched behind the restaurant and all the streets, too. Sent a patrol out. He either found a good hiding spot, or someone came back just in time to get him in a car. Found some blood, but that's about it." Then he lowered his head, unable to look at Julia. "Of course, we have the bloodstains from your blouse, too."

Julia looked down at the clean lightweight sweater Cat had offered her after the police had asked her to remove her uniform blouse. Wishing she could go home and take a long shower to wash away all the fear and doubt, she could only nod toward Adam. "When will you know something?"

"Not sure," Adam said. "It'll take the state crime lab a while to get to it, but we've put a rush on it."

Then he rolled his head, trying to release some of the obvious tension coiling through his muscles. "We've put out an all-points bulletin, and we're checking all the area hospitals for any incoming bullet wounds. We've got roadblocks set up all around the area, too. I'm hoping they'll haul him in any minute now, and I want to be the first person to get at him, trust me." He shook his head, then pounded his fist against the wall. "I let him slip right through my fingers."

Cat gave him a soft smile. "Don't be so hard on yourself. You and Eric did the best you could today. It was crazy, there, after he ran out. Nobody blames you. You and Eric saved Julia from becoming a hostage."

Adam looked at the floor. "There's a lot about this that just doesn't make sense. But we'll get the details figured out. We're running a search right now based on the descriptions we got from other witnesses. The boys will call when they have something conclusive on both him and the weapon. We found the bullet lodged in the front door."

Cat asked, "And Eric?"

"He kept going in and out of consciousness, telling me he was okay, that it didn't hurt too much. Of course that was right before he passed out cold." Hearing Julia's low groan, he said, "Don't worry. He's been through worse playing football back in high school."

Then he glanced over at Cat, causing Julia to wonder if they were keeping something from her. Eric and Cat were close. Just how close Julia couldn't be sure, but she knew they shared a lot with each other.

Feeling left out and afraid, Julia looked at her older cousin. "Cat, is everything okay back at the restaurant?"

"I had to shut her down, of course, so the investigators could look for evidence," Cat said with a shrug, her dark curls shimmering around her face. "Who wants to eat there today, or ever again, for that matter?"

"Ah, now, you can't quit," Adam said, his grin tight with tension. "Who'd keep me fed and watered?"

"You sound like an old mule," Cat retorted, her own smile weak. "I'm not gonna shut down forever. Just…needed to get away from there. The employees are still a tad jumpy."

"We're all jumpy," Adam replied. "And right now

your place is a crime scene, so we had to close the doors, anyway. Technically, I'm on administrative duty only until the Rangers get through investigating." Then he looked down the hall at Harlan. "Hey, why don't I go find us some coffee? I'll ask Harlan if he wants some, too. Won't be as good as yours, of course, Cat, but it might help."

"Yeah, coffee," Cat said. "Just what we need to calm the jitters."

"I'm just offering," he said with a shrug.

"Go on," Cat said, her smile full of understanding. "I'll take mine black. Julia?"

"Nothing for me," Julia said, an uneasy feeling setting her stomach on yet another spasm of jangled, tingling nerves. "I just wish I knew who that man was."

"I'll call and harass the investigators," Adam said. "We all want to know that."

After he'd left, Cat turned to Julia, her big brown eyes full of concern. "So how's Moria?"

Julia looked at her watch. "She's fine. Mrs. Ulmer probably doesn't like me calling every five minutes, though." She was torn between staying here and just rushing to the Ulmers' to get her daughter.

"Adam put a man on her, you know."

Julia's head came up, her heart racing. "Why? Is there something else—?"

"No, honey," Cat said, her hand covering Julia's. "Eric asked him to do it, in one of his more lucid moments just before they put him in the ambulance. Told Adam to send someone to check on your little girl."

"How'd he know?" Julia said, amazed. "How'd he know to do that?" Or that the gesture would set her mind at ease. "You didn't tell him anything, did you?"

Cat chuckled, soft and low. "No, against my better judgment, and because I promised you I wouldn't, I haven't told anyone about your troubles." Then she looked down the hall toward the operating rooms. "But Eric can see things—that's why he's such a good lawman. The man has a sensitive side he hides from the world. He probably figured a mother would be concerned about the safety of her child—I mean after being held at gunpoint. And with the robber still on the loose."

Julia nodded, rubbed her suddenly cold hands together. "I *was* worried. The school's principal couldn't understand why I wanted to pull her out of class, since they have a sheriff's deputy as their resource officer, but I'm glad I did. I'll call Mrs. Ulmer again in a few minutes, but I'm sure Mr. Ulmer will entertain her all afternoon."

"You can count on that," Cat replied. "The Ulmers love Moria like their own grandchildren. She sure is a sweetheart." Then she let out a sigh. "Boy, I'm beat. What a day."

Julia looked at her cousin, grateful for Cat's calming presence. They'd always been close growing up, so when Cat offered Julia a job and a place to live to get her away from San Antonio and all the bad memories, Julia had jumped at the chance to start over in Wildflower. Although Cat was a few years older than Julia's thirty-two, with her stylish curly bob and her big dark eyes she looked younger than her actual age. Petite and becomingly plump, Cat was one of the nicest people Julia had ever met, a true Texan through and through. Cat loved God, people and her job. She loved to cook, especially for all the deputies and police officers who frequented her establishment. Maybe because her own husband had been a lawman and had died doing his job about five years ago.

Working at the café was like having one big, law-abiding family, Julia thought. Cat kept telling her she'd be safe in Wildflower. And living in this quiet town near Caddo Lake did make her feel safe.

That was something she'd never had before.

Thinking this whole thing had probably brought Cat some awful flashbacks, too, Julia leaned close. "Are *you* okay?"

Cat brushed at her hair with one hand. "Me? Yeah, sure. I guess I'm used to all the commotion. I tell you, though, when that man was holding that gun to your head, I 'bout had a heart attack. We just don't get that kind of crime here."

"Eric and Adam saved my life. They saved all of us," Julia said, not sure how to comfort Cat. They'd both lost their husbands, but Cat's man had been a true-blue Texas Ranger. Alfonso Endicott, on the other hand, had been a "yes" man. A hardworking man, but a man always willing to do the bidding of his powerful bosses, nonetheless. She shouldn't hold that against him, but there it was, bitter and heavy, inside her.

Alfonso had sacrificed being with his wife and child to stay at the beck and call of the Gardonez family. And all for the love of money. Alfonso always wanted more, needed more, to prove himself. He'd gone beyond the call of duty in order to keep his high-paying job. The Gardonez family had depended on him to take care of their millions, to make sure everything they did was aboveboard and by the books.

Then why had someone killed him?

Julia had a funny feeling that the motive had to do with money, too, since her husband had been the head accountant for the De La Noche Shipping Company. That brought her thoughts back to today's events.

"Why did that man try to rob us right in the middle of lunch hour, Cat?" she asked, hoping her cousin could put a reasonable spin on things, because Julia didn't want to put her own spin on it. She wasn't ready to delve into all the implications right now.

Cat gave her an eloquent shrug. "I guess he needed some cash. Maybe for drugs, or maybe he just took a wrong turn somewhere. Or maybe he was being stupid. We've never been robbed before, ever, and I've been running the café for over a decade, and my mama before me for even longer than that herself. You've spent enough summers here with me growing up to know that. It's just plain weird."

Julia had to agree. She'd often traveled here with her parents to visit Cat's family. They'd leave her in Wildflower for weeks on end while they traveled around in their RV camper. Julia had loved staying with her aunt and uncle and Cat and helping out at the café. And even though she just had Cat now, she liked working at the café and living right around the corner from her cousin. Or she had up until today.

"I hope we find out something soon about Eric. And that other man, too."

Cat nodded. "Well, just think…you and Eric will both be famous from now on. Adam, too, probably. Even the restaurant, for that matter."

Julia pushed a hand through her hair. "How's that?"

"The *Gazette*, honey. Mickey Jameson is doing a front-page spread about the robbery. He wanted to interview you, but I held him back. Told him to give you a call later today before the paper goes to press." Seeing the look on Julia's face, she put a hand to her mouth. "Oh, my. I wasn't even thinking straight—"

Julia jumped out of her chair. "Front page? I don't want to be on the front page."

But it was too late. The double doors leading from the E.R. driveway swished open and in walked debonair Mickey Jameson himself. "Ah, there's my star witness," he said, smiling broadly. "Got a great shot of you, Mrs. Daniels. Now I just need to finish the story. Cat, I know you said to wait, but I have a deadline. And you know what they say—'If it bleeds, it leads.'"

Julia shook her head, backing away. "I'm not going to talk to you, Mr. Jameson. Not now, not ever."

Eric woke up in the recovery room, his wounded shoulder bandaged but still throbbing. At least now his head wasn't nearly as fuzzy. Finally he could take his time and remember everything that had happened during the robbery.

Lying back, he tried to think things through, but something just wasn't right about the situation. Before he could figure it all out, his father walked in.

"You awake?"

Eric looked toward the end of the bed where his broad-shouldered father stood with his hands in the pockets of his jeans. "I'm fine, Dad. How'd you get in here, anyway?"

"I still have some connections. Managed to sweet-talk a nurse."

Eric grinned at that. "Some things never change."

Harlan didn't dwell on hospital procedure. "Bullet skipped right through you, did it?"

"Yep. I don't know why they even brought me to the hospital. I could have gone home and poured some alcohol on it and been good as new." In spite of the jovial tone, Eric could see the worry in his father's eyes. "Bullet went straight in and out, Pop. Probably still stuck somewhere in the café wall."

Harlan kicked one boot against the other, as if he had mud on his shoes. "Good. That's evidence now."

"Yep. I'm sure they'll find the bullet. I just wish I knew why that guy chose lunchtime to go and rob the place."

"Yep, that is kinda odd. Most wait until closing time." He stood silent for a couple of beats, then added, "Mighty strange how he got clear out of town so fast, too."

"I'm gonna figure it out," Eric said. "I shot the man, but I need answers."

"Just be careful," Harlan replied, rocking back on his worn cowboy boots. "You'll need to rest up for a few days at least."

"I'll be on leave until the department finishes its investigation. Did they call in the Rangers?"

Harlan nodded. "Standard procedure. But you could use a rest, anyway. You've been burning the candle at both ends for a while now."

"I guess I have at that," Eric replied, tiredness sweeping over him. And today, of all days, he'd planned on having a nice, leisurely lunch with his friend just so he could enjoy watching Julia Daniels go about her work. No rest for the weary. "You okay?"

"I'm good," Harlan said, clearing his throat. "Just waiting for them to put you in a room. Then I'll go on home and check on the animals."

"You don't have to come back tonight. I'll probably sleep the night through, then be home tomorrow."

Harlan nodded, his white-haired head down. "That waitress came and sat with me for a while during your surgery. She's mighty grateful."

"Julia? She's a nice woman."

"Do you know much about her?" Harlan put both hands on the steel footboard of the bed. "I mean, it struck me how she didn't want Mickey to put her picture in the paper, didn't even want to talk to him about the robbery and all. Either she's real shy, or she really doesn't want any publicity. Mighty odd to me."

Eric moved his head, his eyes locking with his daddy's. They were both probably wondering the same things. Instincts and natural curiosity made both of them good lawmen.

"No, I don't know a whole lot about Julia Daniels, except that she's related to Cat," Eric replied. "But I aim to find out everything I can." For more reasons than he wanted to explain to his clever father.

He'd been very aware of Julia since she'd started working at the café, mainly because she was pretty and pleasant and, well, he was single and lonely. But now that awareness had changed into concern and suspicion. Eric couldn't answer why, except that today's event had certainly put Julia in the spotlight. And like that nosy Mickey Jameson, Eric had some questions of his own. He didn't want a story for the front page, though. He wanted the truth, especially since it occurred to him that even the usually talkative Cat hadn't given up much information about her pretty cousin.

"I think that's wise," Harlan said, satisfied they'd cleared up that little matter of concern. "Might need to know what all we're dealing with here."

Eric lay back against his pillows, watching as his father threw up his hand and headed out the door.

"You can count on that," he said to himself.

THREE

"C'mon, honey. Time for bed."

Julia tugged on Moria's hand, the sweet soapy smell surrounding her daughter causing her heart to swell with love. Glancing out the window where the streetlight illuminated the whole backyard and Cat's big rambling white Victorian house just beyond, she wondered for the hundredth time today if they were truly safe here.

She *should* feel safe, since Deputy Sheriff Adam Dupont had come by not an hour ago to check on them, and to give her a report on Eric. They would only allow his father in to see him after his surgery. Adam had assured her Eric would be home in a day or so.

He'd also assured her that Eric didn't want her to feel bad about things. It wasn't her fault, Adam kept saying. Eric wouldn't want her to worry at all. He'd be up and about in no time. But not back on the job just yet. His injury and an internal investigation of the shooting would see to that.

"Eric will get in some fishing, at least, while he's on leave," Adam had quipped. "He can toss a line and catch fish with just one hand, easy."

"Easy," Julia said now as she tried to put her uneasiness out of her mind. She focused instead on getting her daughter to bed.

Moria, dressed in a frilly pink nightgown and clutching her favorite doll, stood just inside her bedroom door, her big dark eyes surveying the dainty, feminine room. "I'm not sleepy, Mommy."

Julia prayed this wouldn't turn into another standoff. True, it had become increasingly easier to get Moria to bed since they'd moved here, but every now and then Moria still had a bad night. The rental house that had been originally built for Cat's late grandmother was purposely small, with just a den/kitchen combination across the front, a short hallway with a bath and laundry room to one side and two bedrooms on the other side. There was a clear view of both the well-lit front and back yards. No hidden nooks and crannies, no big deep closets or long winding stairways like those in the house back in San Antonio. She'd sold that gaudy dwelling for way under the appraisal value just to have moving money and a small nest egg to go with Alfonso's life insurance, most of which she'd tucked away for her daughter's future.

Small and safe, Julia reminded herself, glancing around at the clutter-free house. Simple and uncomplicated. Secure. No hiding places. Back at the big house, Moria had loved to play hide-and-seek with her daddy. But here, Julia discouraged that particular game.

Now Julia prayed they weren't about to enter another kind of hide-and-seek. But the man who'd held her at gunpoint was still out there somewhere, she reminded herself. How could he have just disappeared in broad daylight? And where was he now?

"Moria, it's past your bedtime," she said, looking back over her shoulder to make sure the solid front door was dead bolted. "You've had a big day, so I know you're tired."

"But tomorrow's Saturday," Moria pointed out, jumping up onto the ruffled yellow-rose-patterned spread covering her twin four-poster bed. Pushing stuffed animals, fashion dolls and fluffy pillows aside, she added, "Rosa and I aren't tired, honestly, Mommy." She squeezed her favorite doll.

Julia shook her head then laughed. "Mr. Ulmer told me how you and he raced around the backyard today. He said you won every race."

"But I was on my bike," Moria said, her hands wrapped against her midsection. "Mr. Ulmer lets me ride the bike he bought for his grandchildren while he rides his scooter. Rosa sat in the basket."

"That's awfully nice of him," Julia said, silently thanking God for the Ulmers. The couple lived right next door and had immediately taken a shine to Moria. Once they'd heard Julia needed after-school care for those days she worked late at the café, they'd volunteered, no questions asked, even though Mr.

Ulmer had horribly arthritic knees and had to get around with a motorized scooter most days. And they didn't even want any pay. But Julia made sure she did other things for them to compensate, such as bringing home leftovers from the café, or picking up extra groceries whenever she was going to the store. Today, especially, they had managed to distract Moria while the awful details of the shooting had blared across the local news stations.

Including her face and her name, Julia thought, unease causing her next words to come out harshly. "Moria, no more excuses. It's bedtime. You might not be tired, but *I* sure am."

Remembering her brief discussion at the hospital today with the overbearing *Gazette* reporter, Julia let out a sigh. She only hoped the paper wouldn't make too much of this. She wanted to stay low-key. But Mickey Jameson kept pushing, telling her this was big news and readers would want to hear her side of the story. After all, she'd been in the clutches of an armed robber and she'd survived, due to the two deputy sheriffs who'd risked their own lives to save her.

How could she refuse such a request without looking ungrateful? Julia thought. So she'd given him a brief description of how the robbery had taken place, but she'd been very careful not to reveal too much personal information. Besides, her hair was longer now, and she didn't wear the fancy clothes or the expensive cosmetics she'd favored while living in San Antonio. Most days, she hardly recognized herself in the mirror. So maybe no one else would, either. And after Alfonso had died, she'd had her name legally changed back to her maiden name, just as an added precaution. Maybe she'd covered all her bases. She prayed she had, for Moria's sake at least.

"Want to lie on my bed and rest?" Moria asked, her brown eyes going wide as she brought Julia out of her troubled thoughts. "Rosa and I can make room."

Julia grinned, then touched a hand to her daughter's dark curls, seeing the hopeful look in her eyes. "How about I read you a bedtime story?" Julia offered, hoping to distract both of them for a few minutes. "That way I can rest my feet and you can get sleepy."

Moria bobbed her head. "Can I pick?"

"Of course," Julia said, watching as her daughter ran to the small bookcase beneath the window. "But not too long, okay?"

Moria giggled, then found a suitable book. "Rosa likes this one."

Julia nodded, then snuggled up with her daughter, the ever-present doll Moria had named Rosa cuddled between them, her flower-strewn lacy yellow dress and her rose-encased little drawstring purse perfectly displayed.

Alfonso had given Moria the doll for her birthday last year because her dress had matched Moria's yellow rose-decorated bedroom back in San Antonio and because the doll had reminded him of Moria. That had been a few days before his death. Which was probably why Moria clung to the doll from the minute she arrived home from school each day until she fell asleep at night.

Even after they'd moved here, Moria had begged for the same colors in this bedroom. Julia had readily agreed, hoping to make her daughter feel at home. The room looked like a rose garden, complete with a dainty silk oversize yellow rose sitting in a clay pot on the dresser. The rose looked so real, Julia reached out and touched it. Alfonso had loved yellow roses.

Looking down at the doll's beautiful porcelain face and jet-black hair with its miniature combs and curls, Julia once again thought about Alfonso. He'd loved Moria so much. He would have never intentionally put his child in danger. And yet the night he'd been murdered, Moria had been in danger. She'd been in the office with her father, hidden away.

I should have picked her up that day, Julia thought.

But she'd been running late from attending a charity event all afternoon, and Alfonso had been insistent. He wanted to spend time with their daughter, but in doing so, he'd inadvertently brought danger to all of them. At least he'd had the foresight to get Moria out of harm's way once he'd seen that danger coming. He'd given her his phone and dialed Julia, leaving Moria alone but safe. He'd known Julia was at a nearby hotel finishing up with her duties after the charity event.

Now Moria's secrets about what she'd seen or heard that night were also hidden away, deeply embedded inside her child's mind because no one, not the team of therapists or her own mother, could bring it all to the surface for Moria. She kept whatever she knew intact. That is, until she went to sleep at night.

Then, all the horrible scary things hidden in the dark seemed to come out to taunt the little girl.

No wonder her daughter never wanted to go to sleep.

And no wonder Julia was so worried that the secrets locked inside her daughter's mind might bring harm to both of them. Not knowing was driving her crazy.

But finding out the truth might be even more dangerous.

He had to know the truth.

Eric stared at the yellow crime-scene tape slashing across the double doors of Cat's Courthouse Café. He'd come here straight from the hospital, and although his arm was in a sling and he still felt woozy from all the pain medication, it felt good to be out in the bright springtime day with a fresh breeze blowing over his face. His shoulder still ached, but his mind was spinning like the whimsical metallic garden ornament Cat had hanging by the front door. He stood back, leaning against the old-fashioned hitching rail in front of the café, his mind reliving every minute of what had happened here two days ago.

"Got it figured out yet, buddy?" Adam asked as he

came up and handed Eric a bottle of soda. "Thought you could use a drink."

"Thanks," Eric said, taking a long swig of the amber liquid. Then he glanced back through the windows of the restaurant. "He went in through the kitchen, and he brought Julia out through the swinging doors with him."

"That's odd," Adam said, sipping his own drink. "I mean, going in through the kitchen I can understand. But why didn't he just head right to the cash register?"

"Maybe he thought grabbing the first person he saw would give him more cover," Eric replied. "But that notion didn't exactly work out to his advantage. I just wonder where he went. If he bled out or even if he is alive somewhere, we'll never find him now."

Adam must have sensed his remorse. "Don't beat yourself up, old man. You shot him in self-defense, and to protect Julia. We can only imagine what he would have done to her if he'd taken her with him." Then he looked down the street where a few cars passed by now and then. "Besides, I'm the one who let him get away."

Eric thought about that. "He must have had help, someone waiting for him." He didn't like the nasty scene playing inside his head. "I don't want to think about that. I just hate—"

"You don't like having to shoot someone. We've all had to deal with that at times."

"What if he just needed some money? Maybe I should have tried to talk him down more."

Adam shook his head. "You saw the man's eyes. He was too far gone. For some strange reason, he picked a bad day to rob the place." Then he shook his head. "And even though we let him get away, he left a trail of evidence—bloodstains on Julia's blouse and fingerprints on both the outside door and the swinging door from the kitchen."

"Got any leads?"

"As a matter of fact, I think we do," Adam said, handing Eric a printout, then added, "Of course, *officially,* I'm not supposed to have this information. So, *unofficially* and just for your information, we had a sketch artist come over from Longview and talk to several of the witnesses, including Julia, Cat and me."

Eric lifted his chin. "Yeah, I gave a description while I was in the hospital, the whole routine. Tell me something I don't know."

Adam tapped the papers he was holding. "Based on the sketch and the fingerprints we were able to lift, we've established his identity. We found some fresh prints on the back door, ran 'em through AFIS and came up with a positive match. We've narrowed it down, based on the eyewitness descriptions and the sketch. When we hear from the DNA samples, we'll have it confirmed. His name is Mingo Tolar, last known address a seedy hotel in El Paso. And he has a record as long as my arm."

Eric read over the sheet, then glanced at the sketch. "Petty theft, drunk and disorderly conduct, disturbing the peace, trespassing and resisting arrest, possession of narcotics. Why does that not surprise me?" Then he shook the rap sheet. "So if this is our man—and this looks exactly like him—how'd he wind up all the way across the state in a tiny town like Wildflower?"

"Maybe he was a mule," Adam replied. "Just passing through on a drug run along the interstate. Maybe he needed some drug money. He might have sampled the goods, panicked, thought he'd better replace the merchandise. He was high when he hit us, so that means he was also careless. We'll know more when the DNA results from the blood drops we found come back from the CODIS lab in Ft. Worth."

"Did we locate a vehicle?"

"Not yet. He either had someone waiting in a getaway car, or he might have hidden until he could run. He was pretty strung out, best I can remember."

"No wonder he was such a loose cannon."

"All the more reason for us to get Julia away from him before he could take off with her." Adam shrugged, shook out the tightness in his muscles. "I just wish I could have caught him. We searched every building around here and immediately sent out patrols. Amazing how he got away so quickly."

Eric nodded, letting the information settle in his gut. Letting a bad guy slip right through their fingers hadn't gone over very well with the department.

Reminding himself that he and Adam had at least saved Julia, he shifted on his feet. "Something just isn't sitting right."

"Maybe the fact that I'm stuck on a desk job until this is cleared up, and you're on sick leave for a few more days, or that we're not even supposed to be investigating this thing, period?"

Eric looked around, then shrugged. "We were involved. That tends to make a man curious. And… regardless of whether I'm the *official* investigating officer or not, I need some answers."

Adam slanted a look at him. "Talk to me, brother."

Eric closed his eyes, going over the details one more time in his mind. He thought about Julia's expression, about the man's skittishness, about how she'd silently appealed to Eric to help her. There had been something else there in her eyes, something Eric couldn't quite pinpoint.

But Adam's next words brought it all to the surface. "It's like he went straight for Julia, know what I mean? Almost like the money was an afterthought."

Eric glanced from his friend back into the restaurant. "Yeah, I do know what you mean. And you know what else? It's like Julia Daniels had been expecting someone to do just that."

She hadn't expected all this attention. The publicity generated from both the newspapers and the television stations had Julia's head throbbing. And had her even more worried that she'd somehow be discovered. It was bad enough, having to give detailed statements to the investigators, then having to describe the man to a sketch artist.

If she only knew what she'd been running from, she might be able to get a better grip on her sanity. Between the ringing phone and the network crews from both Longview to the west and Shreveport to the east in Louisiana, she hadn't had a chance to even do her Saturday chores and errands. And Moria was asking more and more questions.

Julia glanced out the front window, glad to see the camera crews had left. She wasn't giving any more statements. She was done with this.

But as she turned to go do the laundry, she heard a car door slam. Rushing back to the window, she peeked through the blinds to see who was out there now.

Eric Butler.

Julia's heart went into overdrive. What was he doing here? And why hadn't she combed her hair and put on some makeup this morning? Running her hands through her long tresses, Julia decided she didn't care. She had too much to worry about. The good deputy was probably just checking on her out of a sense of duty.

And she did owe him a lot. At least a cup of coffee and a slice of pie.

But when she opened the door, Eric Butler didn't look as if he were in the mood for either. "Hello," Julia said, trying to give him a reassuring smile.

"Hi, yourself. Got a minute?"

"Of course." She waved him into the room. "I'm glad you came by. I've been meaning to come and see you."

He gave her one of his level, steady looks. "Oh, and why is that?"

Julia's heart sent a warning jolt through her system. "Well, to thank you, of course. You most likely saved my life. I...appreciate it."

He waved his good arm in the air. "Don't worry about that." Then he looked into her eyes, his expression as calm and centered as the still American flag hanging on her front porch. "We couldn't let that man take you with him."

"I didn't want to go with him." She turned toward the kitchen. "Want some coffee? Some of Cat's famous apple pie? She brought a fresh one by just this morning."

Silence.

Julia turned to look at him. "Deputy?"

"Call me Eric," he said, lifting a shoulder off the porch post.

"Okay. Eric, would you like some coffee and pie?"

"What I want, Mrs. Daniels, is the truth."

Swallowing back her surprise, she retorted, "Call me Julia."

"Okay. Julia, we need to talk."

Julia could understand how a criminal would be intimidated by this man. He stood almost six feet tall and right now he was all business. "I'm not sure

I understand," she said, wondering if he'd already found out about Alfonso's mysterious death. Had he also found out something that would incriminate her? "I've talked to just about everyone in the sheriff's department and the police department. What do we need to discuss?"

Eric took two long strides toward her. "I want you to tell me why that man would have come to Wildflower...looking for you?"

Julia gasped, then shrank back. "I don't...I mean...I didn't know he was looking for me." She sank down on a chair, then stared up at him. "What are you talking about? *Was* he looking for me?"

"That's what I'd like to know," Eric replied, his tone gentle now, his expression relaxing. "I'm just trying to figure this thing out, so it can make some sense. I don't believe this was a routine robbery. Got anything you'd like to share with me about all of this?"

"I didn't know that man, if that's what you're asking," Julia replied, praying Moria would stay in her room a little while longer. She didn't want her daughter to hear this conversation. "I'm telling you the truth. I'd never seen him before. Maybe you need to be honest with me, too, Deputy. If I'm in danger. If my daughter is—"

"I didn't say that." He let out a breath. "We're still investigating. We've put out an APB based on eyewitness descriptions and our findings, and we have a rap sheet and a positive ID on someone who fits the robber's description. He's a dangerous man, which is why I'm trying—on my own time—to do a more detailed investigation into his background."

"So I don't have to talk to you, since you're not even supposed to be here, right?"

His gaze swept over her face, then back down. "No, you don't have to tell me anything. But…I'm trying to help you here." He glanced at the picture of Moria sitting on the coffee table. "For your daughter's sake, at least."

Julia couldn't tell him to go away after that. "What do you need to know?"

Satisfied that they understood each other, he said, "His name was Mingo Tolar. Ring a bell?"

She shook her head. "No, I'm sorry, it doesn't."

Eric nodded, then pinned her with another level look. "But, did that man happen to know *you?* That's what I'm wondering. And I'm not giving up on this until I find out what's going on. Because if he did know you…if he did come here looking for you, then yes, you and your daughter might still be in danger."

Julia gulped back her fear, her gaze meeting his. He gave her the same steady, reassuring look he'd given her in the restaurant the other day. Then he looked past her into the hallway, his eyes full of surprise.

Julia turned around to find Moria standing there with Rosa clutched to her chest. And a brilliant fear shattering her big brown eyes.

FOUR

Julia rushed to Moria. "Hey, honey. I didn't see you there." Bringing her daughter into the room, she pulled Moria close as she sat down on the couch. "This is my friend Mr. Butler."

Moria sent a big-eyed look toward Eric. "Are we in trouble, Mommy?"

"Now, why would you think that?" Julia asked, trying to keep her tone calm. She glanced over at Eric, hoping he hadn't noticed the fear in her child's eyes. Or her own, for that matter.

Moria leaned close, her hands going around Julia's neck. "The policemen came yesterday, just like they did when Daddy went away."

Julia's gaze slammed into Eric's. She could see the questions burning there inside his eyes. Pulling at Moria's long hair with her fingers, she tried to laugh. "Oh, that. Well, it's just that something happened at my work the other day and the police are trying to get information. But you and I haven't done anything wrong. We're okay, honey. It's okay. And

Mr. Butler is...he's a sheriff's deputy. That's like a policeman, sorta. And he's just trying to help out."

Moria didn't look convinced. "He scares me. I don't like policemen and I don't like strangers."

Eric's smile was short and quick. "I'm a friend of your mother's. But you're smart to be careful around strangers. Has anyone besides the policemen come by to see you or your mother?"

"No."

"Has anyone who scares you tried to bother you at school or anywhere else, like when you're playing outside?"

Moria shook her head but refused to say anything else.

Julia sent Eric a pleading look. "Can we finish this later?"

His nod was so subtle she almost missed it, but his eyes were on Moria. "You know, I've sure heard a lot about you from your mother. She loves you a lot."

Moria didn't reply; instead she clung to Julia even more. Afraid for her daughter, Julia gently lifted Moria up onto the couch. "Honey, stay right here while I show Mr. Butler out, okay? You can color in that new book I bought you at the grocery store yesterday."

"Okay," Moria said, taking Rosa in her lap. She stared up at Eric with obvious distrust, then went to the small kitchen table where her crayons and coloring book lay.

Julia motioned for him to follow her out onto the

porch. After she'd shut the door, she said, "I appreciate your concern, but…Moria doesn't understand what's going on, and I don't know anything about this man. I only know that I was scared, very scared, when he had that gun aimed at my head. And I am so thankful that you helped to get me away from him." Then a new fear penetrated her already frazzled mind. "You don't think he'd come back, do you?"

Eric's gaze moved over her, glassy and unreadable. "That depends. He's wounded and he's wanted for attempted armed robbery, and somehow he managed to get away. He'd need a mighty good reason to come back to Wildflower, don't you think?"

She *thought* he was fishing again, and Julia refused to give him any more information than necessary. "I think he'd be crazy to do that, but…I want to feel safe. I did feel safe here until this happened."

He leaned back against the porch railing, his quiet gaze moving over her face. "Want to tell me about… your past? Where'd you come from?"

"I don't have to answer that."

"Anyone in your past who might want to do you harm?"

She glanced away, then back. Should she tell him the truth? But what purpose would that serve? Until they found this man, if this was the right man, who knew why he'd come to the diner? Maybe it had just been a random robbery and maybe she was just imagining things because of her husband's horrible death. She didn't want to relive all of that unless she had to.

Finally, she said, "I don't think so."

His harsh gaze made her edgy. "But you're not sure?"

Dropping her hands to her sides, she asked, "How can I be sure? I've tried to live a quiet, normal life. I don't have anything to hide. I just need to protect my daughter."

"From what?"

Impatient, she said, "From the press, from the police asking too many questions. I don't want Moria to worry about me. She's been through enough."

He latched on to that. "Because?"

Letting out a sigh, Julia said, "Her father died last year, okay? Surely you've heard I'm a widow and she's lost her father. We're both still trying to cope with that, but Moria is having a very hard time. I moved here to start over and to help her get through her grief. I just didn't need this on top of everything else. So could you just go, please?"

He stepped back, palms up. "I understand and I'm sorry. Did you tell—"

"I told the sheriff's investigators, the police officer who questioned me yesterday, and…Cat knows, of course. I didn't tell the newspapers and television crews that my daughter has horrible nightmares about losing her father, because it's none of their business. Can we just leave it at that?"

"They'll keep digging."

"I'm afraid of that." She ran her hands through her hair. "And I know you can keep digging. You are a lawman, after all. You can find out anything you want about me. Which means I'll probably have to pack up and move again."

He went on full alert now. "Why would you do that?"

Wishing he hadn't pushed her so much, she let out a bitter laugh. "I just want to get on with my life, and I thought I'd be able to do that here. But I won't have my daughter being harassed because I happened to be in the wrong place at the wrong time."

He lifted off the railing then, his eyes moving over her with suspicion and concern. "Or…maybe you were the right person in the right place at precisely the right time. Maybe that robber knew exactly where you were and how to get to you. Which is why, if you have anything else you'd like to tell either me—off the record—or the official investigators for the record, you'd better do it, and quick. Or you *won't* be able to protect yourself or your daughter."

With that, he turned to leave. But he stopped on the steps to look back at her, then pulled a card out of his shirt pocket to shove toward her. "Take this. And call me if you need anything. Anything at all, okay?"

Julia took the card, her fingers moving over the etched lettering that included his name and work number. "Thank you."

"My home number and cell are written on the

back," he added. "Again, off the record since technically I'm off the case."

She turned it over to scan the scrawled numbers. "Are you always this prepared?"

"I do my homework, yeah."

That sounded like a warning. As in, he wasn't going to give up on this. And how could she expect him to? The authorities were trying to find a man who had tried to commit armed robbery. And she was caught right in the middle. It only made sense that every area of her life would be scrutinized and analyzed until they found some answers. But…she wasn't the criminal, she reminded herself. She just prayed they'd find the man and this would end before she had to bare her past to all of them.

"I hope you find that man," she said as he headed down the steps. "And I'm sorry I couldn't help you more."

He turned one last time, his fingers on the door of his truck. "And I hope you learn to trust me, so *I* can help *you*."

Julia watched as he got in the big black truck and drove away. Could she trust him? She remembered how she'd looked toward him the day of the robbery. His strength had given her courage. The connection she'd felt that day as their eyes had locked had stayed with her, making her think she had found a champion. But she was still afraid to tell him the truth. *What should I do, Lord?*

It was just too dangerous, too risky. Or was she

afraid of more than her past? If she poured out her heart to Eric Butler, she could lose a part of herself all over again, the way she had with Alfonso. And she refused to give control of her life to another person ever again. She wanted to be the one in charge this time around. And that meant protecting her child.

Julia went inside where Moria had her coloring book and crayons out on the kitchen table. "Want a snack, honey?"

Moria bobbed her head. "Is that big man gone?"

Julia had to smile at that description. Eric Butler did cast a tall shadow. "Yes, he's gone." She sat down across from Moria. "Mr. Butler is one of the good guys, Moria. He's very nice and he works hard to help people every day. You don't have to be afraid of him, okay?"

"Okay." Moria's dark eyes looked solemn and unsure. "I wish he could have helped Daddy."

"Me, too, honey," Julia said. "Me, too."

"Will that nice man keep them away?"

Julia's heart went still at her daughter's innocent question. "Keep who away, darling?"

"You know, the mean people."

Wondering if Moria was beginning to remember something, Julia tried not to show the terror holding her heart like a vise. "What mean people, Moria?"

Moria kept right on coloring the picture of flowers in a big basket. "The ones I heard that night Daddy and I played hide-and-seek. They were shouting."

Julia put a hand to her mouth, then pursed her lips to fight the chills moving up and down her spine. "Do you know what they were saying?"

Moria shook her head. "It was angry voices. Loud, angry voices. They sounded rude."

Julia watched as her daughter seemed to shut back down right in front of her eyes. "I'm sorry you had to hear that. We don't allow rude voices, do we?"

Moria kept on coloring, bearing down until Julia noticed that one of the flowers was now a darker pink than all the others. And then, the crayon snapped from the pressure. Julia gasped at the sound, then saw the pain in her daughter's dark eyes.

"I broke the violet one," Moria said, tears brimming over onto her cheeks. "It's my favorite."

Julia rushed to hug her daughter close. "We'll fix it, honey."

Moria began to sob. "It can't be fixed."

Julia's eyes filled with their own hot tears as she hugged her daughter close. Maybe Moria was right; maybe this couldn't be fixed.

Unless she went to the one man who'd offered to help her. Maybe it was time she did learn to trust Eric Butler.

Eric stared out at the quiet, still waters of Caddo Lake, his thoughts swirling right along with the slow-moving water. Julia Daniels was obviously hiding something, but what? And why was it so important that he find out?

Hearing footsteps on the dock behind him, he turned to find his father strolling toward him, two plastic cups of iced tea in his hands. All around them, the bald cypress trees stood silent and watchful, their moss-draped branches drooping toward the water. "Need a drink, son?"

"Sure," Eric said as Harlan made his way across the sturdy wooden deck. "How'd you know I was thirsty?"

"Just figured," Harlan replied, handing Eric his tea. "How's the shoulder doing?"

"Better," Eric said, taking his drink with his free hand. "Still throbs now and then, but I think I'm gonna make it."

"Never doubted it," Harlan said on a chuckle. "Fish biting?"

Eric glanced at his forgotten pole, then looked at the cork bobbing below. "I haven't checked the line in about an hour, so I guess not."

"Somehow, I don't think your mind's on fishing," Harlan said. He set his tea on the dock railing, then pulled in the line. "Nothing on here for a fish to nibble, son."

"I guess my heart's not in it today."

"You still pondering this robbery?"

Eric nodded. "She's hiding something. Now I'm wondering—do I keep digging, or do I just leave things alone and let the boys take care of business?"

"That might be best," Harlan said. He threw the baited line back into the black water, scaring a lazy turtle off a nearby log. "After all, they're looking for a criminal. But you seem more interested in the victim."

Eric looked up at the tranquil azure sky. The tall cypress trees looked like ancient sentinels, their trunks gray and ghostly in the afternoon shadows. Somewhere off in the distance, he heard a splash, then the sound of wood ducks quacking alone the shore. "I'm just worried, Dad. I think Julia Daniels might be in some sort of danger."

"Because of the robbery?"

He nodded, sipped his sweet tea. "That and the fact that the robbery might have happened because of her being here. Her husband died about a year ago, but she wouldn't say how."

"So you think she might have been a target?"

"I do. But I think they sent the wrong man. This Mingo, he didn't have his act together. If someone sent him to find Julia Daniels, he did that. But he sure messed up on taking her back to them…and I'm pretty sure that's what he was aiming to do." Then he turned to give his father a direct look. "Or maybe he just had orders to kill her."

"That's a bit forward, don't you think?"

"I'm thinking all sorts of things right now." He told Harlan about his conversation that morning with Julia. "The woman was as skittish as a barn cat. And the little girl was afraid of me. I could see it in her eyes."

Harlan stood silent for a while. "What do you make of it?"

Eric didn't want to voice the scenario that kept playing inside in his head. But he knew his father would help him sort through things. "I'm thinking domestic abuse, maybe."

"That would explain Julia's need to keep things quiet. And…bad as it sounds…that would also explain the child's fear. But if the husband was abusive, why would someone else be after Julia? Her husband is dead."

"Maybe someone blames her," Eric replied. "Or maybe the in-laws want custody of the child. Who knows?" He looked out over the water. "Or…my worst fear…that Julia somehow had something to do with her husband's death, maybe to protect herself and her daughter."

"This could be tricky, son."

Eric finished off his tea. "Yeah, but if they're in danger, I have to do something."

"I know," Harlan said, resolve steeling his words. "I know, son. But…you need to talk to someone down at the station about this. Let them investigate."

Eric didn't like that plan. "I'd rather handle it on my own. So she'll trust me."

Harlan's shrewd gaze hit Eric square in the face. "Son, do you have some sort of feelings for this woman?"

Eric looked back out over the water. "She's just

someone who needs my help, I think. Someone who's trying to live her life right, you know what I mean?"

"I do, if she's sincere and not a murderer," Harlan replied.

"I can't picture her being that," Eric said, although that thought had crossed his mind. "I just think she's scared."

"And you think you can help her?"

"I don't know," Eric replied with a shrug. "I only know that for some reason, I can't seem to shake this."

Harlan laid a hand on Eric's arm. "You went down this road once before, remember? You can't save 'em all. That kind of involvement can ruin a lawman."

Eric returned his father's stare with one of his own. "No, but maybe I can save this one, Dad. This one. That's what my gut is telling me."

Harlan let his hand fall, nodded, then turned back to his fishing pole. "Hey, looka here." He tugged on the line, then yanked the pole up. "I think I just caught dinner."

Eric laughed, then shook his head at the small, wiggling catfish. "Figures you'd catch something the minute you threw in. And me, I've been trying for an hour now and not a bite."

"The fish were letting you have some thinking time," Harlan shot back. Then he added, "And it sounds like you've got bigger fish to fry, anyway."

Eric had to agree with that. He was going to do a little digging while he was on paid leave. He was going to find out everything he could about Julia Daniels.

Whether she wanted him to know or not.

FIVE

Adam sat down in the worn leather chair facing the sliding glass doors of Eric's log-cabin lake house. "Well, bud, I've got good news and I've got bad news."

Eric shut down the file he'd been reading on the computer screen, then turned to his friend, fatigue settling over him like the sun settling over the water. He'd dug up some interesting things himself. "So do I. You go first."

"We found Tolar," Adam replied, slapping a file down on the coffee table. "Well, *I* didn't find him, but the authorities way across the state did. That's the good news."

Eric hated to even ask. "And the bad?"

"He won't be talking. He's dead. Been dead for about a week, according to the San Antonio investigators."

Eric stood up to stare out at the big, sloping yard and the water beyond. "Dead? In San Antonio?"

"Yep. But, the other good news is that he didn't

die from the slug you put in him. He was stabbed. And the other even better news, we've both been cleared to return to full duty—me right now, you whenever the doc tells you you're good to go. And the even better news—they found Tolar's gun. We should be able to match the slug to the weapon, at least. Case solved."

Eric nodded, his teeth biting into his bottom lip, thinking that wouldn't solve what was really bothering him. "Tolar was found dead in San Antonio, from a stab wound?"

"That's about the gist of it," Adam replied, a long sigh emitting from deep within. "That bites, doesn't it?"

Eric swung around, glad that they were alone in the big house. His father usually walked across the yard each day to eat dinner with Eric, but tonight Harlan had gone into Longview to eat with some of his fishing buddies. "Sure does, especially when I've just researched a whole lot of interesting things on Julia Daniels."

Adam looked up at him with a squint. "Such as?"

"Such as, she lived in San Antonio for about ten years before she came here. And she used to go by the name Julia Endicott."

"For real?"

Eric nodded. "She was married, but her husband, Alfonso, died. The official report is that he was working late one night and an intruder broke in to the office and killed him."

"But...you got something to add to that?"

"Yep, he was the CFO for the De La Noche produce company." He twirled his ink pen between his fingers. "And...Julia was briefly considered a prime suspect in his murder. Although it's never been solved, she's been cleared."

Adam let out a whistle. "Wow."

"Yeah, wow," Eric replied, almost understanding Julia's need for anonymity. "Apparently the police put her through the ringer—based on what little I could find out from phone calls and transcripts. The San Antonio boys aren't talking a whole lot."

"Maybe because the Gardonez family has put a lid on things?" Adam asked, musing out loud.

"A very tight lid, apparently."

Everyone in Texas knew about the wealthy San Antonio family that ran a national food conglomerate. The Gardonez family was well-known and powerful, with members ranging from doctors and lawyers to senators and executives. Through the years, they'd branched out to buy up all kinds of companies—anything that had to do with flowers, fruits and vegetables. They ran a clean business and kept a tight rein on their private lives. So mostly nobody messed with them. The head honcho now, however, had married into the family. From what Eric could find, Luke Roderick pretty much ran the entire operation that his in-laws had inherited and nurtured. But the news wasn't all good. There had been some tension within the ranks over the last few years.

Adam tapped a hand on the arm of his chair. "Murdered while at work for the Gardonez clan? That sure doesn't make any sense. That company has some of the tightest security known to man. How did anyone get inside the building and murder Julia's husband?"

"That's what I'd like to know," Eric replied. That and why Julia hadn't told him the truth right from the get-go.

Adam got up and headed to the kitchen. "Can I have a soda?"

"Sure," Eric replied. "Bring me one and we'll go outside on the deck so I can fill you in."

Adam nodded. "Yeah, 'cause I sure need to hear the rest of this story."

Cat sat down across the table from Julia, her dark eyes wide. "I really think you should tell Eric the rest of the story."

"I can't," Julia said, careful to keep her voice low. Moria was just out the back door talking to Mrs. Ulmer while she did some yard work. Since there was no fence between the two yards, Moria had the run of both of them and Cat's huge garden, too. "I don't want to get all caught up in being paranoid again."

"Honey, someone killed your husband and you don't even know the who or the why. Now would be a perfect time to bring the authorities here in on that little tidbit."

Julia touched a finger to the condensation on her glass of lemonade. "I've thought about telling Eric all of it, but what if I'm just imagining things? The police in San Antonio thought I had made it all up— the hang-up calls, the feeling that someone had been inside my home, even being followed—and maybe I did just imagine those things. I don't have any proof that someone was trying to scare me, and we both know how the police there treated me. What's to say the authorities here won't react in the same way?"

Cat tapped her long red nails against the table. "Well, you sure didn't make up the part about your husband being murdered not ten feet away from your daughter. And Moria didn't make anything up. She was there that night."

"Exactly," Julia said, getting up to pour her tepid tea in the sink. "And that's why I don't want to go back through this. She was just getting to the point of feeling safe again. I don't want to drag her into something that most likely has nothing to do with my past."

"But what if it does?" Cat asked. "That man just showed up here and...well, he came right for you, honey. And now rumors are flying faster than fishing line."

"What kind of rumors?" Julia turned from the window to stare at Cat. "What have you heard?"

"Oh, you know. That you were the target. That the man got away because someone helped him." She shrugged, then lowered her voice. "And something big must have happened today. Adam was in such a mood when he came into the diner. He wouldn't so much as blink any department tips, then he headed right off to find Eric."

Julia's heart thumped a consistent warning. She felt as if her shoulders were wired tight to her neck, the tension in her muscles so flexed it made it hard to breathe. "But…we haven't heard anything for over a week. I thought…I thought they were still looking for the robber."

"Oh, they are," Cat said, getting up to help with their dinner dishes. "The other cops and deputies might give up, but Eric and Adam won't rest. This happened to all of us —you, me and them. Not to mention all the other people in the diner that day."

"I'm sorry," Julia said as she dropped dishes into the dishwasher. "I don't want people to think I've brought trouble into Wildflower."

Cat touched a hand to her arm. "Then maybe you need to do something to fix that trouble."

Julia looked at her cousin. "You think this was intentional? You believe this man came here for me?"

"I've just got this feeling," Cat said, rubbing her hands over her arms. "Just like when Nathan went out on that call five years ago. I had this same bad feeling then, too. And I was right. My husband never came back home."

Julia turned to stare out into her backyard, watching as Moria laughed and played with Mrs. Ulmer's tiny Chihuahua, Fred. The wildflowers along the

back alley between her house and Cat's were beginning to bloom in vivid blues and lush mauves. Moria
was looking forward to the upcoming Wildflower
Festival that was held on the town square each year.
Julia shut her eyes, trying to imagine what would
become of her world if something happened to her
daughter.

"Maybe I should just leave," she said, tears pricking at her eyes.

"And go where?" Cat asked. "I'd worry about
you day and night. You can't go to your parents in
Kentucky. Y'all aren't exactly on speaking terms,
as we both know, and they're too old and feeble to
take you and Moria in. And besides...you've never
been one to just up and run from a fight." Then she
looked out at Moria. "And...well...I'd miss you both
so much. Having you here has helped me more than
you realize."

Julia shook her head. "And you've helped us.
But—"

"But nothing," Cat replied. "You can't keep running from something you're not even sure of, Julia.
And you *are* safe here, whether you want to believe
that or not. Just let Eric help you. Tell him the truth
about everything. If you don't want the local law
involved, Eric won't bring them in. But he can help
you. He's very good at his job. If someone is out
there looking for you, Eric will find them before
they get to you."

"But what if it's too late?"

Cat looked out the front window. "I don't think it is. Eric and Adam just pulled up in your yard."

"The boss will have our hides for this," Adam said, his expression holding a frown. "The sheriff is already fuming because Tolar got away, and never mind that this is a very small town and he has a pretty good hunch that we haven't been heeding the rules on this already. If he finds out we came over here to talk to Julia before we got the all clear for full duty tomorrow, we'll be on leave for a very long time."

"I'm on leave *now*," Eric replied. "Nothing in the books says I can't visit a woman's house. And you did get cleared for regular duty today, right?"

"Right, on both. Except that the woman you are visiting is involved in a case where you got shot—a case we're not supposed to be investigating. The sheriff turned it over to his other deputy, remember? And have I failed to mention the Rangers are still involved? We both know how dicey that can be, even if their investigation did clear both of us of any wrongdoing."

"Then why did you bring me this latest information?" Eric asked, slanting his friend a glance as he slammed the truck door shut.

"Because I was trying to be a good friend. I thought you'd like an update—not a date with the woman right in the middle of all this mess."

"Maybe I'm just trying to be a friend, too," Eric retorted.

"Okay, all right," Adam said, a hand in the air. "I see Cat's here. I'll just pretend I came to see her."

"Good idea," Eric replied, "since everyone in town knows you've got a major crush on her."

"Who? Me?" Adam shrugged. "I do not."

"Please," Eric countered. "You're about as subtle as a porcupine."

Adam frowned. "The woman is five years older than me."

"Since when has age stopped you?"

They'd reached the open front door, so Adam couldn't respond. Instead he looked up at the two women staring through the screen at them. "Hey, Cat, Julia. How y'all doing?"

"Out cruising around, boys?" Cat asked, a soft grin forming on her square-shaped face as she gave Adam the once-over.

"Something like that," Adam said, giving her a look that Eric interpreted to mean anything but.

"Can I talk to you?" Eric asked Julia, waiting as she stared at him with open anxiety through the wire separating them.

Julia looked spooked already and he hadn't even told her about Tolar being found dead. Then he glanced at Cat, realization dawning. Cat knew whatever it was Julia was trying so hard to keep a secret. But then, so did he now. Or he knew some of it. Was there more?

"What's this about?" Julia asked, clearly afraid to hear his news, whatever it was.

Adam nodded toward Cat. "Hey, Cat, let's go around back and see how Mrs. Ulmer's tomatoes are coming along. I saw her back there. She could probably use a hand with pulling weeds."

Cat lifted a brow, obviously about to tell him no thanks. But when both Eric and Adam gave her a long, steady look, she took the hint. "Oh, all right. But you know I don't like to sweat."

"Yeah, I know," Adam retorted as he watched her saunter out onto the porch. "But you sure look pretty when you glisten."

"You are such a teaser," Cat replied, sticking her tongue out at him as they headed down the front steps and around the house. Then she called back to Julia, "Take your time. I'll watch Moria."

Eric waited as Julia moved toward him. She seemed in slow motion, as if each step were a struggle.

"You look beat," he said, his gaze moving over her face.

"Thanks," she quipped. "Lack of sleep does that for a girl."

He could see the dark smudges underneath her eyes. "You're having trouble sleeping?"

"Yes, but then, you probably know that. I hear everyone in town is talking about me, speculating on what type of dire things I've brought down on Wildflower."

"Do you think you've brought us trouble?"

"I think," she said, a long shudder of a sigh moving through her as she pushed at her ponytail, "that I need to move on."

"Why?"

"Why?" She glared at him, her eyes going from gold to green like heat lightning at dusk. "Because I'm worried. Moria is so...confused."

"We can get her help. We can get both of you help."

They moved through the front yard. Eric purposely took her away from the house so no one would listen to their conversation. "Do you hear me?"

She gave him a look of resolve, but her standoffish demeanor showed her hesitation. "I hear you. We've had help. And I've already taken her to therapists in both Marshall and Longview. I know what I need to do for my little girl. She misses her father, she has nightmares and she seems to cling to the things he gave her. Sometimes she even hides the few special gifts Alfonso gave her. She tells me they used to play hide-and-seek at our other house. Then she'd pick special things around the house to hide, and Alfonso would try to find them. She still does that sometimes." Eric saw the shiver she tried to suppress. "I don't like playing hide-and-seek anymore."

He leaned against the bumper of his truck, then turned to look into her eyes. "Why didn't you tell me your husband was murdered?" He wanted to add

"And that you were a suspect?" But he kept that information to himself for now.

Her gasp of shock didn't surprise him. "How did you—" Then she shook her head, her eyes full of distrust and disappointment. "Never mind. Stupid question."

"I've had a lot of time on my hands," he said by way of an explanation. "I did my own background check. Alfonso Endicott—thirty-five years old, successful CPA, head of accounting with the De La Noche produce company, San Antonio, Texas. Mother, Regina, now lives in San Juan, Mexico. Father was a successful Texas businessman, but died from cancer about a year before Alfonso was killed. Murderer was never found and no motive other than a random robbery was ever established."

"Are you finished?" she asked, her hands shaking, her eyes flashing. "Are you satisfied?"

"No, I'm not finished," he said. Then he leaned toward her. "And I'm sure not satisfied."

"I'm going to leave this place," she said, wiping at her eyes. "I can't deal with this."

"Where will you go?"

"My folks…live in Kentucky. They're retired and they have a lot of health issues, but I'll go there. I should have gone there to begin with. I can help them. They need my help, but they insist on trying to be independent."

Eric heard her trying to convince herself, but he wasn't buying it. "Why do you have to leave, Julia?"

She crossed her arms, her whole stance defiant. "You mean you haven't figured that out yet?"

"I think I might have a hunch," he said, hoping she'd just go ahead and tell him. "Are you afraid because your husband was murdered? Did he abuse you?"

Shock once again colored her face. "Alfonso? Abuse me? No...it wasn't like that. Alfonso didn't have a mean bone in his body. He was a hard worker and a good husband. He loved his family. But he also loved his job, too much." Shaking her head, she said, "It wasn't abuse. Nothing like that."

Relief pulsed like fast-moving water through Eric's system. "I thought maybe—"

Then she gasped, realizing what had been worrying him all along. "That I'd killed my husband, or had him killed?" Putting a hand to her mouth, she moaned low in her throat. "I loved him. He was the sweetest man in the world, and he tried to give me the world. *That's* what killed him."

She came around the truck, then sank against the passenger side, her hands on her knees. Glancing up and down the street, she said, "I'm afraid for my daughter." Then she turned to look at him. "Moria was in the building the night Alfonso was killed."

Eric felt as if he'd been gut punched. Sucking in a breath, he said, "I did not know that."

"Not many people do." She glanced toward the sounds of laughter coming from the backyard. "The police kept it very quiet, to protect her, and to save the Gardonez family any further publicity, of course. We…we weren't sure what she saw or heard that night."

Eric didn't like the ugly scene playing inside his head. "Where was she?"

"In a bathroom, with Alfonso's cell phone. He'd dialed my phone for her and told her to stay right there and tell Mommy to come quick. She thought it was all another game of hide-and-seek."

"And when you got there?"

"I had someone call the police while I stayed on the line with her, but by the time I got there, about ten minutes later, they had already found Alfonso. He'd been stabbed several times." She gulped, closed her eyes. "Moria was sitting in a chair in the women's bathroom, playing with her doll."

Eric came around the truck to hold her, only because she looked as if she might collapse right there in the street. "I'm sorry. No wonder you're so on edge. So this is why you refused to tell us about your background."

"I don't know what to do," she said, tears streaming down her face. "I don't know if Tolar was after me…or Moria. Or maybe both of us. Eric, I'm telling the truth. I don't know what happened that night, and I don't know if Tolar was here because of me."

Eric pulled her close, the sweet scent of her shampoo clashing with the bitter tone of his words. "You don't have to worry about Tolar anymore. He's dead."

Julia drew back, shock coloring her pale face. "Are you sure?"

He nodded. "Yep. But…Julia, he didn't die from the shoot-out during the robbery. They found him in San Antonio, in a back alley. He'd been stabbed repeatedly."

She looked up at him, her eyes wide with horror and doubt. "Just like Alfonso. Who? Why?"

"We don't know."

Her next words were barely above a whisper. "Is it over, then?"

Eric couldn't lie to her. He held her, steadying her. Then he said, "No, I think it's just beginning. I think whoever killed Tolar will send someone else to finish the job. And that means you're still in danger."

Julia slumped back against the truck. "I can't go through this again. This can't be happening."

"But it is happening," Eric said, his hand on her chin so she was forced to look him in the eye. "And you can't keep running. If Tolar has some sort of connection to your husband's murder, then it's even more dangerous now that he's dead. Whoever is behind this will only send someone else to find you. You've got to level with me, Julia. Right now. I need to know everything you know, so I can help you. Before it's too late."

SIX

The next morning, Julia stood in the kitchen at the Courthouse Café, remembering the day a few months after Alfonso's death when she'd called Cat to ask if she could come and visit. Cat had immediately picked up on her anxiety.

"Come and *live* here," Cat had suggested. "And if you need work, well, I can always use another waitress. You worked here when we were teens. I'm thinking you can work here again. Just until you decide what you want to do." When she'd offered her deceased grandmother's vacant house, as well, Julia had taken that as a sign that her prayers had been answered.

So Julia had sold off all the fancy designer furnishings and the big house in San Antonio, taking that money and the insurance settlement to start a new life here in the quiet piney woods of East Texas.

She had certainly thought about going back to Kentucky, just to get as far away from Texas as possible. But Cat's offer had seemed like a good place to start, since her parents had practically disowned her when she'd married Alfonso. They hadn't appreciated the way the Texan had come to town and swept their daughter off her feet. Maybe they'd seen something in her future husband that she'd been too blind to see.

Whatever it was, her parents hadn't reached out to her since she'd left Kentucky, not even after she'd become a widow with a child. They came for the funeral and they kept in touch, but they didn't visit at all. They sent Moria Christmas and birthday presents, but anything beyond that was strained and awkward. So she'd settled here in this beautiful, quiet little town, hoping for a new start.

She and Cat had always been close, and Cat understood her need to be independent, to do things her own way. Cat would come if Julia called, but she wasn't overbearing or pushy. She was a relative, but she was also a good friend.

Which was why it would be so hard to leave. But after talking to Eric yesterday, she didn't have a choice. She was scared—scared of this threat looming over her head and scared of the way she wanted to give in to her need to depend on Eric Butler for help.

Julia turned to stare out the kitchen window toward the back alley. Even there, where few people needed to venture, Cat had planted a climbing rosebush against a white trellis. The tiny red roses were budding all over the place in anticipation of the long summer days ahead.

But she wouldn't be here for that, Julia decided. She'd only come in today to give her notice and collect her check. She wouldn't risk Moria's safety by staying in Texas, no matter how much she loved living in Wildflower. No matter how much Eric Butler had promised to help her.

She heard the swinging door fly open, then turned to find Cat standing there, her hands on her hips. "So you're bailing out on me, huh?"

Julia shook her head. "I've caused enough trouble. I don't want to bring more down on you."

"I can take care of myself," Cat said, a scowl on her face, her lone-star earrings dancing. "And I'm pretty sure among all of us around here, we can take care of you and Moria, too."

Julia turned back to stare at the climbing roses. A sparrow landed on the trellis, hopping back and forth along the tiny ledge at the top. "But you shouldn't have to look over your shoulder, wondering if someone else will come searching for us."

Cat let out an unladylike snort. "Jul, I'm surrounded by lawmen here. I was married to one. I'm always looking over my shoulder."

"But…this isn't fair to you, this having to watch out for me, too," Julia retorted. "I'll just go back home to Kentucky. For a little while, at least."

Cat tilted her head. "So…your solution to all of this is just to keep on moving around? What kind of life is that? And what about your parents? Won't you be putting them in danger, too?"

Anger poured over Julia as thick and heavy as the maple syrup they served with the pancakes each morning. "It's the only life I have right now. These people—"

"You don't know who they are," Cat said, hitting her hand against the stainless-steel counter. "You don't know for sure that they're after you or Moria."

"I know that man—Tolar—was murdered in San Antonio. That's all I need to know."

"Honey, he was a thug. He messed with the wrong people."

"But…he wound up in San Antonio for some reason. Why did he end up there of all places?"

Cat shrugged, then turned to start dragging out the supplies for the day. "I can't answer that. But it sure doesn't make a bit of sense for you to just up and leave because of it. Why don't you let the sheriff and his men do their jobs, then decide what's best?"

Julia ran a hand through her hair. "I can't take that chance, Cat. Not when my child is involved."

Cat yanked down bowls and grabbed at utensils, her actions making a lot of noise. The cook who'd been with the café for over twenty years rolled his eyes as he hurried by with a carton of eggs. The early-shift waitresses gave Cat a wide berth as they clipped their orders on the wire over Cat's head. Even a few of the early-morning regulars glanced up from their coffee and toast.

"Hey, what's all the commotion back there?"

Both women looked out of the open pass-through to find Eric standing at the counter. "Hey, there," Cat said, turning to give Julia a long, hard look. "I was just trying to convince my stubborn cousin here to hold her horses before she goes running off to the wild blue yonder."

Julia glared at Cat, then pushed through the swinging door. "Can I get you something, Deputy?"

"Whoa, somebody got up on the wrong side of the bed," Eric said, but he wasn't smiling. "Will you sit down and have a cup of coffee with me?"

Julia looked from him to Cat. "I...I'm not working today. I just came by to give my notice and collect my last check."

Eric was still wearing a sling, but he managed to lift his fingers in the air toward her. "You can't leave town, Julia."

Julia's mood went from bad to worse. "And why not?"

"Well, this case is still active as far as I'm concerned. In fact, Adam and I just got word yesterday that we're cleared for full duty again. But until I get my doctor's consent to go back, I intend to keep digging on my own. Even though Tolar is dead, we're still trying to figure this thing out, and we need you around for that."

"So you're going to force me to stay on a technicality?"

"I can't force you to do anything, but it would

be wise for you to keep a low profile until we know you're safe."

"I can do that—far away from here," she replied. Then she grabbed her purse from behind the counter. "Cat, I'll be back later for my check. I have some packing to do."

Cat let out a groan. "Eric, talk some sense into her, will you?"

Eric lifted his chin toward Cat, then grabbed Julia by the arm. "C'mon."

She halted, pulling away. "I told you, I have to go."

"You're going all right. With me."

"But—"

"Is Moria in school?"

"Yes, but—"

"Good, then we have the whole day." He didn't give her time to argue. He just pulled her through the café and out the front door until he'd reached his truck. Opening the passenger-side door, he said, "Get in. We're going for a little ride."

Julia didn't know what to do. He had a look about him that told her it would be useless to try and get away. "I could scream," she said, determination giving her strength.

"Go right ahead," he replied. "People will just think I'm hauling you in for bad behavior."

She watched as he slammed the door then came around the truck, his expression full of dare and thunder. Her mouth was still open in shocked silence when he cranked the truck and spun out onto the street.

* * *

Eric didn't know why this woman infuriated him so much. But she seemed determined to sabotage any form of help or hand out, so he decided he could be just as stubborn as her and twice as mean. He wasn't used to manhandling women, but this one needed a good talking-to.

And he was just the man to do it, since he couldn't work because of his injury, and because all he could think about was her and this bad situation.

"You need to take me to my car," Julia said, her voice shaky in spite of the defiant tilt of her chin.

"Not just yet."

He kept driving until they were out of town and moving past the lake. He didn't stop until he was at his cabin.

"Where are we going?" she asked, craning her neck to see the house and the woods. "I don't like this."

Eric didn't bother to answer. He just parked the truck, then got out and came around to her side. When he opened the door, he was met with a steely golden-green glare.

"I'll just call someone to come and get me," she said as she slid off the seat.

"Try it." He knew not even Cat would bother them now. "You refused to talk to me yesterday when I told you about Tolar. But today's different. You're thinking about leaving and that would be a really bad mistake."

"What do you want?" she said, screaming out the words, the echo scaring a pair of mourning doves out of the nearby bushes.

"I want to help you," he said. "But you seem dead set against that notion." He held a hand in the air. "For the life of me, I can't understand why a woman who strikes me as smart would want to take off and put herself and her child in even more danger."

"I just want to leave," she replied, her arms crossed, her booted foot hitting the dirt. Then she seemed to go limp. "I just need to leave."

"That could be very dangerous," he said, inhaling one calming breath as he repeated himself. "You don't know what's waiting out there."

"But I sure can see what's right here—you badgering me, the press hounding me and…someone obviously sent that man to do me in. I can't stay here, Eric. They know where I am now."

"You can't go, either," he said. "And for that very same reason."

She stared him down for a full minute, then said, "So what do you suggest?"

Relief washed through him. "Now that's better. Are you willing to listen to me?"

"I don't know," she said, shrugging. "I just don't know who I can trust right now."

He touched his free hand to her arm. "Look, we can start from the beginning. We can start with your marriage and everything you can remember about your husband—his work, his social connections, anything or anybody. We need to figure out why he was murdered. And then we'll figure out why you're so afraid."

She looked up at him, all the hostility gone from her eyes. She looked sad and defeated. "Why are you doing this?"

Eric chuckled, then looked out at the dark waters of Caddo Lake. "You know, I keep asking myself that question."

"You could get into trouble with the sheriff. I've heard he's already read you and Adam the riot act for endangering everyone in the café that day."

"Honey, I'm always in trouble with my boss. So just put that notion out of your mind."

"Do you think I'm lying to you?"

"Are you?"

She shook her head. "No, but...honestly, I don't hold out much hope on this. The police in San Antonio didn't believe me."

"What didn't they believe?"

She turned toward the lake. Eric took that as a sign she was ready to talk, so he grabbed her by the elbow and guided her toward the back of the cabin and the deck out over the water. "This is my place. You're safe here." He pointed to the smaller cabin a few hundred feet from his big sprawling cedar one behind them. "That's my dad's place, and I live here in this one. Let's go sit."

She nodded but kept quiet as her gaze moved across the grounds and the water.

"Do you want something to drink?"

She shook her head.

Eric guided her toward two lounge chairs centered on the big deck. "Here."

She sank down across from him, appearing waif-like in her jeans and light sweater. Then she looked over at him. "You don't need to babysit me."

"I'm not doing that," he retorted. Then he leaned up in his chair. "I *like* you, okay? I really like you. And I hate to see you so worried. And I sure don't want you to leave Wildflower."

She slanted her head, her gaze touching on him with a hesitant smile. "You *like* me?"

"Yes, I do. I had even thought about asking you out before all of this happened. So just consider this a date."

That made her laugh. "Being practically kid-napped and taken to a remote location to be interro-gated? That's your idea of a date? It's a first, I have to admit."

"We could have lots of firsts together," he countered, holding her gaze. "That is, if you stick around long enough to get to know me. And if you allow me to get to know you."

"What do you want to know?" she asked, her eyes going soft.

Eric considered that question a victory. But he knew he had a lot of battles to go before he'd won this war.

* * *

Two hours later Julia had told Eric Butler everything she could remember about Alfonso and the company he worked for. She didn't know if it was the tranquil waters of Caddo Lake or the calm way he managed to question her without making her feel cornered, but she poured it all out to him—all the horror and pain of the last year, all the nights she'd sat up with her daughter, holding Moria because neither one of them could sleep. She'd told him all about the police investigation, the counselors and social workers who'd tried to help Moria remember, and she'd told him all about how Alfonso worked so hard at times that he'd just come home and collapse on the couch and stay there all night.

"We were happy when we first came back to Texas," she said now, as they walked back toward the truck. "It's just that…he had worked for the company since high school, and they'd put him through college, then kept moving him up in the chain of command. It was his life. He was very loyal to the family because his father had also worked there—as a truck driver. Mr. Endicott wanted more for his son, though. So Alfonso became a part of the inner circle. But something was bothering him toward the end. I don't know if he was under too much stress, or if he just had this big weight on his shoulders and he didn't know how to get rid of it."

"But from everything you'd said, the Gardonez family was good to him?"

"Yes. He loved his job. They paid him a generous salary and we lived a good life in a nice neighborhood. We attended church with the family. I just can't believe anyone in that family could have been involved in his murder. That doesn't make any sense." She glanced up as a hawk circled over the tree line. "De La Noche is a solid company, with produce distribution all over the world. Not to mention the nurseries and flower shops. That's how we met—he'd come to Kentucky to oversee an opening for a new distribution center. They trusted him. They were very generous, especially with people as loyal as Alfonso."

Eric followed her gaze on the hawk. They both watched as the graceful bird dived to catch his prey. "Maybe someone else within the company—someone not related to the family?"

Julia thought of Luke Roderick, but she blocked that out of her mind. Even if he'd seemed condescending and superior at times, Luke was a member of the family; he knew the Gardonez way of life and, to his credit, he'd worked hard to rise to the top spot within the company. There was no need to tell Eric that Luke was also a womanizer and that Alfonso had been jealous at the way his married boss hovered around Julia. "I can't think of anyone."

"And what about your suspicions regarding Moria? You do believe that she might have heard or seen something that night?"

"Yes, I feel that in my heart, even if the police

never took me seriously. But…she's not talking. I can't prove anything, but right after his death, I just had this feeling that whoever killed Alfonso was still after us."

"And now do you think Tolar came looking for you?"

She nodded. "I didn't want to believe that at first, but I think it's obvious now." Then she looked over at him, her hand on the truck door. "You knew that the day it happened, didn't you?"

Eric didn't even try to deny it. "I could sense something wasn't right, yes. But…I had no idea just how wrong it would turn out to be." Then he rubbed a hand down his jaw "And you're not alone in your concerns. Nobody back at the sheriff's office except Adam knows or even suspects this link between Tolar and you, not yet anyway. I didn't want to say anything until I confirmed some of this with you. The boss doesn't always move on just my gut instincts alone."

"Cat told me you have good instincts," she said. Then she smiled. "She said you're sensitive, but you don't like to let that show."

He grinned, the strain of the past few hours disappearing from his face. "That would certainly ruin my reputation."

Julia was just about to tell him how much she appreciated his sensitive side when her cell phone rang. She hurriedly dug it out of her purse. "Hello?"

"Julia, this is Mrs. Ulmer. I was just worried about you, darling."

"Why? What's wrong?" Julia immediately thought of Moria. "Did the school call?"

"No, no. But...something funny is going on over at your house. I heard Fred barking out on our screen porch and when I went out to have a look-see, I saw a fellow nosing around over there at your place, so I asked him if I could help him."

Julia held a hand up for Eric to wait. "What did he want?"

"He said he was there to repair the cable or something like that, but after I questioned him, he took off on foot. I just wanted to check."

Julia glanced toward Eric. "I'll be there as soon as I can." She hung up, her pulse echoing at a dangerous pace inside her head. "Mrs. Ulmer said there's a man snooping around my house. I need to go—"

"I'll get you home," he said, hurrying around the truck. After slamming the door, he turned to Julia. "Buckle up. I'll be breaking the speed limit."

"I can't believe this," she said, a sick kind of dread pooling inside her stomach. "I have to go to the school. Eric, I have to find Moria."

"We'll send someone to get her," Eric said, his gaze brooding. "You're going to be okay, Julia. Both of you. I intend to see to that personally."

Julia held on as he sped along the country road toward her house. She wanted to believe him, because for the first time in a long time, someone was willing to believe in her. And for that reason alone she knew she couldn't run this time. Even though she wanted to.

She asked God to give her the strength to stay and fight this until it was resolved, one way or another. And she prayed Eric was right, that he could help her.

"What exactly did Mrs. Ulmer say?" Eric asked.

She filled him in, then said, "He told her he was a cable guy. But I didn't call anyone from the cable company."

Eric gave her a grim look, then gunned the engine.

SEVEN

"Cat's checking Moria out of school right now," Julia told Eric. "She talked to the resource officer on duty and explained we had a possible threat, so he's waiting with Moria."

They'd reached her house in record time. Eric slammed on the brakes and put the truck in Park, then hopped out to come around for her. "She'll be okay, then. The school knows Cat is listed in case of an emergency right?"

"Yes, thank goodness," Julia said, her breath catching in her throat. "I just need to see Moria to be sure, but they're going back to the café for now."

Eric guided her up the steps to her house. "Good idea. Moria doesn't need to be here until we find out what's going on."

Julia understood. "As long as I know she's safe—"

Mrs. Ulmer was waiting on her front porch, and now she came rushing over, leaving her husband there to watch from his scooter chair, Fred barking and dancing around by his side. "I'm so sorry for scaring you, Julia. But I declare, when I looked out my back window and saw a strange man coming out of your back door, well, I just knew something wasn't right. Gus heard me calling out to the man, so he naturally wanted to go over there and confront him, but I told him no. We didn't see any type of repair truck, either. That's when I called you."

"Is he still in there?" Eric asked, his voice low.

"I don't know," Mrs. Ulmer said, her lips pursed. "One minute he was there on the porch and the next, he seemed to just disappear around the other side of the house. I didn't get a very good look at him, either. I think Fred's barking scared him off."

"Thanks, Miss Nina," Julia said, her hand on the door.

Eric tugged her back. "Let me go in first."

She nodded, hoping against hope that there truly was some sort of repairman inside her house. But when Eric opened the door, he was immediately met with some resistance. Frowning, he pushed hard until he almost fell into the room.

And that's when both Julia and Mrs. Ulmer gasped at the sight before them. Julia's house had been ransacked. Furniture and magazines were scattered all over the place. A huge sofa pillow was shoved against the door. Even the tiny television had been thrown to the floor.

"Oh, my," Nina Ulmer said, her plump hands going to her mouth. "I should have called the police the minute I saw him. At least Eric is here now."

"Stay out here," Eric warned. "I'm just going to go in and check things out."

"Should I call for help?" Mrs. Ulmer asked in a shaky voice.

Eric looked at Julia. He must have seen her anxiety, since she was shaking all the way from her head to her toes.

"No, not yet. I doubt he's still here. Just stay out here and be quiet. I'll be fine."

Julia wasn't so sure about that. "But your shoulder—"

"I'm well enough to put up a fight," he retorted, his finger going to his mouth to quiet her. "Just stay back."

Julia did as he told her, her hand grabbing Mrs. Ulmer's. Nina waved to her frowning husband to reassure him, even if neither of them felt all that reassured themselves.

Then Nina picked up a small garden shovel Julia had left on the porch. "Take this, at least."

Eric frowned but took it, then he pushed inside the door. "Wait right here."

While they waited, Julia held her breath and asked God to help her. It had been a while since she'd turned to God for any favors or pleas. Probably since the night the police had told her that her husband was dead. Not once during all her fears and trepidation in San Antonio had she relied on God to calm her or guide her. But standing here, in this rental house in Wildflower, with the sun shining in a piercing deception of peace and tranquility all around her, she knew she needed God's help in dealing with this. And she was beginning to believe God was sending her that help in the form of one very brave hero.

"I pray Eric doesn't find anything bad in there," Mrs. Ulmer said.

Julia nodded. "So do I." And this time she meant it.

When her phoned beeped, she almost jumped out of her skin. "Julia, it's Cat. Moria is at the café with me and Adam is staying close. Is everything all right at home?"

"I don't know. Eric's checking it out. Someone broke into my house."

"Oh, honey, that's not good. I'll keep Moria here until I get the all clear from you, all right?"

"All right. I'll call you." She heaved a breath. "And Cat, please keep an eye on her."

"You know I will. She can help me make the pies for tomorrow's lunch crowd."

Julia closed the phone just as Eric emerged from inside her ruined living room. "He's not in here. He must have been leaving when you spotted him, Nina. Your dog must have spooked him, so he tried to get away without anyone seeing him." He gave the older woman a gentle look. "Do you think you could identify this man?"

Nina shook her head. "I don't know, Eric. I didn't have on my glasses."

Eric nodded. "We'll worry about that later, then."

Both women let out the breaths they'd been holding. "I'll go tell Gus what's going on," Mrs. Ulmer said. Then she turned around, her paisley-printed apron flying out. "I'll come back and help you clean up, suga'."

"Don't touch anything. I have to call this in first," Eric said, his gaze resting on Julia. "I have to."

She knew what that meant. Even more scrutiny on her private life. But…she really didn't have a choice now. Someone was obviously searching for something. Her husband had died because of this. Mingo Talor had possibly died because of this. She didn't want to think about what these people would do next.

"I know," she told Eric as she stepped inside the clutter of her home. "I know. I just wish—"

"Look, I'm going to Sheriff Whitston with all of this." When Julia held up a hand in protest, he added, "And since I'm not clear for full duty until my arm heals, I'm going to ask him to assign *me* to *you*."

"What?" Julia shook her head. "I don't need a bodyguard, Eric."

"Yes, you do. I think you and Moria are being targeted, Julia. And until we find out why and by whom, you need protection."

"So you're just going to camp out on my doorstep?"

"No, not exactly," he said, his gaze sweeping over the broken dishes and strewn food in her kitchen.

"But you *are* going to be with me 24/7. You and Moria are coming to stay at the lake with Dad and me. And that's final."

Later that afternoon, Julia was once again on the big deck stretching out over Caddo Lake, the silhouette of Eric's spacious cabin behind her as she allowed the gentle spring wind to play through her hair. Too numb to think about how most of the few possessions she'd brought from San Antonio were now destroyed, she just thanked God that Moria was safe. At least she'd stored some of her more prized possessions in Cat's big attic.

Of course, she'd had to dig in her heels with Eric. She wasn't going to stay out here on the lake day and night, and *that was final,* she'd informed him earlier. However, she was willing to come out here for dinner tonight, just to keep Moria from seeing their house. Cat had agreed to let Julia and Moria stay with her for as long as they needed. After all, Cat had reminded her, she'd wanted them to stay with her when they moved back, anyway, but Julia had insisted that would be imposing. Now Julia felt trapped between two very dynamite forces—her cousin and the man who kept coming to her rescue. They'd reached a compromise of sorts, at least. When she wasn't working at the café, she and Moria would be with either Cat or Eric, or both if need be. They wouldn't be alone until Eric could make sure they were safe again.

"I like it here, Mommy," Moria said from her spot near the railing. "I like the turtles. Do we get to stay a long time?"

"I'm not sure, honey," Moria replied, careful to keep her tone light. "Probably just for dinner, okay?"

Moria nodded. "Why can't we go back home?"

Julia would like to know the answer to that question herself. "I don't know yet. Remember I explained how some things had been damaged at our other house? We have to get that fixed first. We'll visit with Eric and his dad, then we'll stay with Aunt Cat for a while. It'll be fun, since you're out for spring break next week."

Moria clung to her doll. "Rosa likes it here, too."

"I'm so glad," Julia said, turning to touch a finger to the doll's glistening hair.

At least Moria's favorite toy hadn't been destroyed by the burglar. Eric seemed to think the man had heard Fred barking, or something else had alerted him before he'd searched the whole house. Then when he'd seen Mrs. Ulmer, he'd run off. Julia's room had been plundered, but it looked as if the man had stopped midway and left. Moria's bedroom was untouched.

"That just means they'll be back again," Eric had reasoned earlier after the whole place had been dusted for prints.

Hearing footsteps on the deck, she turned now to find him coming toward them, a look of fatigue shadowing his face. Whispering low, he said, "We'll have to wait to hear on the prints—if there were any new ones. That's all we have to go on right now. Whoever did this, they didn't leave behind any evidence."

"That doesn't surprise me," Julia said. "I have a feeling whoever is behind this is desperate."

Eric leaned close. "Exactly. Even more reason to take extra precautions."

Moria ran up to Eric. "Mr. Eric, I've seen six turtles so far. No alligators, though."

"I wouldn't count on seeing an old gator," he said, running a hand over Moria's head as he stepped close. "They like to lay low. Just remember what I told you—don't ever go out to the dock by yourself, okay?"

"Okay," Moria said, looking back out at the water. "I won't."

Eric's smile was indulgent. "Supper is almost ready."

"I could have helped," Julia said, feeling awkward and out of place with nothing to occupy her time.

"Dad doesn't allow anyone near when he's making his famous chili dogs." He grinned over at Moria. "Hope you like tater tots."

"I love them," Moria replied, her smile shy.

Eric looked back at Julia. "Everything is set. Dad and I both are on active watch now. One of us will be with you or near you at all times. The school has been alerted and they know the routine. You are the only person who can give approval to check out Moria until this is resolved. Nobody else, not even

Cat, not even me, you hear? It's important to stick to your routine, no matter how hard that is."

"Then why did I have to leave my home?" she said on a low whisper.

"Because your home is uninhabitable right now. And because you're much safer out here where I have a built-in security system and a bulldog of a daddy. We'll keep you here and at Cat's house, with Dad, Adam and me taking shifts. The normal routine will begin again once school starts back after spring break. But hopefully, between the authorities in San Antonio, and with our department here working on things, this will be cleared up by then."

Trying to find some humor, she shrugged. "And here I thought this was just your way of getting to know me better."

"Maybe that's part of it, too." His expression changed from amused and interested to deadly serious. "I need to keep you safe and it's just easier on everyone to do that here as much as we can. We're off the beaten path, and we have more room, more distractions for Moria and…as I said, my dad as backup."

She nodded. "Don't worry. I understand. But I'm going back to Cat's house each night. I don't want to disrupt Moria's life too much and we hang out at Cat's house all the time as it is."

"Which we need to consider," he said, shaking his head. "Someone might be aware of that routine."

Julia shuddered. "I can't just stop my life in midstream."

"True. Okay, I can live with that as long as Adam can help with checking on all of you. Cat knows how to use a weapon. And we'll assign an additional man to watch the school if we haven't figured this out by the time Moria is due back, okay?"

Forcing herself to relax, she said, "Well, we don't have to worry about school for another week, at least. Spring break on the lake—reminds me of high school."

He gave her that tight little smile again. "Cat said y'all used to have some fun times every summer. I wonder how I never got around to knowing you back then. I guess I was away at college part of the time."

"We probably ran in different circles. Cat was older, wiser, smarter, I think. She kept me out of trouble." And he would have been serious trouble, she thought to herself.

"Cat's good at that."

Julia watched as Moria threw pebbles into the water. "Are you sure your dad's okay with this female invasion?"

"He's just fine. He and Moria have already established a nice bond."

"She doesn't take to everyone. Your dad is a very nice man."

"Thanks. I inherited that trait."

She saw the amusement surfacing in his dark eyes again, and in spite of all the tension surrounding them, she felt a little ray of hope…and a big jolt of awareness. "I think you did."

"So…are *you* okay with all of this?" he asked. "My dad will serve as chaperone and disciplinarian if I get out of hand," he added, nudging her elbow. "Just like high school again is right. And the more I'm around you, the more out of hand I could get."

"You can't flirt with me until this is over," she said as she shifted away. "We agreed on that back at my house when you talked me into this, remember?"

"I don't remember any such agreement. But considering how I got a lecture from my superior about withholding information and going behind his back to investigate a case that was clearly not mine to investigate, I'd say flirting is definitely out of the question right now. But…that'll just make it all the better later, when things are back to normal."

"And will things ever get back to normal?" She had to wonder at that. Lowering her voice so her daughter wouldn't hear, she said, "I mean, I've forgotten what normal *is*. It's been so long since I've felt that way."

He moved closer, the warmth in his eyes glistening right along with the sunset over the water. "I wonder about normal myself. I try to imagine this house full of love and laughter, with a family of my own."

She shook her head. "And yet, you've obviously never married, right?"

"Right." He shrugged, then his eyes turned hazy

with memories. "I've dated a lot, and one or two times it looked serious. But…once I got settled into the routine of my job, my personal life kind of fell by the wayside."

"Did you ever have someone special? I mean, really special?"

He looked away. "Once, but that was when I was in college. And it was over before it even got started."

Julia looked out at the water, watching as a dragonfly buzzed over the surface. Maybe he didn't like talking about his personal life. "I loved being married, being a mom. I had it all. Or so I thought."

Eric gave her a measured look. "You seem to be good at the mother part."

Glancing back toward where Moria sat fussing over Rosa, she hoped that was true. "Everything changes when you have a child. Your whole perspective shifts."

He drummed his fingers along the railing. "I certainly understand that. Sometimes I envy my dad. He's had all of that, and even though my mom died a few years back, now he gets to sit back and take it easy, knowing he's a blessed man."

"Or at least he did," she said, "before we were forced on him."

"My dad is tough. He can handle you two. Besides, he has his own place. He can retreat to his cabin anytime he wants."

"I hope so. I don't think he's as thrilled as you seem to be about having us here."

She saw him hesitate before he responded to that. Then all doubt was gone. "My dad always does the right thing. Let's go eat, or he will be mad at all of us."

Later, after Moria had fallen asleep on the couch and they were all three sitting around the spacious paneled den with a perfect view of the lake, Eric wondered if Harlan did resent having Julia here. But then again, his dad hadn't hesitated one bit when he'd called earlier to explain things to him. Eric figured his dad was just trying to protect him, on both a professional and a personal level. His dad sure had seen the ups and downs of Eric's pathetic love life and the ups and downs of being a lawman. And Harlan didn't have to tell Eric that he was in way over his head with this particular work-related project. But they both knew Eric couldn't turn away from Julia now.

Hoping to break the ice between his dad and the woman who was somehow fast becoming an important part of his life, Eric chuckled. "It's been a long time since I brought a girl home to meet my dad, huh, Pops?"

Harlan glanced up from his newspaper. "You can say that again. I thought we were both destined to remain two grumpy old bachelors."

Julia shifted in her spot on the couch. "Let's not get ahead of ourselves here. I'm not moving in—just spending some time here."

Harlan kept on reading, his bifocals jutting out

from his nose. "That's what my Patsy said when we first started dating. Told me she wasn't interested in me, no way, no sir."

Eric winked over at Julia. "Well, I'm sure glad you convinced her to marry you, since I wouldn't be here if you hadn't."

Harlan shot his son a deadpan look. "Believe me, I've considered that through the years." Then he looked at Julia. "This one is famous for his hare-brained schemes."

Julia gave Harlan a questioning look, her slanted eyebrows lifting up. "Such as bringing a woman and her child home for dinner?"

Harlan didn't even blink. "Yep. This has got to rank right up there with the time he brought home two baby wood ducks and a bullfrog but forgot to tell his mama they were all cozy in the bottom of his closet. Boy, that caused a regular ruckus around the house."

Julia looked embarrassed until Harlan shot her a grin. "But, honey, you are much prettier than that old bullfrog and a lot less noisy than those scared little ducks, let me tell you."

They all laughed, and Eric breathed a sigh of relief. Leave it to Harlan Butler to get things rolling. "Dad, I appreciate your help on this. I don't think I need a chaperone at my age, but I know you'll make a good one."

Harlan put down his paper, then turned toward them. "I can't say I understand your tactics, son, but I don't cotton to a woman and her child being threatened or harassed. So you both can count on me. Now, let's consider that the end of that particular discussion."

Julia sat up to clutch a throw pillow Eric's mother had cross-stitched years ago with Bless This Mess. "I don't intend to hang around here all the time, Mr. Butler. And while I didn't want to resort to leaving my home, I want to thank you for tonight. I can rest better knowing Moria is in good hands for a little while, at least."

"Call me Harlan," Eric's dad said, pushing up out of his chair, his smile gentle as he looked down on where Moria lay nearby. "Now, I'm old and I'm tired. So I'm going to go across the yard, feed my dog and go to bed. Eric, you'll make sure she gets safely to Cat's, right?"

"Of course," Eric replied, smiling up at his dad. "Get a good night's sleep."

Harlan held a hand up in parting. "Same to you."

After his father had left the room, Eric turned back to Julia. "Finally, we're alone."

She frowned over at him. "Was this your plan all the time, Deputy?"

He slid closer to her on the couch. "Maybe."

He watched as her gaze moved from him to the moonlit night. "Hard to imagine that someone could be out there, watching my every move."

"Not so hard to imagine," he reminded her. "I saw

your house today. I'm just glad you weren't there when that man decided to search the place."

She let out a little gasp. "I don't even want to think of that. I just want this to be over."

"Me, too," Eric said as she glanced back at him. "For more reasons than one."

He could see the becoming blush rising up her neck. "No flirting," she reminded him. "For lots of reasons."

"Want to tell me some of those reasons?"

"Not tonight," she said. She got up, pointing toward her sleeping daughter. "It's time to take us back to Cat's."

She moved toward Moria, leaving Eric to wonder what other obstacles he'd have to face once he'd caught the bad guys.

EIGHT

"Ready to go home?"

Julia grabbed her purse off the table at the café, her gaze edging toward Eric. He'd brought her in to see Cat and get something to drink, but now she just wanted to get out of here. She'd spent two hours at the sheriff's office answering questions, and she had gotten the distinct impression that they all thought she had somehow imagined the danger she thought she'd left back in San Antonio. "I am so very ready to go…wherever home is right now."

"I know being questioned was tough," Eric said as she got up, "but at least now we've got everything out in the open. We have your official statement and now we can compare notes with the authorities in San Antonio. This should get things moving."

Cat followed right on their heels. "I sure hope so. Those big city boys were tough on Julia after Alfonso was killed, from what she's told me about their interrogation techniques." After Julia shot her a warning look, she changed tactics. "Anyway, Julia's been through enough. She was nearly exhausted when y'all came in."

"I understand," Eric said, "and I'm sorry it had to be today. But we got everyone together to get things rolling. The sooner we get moving on this, the safer you'll all be."

"If they even believe me," Julia replied, shaking her head. "It does sound farfetched."

"But Tolar's trying to kidnap you and someone breaking into your home was real," Eric reminded her. "And until they prove otherwise, I think there's a connection and I think you're in danger."

Cat patted her big purse. "Well, *I've* got a permit to carry a concealed weapon. And I know how to use it if they come knocking at my door."

Eric lifted his eyebrows. "I just hope Adam *taught* you how to use it."

"Adam, smadam," Cat retorted. "My daddy taught me how to fire a gun a long time ago. I was just out of practice, is all."

Julia shuddered. "I don't like guns. I don't want Moria around them."

"Well, honey, Eric and his daddy have lots of guns out in their cabins." She shot Eric a suspicious look. "Which is why I've been trying to convince Julia all day to just stay in town with me for dinner. I don't see why she has to traipse out to the lake and stay there all day long, every day."

"She's safe spending some time out at the cabin. It throws any watchers off the trail," Eric countered.

"And the guns aren't an issue. Dad has all the weapons locked up tight in his office, which is also locked. And I only have my service revolver, which is right with me at all times whether I'm at home or on duty."

Cat nodded. "Uh-huh. I just think you want her all to yourself. I think this is about more than just finding a criminal. You've had dinner with her for two days straight now."

"Cat!" Shocked, Julia headed toward the door. "You are impossible sometimes."

"I call 'em like I see 'em," Cat retorted. "And I don't recall Eric Butler ever being so nice and accommodating before. He usually runs the other way when a woman even smiles at him."

"I'm a very nice person," Eric said, his expression blank. "And this is different—I'm trying to do my job here. And besides, since when are you so worried about my actions?"

"When it involves someone I care about," Cat said, turning off lights and setting up chairs as she moved toward the front doors. "Like I said, Julia's been through enough."

"Don't you trust me to take care of her?" Eric asked.

Cat planted a hand on her hip. "Of course I do. I just don't like you hogging her all the time."

Eric let out a groan. "Fine, then, I'll just have dinner with all of you at your house tonight. Just to be sure you get equal time."

Julia whirled around. "Cat's right. I've had about

all I can take for one day, okay? Cat, we've had this discussion already. I like it out at the lake. Moria can roam around out there. Your place is big and creaky and not exactly childproof, so we can't just stay hidden inside your house all the time."

"My house is not that bad," Cat retorted. "Moria brought half her stuff over there anyway. And she loves exploring my house, especially the turret room."

Julia looked over at Eric. "Moria seems to want to cling to her special things, so I didn't have the heart to tell her no. She brought her doll Rosa and a few other things to decorate her room at Cat's house."

"And she likes to hide things all over the house when she's exploring. She wants me to come and find her and then we have a treasure hunt of sorts," Cat added, laughing. "Which I happen to have the perfect house for, thank you very much."

Julia's gaze locked with Eric's. "I don't like her playing hide-and-seek. It scares me when she won't answer me or come out of hiding when I can't find her."

"You should keep an eye on her even when she's exploring," Eric warned. "That's why the lake is safer. We can all watch her out there, but she still gets some fresh air and sunshine."

"I just want to help, too," Cat said, glaring at Eric. "People will talk if y'all keep leaving the city limits together at dawn and don't come back until dusk."

"I'm on vacation for a few days," Julia reminded

her. "Which is why I came in today to talk to the sheriff. I just want this to be over."

"This is a very small town, honey. Y'all can't keep this a secret much longer."

"We can if no one talks," Eric said, shooting Cat a warning. "And I mean not even you."

"I'm not talking," Cat said, raising a hand. "I know how things work."

"I'll be fine," Julia said. "Right now, I just want to get back to Moria. I'm sure Harlan is tired of babysitting."

"Adam's with them," Eric said to reassure her. "And Cat, if you're so worried, you can call him to bring Moria to town for supper with us." Then he grinned. "We'll be like one big, happy family. I'll even cook."

"I've had your cooking," Cat replied. Then she patted her booted foot on the floor. "But if Adam's willing to bring Moria back, then Julia won't have to go all the way out there tonight—"

"And you'll get to see Adam. Who's working this angle now?" Eric asked, winking at her.

"Adam and I are good friends," Cat said, slinging her purse over her shoulder with a huff. "And since I've cooked all day here, somebody else can certainly provide the meal. As long as it's not you—"

"I'll grill chicken and some vegetables," Eric said as they walked out the front door. "I do a passable job on the grill. So are you in or not?"

Cat glanced over at Julia. "I guess I'm in. I'd just sit home worrying if y'all leave me all alone."

"Good, we'll have a nice, quiet dinner at your house then."

"I doubt that," Julia said, heading toward Eric's truck. "Not with you two fussing over me." Then she turned as she waited for Cat to lock up. "But…I just want you both to know I appreciate being fussed over." And she appreciated that they both seemed to believe everything she'd told them about her past.

Cat double-checked the door, then turned to give them a reluctant smile. "And I want you to know, honey, if I had to handpick the one man I'd trust to guard you with his life, it'd be this man standing right here." Shrugging, she added, "I just had to mess with him a little bit, to make sure he knows I'm keeping my eye on this situation."

"Everyone is well aware of the situation," Eric added. Then he looked up and down the sleepy street. "Except Mickey Jameson at the *Gazette,* of course. We didn't give out the details of this latest incident and we don't want any publicity on Julia's whereabouts, for her own protection."

"Then we'd better get going," Cat said. "You know how that Mickey can smell a story a mile away."

Julia looked around, a chill moving over her like a cold wind. "I agree. His article in the paper after the robbery didn't help at all. Anybody in Texas can find me here now."

"The paper's office is closed up tight," Cat said.

"And Mickey's souped-up Mustang isn't in his usual parking spot."

"Good, let's get gone ourselves," Eric said as he opened the door for Julia. Then he nodded to Cat. "Call Adam and tell him our plans."

Julia got inside the big truck, still cold in spite of the warm spring afternoon. She couldn't stop the feeling that even though the streets were deserted, someone was watching her every move.

An hour later, Eric and Adam stood watching the paprika chicken and sliced squash and potatoes sizzling on the gas grill.

"Cat's got a nice place here," Adam said as he looked around the big fenced yard. "Her folks always did take good care of their property."

Eric followed Adam's gaze. The big square yard looked like some sort of secret garden with all its white-lace wrought-iron furniture and the octagon-shaped white gazebo down by the koi pond. "Yep. She's worked hard to maintain this old house and this garden. They don't build 'em like this one anymore."

"One hundred years and counting," Cat said as she came out onto the big cedar deck she'd had built around an ancient pine tree on one side of the yard. "It's a pain to keep up, let me tell you. Always something popping or cracking around here. And the utility bill is outrageous, in spite of all the updates with the heating and air."

"You love it, though," Adam said, grinning over at her.

Eric decided there was more sizzle between these two than on the grill. Adam had been dancing around Cat Murphy for a while now. And it wouldn't take much for him to get all gung ho about taking things a bit further with her.

Eric prayed his two friends would realize that they'd make a good team. Then he glanced around as the screen door from the kitchen swung open, Moria's laughter echoing out into the yard as she ran down the steps. Julia followed, looking more relaxed now that she'd changed into walking shorts and a button-up blouse.

Watching them laugh and frolic, Eric felt a tug of pleasure inside his heart. They sure made a pretty little picture there amongst the just-blooming clematis running up the porch columns. He wanted to keep them happy and safe. That was his job.

But his heart was telling him to keep them near for other reasons. He liked being around Julia; admired her determination and her need to be independent. And he loved Moria. The child was slowly warming up to him, but she'd really taken a shine to Harlan. Moria and his daddy had taken to walking hand-in-hand around the trails along the lake. They were good for each other. And Julia was good for him.

He turned back to the smoking meat, flipping the

pieces with his tongs. He'd better concentrate on the meal, or they'd be ordering pizza for dinner.

"That smells great," Julia said as she came to stand beside him. Then she looked out over the camellias and azaleas blooming underneath the tall pines. "It's so peaceful back here. Like a retreat. Hard to imagine that there could be anything wrong just beyond this fence line."

Eric put down the tongs, then turned to face her. "Maybe we'll hear something back from San Antonio. They'll reopen the case and go over the files. They could find something to help us."

She pushed at the deck railing. "Or they might come up empty-handed. They never took me seriously when I reported any of my concerns to them before, so why should they believe there is a connection now?"

"Because we do have a connection now. Tolar was here, holding you at gunpoint in front of several witnesses, and now we've matched his gun to the bullet we found in the café wall. He kept saying he had to take you. Then he wound up dead in San Antonio. That's a stretch but it's still a connection."

"But it doesn't mean he's connected to the Gardonez family."

"We'll just have to keep digging until we can find some solid evidence," Eric replied.

She lifted her chin in acceptance. "At least things have been quiet since the break-in."

Eric looked toward the gate to her house, which

in the past had been thrown open for Moria to run back and forth. Not anymore. They were more contained with the gate locked. "Why *did* you move into the cottage instead of living here with Cat? She certainly has the room."

Julia shrugged. "It's hard to explain. I love this house and, yes, Cat has plenty of space. But…we lived in a huge house in San Antonio—it was very lonely for Moria and me. It just seemed so vast, especially after I started finding things that had been misplaced or rearranged. I know someone had been inside my house. But I could never catch anyone in the act or even begin to prove it to the police."

"So when you moved here, you wanted something more compact?"

"Yes. I wanted a small space, so I could feel secure and in control. That's ironic, since Alfonso always wanted bigger and better. I loved our house, but it was way too big for three people. And after his death, I just couldn't live there anymore. Too many rooms, too many doors and windows and hiding places. I couldn't sleep, couldn't take the tension and the stress. So…the cottage was perfect. We stored our extra things in Cat's attic and took what we needed to move into the cottage. It gave everyone privacy, but we're right over the fence from Cat. Moria can play between her yard and mine. And she has the Ulmers right next door. We walk to church. It's a good environment for her."

"You always put her first, don't you?"

He saw the motherly love glowing in her eyes as she watched her daughter playing chase with Adam and Cat. "Yes, but then, that's what parents do. Some parents, at least."

Wanting to know more, he said, "Meaning?"

"My parents...didn't want me to leave Kentucky. They didn't trust Alfonso. Said he was a smooth talker and a stranger. They expected me to marry a local boy." She glanced down at her shoes. "It always seemed they put their own hopes ahead of what I wanted for myself. And when I met Alfonso, I fell in love and wanted a life with him. They still resent me for it."

"How'd you two meet?"

"He came with a whole team to the community college, looking for people to work in the distribution center De La Noche was building. It meant good jobs for a lot of people, and since I wasn't sure what I wanted to do with my life after college, I applied for a position as a secretary in the front office."

"I take it you got the job."

Her smile was bittersweet, her eyes a shimmering gold green. "I took the job and won over the boss."

"I see," Eric said. But he didn't want to see. It felt odd, thinking of her with someone else. Odd and not very rational. He was fast becoming possessive of this woman. Of course, he reminded himself, that back when she was falling in love with Alfonso, he was falling for another blonde. The one he hadn't been able to save.

Julia tugged at the loose sleeves on her blouse. "Anyway, my parents didn't approve of the relationship. They tried to convince me I was making a huge mistake. But…we got married anyway and I came back to Texas with Alfonso. Since then things have been shaky between my parents and me."

"But they have to care about Moria."

"Oh, they do. They send her gifts on all the right occasions, just as her paternal grandmother in Mexico does. But they're too old to travel and I just can't seem to find the right time to take her there. One day soon, though. I'm hoping I can mend things with them before it's too late. She should know her grandparents."

"That sounds like a good plan," he replied, wishing that for her. "She's a great kid. Dad is in love with her already. She's a nice distraction for him."

"Your father is a very understanding man. I admire the bond you have with him. You two seem so centered, in both your lives and your faith."

He smiled at that. "Our faith *keeps* us centered."

"I need to work on that area, too," she said. "I didn't think faith was a priority in San Antonio. I was too busy living a fast-paced, high-profile life of parties and fund-raisers. We went to church, but it was all about being seen with the right people. I wanted to be the perfect wife for my executive husband. I wish I could have helped him somehow. I wish I had turned to God to help all of us."

Eric looked at the woman standing beside him.

"I can't see you in that kind of role—the rich society woman. I mean, you seem so down-to-earth."

"I changed to accommodate our lifestyle and now I've changed again since Alfonso's death. I think I've gone through three lifetimes. And now this. I'm tired of changing. I want to be settled and secure."

"I can certainly understand that."

She turned to face him. "Then you can also understand why I'm so hesitant around you."

He had to admire her honesty in this area at least. "You're not ready to take the plunge and get all tangled up in another relationship yet?"

"No, I'm not. I'm still grieving. Not just for my husband, but…I'm grieving the loss of my own naiveté and…my daughter's innocence. It's so hard, knowing that she seems okay on the surface but that deep inside she's hiding some sort of silent pain."

Eric touched a finger to her sleeve. "And so is her mother, I think."

Julia looked up at him then, her eyes shimmering with hope and regret. "I want to be whole again. I want to laugh again, really laugh again." Then she stepped back. "And…I'd like to get to know you better—not just as my bodyguard, but as a friend."

"We'll make it happen," he said, wishing he could kiss her. "I promise."

Adam's voice jarred them out of the moment. "Hey, can you make that chicken cook any faster? I'm starving."

Eric glanced around to find Cat, Moria and Adam all staring at them. "What?"

"You tell me, bro," Adam said, grinning. "I think y'all got more cooking over that grill than just that poor chicken."

Eric checked Julia to see how she'd react to that assumption. After all, she'd opened up to him just a little bit more. Maybe she really did want to get to know him better, as she'd said.

But Julia didn't give anything away, even though Cat and Adam gave them a knowing, questioning look. She blushed a little bit, then shrugged. But she shot him a soft smile before she headed toward her waiting daughter.

Which told Eric her real secrets were still intact.

NINE

Julia woke with a start, her breath coming in shallow gulps. Her heartbeat hit against her temple like a mallet and her skin felt clammy and hot. Had she been dreaming?

Sitting up, she checked the dainty clock on the bedside table: 2:00 a.m. The vast upstairs bedroom of Cat's house was lit by moonlight, the shimmer of the night filtering through the white lace sheers. Hurrying across the hall to check on Moria, she grabbed a lightweight robe and padded barefoot toward the open door between their rooms.

And that's when she noticed the eerie glow in the sky.

Rushing to the window, Julia let out a gasp. The cottage was on fire. Turning to grab the phone, she called 911, then hurried to wake Cat, fear gripping her with a terror that seemed to suck the breath right out of her lungs.

What if she and Moria had been inside that house?

After quickly glancing in on her sleeping daughter, she rushed down the hall toward Cat's bedroom. The door was open, so she hurried in. "Cat, Cat, wake up."

Cat groaned, then rolled over, squinting toward her. "Jul? What's wrong?"

"Fire," Julia said. "The cottage. I've called 911. Get up, Cat!"

Cat rolled out of the bed with a precision that lived up to her name, landing straight up on both feet. "Oh, no. The cottage? But—" She grabbed at Julia. "Mercy me, somebody set your house on fire?"

"It looks that way," Julia said. "I didn't have much left and this will take care of what I did have. Thank goodness we stored some things over here."

Cat grabbed a pair of pink fuzzy slippers and a chenille robe, then searched for her cell phone. "Let's get down there."

"I'm calling Eric," Julia replied, shock washing over her.

"What about Moria?" Cat asked. "We can't leave her alone."

Julia pulled Cat toward Moria's room. "I'll get her. I'd rather she was with us."

"This will upset her," Cat said as they jogged up the hall.

"I know, but I'm afraid to leave her here," Julia replied. With shaky hands, Julia managed to get on her sleepy daughter's slippers and robe, the scent of burning wood permeating the air as she urged Moria up.

"What's wrong, Mama?" Moria asked on a groggy wail.

"Just a problem, honey. We have to get up now. It's okay. C'mon, Mommy will hold you tight."

Moria didn't protest anymore. She fell into Julia's arms and held on to her neck as Julia and Cat rushed down the long stairway toward the front door.

They could hear the sirens shrilling into the night, but Julia knew it was too late to save her home. The tiny cottage was engulfed in flames. Sparks and ember floated up into the night all around the house. "Oh, Cat, I'm so sorry."

"For what?" Cat huffed as they reached the gate to Julia's yard. "Forget the house. I'm so thankful you and Moria were with me."

Julia looked at her cousin, seeing the bright tears in Cat's eyes. "Me, too." She hugged Moria tight, trying to shield her daughter from the brilliance of the fire. They were helpless against this—the fire, the night, whoever wanted them dead.

Julia needed God's guidance now more than ever. Because she had become so weary, so fearful. How could she go on, she wondered, as she watched the firemen moving about, trying to save her house. Soon the entire neighborhood was awake and outside watching.

Including Mickey Jameson from the *Gazette*.

"Ms. Daniels, isn't this your house?" the reporter asked as he came running up to Julia and Cat.

Julia nodded. "This *was* my house, yes."

"What happened?"

Cat stepped between Julia and the reporter. "Mickey, can this wait? We just realized the house was on fire."

"Good thing you were able to get out," Mickey said.

"Yes, good thing," Julia replied, too scared and tired to give the man an exclusive.

"What caused the fire?"

Then they heard tires squealing in Cat's driveway.

"Eric," Cat said, nodding toward her house. "He made it in record time."

Ignoring Mickey, Julia glanced from her burning house back toward Eric's truck. He came running toward them in a long gait, his gaze centered on her. "Are you all right?"

"We're fine," she said, glad to see him. She resisted the urge to fall into his arms. "We're okay."

Eric stared up at the roaring fire. "This has gotten serious."

"So you think it was deliberate, just like I do?" Cat asked, her hands on her hips.

"Very deliberate." He touched a hand to Julia's arm. "Let me take Moria."

She resisted at first, then finally gave her daughter over to him, silent tears falling down her cheeks.

"Did you say this was deliberate?" Mickey asked,

moving closer. He snapped a couple of pictures of the burning house, then turned back to Julia. "Ms. Daniels, did someone set fire to your house on purpose?"

"Hey, Mickey, no more questions, okay?" Eric said, nudging the other man to move on. "Not right now."

Moria lifted her head to stare at Eric. "What's wrong, Mr. Eric?" Then she turned toward the cottage, her big eyes going wide. "Mommy, our house is on fire. Mommy?"

"I'm right here, honey," Julia said, wiping at her face. "We're okay. Aunt Cat is right here and we're going to be just fine."

Eric patted Moria's back. "That's right. I won't let anything bad happen to you, Moria, you understand me?"

Moria nodded, her eyes bright. "I don't like bad people. Did bad people do this?"

Eric watched Mickey's inquisitive expression, then shot a look at Julia. "We'll have to figure out what happened, sweetheart. But you don't need to worry. Just rest, okay?" Then he gave Mickey a hard stare. "I said to leave, right now. You'll get the official report whenever the fire chief finds out what happened."

Watching the reporter stalk away, Eric held Moria tight. "It's all gonna be okay, baby."

Moria nodded, then dropped her head against his shoulder. Julia watched as her daughter's tiny arms went around Eric's neck. It was the first time in a very long time that Moria had allowed anyone besides Julia to be that close. She trusted Eric with her bruised little heart.

And now, Julia knew *she* had to trust him, too, not only with her heart, but with her life.

"It was arson," Adam said the next morning. "No doubt about that now."

Eric glanced down at the report Adam had just snagged from the fire chief. "Gasoline as an accelerant? Well, that's a stretch."

"Yeah, ain't it though. These people are either very bold or extremely dumb. They've messed up each time they've tried to get at Julia," Adam said, slinging down in the chair across from Eric's desk. "I don't get it."

Eric read over the report. "I think I do. Someone keeps sending underlings to do their dirty work. And so far, they've botched things. And that's got me worried."

"Because?"

"Because sooner or later these people are going to send in a big gun. I just wonder who that will be and how they'll plan to strike."

"We can beef up security around Julia and Moria," Adam said. "I can sleep on the couch on the sunporch at Cat's house."

"I've already offered to do that," Eric replied. "But we could both stay at the house and take shifts. Might make it easier."

"I'm in," Adam said, his dark eyes full of woe. "I mean, this involves Cat, too, now."

"Yeah, especially since Julia has no choice but to live with Cat from now on—or at least until she can find another place."

"When it's safe again," Adam replied.

"Yeah. When it's safe again."

Eric wondered when that time would come. He was even more worried about Julia and Moria now, but not just for safety's sake. This fire had really done a number on Julia. She was quiet at the moment, resigned and watchful, her eyes dark with fatigue. He didn't see how she could continue on with this kind of stress in her life.

Watching her this morning as they'd walked through the ruins of the cottage, he knew she was near the breaking point. It would be just like her to up and leave during the night, simply because she thought she had to put everyone else ahead of herself. And to protect Moria. But leaving wouldn't protect either one of them. It would only put them both in more danger.

"Look," he said, getting up to come around the desk. "I'm taking Julia and Moria to church tonight, to the social supper that kicks off the Wildflower Festival. Maybe that'll at least cheer them up." And give him one more excuse to keep them near. He shrugged, rubbed a hand on the back of his neck. "The house is gone. And we've searched through the rubble. Not much else to do but get the lot cleared. At least Julia had some things stored in Cat's attic."

"Did she agree to go to the kickoff dinner with you?"

Eric slanted his head. "Not at first. I had to do some persuading. She's afraid to leave the house."

"Can you blame her?"

"No, but…we've got a lot of manpower on this now. She's covered from every angle. So…I'm taking her out to get her mind off all of this."

Adam lifted out of his chair. "Yeah, I asked Cat to go with me."

That brought a smile to Eric's lips. "So…you finally took the first step, huh?"

"Yep," Adam said, his expression sheepish. "We had a long talk after the fire the other night. I mean, things like this kind of bring life into perspective."

"They sure do," Eric replied. "I'm liking you and Cat together. I think you'll be just fine."

Adam shrugged. "I hope so. She's as stubborn as a fence post, but she's also cute as a button." Then he turned serious. "Do you think I'm too young for her, Eric?"

Eric let out a long sigh. "Remember that quote by the famous baseball player. 'Age is mind over matter. If you don't mind, it don't matter.' I think that's between Cat and you."

"And God," Adam interjected. "I've sure done my share of praying about it." Then he grinned. "And I've done my share of thinking about Cat, too."

Eric had to smile himself. "Seems to be in the air around here. I can't stop worrying about Julia."

"Oh, you mean—thinking about her in terms that go beyond this case, right?"

"Right," Eric replied. "But I'm not holding out much hope. Julia is in a bad place right now. She doesn't trust anyone, she's still torn up about her husband's death and she's afraid her daughter is holding some sort of information about the murder. Not to mention, of course, that someone seems to be intent on doing them both in."

"No room in there for you, right?"

"No room at all. And I can't really blame her," Eric said. "But…I'm not gonna give up. I like the woman."

"Same here with Cat," Adam admitted. "I think I've been half in love with her for years now." He tapped his hand against a table. "Just watching her at Nathan's funeral—my heart went out to her. I kind of decided right then and there I'd watch after her."

"That's mighty nice of you," Eric said, slapping Adam on the back. "But in case you haven't noticed, Cat is a pretty independent woman. She can take care of herself."

Adam followed him out into the hallway. "Yeah, and that's the biggest problem between us. She doesn't necessarily take me very seriously."

"You'll just have to keep at her."

"I intend to," Adam said. "Same with you and Julia."

"Yeah, right. We can compare notes later, see how that's working for us."

"Good idea," Adam said. "And in the meantime, I'm gonna stay real close to all of them."

"I'll be right there with you," Eric said, his pledge to protect Julia turning to a prayer for help from above. "Me, too."

"I don't feel like going."

Julia looked down at her daughter, her heart breaking all over again. Moria had been through so much loss and pain that she was afraid she was going to lose the child forever. She didn't feel like getting out, either, but Eric had convinced her it might be good for both of them. And Cat had chimed in, saying she wouldn't go to the festival kickoff without them. So now Julia had to convince herself and her daughter. "But…you love going to church. And you know all of your friends will be there. Plus, Mr. Harlan and Eric, too. Even the Ulmers and Fred."

Moria plopped down on her bed, her dark gaze moving over the purple and white swags hanging across the big bay window. "I miss my room at our house. I want my yellow roses back."

Julia sat down on the bed, then ran a hand over Moria's curly hair. "I want all of my things, too, honey. But the fire took everything except some of my dishes and other things we stored here. Did you check the box of goodies Mrs. Ulmer brought over?

She went out and bought you a whole set of new books and toys."

Moria bobbed her head. "That was nice of her. I love Miss Nina."

"I love her, too," Julia said, amazed at how gracious everyone had been to them. In a matter of hours, they'd had clothes to wear and all the necessities they'd need to get them through the next few weeks. She was thankful for all of it, but she didn't know how to explain to her daughter that their lives had once again been disrupted. And she didn't know how to convey any hope to Moria.

Glancing around, she spotted Rosa sitting on the dresser. "At least you still have Rosa with you."

Moria got up and grabbed the doll. "Rosa was so scared of that fire."

"I was scared of it, too," Julia admitted. "But we're okay. Aunt Cat loves us and we can live here as long as we need to."

"I like it here, but I miss my bedroom."

"I'm glad you like it. And one day, we'll get back to having our own place."

Julia watched as Moria touched a hand to her other favorite possession. "And you do have the flower that Daddy gave you. I'm so glad you thought to bring that over here with us when we came to stay with Cat."

"I had to," Moria replied. "I promised Daddy. He called it a Texas rose."

Julia's heart burned with that reminder. "Your daddy loved his roses, didn't he?"

"He told me this one would never die, ever," Moria said. "He told me to take care of it and love it, even if it was just silk."

"Daddy wanted you to have beautiful things," Julia said, her frazzled mind too tired to conjure up bitter memories right now. "And he'd want you to have a good time at church tonight. So…will you go with me?"

"I guess," Moria said, her fingers touching the big silk petals of the flower sitting in its sturdy white vase on the vanity table.

Julia watched as Moria ran her fingers over and over the silky yellow material. "How about we plant a yellow rose in Aunt Cat's backyard, as a way to thank her for being so generous to us? And as a way to remember Daddy?"

"Can we?" Moria asked, suddenly excited again. "I know how. Daddy taught me. He said you have to make sure the roots are just right."

"Good, then," Julia said, getting up to straighten her floral dress. "But right now we need to go downstairs and wait for Mr. Eric to pick us up, okay?"

Moria bounced ahead of her, her mood changing from morose to happy again in typical childlike fashion. But Julia had to wonder if her daughter would ever be a typical child.

Help me, God, she prayed. *I need You to protect my child. I don't know who's out there, or why they want to harm me. But Moria is innocent. Please watch over her.*

She reached out to touch the artificial flower Moria so loved. Her daughter had a way of becoming too attached to things. They'd lugged a whole box of stuff over here before the fire, but now Julia was glad they had. At least Moria had those special things to comfort her. Julia thought about one of her own favorite things—her tea set collection. She'd almost sold it off when they moved, but for some reason she couldn't bear to part with all the dainty teacups and matching pots she'd bought here and there through the years. Maybe because Alfonso always bought her special additions to the collection on her birthday each year. She'd planned on building some shelves in the cottage to display them. But what would happen to her collection now that they didn't have a home of their own? she wondered.

And what would happen if Julia kept spending time with Eric? Would it be the same with him? Would Moria become too attached? Julia didn't want to move too fast, but Eric was a constant, steadying presence in their lives these days. This situation had forced them together. But she had to wonder if in the end, it might also tear them apart. Julia didn't want to become too attached, either.

"I need to go to church," she told herself. "I need to find some sort of peace."

But that wouldn't be easy right now. Because she

felt the same as Moria. She wanted her life back. One way or another.

She went downstairs to find Moria and Cat, then heard them out on the big front porch. Glancing through the window, she saw them sitting together in the swing.

Then her cell phone rang inside her purse.

"Hello," she said, watching Cat and Moria as they petted the big neighborhood cat everyone called Prissy.

"Julia, is that you?"

"Mrs. Endicott?"

"Yes, it's me. I'm worried about you. You haven't called me in a while."

Surprised that her mother-in-law was calling out of the blue, Julia stepped away from the open front door. "How are you, Regina?"

"I'm just fine. How's Moria?"

"She's okay. We're…we're doing all right."

"Are you sure? You know I miss both of you so much. I've just had a bad feeling."

Julia didn't know whether she should tell Regina anything about what was going on or not. If she told Alfonso's overprotective mother that they were in serious trouble and fearing for their lives, Regina would certainly fret and worry. But she couldn't keep everything from her. Moria might accidentally let something slip.

"We…did have a scare a couple of nights ago."

"What happened?"

Imagining the petite woman clutching a hand to her chest, Julia took a deep breath. "Our house caught on fire."

"Oh, no. How awful. Are you sure you're okay?"

"Yes…we're fine. We're staying with Cat." That much was true, at least.

"You're blessed to have her right there, and with that big, rambling house, too."

"Yes, we certainly are. So, don't worry. We're going to stay with her until we decide what to do."

"I see. So…indefinitely, then?"

"Uh, yes, just until we can figure something out." Julia had never felt comfortable around Regina Endicott, but she knew Regina loved Moria. "Cat and I are close, and Moria loves her."

"You'll take good care of my granddaughter, won't you?"

"Of course," Julia answered. "So…how are you doing?"

"I have my moments," Regina replied. "I miss my son."

"I miss him, too," Julia said. "It's hard."

"Yes, very hard. A mother's love is so strong."

"Would you like to speak to Moria?"

"Could I?"

Julia went to the front door. "Moria, it's Abuela Regina. Talk to her for a minute before we go to church, okay?"

Moria's eyes lit up as she rushed to take the phone. After she went into an animated discussion about the fire and her new toys, Julia turned to Cat. "Now why would Regina call us?"

Cat shrugged. "She's a grandmother. They call all the time."

"Not this one. We haven't heard from her in months."

"Maybe she's been busy."

"Yeah, maybe."

Julia stared at her daughter, hoping Moria wouldn't give Regina too much information. The last thing Julia needed right now was an overbearing mother-in-law asking her all sorts of questions.

Especially one who'd never approved of her to begin with.

TEN

A quartet was singing an old-fashioned gospel hymn underneath a great live oak while church members and guests strolled around the church grounds. It was a warm night, balmy with a nice breeze, the buzz of mosquitoes humming in the air. The smells of honeysuckle and jasmine mingled with the scent of roasting chicken and sizzling hamburgers.

Julia took a deep breath, embracing the peace that washed over her each time she came to this old church near the lake just on the edge of town. She loved the white clapboard chapel with the tiny steeple over its big oak double doors. Everyone here tonight was in a festive mood.

She wanted to feel the same, in spite of all the worries crowding her mind. But her conversation with Regina had left her feeling alone and guilty. Maybe she should try to visit Alfonso's mother sometime soon, so Moria could see her grandmother at least. And…Julia told herself, she needed to make peace with her own parents. If nothing else, she'd learned that time here on earth was very precious and fragile. And so were the people you loved while you were here.

But right now she forced herself to enjoy this nice spring night. Still in shock over the fire and the report that it had been deliberately set, she wondered how she was supposed to pretend everything would be okay. Eric had convinced her that coming here tonight would help put aside any rumors that might be circulating about the fire. But this was a tight-knit community and the front-page story in the *Wildflower Gazette* had only added to all the questions and suspicions surrounding her, especially since the headline had read Waitress Involved in Café Robbery Loses Her House to Mysterious Fire. People already thought she'd only brought trouble to this little town. How could she defend herself against the obvious?

Determined to put on a good front for Moria's sake, she asked God to grant her a reprieve against all that had happened to her lately.

"You look pretty," Eric said as he handed her a cup of lemonade.

Julia smiled. "I was actually working on having a moment."

"Want me to leave you alone so you can keep working on it?"

She glanced over at his hopeful expression, something sweet and newborn clutching inside her heart, some strange emotion that made her want to fight for this man. "No, you can be a part of it. Just let me stand here for a minute and pretend that my life isn't falling apart."

She closed her eyes again, imagining his clean-shaven face and his dark, somber eyes. She could smell the sandalwood of his aftershave mixing with the clean scent of his fresh-washed shirt. "I'm thinking that this is a normal night, and we're here to enjoy the kickoff of the Wildflower Festival this weekend. You and I have a date. We'll take a long drive along the wildflower trail, and we'll stop just at dusk to take a stroll through the daisies and red clover. Then we'll sit down on a bench and enjoy the Indian paintbrush and the bluebonnets. You might even kiss me—"

She stopped, opened her eyes, gasping as heat seared up her neck and onto her face. "I'm so sorry."

Eric was watching her with that same warm heat in his eyes. "Sorry for what?" he said, his voice low and gravelly. "I was enjoying that story, a lot. Especially the part where I kiss you."

Julia gulped down her lemonade. "I shouldn't have said all of that out loud."

He leaned close. "And why not? I mean, if you were thinking it—"

She tossed her empty cup into a nearby trash can. "That's just it. I shouldn't even be thinking such things. I shouldn't even be here, trying to celebrate anything. I might be putting everyone here in danger, right along with myself. My house burned to the ground. Someone is after me for a reason I don't even understand. And yet, here I stand, dreaming about a life I'll never be able to have."

"First of all," he replied, lifting a hand in the air, "we've got deputies walking the entire perimeter of the church grounds, and second of all, why can't you have that life you just described? Why can't *we* have that life?"

She glanced around, careful to keep Moria in her sights. Seeing that her daughter was at the Go Fishing kiddie booth with Adam and Harlan, she looked back at Eric. "You know why. I can't dream beyond the nightmares I've been having since this all started up. Eric, I'm so grateful that you want to help, but I still think the best thing I can do is leave Wildflower...for good."

He held a hand on her arm. "And let them come after you? I don't think so. If you just try to trust me and listen to me, I think we can end this. Sooner or later, they're going to slip up and we'll figure it out."

"But what if it doesn't work out that way? What if something happens to Moria? Am I a target, or are you just using me for bait?"

"Yes, you are a target," he said, his tone as heated as the brisket roasting on the big grill up near the church. "But we're *trying* to keep you out of danger, not set you up as bait."

"I don't like my daughter being so exposed. We should be in hiding somewhere, not out here walking around in the open."

"I won't let anything happen to Moria," he said.

"Julia, we've been watching Cat's house around the clock, and even the sheriff is in on this now. Anybody would be crazy to try something in a crowd such as this. You have to let us do our jobs. We all believe you."

She shook her head. "I don't know—I've gone back over everything in my mind. None of it makes any sense. I've even tried to do research on my own. I've checked the De La Noche website, tried to remember if I stored any of Alfonso's files anywhere, but I can't find anything to help us."

Eric put his hands on her shoulders. "Don't go snooping too much. That could only lead to more trouble."

"Right, so I'm just supposed to sit around, while everyone here tries to protect me. That's not how I operate, Eric. I'll go mad. I just don't know what to do next."

"Well, I do," he said, motioning toward Cat. "C'mon, we're going to take that stroll through the wildflowers so I can convince you that you're safe doing nothing right here with me."

Before Julia could protest, he dragged her past Cat. "Stay with Moria. We're going for a walk."

"Yes, sir," Cat said with a big grin, saluting him.

Julia took a look at her daughter, then followed Eric toward the water's edge. "I don't want to go far."

"We'll be right here," Eric said. "Just try to relax."

She glanced back toward the crowd, making sure she didn't see any strangers. "It's hard, looking over my shoulder all the time. I don't think I've really relaxed since Alfonso was killed."

"Who could blame you?" he said, taking her hand in his. "But we're going to work on that. We're still waiting to see what the authorities in San Antonio find out about Tolar. He has to have some sort of connection to De La Noche, but your friend Luke Roderick isn't cooperating."

She turned to look up at him. "Why are you doing this for me, Eric?"

He looked surprised. "You know why…."

"Yes, you keep saying it's your job. But…you have to admit this is going beyond the call of duty."

"You're a citizen of this county and our town, Julia. And you've been threatened. We have to protect you." He leaned toward her, his dark eyes luminous. "And…I told you, I like you."

She couldn't stop her smile. "You've said that a couple of times."

"Then why don't you believe me?"

She wandered to a bench near the water, then sat down. The wind played through the tall cypress trees, causing their branches to do a lazy dance over the lake. Down in the shallows, two egrets strolled gracefully through the water lilies.

Waiting for Eric to sit down next to her, she said, "I do believe you. I just don't want you to think there can be much more than friendship between us."

He shook his head. "Even though you were just daydreaming about kissing me."

"That was a silly dream."

"I don't think it's silly."

Julia didn't know how to tell him everything in her heart. She'd married Alfonso because she loved him. They'd had a beautiful daughter together, but there had been so much left unsettled between them at the time of his death. She wasn't sure she could ever make that kind of intimate commitment again. But when she looked at Eric and saw the goodness there inside his eyes, she wanted to hold out hope that maybe God had brought them together for a reason.

"You're fighting against something besides me, aren't you?" Eric asked.

Julia swallowed back her fear, tentatively reaching toward that trust he hoped to gain. "When Alfonso died, the police...at first, they thought I was a suspect. They found out we'd been going through a very rough time in our marriage."

He lifted his chin a notch. "I see."

"No, you don't see," she said, wondering how to explain, wondering just how much he already knew. "Alfonso was dedicated to his work. He wanted the American dream and he worked hard to get it. His parents weren't very wealthy, but his father was a truck driver for the De La Noche company, so the company helped to give Alfonso a good education. He tried to repay them in every way. Then his father died. After that, Alfonso became depressed and moody. I believe something about work was bothering him, but he refused to talk to me about it. He would pace the floor at night, and he'd leave the house without even kissing me goodbye. Moria was the only light in his life. He loved her so much. Before, when I told you everything, I left that part out. I was ashamed to admit my marriage was failing."

"What happened between you two?"

"We fought a lot. All the time." She looked out at the ducks moving across the lake. "People talked. The rumor was that he was having an affair, and I was jealous. But it wasn't an affair. He was too involved in his job, and in spite of how he treated me before he died, he was an honorable man. Alfonso wouldn't have done that to me."

"But you don't know what was wrong?"

"No. And, honestly, I can't believe anyone within the company would have been doing anything illegal. The family was as honorable as my husband. They still are. They all seemed very distraught when Mr. Endicott passed away and when Alfonso was killed. And to their credit, they stood by me, even when the police doubted me."

"We have to keep digging," he said. "Maybe we're looking at the obvious here. We think it's the family because they've got the power to come after you, and they might have something to hide, but maybe we should focus on someone just outside the family."

Julia looked over at him as a quiet settled between them. "You didn't ask me. You've never once asked me."

"Ask you what?"

"If I killed my husband."

He gave her a smile, but his eyes held disbelief. "Are you trying to tell me something?"

"You're a lawman. You have to wonder. When you first came to see me, to question me about the robbery, I could see it there in your eyes. You didn't quite trust me. Is this why? Did you already know the truth? That I was a suspect in my husband's murder?"

He got up, putting his hands in the pockets of his jeans. "Julia, I know you didn't kill your husband. Is that why you were so afraid to tell me the truth? Did the police back in San Antonio harass you to the point that you can't even trust me?"

"They didn't make my life easy," she replied. "They questioned me over and over. I'm surprised you haven't seen the official reports."

"They don't really want to release all the information to us," he said. "They gave us a very generalized overview and told us that you'd been cleared, but the case was unsolved. They'd chalked it up as a cold case."

"My husband is cold in his grave," she said, the bitterness and helplessness getting the best of her. "That's all I know."

"That and the fact that someone might want you to wind up the same way," he added. "You didn't kill Alfonso, so you can relax if you're worried I might actually think that." Then he turned to stare down at her. "And if you think I'd believe something like that, then you don't know me."

Seeing the anger rising in his eyes, she stood. "I just wanted to tell you that, just in case."

"Just in case it might push me away from you? Is that what you wanted? You thought I'd be disgusted by that information, disgusted enough to…not care?"

Shocked that he'd even think such a thing, she backed away. "You've been asking me to open up to you, to be honest And the one time I put everything on the line and tell you about one of the worst times of my life, you get angry at me for doing it? Eric, what do you want from me?"

When he didn't answer right away, she turned to go back toward the church. "I have to find Moria."

She heard him stalking after her. "Julia, wait."

But she couldn't face him. She was afraid she'd blurt out the one truth that still haunted her day and night each time she thought about the horrible turn her life had taken.

Had she somehow caused Alfonso's death?

Eric watched the dwindling crowd. Everyone was full of grilled meat, fried catfish and homemade pie and cake. Darkness had fallen over the churchyard and it was time to go home. Glancing around, he searched for Julia and Cat, then saw them sitting at a picnic table with Adam. Moria was playing with some other kids nearby, Harlan right near her.

Feeling sheepish and embarrassed, Eric marched

toward them, hoping to salvage the rest of the evening with Julia.

She looked up as he drew near, her eyes full of hurt and sadness. "We were about to leave," she said, glancing toward Cat. "Right, Cat?"

"Uh, yes, right." Cat gave Eric a pointed look. "Unless you want Eric to drive you home."

"No, I don't," Julia said. "And you know something else? I really don't want Eric to stand guard over us tonight. Or you either, Adam. I'm tired of all of this. I want my life back. I'm tired of questioning my own sanity."

Cat lifted her gaze toward Eric, then back to Adam. "Julia, it might not be safe yet."

"It might not ever be safe," Julia retorted. "But I can't expect these two to just move in with us, now, can I?"

Adam grimaced. "What exactly did you two talk about on that long walk?"

Eric stared at Julia. "Not much. We went over the case again. Same old stuff."

"Y'all were supposed to take a night off," Cat said, glaring at him. "Obviously that didn't go over real well."

Adam pushed away from the bench. "Look, people, this is tough on all of us. But we're a team, here—the four of us. We can't fall apart at the seams now."

Julia started tossing their paper plates in the trash. "We can if Eric thinks every time I turn around I'm trying to distance myself from him." Then she wiped her hands together. "But how could I possibly do that when he won't let me out of his sight? I've gone over all the details as I remember them, but we can't seem to figure out who's after me, can we? We have no leads, we have no clues and we can't find a connection between my old life and the new one I thought I had. I can't make Eric see that I need some space… and maybe that means I need to get out of Wildflower."

Cat motioned to Adam. "Let's go get Moria. She's with the preacher and Harlan."

"Right." Adam finished clearing the table, then the two of them scurried away.

"I sure know how to break up a party," Eric said, leaning down, his knuckles pressed against the aged wood of the table. Then he focused on Julia. "I'm sorry, all right?"

She put her head in her hands, then took a long breath. "No, I'm the one who should be sorry. I had no right to get so upset with you. I know you're trying your best to help me."

"Yes, I am. And I haven't been completely honest with you, either."

She frowned. "Well, I think it's time we just get it all on the table between us."

"Good idea." He sat down across from her. "You asked me if I'd ever had anyone special in my life. Well, I did, my last year of college. I knew I was coming back here to be a sheriff's deputy and I had this girl in mind to be my wife. But she was torn between another man and me. And she wasn't so sure she wanted the small-town kind of life." He closed his eyes, remembering her beautiful face. "She picked the other man, and he abused her even before they got married. But she refused to leave him. She called me one night, crying, and I went to help her. But it was too late. She died because no one would believe the man she loved could do such things." He lowered his head, his voice going low. "Not even me. I didn't believe her."

Julia's expression only mirrored what he felt in his heart, shock and disgust. "But you said you tried to help—"

"I did, that night. But if I'd listened sooner, if I'd tried to reason with her to let me help, she might still be alive." He sat down beside her. "So if I seem overbearing and determined, well, that's why. That's the reason I'm a bulldog at my job. I don't want to ever feel that way again, or to go through that kind of pain again. And that means I'm going to do my best to make sure something like that doesn't happen to you. Got it?"

The color had drained from her face. "Eric, I'm sorry. You should have told me this from the beginning."

"Yeah, well, you should have leveled with me from the beginning, too. But you didn't. Now we're even. But I had no right to imply that you were deliberately trying to turn me away. I understand that you're scared." He knew he had to be honest with her or she'd bolt like a doe. "And, Julia, I learned from talking to the authorities in San Antonio that you were on the suspect list for your husband's death. Apparently, you were the only suspect for a while there. I should have told you that I already knew. But I don't think that's why you're pushing me away."

She held a hand against her chin. "I wasn't deliberately trying to push you away, honestly. It's just that…I was so ashamed that the police would even think such a horrible thing about me, that I'd even be considered a suspect in my husband's murder. I didn't know how to tell you that. I was afraid you would think it was true, or that the police would gladly tell you that just to harass me a little more."

"Because you tried so hard not to tell me anything to begin with, right?"

"Right. I was honestly surprised you hadn't already found out the truth. I thought maybe you knew and you were just testing me." Then she gave him a direct look. "Were you testing me?"

"I'm not like that, Julia. I wouldn't hold back. I'd want to question you on something like that if I really believed you were capable of doing such a thing. But I don't believe that for a minute. I've seen you with Moria, I've heard you talking about your husband. I know the truth."

She kept her gaze steady on him. "So you weren't suspicious about me? Not even a little bit?"

He had promised her honesty, so now he gave it

to her. "At first, yeah. It just didn't add up. But now that I'm slowly getting to the truth, I can see why you'd want to hold back on talking to anyone about this. Especially a deputy sheriff. You don't trust the cops, so why should you trust me?"

She touched a hand to his, the warmth of her slender fingers surging throughout his system. "I do trust you." Then she stood up. "But you have no idea how hard it was for me to admit that."

He took her hand, seeking the connection for just a while longer. "Oh, yes, I do. You said you saw my doubts there in my eyes, remember? Well, I saw something there in you that day Tolar held you at gunpoint. You looked at me, Julia, and I could see all the fear right there in your eyes and it reminded me of all my own shortcomings. But I also saw something else."

Right now he watched as tears formed in those same eyes. "What?" she asked, her tone a whisper.

"You trusted me that day. You wanted to live to be with your little girl, and you turned to me to help you. So, trust me now to make that happen, okay?"

She didn't speak. Instead she stood there looking up at him, a kind of awe shining through her tears. "I'm trying," she said. "And I'm really sorry you lost the woman you loved. But saving me can't bring her back, Eric."

Then she pulled away and rushed toward her daughter. Eric's heart bumped against his ribs as he remembered the agony of knowing he'd failed once.

But Julia was wrong about one thing. He didn't intend to lose the woman he loved. He wanted her to look at him and know that she could always trust him—this woman who'd come here to find hope again.

Julia was the woman he loved now.

And still he wondered if she'd ever trust him enough to tell him all the secrets of her heart.

ELEVEN

The next morning, Eric's cell phone rang just as he was about to leave the cabin. Answering it as he stepped outside, he saw his daddy walking out to get the paper they both shared.

"Butler," he said into the phone.

The call was from his contact in San Antonio, and after Eric listened to the man's short, concise report, he had no doubt that someone from that city was definitely after Julia Daniels. Turning as Harlan strolled over, he shook his head. "It's like we thought, Pop."

Harlan unfurled the paper, then asked, "How's that?"

"Tolar. He once worked for the De La Noche company."

"You don't say?" Harlan nodded toward his house. "You got a minute or do you need to go?"

"I can take time for another cup of coffee, I reckon."

He followed Harlan back to the tiny porch overlooking the lake. A pot of fresh-brewed coffee sat in an old percolator on the table. Harlan poured two cups, used to this morning ritual before Eric headed off to work.

"So…Tolar was connected with the Gardonez family, after all?"

"It looks that way. My source said he worked for them about two years ago. That means he was there right before Alfonso Endicott got killed."

"Think Tolar did the deed?"

Eric ran a hand down his face. "It sure looks that way, but the authorities didn't make the connection during the initial investigation. There's no proof. But why would a low-life like Mingo Tolar kill a high-up executive? I mean, you'd think robbery, but nothing was taken that night. At least, nothing obvious."

Harlan swigged his coffee, then set his favorite fishing mug down on the cedar table. "Then you need to look for the not so obvious."

"That's what I told Julia the other night. The family is too obvious and too exposed to pull off something like this. I've even tried to pin it on the son-in-law, Luke Roderick, but so far the main man comes up clear as a whistle." He looked out over the dark, calm waters of the lake. "So let's say it was Tolar. Maybe he hoped to rob Endicott and it went wrong."

"Could be. If he was an underling and he needed drug money, I wouldn't put it past him to try something real stupid, same way he tried to take Julia hostage right in front of everyone in that diner."

"The man didn't seem very rational, but not even an idiot like Mingo Tolar would have the nerve to walk into a highly secure, wired building to rob one of its top executives. Unless, like you say, he wasn't there specifically for money."

Harlan lifted his bushy eyebrows. "Bingo. There must have been something else in that accountant's office. Something someone didn't want the world to see." He took another drink of coffee. "Or…maybe somebody sent Tolar to do the job and things went wrong somehow."

Eric thought about that. "That fits with our theory that someone else sent him here. And if that same someone sent him that night, but Tolar failed to get what he went after, then that also fits our theory that they now think Julia has the information—maybe an incriminating file or some sort of bank statement that would expose the company as corrupt?"

"That would make sense," Harlan replied. "But I don't think Tolar would have the sense to know something like that if he saw it."

Eric finished his coffee. "Which means we're right and that someone who is smart is behind all of this."

"There's your connection," Harlan said. "Now all you need to figure out is what he was after that night and who sent him."

Eric nodded. "And where is that information now?"

He had a bad feeling that these thugs thought Julia

had that information. Or worse, that her little girl had something they needed to find.

"I'd better get into town and pass this on to the sheriff," he said. "Thanks for the coffee, Daddy."

Harlan lifted his cup in salute. "Hey, Eric?"

Eric turned on the steps. "Yessir?"

"How are things between you and the waitress?"

"She has a name, remember. It's Julia."

"I know the woman's name. Just tell me what was going on last night at the church."

His daddy never missed a thing, which had made it hard for Eric to ever lie to his parents growing up. "We had a fight."

"That much was clear."

Wishing this town wasn't so nosy and busy-bodied, Eric shrugged. "We talked it out. This case has all of us nervous. Julia is feeling the brunt of this. She's been held at gunpoint, lost her house to an arsonist and she's trying to stay sane. It's enough stress to cause anyone to lash out."

"And she lashed out at you?"

"Yes, but only because she's afraid to trust me. The police gave her a hard time after her husband's death."

"Because they went after her?"

"Yeah, they immediately looked toward the surviving spouse. There was trouble in the marriage."

Harlan nodded. "Just be careful, son."

"I'm a big boy, Daddy. I can handle this case."

"I'm not talking about the case. I'm talking about you."

"I know what you're talking about. I'll be just fine."

Harlan looked skeptical. "Then get on with it."

Eric waved a hand. "Try not to catch too many fish."

"Try to catch at least one criminal," Harlan hollered back, used to the teasing.

It was an unspoken rule between him and his father. They didn't talk about the one woman Eric hadn't been able to save. The one woman he'd loved a lot and still grieved for.

But that had happened a very long time ago, and just as Julia was reluctant to discuss her past and her marriage, Eric didn't like to talk about the college sweetheart who'd died in his arms one spring night so long ago. Not even Cat or Adam knew that particular story.

But he'd told Julia last night. Not the awful details, but enough to help her see that he couldn't let that happen again. Not to someone he cared about.

Cranking his truck, he sat for a minute with the motor idling, thinking about what had driven him to follow in his father's footsteps. He'd failed at his job once when he was young and inexperienced, but this time things would be different. This time he was older and wiser and he was an officer of the law, not just a kid hoping to become one.

This time he was determined to help Julia and her

daughter stay alive. Because he wanted them both in his life for a very long time.

"So we've determined that Tolar was indeed connected to the Gardonez family," Eric told Julia later that day at Cat's house.

Now that he was back at work, he couldn't use the excuse of bringing her out to the lake each day to protect her. And next week, Moria would have to go back to school. Which meant their time was running out, since the sheriff wasn't too keen on sending an extra man to the school to watch over the little girl.

"I can't believe it," Julia said as she sank down on the back steps of Cat's house. "This means he was sent here for a reason, just as we thought. And that reason had to be that he wanted to take me, to kidnap me. But why? I don't know anything."

Eric took her hand, rubbing his fingers over her knuckles. They were here alone since Adam and Cat had taken Moria to the café with them earlier. The kid was never alone, and that at least was a blessing.

"We think maybe your husband knew something, though. Since whoever killed him didn't take anything, we believe they must have been sent to find one specific thing—a file, or a computer disc of some sort. Something that would contain evidence or incriminating information, maybe. Can you think of anything like that—something your husband would feel the need to protect with his life?"

She blinked, shook her head. "I can't imagine.

Alfonso handled a lot of things for the company. Even though he was listed as head of the accounting department, he did more than just watch over the books. The family trusted him with their most-guarded secrets, everything from food distribution and production to new product placement."

Eric zoomed in on that. "Could there have been some sort of product that the Gardonez family didn't want made public?"

"How would I know?" she snapped, waving her hand in the air. "My husband never talked to me about his work."

Eric let her stew while his mind whirled. "Maybe because he didn't want to put you in harm's way?"

"Oh, so that explains why he insisted our daughter go with him to the office the night he died? None of this makes sense. He wouldn't have put either of us in danger."

"Are you sure?"

She got up, stomped a few feet away to pace in the yard. "I don't know. Alfonso was cold and distant in the months before he died, so, yes, I believe he was hiding something. And I also believe he didn't do it to protect me, more like because he didn't have any choice." She let out a sigh, chased a buzzing mosquito away from her ear. "He was very loyal to the company."

"Maybe too loyal," Eric said. "He took his secrets to the grave." He got up to stop her, putting his hands on her arms. "Someone is trying to silence you, too, Julia."

"Tell me something I don't know," she said, her tone full of anger and irritation. "It's just that I don't have any more secrets. I've told you everything I can remember."

Eric steadied her, watching as her expression changed from angry to frightened. "But, Eric… Moria *can't* remember. Moria might know exactly what they're trying to find, only she can't remember. Or…she's afraid to tell anyone, even me." She gasped, putting her hands to her mouth. "It's my worst nightmare, what I was so afraid of all along. They aren't targeting me—they want my daughter."

When he didn't try to deny it, she fell into his arms. "They want Moria. And that day, when Tolar kept saying he had to take me —"

"He was probably going to use you to get to Moria," Eric finished, a burning sensation tearing through his gut. "They think she knows something. They don't know either way whether she can remember anything or not. But they're trying to find out. And if she's hiding something…they'll try to look for it or destroy it."

"The fire," she said, her skin going pale. "Oh, Eric."

"The fire and the way they ransacked your house. They won't give up." He held her closer. "We have to prove the connection between Tolar and De La Noche."

"Oh, I think I'm going to be sick—" She pulled away from him and rushed into the house.

Eric heard the slamming of a door as he followed her inside the cool, spacious house. He heard her in the downstairs powder room, sobbing and retching. When she came out, he was ready with a clean wash towel and a glass of water.

He motioned toward a kitchen chair. "Sit here." Then he handed her the water. After she took a sip, he wiped her face then handed her the cloth.

She took another drink, her face pale, her eyes swollen from crying. "I want my child here with me." She grabbed his hand. "Eric, call Cat to bring Moria home, please."

"I will," he said, trying to reassure her. "I will."

Holding her with one hand, he punched numbers in his cell to reach Adam. "Bring Moria to Cat's house right now. Her mother is worried." Then he turned away and whispered, "And so am I."

The little group sitting in the comfortable den at the back of the big house was quiet. The mood was somber. Julia couldn't speak, couldn't think past the fact that someone would want to harm an innocent child. But why?

"Do you want some soup?" Cat asked, her voice low and grainy. She'd been just as shocked as Julia after Eric had explained his theory to her and Adam. Even though they'd all suspected this, hearing it with all the circumstantial evidence to back it up made it jarringly real.

"I'm not hungry," Julia replied, her hands together in her lap. She felt so cold, so tired. "It was always there, this fear that they might be after Moria, but now that we're getting closer to the truth, it's so real."

"Why don't you go on to bed?" Eric said, giving her a steady look.

"I can't sleep."

He gave Adam a knowing nod. "I think we should take a little trip to San Antonio, maybe shake up the boys down there."

"Do you think they'll cooperate?" Adam asked, glancing from Cat to Julia.

"Only one way to find out," Eric replied. "I'll talk to Sheriff Whitston first thing in the morning. At least we can go over the files there—see if anything sticks out. Maybe talk to someone in the De La Noche building."

Julia rubbed her hands down her arms. "They won't talk. They didn't want any publicity when Alfonso was murdered. Why would they want to drag it all back out now?"

"They will if we get a warrant to search their records," Adam said.

"Well, now we're at least taking action," Cat said, getting up to stalk around the big, airy room. "I can't stand this sitting around doing nothing. When do we leave?"

"You two aren't going anywhere," Eric said, his eyes on Julia. "Especially not to San Antonio."

Cat made a face. "I probably shouldn't leave the café anyway. Not with all of this going on."

Julia pinned Eric with a pleading look. "Will you assign someone else to watch out for Moria?"

Adam shook his head. "Let me go to San Antonio. I'll take another deputy with me. We'll find out what we need to know. That way, you can stay here and watch out for Moria."

Eric looked torn. Julia prayed he'd stay without her having to beg. For Moria. Julia might not trust the man with her heart yet, but she did trust him to protect her daughter. Him and no one else right now.

His gaze held hers much in the same way he'd looked at her the day of the robbery. Finally he nodded. "Okay. I'll clear it with the sheriff. You go and I'll stay."

Julia let out the breath she'd been holding. "Thank you, Eric."

Cat motioned to Adam. "Let's go check on Moria. Then I'm turning in. I'm so tired I can't see straight."

Adam followed her. "I guess I get to spend the night out on the sleeping porch again, right?"

"Right," Cat replied. "You're not scared of mosquitoes, are you now?"

"Only the really big ones," he retorted. "I just hope the neighbors don't get the wrong idea about all of this."

"That's why I have the big fence," Cat retorted as

they headed up to Moria's room. "Besides, thanks to that nosy Mickey Jameson, everybody in town knows y'all are guarding my house. And since he gave out some of the details, the neighbors know Julia and Moria are in some kind of danger."

"They're speculating about me being in trouble," Julia said after the others had left the room. "I still think the best thing I can do is get out of here, go somewhere no one knows me."

Eric dropped his hands on his knees, then frowned. "They'd still find you. These kinds of people don't give up."

"Exactly what kind of people do you think we're dealing with?"

"The worst kind," he replied. "The kind who have something to hide."

In about two minutes Adam came back down the stairs. "Moria is out like a light. Sleeping away in that big frilly bed." He waved his own good-night, then headed to the back of the big house to the screened-in porch where Cat had a sleeper sofa made up for him and Eric to take turns resting. "Eric, wake me up around two and I'll relieve you." Then he whirled at the door. "Oh, and we've got a cruiser patrolling the street every thirty minutes."

"Got it," Eric said, waiting until Adam had closed the door off the side of the kitchen. Then he moved to sit on the couch with Julia. "Want to watch a movie?"

She wanted to fall into his arms and let him make her feel safe again. "No."

He tugged her hand into his. "We have a lead now and a plan, at least. We'll figure this out. We'll keep pounding away at it until we crack this thing. Somebody will remember something, or somebody will slip up. And then we'll nail 'em."

"I hope so."

As if he'd read her thoughts, he tugged her close, cradling her in his arms. "How 'bout we just sit here in the dark?"

"That would be nice."

He didn't speak again. He just held her there until her head was resting on his broad shoulder. Julia closed her eyes and pretended this was a typical springtime night, with mosquitoes buzzing and night birds rustling, a night where the world was sweet with fragrant flowers and the hope of a love so strong, nothing could break it.

That's the kind of love I can give you.

Julia thought she heard those words coming straight from the Lord to her. And for some reason, they gave her a tiny bit of peace and strength. As worried as she was about Moria's safety, knowing she had Eric and God both on her side gave her a measure of confidence. She couldn't run away; she had to stay and fight for her daughter.

She must have sighed or dozed, she didn't know which. But soon she was curled up against Eric's warm chest. She opened her eyes to find him looking down at her with eyes as dark and dangerous as the night. But she trusted those eyes. It seemed so natural to reach her hand up to touch his face. It seemed so natural to pull his head down to hers and kiss him.

And within that soft, gentle kiss, the world seemed far away and she felt safe and normal and...loved.

Until her daughter's screams coming from upstairs jarred Julia straight up out of Eric's arms and back into the cruel reality of her nightmares.

TWELVE

Julia rushed into Moria's room, followed by three people—all with guns drawn. Eric and Adam quickly did a scan of the tall windows, then checked the closets and the bathroom next door.

"Clear," Eric said. "Let's take a look around outside."

Adam nodded, then followed him out while Cat stood there with her gun aimed toward the ceiling.

"Put that away," Julia whispered as she hugged her daughter close. "It's okay, baby."

Moria sat straight up in bed, clinging to her doll, her eyes bright with tears. "Mommy!"

"I'm here, darling," Julia said as she pulled Moria into her arms again. "It's all right. We're all here."

Moria clung to her, her hands gripping Julia's shoulders. Julia could feel the tiny, erratic beats of her daughter's heart. Pulling Moria around so she wouldn't see Cat's pistol, she tried to soothe her. "Did you have a bad dream?"

"Uh-huh." Moria bobbed her head. "The mean

people were chasing me. They shouted at me. Grandma was crying. And you were trying to help me, Mommy."

Cat came to sit down beside them. "We won't let any mean people get in here, honey. I promise."

Julia wished she could be so sure. Moria had been doing fine until all of the harassment had started up. First thing tomorrow she would make an appointment so they could talk to the therapist in Longview again. Maybe Moria would open up more now. Or the little girl might retreat even further into her nightmares. But Julia knew she had to continue getting the proper help for her daughter.

She pulled back to smile at Moria. "I think we need to talk to that nice lady I took you to see before. The one who works in Longview. Remember when we went and talked to her after we moved here. Would you like to do that again?"

"I don't want to talk to anyone," Moria said, clinging to Rosa. "I don't like mean people."

"None of us do," Cat said, shaking her head. Thankfully, she'd placed the gun on the dresser. "But your mama wants to make you feel better. And sometimes that means you have to talk to another person, so that person can help you to remember things."

"Don't want to remember."

Julia sent Cat a look over Moria's shoulder. "It's okay, honey. We'll figure that out in the morning. Why don't you lie back down now and try to go back to sleep?"

"Can I have some juice first?"

Cat stood up. "I'll go down and get some right now."

Julia thanked her, then turned back to Moria. "What happened in your dream?"

Moria's eyes grew big again. "I was running inside Daddy's building. The way I used to run when he and I would play hide-and-seek."

Surprised, Julia pushed curly brown hair away from Moria's forehead. "You and Daddy played hide-and-seek at his office?"

"Uh-huh. Just like at home. Daddy let me hide things, then he'd try to find them."

Julia filed that information away, wondering what else she didn't know about her husband. Apparently, a lot. But right now, she wanted to see if Moria would tell her anything that could help them. "Why were you running in your dream?"

Moria rolled her eyes. "'Cause Daddy was telling me to run, run fast. I couldn't see Daddy, but I could hear them coming down the hall. I hid just like Daddy told me." She shrugged her tiny shoulders. "I tried to find you, Mommy."

Julia's heart stilled. Had her husband had some sort of practice drills with Moria, teaching her how to be safe? Or trying to help his daughter escape in case something bad happened to him?

"And where did you try to hide in your dream?"

"In the bathroom, like Daddy told me. He always said if I got scared to run to the bathroom and hide behind the sofa in there—he said to go to the women's lounge."

"I see. And in your dream, did Daddy give you his cell phone?"

Moria shook her head. "No, Mommy. He only did that in real life. That one time we were playing the game and then he never came back." She grabbed Rosa and hugged her close. "That's why I was scared in my dream. Daddy wasn't there."

"And neither was I," Julia said, a great surging hurt tearing through her body. "I'm sorry, honey. I'm so sorry I wasn't there when the bad people came to see Daddy."

Moria stared up at her with big, dark eyes. "I'm glad you weren't there, Mommy. Or else you might have gone away with Daddy and then I'd be all alone."

Julia sank back on the bed, a gasp leaving her body. Moria was right, so right. If Julia had been on time that night, if she'd gone by Alfonso's office as she'd thought about doing, to pick up Moria, she most likely would have walked in on the murderer.

And she, too, might be dead.

A shudder went through her body as she tugged Moria back into her arms. "You are a very wise little girl. And I want you to remember this—I will never leave you like that again, ever. That's why we're here with Aunt Cat, so you will always have an adult who loves you nearby to help you and protect you. Do you understand?"

Moria nodded. But her next words shattered Julia all the way to her soul. "Because the bad people will find me, won't they? That's why Daddy played hide-and-seek with me. He told me he didn't want the bad men to find me. Only, I think they might find me, anyway. And I'm so scared, Mommy."

Eric turned away from where he'd been standing at Moria's bedroom door, her whispered words twisting his guts into tiny jagged nerves. What kind of nightmares did this child suffer because of something beyond her control? And how could he keep reassuring her mother when he didn't have all the answers and not nearly enough evidence to prove who might be tormenting both of them?

He heard Cat coming up the stairs, then turned to face her. "We didn't find anything outside."

Cat nodded. "Adam told me. He's taking another look."

She went on into the room to give Moria her juice. Eric stayed where he was, but he looked toward Julia to see how she was holding up.

Not too good, from the looks of her. Her features were pale and drawn in the moonlight, the light from the bedside table slanting across her face with an eerie yellow glow. And to think that just a little while ago she'd looked relaxed and at peace. And she'd kissed him with such a sweet longing that Eric knew he'd never be able to forget her lips on his.

"Everything all right in here?" he asked now, trying to keep his voice even and calm for Moria's sake.

"We're doing okay," Julia said, her smile shaky. "Just a bad dream."

Moria sipped her juice, then handed the cup back to Cat. "Will you leave the light on, Mommy?"

Julia nodded. Eric didn't think she could speak.

Cat pulled back the quilted comforter. "How about I read to you until you get sleepy again?"

Moria looked at Julia. "Will that be okay?"

"That's fine, honey. As long as you promise to try and go back to sleep. You only have a few more days of spring break, remember?"

Moria lay down on the flower-etched pillow, tucking Rosa in beside her. Cat grabbed a book out of the basket Moria had insisted on bringing to her house. "Let's see what happens to the princess. Maybe she winds up rescuing that handsome prince, huh?"

Moria giggled. "Can a princess do that?"

"Of course she can do that," Cat said, her eyes going wide. "Why shouldn't a good, strong woman take care of the world around her? I do believe you are exactly that kind of princess. You can take care of yourself, just like your mama."

Julia kissed Moria, then tugged her covers back around her. "Are you sure you're all right now?"

"I'm better," Moria said. She glanced shyly toward Eric. "You scared the bad people away."

Eric's gaze met Julia's. "We sure did." Then he stepped close, a hand on the floral comforter. "But

I think they were only in your dreams, sweetheart. So maybe you scared them away yourself by waking up."

Moria's big eyes searched his face. "I'm afraid to go back to sleep."

Eric heard Julia's sharp intake of breath. He touched a hand to one of Moria's dark curls. "You can sleep, honey. You'll be all right. You know what my mama used to tell me when I had a nightmare? She'd tell me to think of something fun and good right before I'd go to sleep. You know, like going to the beach or riding your bike, maybe fishing out at the lake with Mr. Harlan. Just think about something like that and you'll have good dreams."

Moria looked doubtful, but she bobbed her head. "I'll think about the Wildflower Festival."

"Good idea," Cat said. "Now let's get on with the adventures of our princess."

Eric took that as his cue to leave. "Good night."

Julia walked toward him, her eyes bright. They silently made their way downstairs, then she turned to face him. "Did you see anybody outside?"

"No, nothing. She must have been dreaming."

"Her dreams are beginning to tell me a lot about what happened that night. I think Alfonso had been preparing her for this. I think he knew something could happen, so he wanted Moria to be able to get away. And she did just that. He got her to safety, at least. But she's remembering that and it's all mixing together—her nightmares and the reality of what actually happened."

"Maybe she'll be able to give us a clue soon," Eric said. "I know we can't push, but she's safe and she seems to trust me more and more, at least. That's a good sign."

Julia took his hand in hers, her eyes warm. "I'm beginning to trust you more, too."

He pulled her close, his forehead touching on hers. "That is a very good sign."

She gave him a peck on the cheek. "I'm still so worried about her, Eric. She seems so fragile at times. And tonight, well, she said something that ripped my heart out. She said she was glad I wasn't there that night. It's as if she knew—"

"But why would he have her there then? If I thought someone was gunning for me, I'd try to keep my family as far away as possible."

She pushed at her hair. "I don't understand that either. I do remember that he had become very possessive over the last few weeks before he died. He wanted Moria near him a lot more than normal. They always had a good relationship, and he was a very involved father. But he seemed to be trying to get in as much time with her as possible. And the way he insisted on picking her up that day." She shrugged. "It's almost as if he'd been waiting for the right time, a time he knew I'd need him to pick her up. I just wish I knew what really happened, what he went through."

"We're going to find out," he told her, lifting her chin with his finger. "I want this over as much as you do. I want you and Moria safe and sound—but my reasons are purely selfish."

She managed a soft smile. "Oh, and why is that?"

He leaned close again. "Because I want you to be able to stop pretending those little happy moments, Julia. I think that's how you cope—you go into a nice, quiet daydream, trying to imagine what life could be like for you and Moria when things are back to normal. And that's what I want for us—normal. Nice and steady and good. And the next time you kiss me, I want it to be real and I want it to be forever. Because this isn't about the woman I lost a long time ago. It's about the one I'm looking at right now. The one I aim to keep…forever."

He could tell he'd shocked her, confused her. Julia didn't like to rush things. And usually neither did he. He was about to kiss her again, in spite of his pledge to make it real when the time was right, but Adam's footsteps in the kitchen pulled them apart.

"See anything?" Eric asked, turning to face his friend.

Adam shook his head. "All's quiet out there. Not even a breeze stirring. Nothing."

"It's too quiet," Eric said. "We'll just have to keep watch."

Adam nodded. "I'll be out on the sunporch if y'all need me."

Eric watched as he left, then he turned back to

Julia. "We could take up where we left off before Moria woke up."

"We could," she replied. Then she touched a hand to his face again. "But I think I should go on up and at least try to rest. Plus I want to be nearby in case she wakes up again."

He gave her a reluctant smile. "Probably wise." Then he pulled at her hair. "Try to rest."

"I will," she said, pivoting back toward the stairs. "You should do the same."

Eric nodded, but he doubted he'd find any rest tonight. He was determined to piece all of the puzzles of this bizarre case together, and the sooner the better.

So things between Julia and him could turn from daydreams to reality.

Julia had her own nightmares. Her dreams moved with lightning speed from laughing and happy, with Moria and Alfonso walking toward her along the Riverwalk in San Antonio, to her standing alone, searching for her daughter amid thousands of wildflowers. In her dream she called out for help. She called Eric's name. She turned but she couldn't find him. And she couldn't find Moria, either. This scenario seemed to loop over and over in her dreams, with the faces changing and shifting all the time. At times she'd be just within reach of Moria, but then Alfonso would appear and tell Moria to run, run. Julia would cry out, but her voice couldn't be heard.

Moria would run away from her, and then things would change and the wildflowers would be back, beautiful and lush, and…so frightening because Julia couldn't find her daughter anywhere.

She woke to the morning sunshine streaming into her room and the cell phone on her bedside table jangling for her attention. Bleary eyed, disoriented and drained, Julia grabbed the annoying phone. "Hello?"

"Julia, it's Regina."

"Uh, hello." Surprised that her mother-in-law had called twice in one week, Julia sat up and tried to stifle a yawn, her mind still reeling from her troubled, dream-filled sleep. "Is everything okay, Regina?"

"Just fine," Regina answered, her laugh brittle. "I just wanted to let you know that I'm packing up right now and I should be leaving within the hour. I'm taking a taxi to the airport and I'll be flying into Dallas."

"Oh, where are you going?"

There was a brief pause, then Regina laughed again. "I'm just so worried about my granddaughter and since we haven't seen each other in such a long time, I've decided to come there for a little visit."

Julia stood up, her heart accelerating, panic lifting the last of her sleepiness away. "You're coming here?"

"Yes, I am," Regina replied. "I've already arranged for a rental car to drive from the airport. I'm coming to Wildflower to spend some time with

Moria. I just feel like she needs her *abuela* right now. If all goes as planned with my flight, I should be there late this afternoon."

THIRTEEN

"This should be interesting."

Julia scanned the street outside the café, wondering if Regina would get there before dark. "I don't understand why she decided out of the blue to come now, of all times."

Cat attacked a large enamel baking pan with a steel-wool pad, taking out her agitation on the cookware. "Neither do I. Maybe you should have leveled with her and told her it wasn't so smart to visit right now. Just one more person to worry about."

Julia pivoted away from the pass-through to stare at her cousin. "I imagine you're pretty tired of all of this yourself."

Cat scrubbed away, her yellow gloves covered with grease stains. "Now, don't go getting all guilty on me. I don't mind one bit that you and Moria are living with me. I wanted you to do that in the first place, remember? So just put that notion right out of your head. And if you're worried about my granny's house, the insurance is going to cover that just fine."

Julia put away silverware. "But that won't bring back some of the antique furniture you had in the house."

Cat dropped her scrubbing pad. "Look, I'm just glad you and Moria weren't in that house, so hush up on that. And I don't mind one bit housing your mother-in-law, even if it does seem odd that she'd just pop up."

"You don't know Regina. A complete stranger in your home? Won't that be uncomfortable?"

Cat laughed. "Not really. It's a big house, Julia. We'll put her down the hall from our bedrooms." She wiped her brow across the sleeve of her T-shirt. "Besides, I can see what it's like to own a bed-and-breakfast. You know, everyone thinks I should turn the house into one—just to bring in more people for the Wildflower Festival each spring."

Julia smiled at that. "Well, you're sure getting a dry run. The whole town thinks Eric and Adam have rented rooms, and now my mother-in-law." She picked up the tray of dishes she'd been clearing away. "I'm glad she's coming to see Moria, but I hope she doesn't upset her. Regina likes to talk about Alfonso and, well, she says things sometimes that make me think she blames me for his death."

"That's silly," Cat said, finishing up on the pans. "Do you think she knows that the police had you listed as a suspect at first?"

"I don't know," Julia replied. "Regina has never been very chatty with me. She saves all her love for

Moria, which is fine by me. I just don't need this extra stress right now."

Cat patted her hands dry on a fluffy towel, then started helping Julia refill the sugar containers. "Well, look at it this way. You'll have even more help with Moria."

Julia couldn't argue with that. Moria was surrounded with loving, concerned people here. Julia thanked God for that. Right now, Moria was with Harlan and the Ulmers. Harlan had insisted on taking Moria out to the lake while Julia worked the morning shift, and he'd invited his friends the Ulmers to ride out with him, probably just to keep Julia from worrying too much. Even though Julia knew Moria was in good hands, she'd still been tense and on edge all morning. The sleepless nights were catching up with her, not to mention the constant worry of wondering when these people would strike next. And when she added Regina Endicott to that mix, well, no wonder she was getting a throbbing headache.

"I hope Eric reports back with some news," she told Cat. "Maybe Adam will call from San Antonio soon."

"He might be down there awhile," Cat said. "Adam is nothing if not thorough."

Putting her own problems aside, Julia grinned at Cat. "He seems very thorough when he's around you."

"We're…getting closer, yes," Cat retorted, careful to keep her voice low so none of the other workers would hear. "But I'm not ready to jump into another relationship with both feet."

"I know what you mean," Julia said. "Same here."

Cat stacked menus on the pass-through ledge. "Funny, how all these weird happenings have brought us all together."

"Misery loves company."

"Or maybe it was just time for both of us to let go of our misery," Cat said. "That is, if we ever get past fearing for our lives."

"Yes, there is that," Julia said, that strange feeling of doom washing over her again. "At least today has been quiet." Her constant prayer for her daughter's safety had helped to settle her nerves, but she kept her worries at bay.

"Looks like the lunch crowd has died down," Cat said, coming around the counter to take a patron's twenty. Smiling at the familiar face, she looked toward the front door. "You spoke too soon. Brace yourself. Here comes Mickey Jameson."

Julia didn't glance up. Mickey was a nice enough man. But he sure liked to badger her about what was going on. She wondered just how much he knew. She wasn't planning on giving him the exclusive details.

"Could I get a to go of spiced iced tea?" he asked, his smile indulgent. "That is, if you two aren't too busy chasing away would-be criminals."

Cat stared him down. "Nah, today we're back to being regular people, Mickey. Wish I could say the same for you."

Mickey put a hand to his heart. "Ah, now, Cat, you pain me. A man has to do his job."

Julia tried to ignore him. But Mickey wasn't through with them. "I hear Adam took a trip down to San Antonio. Trying to find some leads, right? But the robber is dead now. What's the point?" He looked right at Julia when he asked this question. "Unless, of course, there is some sort of connection between you having lived in San Antonio, Mrs. Endicott, and that man Mingo Tolar coming here. Care to comment on that?"

Julia turned to face him, a dishrag in her hand. "It's Daniels now. Ms. Daniels. I took back my maiden name."

Mickey's dark gaze centered on her while he paid Cat for his tea. "And why is that?"

"That is none of your business," Julia said, her smile tight. "I've told you everything you need to know. There's no story here."

"That's not what I'm hearing around town," Mickey replied, moving his straw up and down through the cup lid, the squeaking seesaw sound grinding away on Julia's nerves. "I think there's a very big story here. Only, no one's willing to talk about it. A man holds you at gunpoint, then he gets stabbed all the way across the state in another town. Two sheriff's deputies seem to have become your permanent bodyguards, not to mention your house was ransacked and later burned to the ground. Don't you think the taxpayers have a right to know why armed deputies are watching Cat's house around the clock?"

Julia slapped her dishrag down on the counter. "You just summed it up, didn't you? We don't know who set fire to my house. Cat was kind enough to let me stay with her until I can decide what to do next."

"And kind enough to let Deputies Butler and Dupont hang around at all hours, too. My readers have a right to know if they're in danger."

Then came the reply from a deep voice behind Mickey. "Your readers are safe."

Julia looked up to find Eric standing inside the front door. Letting out a sigh of relief, she nodded toward him. "I don't have anything to say, Mickey. Why don't you talk to Deputy Butler instead?"

Mickey laughed. "Good idea."

Eric walked toward them. "I'll be happy to brief you, Mickey. This is a pending case, so I can't divulge the details. However, we're still working on finding out who burned down Julia's house. And right now some of our leads are taking us to other towns to investigate."

"And why are you guarding Mrs. Daniels so heavily?"

"Because she's been threatened twice now. But I can't tell you anything beyond that."

Mickey didn't seem satisfied. "I'll find out the truth, Eric. I always do."

"You're real good at your job," Eric replied. "But then, so am I. Remember that."

Mickey waved a hand as he headed toward the door. "I'll get to the bottom of this story, don't worry."

Julia looked at Eric. "That's what I'm afraid of. If he digs up my past and prints all the sordid details on the front page, I'll have to leave for sure. People will brand me without even knowing the truth."

"He won't get far," Eric said. "But hopefully, Adam will find something to help our case."

Julia hoped so. "No word so far?"

"Nope. But he just got there. Let's give him a day or two." Then, as if to reassure her, he added, "By the way, I just called Dad to check on Moria. She's fine. All's quiet at the cabin. We've got diligent neighbors—everyone's on the lookout out there."

Relief washed over Julia. "Thanks for checking on her. She has to go back to school Monday. I'm concerned about that."

"You can always keep her at home."

Cat came by, carrying a tray of salt and pepper shakers. "Yeah, and maybe your mother-in-law can help with babysitting duties."

Eric looked surprised. "Mother-in-law?"

"She called this morning to let me know she's coming for a visit."

"And you didn't try to stop her?"

"Should I have? If I'd told her the truth, she would have insisted on coming, anyway. She's the worrying kind, and I guess since I told her about the fire, she thought she had to come and see for herself if Moria is okay."

"Do y'all get along?"

"We…tolerate each other," Julia said, wishing she could say differently. "She doted on her son. Now he's gone. Things have been rocky between us since his death. She went to Mexico to get away from her grief, and I have no idea why she's coming here, other than she wants to see Moria."

"Great." He took off his hat and rubbed a hand through his crisp, dark hair. "Just what you needed, right?"

"Right. But I only agreed for Moria's sake. Regina will at least be a happy distraction for her." Julia looked past him out onto the street. "And if I'm not mistaken, she just pulled up. I told her to meet me here."

"You sure you're up for this?"

"No, but it will be a nice surprise for Moria."

At least her daughter would find some comfort in Regina's unexpected visit, whether Julia did or not.

"Grandmama!"

Moria burst up onto the porch at Cat's house, her eyes bright after she spotted Regina sitting in the swing.

"Hello, my little one," Regina said, taking Moria in her arms to give her a long hug. "Sit here beside me. Tell me where you've been all day."

Moria lapsed into a long account of how she'd

gone fishing with Mr. Harlan and her favorite people, the Ulmers, and how Fred, Mrs. Ulmer's little Chihuahua, had barked at the fish and tried to chase turtles.

"It was really fun. I've been out to the lake a lot. I'm on spring break. But I have to go back to school after the weekend."

"My, my, you sure have been busy," Regina replied, her dark eyes sparkling as she scrutinized her granddaughter. Running a hand over her short, clipped brown hair, she said, "And here I was, so worried about you."

"Why?" Moria asked. "Mr. Eric makes sure no bad people bother me."

Regina's gaze quickly moved to Julia. "What is this child talking about? Who is Mr. Eric?"

"He's our bodyguard deputy sheriff friend," Moria said before Julia could explain. "Because of the bad people."

Regina's smile turned into a pinched frown. "What bad people? What on earth are you talking about?"

Moria looked at Julia, her eyes wide. "I'm sorry, Mommy."

Not understanding why Moria felt the need to apologize, Julia nodded. "It's okay, sweetie. Why don't you go and wash up for dinner? You and your *abuela* can have a nice long visit later."

Moria hugged Regina again, then bounced inside the house, the screen door flapping shut behind her.

"What's going on around here?" Regina asked. "You seem so drawn and tense, and now I hear some strange man is your bodyguard. Is my granddaughter in some sort of danger?"

Julia sank back in the white rocking chair across from the swing. "You know about the fire. We think it was deliberate. So Cat let us move in with her. My friend Eric is a deputy sheriff. He's been looking out for us. All of us. It's just a precaution until we can find out more about the arson—"

"I can't believe this." Regina fanned a hand in front of her eyes. "You should have stayed in San Antonio. You had friends there, connections. Moria went to a wonderful school. The Gardonez family would have taken care of you."

"We were lonely there," Julia replied. "I have family here."

"I'm your family," Regina said, her tone bitter. "You could come and stay with me in Mexico."

"I can't do that," Julia said. "I like it here. And eventually I want to take Moria to Kentucky to visit my parents."

"But you could send Moria to visit me for a few weeks. She would be such a comfort to me. Maybe this summer?"

"I don't think so," Julia said, appalled at the thought of Moria being so far away. "She's still working through things…about her father. We need to stick together right now."

Regina rubbed her plump arms with her hands,

as if she were cold. "At least you honor her father's memory. I wondered if you'd forget about him completely."

"Why would you think that?" Julia asked, shocked. "You know I loved Alfonso."

Regina's frown creased her olive skin. "I hear things. My son was not happy before his death. I wish someone could explain that to me. I've tried to talk to Luke about it, but he's banned me from the De La Noche building. What did you do to them before you left?"

"I didn't do anything," Julia replied. "I haven't talked to Luke Roderick in months." But she could almost sympathize with the man regarding Regina. The woman always did ask too many personal questions and she was good at making demands. Alfonso had always tried to accommodate his mother's demands and now Regina had no one. Maybe that was why the sudden visit. Wondering why Regina would even want to visit Luke Roderick at his office, Julia said, "I didn't realize you and Luke were so close."

Regina moved the swing back and forth. "We aren't close, but he was good friends with Alfonso and he was very kind to me after both my husband's and my son's deaths. Now he's changed completely. Somebody needs to find out why he's been so distant lately."

"Well, I can't give you any answers about Luke," Julia said, wondering how long she'd have to put up with Regina's disapproval. "But as for the rest, Alfonso and I had our share of problems, but I loved him. And he loved me. I know it's been hard on you. But I'm glad you came to see Moria. She needs a lot of support right now."

"I can see that." Regina relaxed a bit, then added, "But I can also see that you are providing her with a good home and a secure life here. She seems happy in spite of everything."

"She is happy. She still has nightmares, but I've made an appointment with a very good child therapist in a town just west of here. I'm taking her in next week for a follow-up appointment."

"You think my granddaughter is loco?"

"No, I don't think that. But I think she needs some help to sort through her emotions and her memories."

Regina's head shot up. "What do you mean? Has Moria remembered something else from that night?"

"Nothing," Julia assured her, not wishing to discuss the details of her daughter's nightmares. "And she might not ever remember anything. We just don't know what she saw or heard."

"Maybe you're just overreacting."

"Maybe. But she's been through a trauma. That much I do know."

Regina relaxed back in the swing, her eyes on Julia. "And so have you. Did coming here help you any?"

"I'm happy here," Julia admitted. "Or at least I was until we lost our house. I'm feeling a bit unsettled right now."

"All the more reason to let me help," Regina said, getting up to stare down at Julia. "I'll make dinner."

"You don't have to do that."

"It's no problem. You and your cousin work in that café all day. Let me take over for now."

That sounded good to Julia, but she didn't want to get used to Regina being around too much. She wanted her life back. And she didn't want Alfonso's well-meaning mother to stir up things with Moria.

Regina turned at the screen door. "Meantime, think about my offer to take Moria for the summer. It would do my heart so much good."

Julia didn't respond. She couldn't let Moria go back to Mexico with her grandmother. She just couldn't. But she had the sneaking feeling that Regina had come here with that very purpose in mind.

And why now, of all times, had Regina suddenly decided to become so involved in Moria's life?

FOURTEEN

"It's been a few days now, and so far so good."

Eric smiled over at Julia, hoping to convince her that she and Moria would be okay going to the Wildflower Festival on the square in town on Saturday.

Julia looked over her shoulder toward where her house used to be. "A few days can't put that image out of my mind. I just want to keep Moria locked inside." Letting out a sigh, she said, "But I did promise her we'd go. And she's been telling Regina all about the festival. She wants to try all the kiddie rides and the pony rides, too. Do you think it'll be safe?"

Eric didn't want to promise her too much. "I can only say that I'll be close by, and that all the other deputies are well aware of your situation. We're all on high alert, and that includes the police department here in town, too."

She grinned. "You mean the three-man police department?"

"Well, they're still a department, even if they are tiny. And they're just as concerned as the rest of us.

We tend to handle big cases by cooperating with each other. Just makes things easier on all of us."

Julia lifted a climbing honeysuckle vine near Cat's gazebo, sniffing its fragrant scent before she spoke again. "I wish we'd hear something from Adam. Maybe we sent him on a wild-goose chase."

"If anyone can get to the bottom of this, it'll be Adam," Eric replied. "He won't back down." Tugging her close, he added, "And neither will I. The festival will be heavily patrolled, anyway, and Moria has been looking forward to it. The odds of someone trying to do anything in such a public venue are very slim. I say we go and spend some time there and try to relax."

"I could use some down time. Regina and Moria are having a great time together, but the woman puts me on edge. It's obvious she doesn't approve of me."

"Is she still trying to convince you to let her take Moria for the summer?"

"Oh, yes. It comes up in just about every conversation. And now, she's got Moria wanting the same thing. I think she's trying to brainwash my daughter."

"I don't think she cares very much for me, either," Eric said. Most of his time spent around Regina Endicott had been strained to say the least. The woman didn't try to hide her hostility or her disdain.

"She doesn't understand why you're always around," Julia replied. "I've tried to make her see that you're just watching out for us since the house burned. I haven't gone into detail about all the rest."

Then she shook her head. "But you have to admit, you can't keep watch over us indefinitely, Eric."

"I can and I will."

"You had a life before all of this. I'm sure you want to get back to it."

He laughed. "Yeah, I had a life. I fished and I watched ESPN with my dad. And I worked. But this case is big for us, Julia. Wildflower is not used to being caught up in big-city espionage."

"My point exactly. You don't have to guard me all the time. I think when Moria starts back to school, you and Adam can go back to your normal routines. As long as I know she's being looked after, I'll be fine. And since we've already notified the school, and the sheriff has agreed to put a deputy there with the full-time resource officer, I'm hoping Moria will get through this without even realizing she's being guarded at school. I'm taking her to see the therapist next week, so that should help some with her nightmares and maybe give us some answers, I hope. And as for me, I'm usually with Cat all the time anyway. And you've seen her gun."

He grinned at that. "Okay, we'll think about what to do next. You might have a point. Maybe the fire was the end of this. They might think they destroyed whatever they thought you had. But we can't get too complacent. If someone is watching and waiting... well, we just can't slip up now. Not when we've been so careful already."

He saw the shudder moving through her body.

She gave him a direct look, her eyes sparkling in the late-afternoon sunshine. "I can't seem to enjoy anything anymore. One minute I tell myself to relax and not worry, but the next I think of what could happen if I let my guard down. At least having you around keeps me sane."

"That's why I'm here. And if I admitted the truth, then I like having an excuse to be around you a lot."

She leaned her head on his shoulder. "Well then, I have to admit I've enjoyed spending time out at the lake and here with you." She looked up at him again. "I can't believe it took my life being threatened and my home being destroyed to make me see what a wonderful man you really are."

"I was working my way around to that," he said, stealing a soft kiss. "I had this elaborate plan to win you over, one way or another."

Her eyes turned luminous. "I wish you could have followed through on *that* plan, instead of having to deal with this constant threat." She closed her eyes. "I'm having a moment. I'm imagining you coming into the café to ask me out on a real date. I'd say no at first, but you'd be very persistent. You'd bring me a cluster of wildflowers and take me to a really sappy movie. Then we'd go back to the lake and sit out on the dock in the moonlight and—"

Eric's heart turned to liquid fire as he watched her sigh with longing. He felt that same longing. "And?"

They heard the back door slam. Julia's eyes flew open and Eric stepped back. Moria came running toward them, her dark eyes bright. And Regina slowly made her way down the steps, a frown on her face as usual.

"I guess your moment is gone for now," he whispered. Then he added, "But hold that thought. Don't let it get away."

"Mama, *Abuela* and I made sugar cookies."

"Did you? May I have one?"

Moria giggled. "Yes, you may. You, too, Mr. Eric."

"That sounds good to me," Eric said, reaching down to pick up Moria. She giggled again, the sound of her little-girl laughter warming Eric's heart.

But when he looked at her disapproving grandmother, a cold chill filled his soul. There was something in Regina Endicott's eyes that put Eric on alert. Telling himself he was being paranoid, he nevertheless decided he'd have to watch that woman very closely.

"I don't think it's wise of you to be flirting so much with that man," Regina said to Julia later that night.

Julia counted to ten for patience. This, too, had been an ongoing thread of conversation since Regina had arrived. "I told you, Eric and I are good friends. I care about him a lot."

Regina's thin lips were pursed together as she wiped away at the kitchen counter. Cat had escaped early, since she was on one of the committees to get things set up for the festival. And thankfully Eric was in the den watching an animated video with Moria.

"Are you trying to replace my son so soon?"

Julia whirled to look at Regina, trying with all her heart to understand the woman's frame of mind. "I'm not trying to replace Alfonso. Eric has been a good friend to me and he's helped me through a rough time. He's also helping me to protect Moria. I would think you'd appreciate that, at least."

Regina threw down her dish towel. "Protect her from what? I keep wondering what's really going on around here. No one will tell me the truth."

Julia placed her hands on the counter. "We've had a few scares. For a while now I thought someone might be stalking me. But now things have settled back down and I hope it's over." If she told Regina about her fears for Moria, the woman would go hysterical and scare Moria even more.

Regina's shock was evident. Her olive skin went pale. "Who would be stalking you?"

"I'm not sure. But Alfonso was murdered. We think there might be a connection. I'm trying to keep all of this from Moria, so please don't scare her."

Regina's dark gaze scanned Julia's face. "Do you know something about my son's death?"

"No. I wish I did. I wish I could relax. The best thing you can do is to continue supporting your granddaughter until we find some answers."

"So that man intends to hang around forever, then?"

"No. As a matter of fact, we had a long talk about that earlier—"

"You mean, when he was trying to kiss you out in the garden?"

Julia didn't hide her anger. "Were you spying on us?"

"You certainly didn't try to hide."

"Look, Regina, I'm a grown woman. I have every right to start dating again."

Regina grabbed a glass from the dish drain, then poured herself some water. "So you admit you are dating this man?"

"We're close, yes."

"Do you think he will be good to Moria?"

"He is good to her. She talks to him and trusts him. She's come a very long way since Alfonso's death. Or at least, she was improving until our lives got turned upside down again."

Regina drank down her water, then washed the glass, her actions full of anger. "You will let her forget her father."

Julia came around the counter. "I tell Moria things about her father every day. She will always remember him, Regina. She was there the night he died, so I'm trying to help her think of all the good times, not that one horrible night."

Regina turned contrite then. "I'm sorry. I know you've both been through a terrible experience. I guess I need to accept that you must move on with your life."

"Yes, you should do that." Julia took a calming breath. "It's taken me months to even begin to think about moving on. I came here for that very reason. I hope you'll try to understand."

Tears formed in Regina's eyes. "I do. It's just that Moria is my only link to my son."

"And you're welcome to visit with her, but don't judge me so harshly," Julia said. "Moria will always come first with me."

Regina lowered her head. "Forgive me." Then she stood back, her spine going straight. "Catherine was telling me she has some old cookbooks stored in the attic. I thought I might look them over and find something new for dinner tomorrow night."

Thrown by how quickly she'd changed the subject, Julia nodded. "Cat and I both have things stored in the attic. I can go up there and look for you."

Regina raised a hand. "No, no. You go on in the den with Moria and Eric. Catherine said they are right by the attic door on a shelf. I'll find them and take them upstairs to my room. I'll pick out what looks good and get the groceries tomorrow."

"Remember we'll be at the festival most of the day," Julia said. "I don't want you to have to cook."

"It won't be a problem. I can come back here early and get started. If we don't eat it tomorrow night, we'll just have it Sunday after church."

Julia was hoping Regina would be leaving Sunday, but that didn't look promising. Her mother-in-law had hinted she might stay a whole week. Sending up a prayer for strength, she watched as Regina slowly walked toward the tiny attic stairs just off the kitchen. "Are you sure you don't want me to go up there for you?"

"I'm fine," Regina said, shooing Julia away. "Go on. I'll be down in a few minutes."

"Well, be careful."

Julia watched to make sure Regina found the light right by the attic door, then turned to go into the den. She could hear Moria giggling and Eric laughing. They were good for each other. Moria seemed to have taken a shine to both Eric and his daddy. And Julia had certainly taken a shine to Eric. But she was afraid to hold out hope for anything permanent. She had to be sure all the nightmares were behind her and Moria before she could give her heart over to Eric completely.

She'd just rounded the hallway and was walking toward the front of the house when a piercing scream sounded through the house.

A scream that was coming from the attic.

Eric's gaze locked with Julia's. He was up and running toward the back of the house in a matter of seconds.

"It's Regina," Julia said, hurrying after him. "She was going up into the attic to look for old cookbooks."

Moria came running, too. "Where's *Abuela?*"

Julia grabbed her daughter. "Let Mr. Eric go, honey."

"I want my grandmother," Moria said, squirming against Julia's jeans.

"Not yet," Julia said. "C'mon." She took Moria by the hand and went into the kitchen, then peeked around the corner. After waiting for what seemed an eternity, she called out, "Eric?"

"It's okay," Eric said, guiding a frightened Regina back down the stairs. "She's all right."

Regina's eyes were wide with fear. "I didn't mean to scare anyone. It's just that—"

"You're all right, aren't you, *Abuela?*" Moria asked, rushing to her grandmother's side.

"I'm fine, just fine," Regina said, her gaze meeting Julia's. "Go up with Eric."

Julia looked confused. "What?"

"Just go," Regina said, hugging Moria close. "I'll be right here with Moria."

Julia did as Regina told her, her gaze locking with Eric's. "What's wrong?"

Eric guided her into the attic, the dim light shining over the jumble of boxes and shelves. "This," he said, pointing to a far corner where the tiny attic window stood open, the white curtains flapping in the wind.

Julia let out a gasp as her gaze traveled from the window to the floor. "My teapot collection."

Every box of her prized teapots and matching

cups had been overturned and emptied. And everything was shattered and broken, ruined.

"Oh," she said, reaching for Eric. "Oh, no. What happened?"

Eric shook his head. "Regina said she saw a man in here. She said he left through the window, but when I looked out I didn't see anyone. I alerted the street patrol."

"But how? Who?"

Eric's expression was grim. "Isn't that obvious? Our troubles haven't settled down one bit, Julia."

She put a hand to her mouth. "You mean, in spite of everything, someone managed to get inside this house and do this? But we were here all night. I never heard a thing."

He nodded. "I don't know how they did it, but it looks that way. We had the TV loud, watching that movie, and we had supper up front in the dining room. But you're right. We would have heard dishes breaking up here." Then he kicked an empty box, his frustration erupting. "Maybe they did the job when we were out of the house and Regina stumbled on them coming back for one more look. It's not over yet."

"It won't ever be over," Julia said, leaning on a wall to stare at the dainty broken floral cups and the shattered teapots. "I've been collecting these since Alfonso and I got married. It wasn't so much that they were valuable. They just meant a lot to me. Every time we traveled anywhere, I'd buy a new tea set. Alfonso ordered some of them for me on special occasions. I was saving them for Moria."

"I know," Eric said, coming to stand in front of her. "And I'm sorry."

"What now?" she asked, hysteria slowly overtaking her shock. "What now, Eric? We've tried everything. I can't...I just can't keep doing this."

The same defeat she felt shone in his eyes. He was giving up, too. "I don't know," he said, dropping his hands down. "We wait and we hope that Adam figures something out. We just need a tidbit, a connection. We wait and keep trying to nail these people."

"I'm so tired of waiting."

He pulled her into his arms. "I'm not going to stop until we find out who's doing this, Julia. I promised you that, and I intend to keep that promise."

"No," she said, backing away. "No, this is crazy. I'm going to take Moria and I'm going to leave. I'll go somewhere where they'll never find me. It's my only hope."

The defeat she'd seen minutes before in his eyes was gone now, to be replaced with a grim determination. "I won't let you do that. I won't. I'll go with you, if I have to. I mean it. If Adam can't give us a good lead, then I'll take both of you away from here until we capture these people."

Julia wanted to believe him, wanted to tell him yes, he could come with her, but she couldn't ruin his life. "No, Eric. We've done everything. It's time I accept that this isn't going to go away. I don't want to run, but we have to get out of Wildflower. Permanently. And without you."

He tugged her into his arms to kiss her. "I can't let you do that. Not yet. I'll figure something out, okay? I'll figure something out, somehow. I don't want you to go."

Julia didn't want to leave him, but what choice did she have? Someone had destroyed her tea sets on purpose. It was deliberate and it was cruel. But...it could be just the beginning of an even worse cruelty.

Because the next thing they destroyed might be more valuable to her than any kind of collection or possession. The next time, they might finally come after Moria.

FIFTEEN

Eric looked around the attic. "I think we got all of it."

Julia lifted the box of broken china, handing it over to him. "I sold everything I could, but this. Why would someone want to destroy it?"

"They were looking for something," Eric replied. He felt weary down to his bones. This case was baffling, no doubt. The uncertainty of it all was about to get to him, but he wasn't giving up just yet. "Like everything else that's happened, this doesn't make much sense. If someone came into the attic and destroyed your dishes, why would they return to the scene?"

He watched as Julia swept the floor clean to make sure no shards of porcelain were left on the aged hardwood. Leaning against her broom, she said, "Who knows? They didn't get to finish searching the cottage, so they torched it. Now this." Her gaze lifted to Eric. "You don't think they'd set fire to Cat's house, do you?"

Eric didn't want to tell her that his gut was churning with that very worry. "Not with me here," he said, but he was fast losing confidence in his ability to protect her. Maybe it was time to get her and Moria out of town.

Julia lifted the dustpan over one of the boxes, then dropped the contents on top of the broken dishes inside. "Well, that's the last of that. I'm going to check on Moria and Regina. I think Regina was more shaken than she let on. And I hate that she's now gotten caught up in this mess, too."

Eric watched her stomp across the attic, her shoulders bent in defeat and frustration. After securing the window and making sure the board he'd found to wedge against the glass would hold until he could talk to Cat about fitting new window locks, he left the attic and headed down the stairs to the kitchen. Apparently, the old attic window hadn't been locked at all, since the hinges were rusty and broken away. And someone must have found an easy way into the house simply by climbing up one of the porches and using an old oak limb for leverage to the roof and the attic.

His cell phone buzzed just as he reached the last step.

"It's me, buddy."

"Adam. Please tell me something good."

He heard a long sigh. "I think I might have stumbled on something."

"Talk to me," Eric said, turning to stare across

the room to where he and Julia had placed the boxes full of broken china.

"Well, our man Luke Roderick finally agreed to talk with me earlier today. He's clean, Eric. A bit arrogant and he has an ego the size of Dallas, but he's clean. He told me that Alfonso Endicott was a good man with nothing to hide. He also said that Mingo Tolar had worked for De La Noche at the time of Endicott's death and that yes, the police knew that. But he remembered something he'd never connected before. Tolar had done some yard work for the Endicotts, just to make money on the side. He remembered after I showed him Mingo's picture. An easy oversight, since he wasn't one to keep up with the grunt workers of the company by name or face."

"How would he know that, or suddenly remember it now?"

"He and Alfonso played golf together on a regular basis. That's how Mingo got hired on at De La Noche—Alfonso recommended him for a job on the loading docks. Roderick never met him at the office or at the docks, but when I showed him a picture and told him it was Tolar, he was surprised. He said he remembered seeing Tolar working one day in the Endicotts' garden. And it was not long before Alfonso died."

"Then why didn't Julia recognize him?"

Adam grunted. "Because Tolar wasn't working in Alfonso's yard. Roderick saw the man when he went by to visit Alfonso's father during his fight with cancer. Tolar was working for Alfonso's parents."

Eric's indigestion burned all the way to his throat. "So we have a solid connection between the man who tried to kidnap Julia having worked for both De La Noche and the senior Endicotts. Interesting." Very interesting, considering that Julia's mother-in-law could possibly be able to ID the man. "But the police didn't know about Tolar's moonlighting for the Endicotts?"

"Nah. The old man died right after that visit, and then a year later, Alfonso died. Roderick never made the connection." He huffed a breath. "But now he has a theory."

"Which is?"

"Luke thinks Mingo saw and heard all about the good life of his friend Alfonso—through Alfonso's parents who were proud and braggadocios—and decided to try to cash in on that life by robbing the company. He thinks Tolar had somehow memorized one of the security codes and intended to break into one of the safes but was surprised to find Alfonso at the office that night. He panicked and killed Alfonso."

"Why haven't the police made this connection?"

"They never knew there was a connection until now. Roderick was willing to tell them exactly what he told me. He easily identified Tolar and suggested he was Endicott's killer."

"So why is this good news?"

"Well, now that I've talked to the folks here and explained that one Mingo Tolar came to Wildflower and held Julia Daniels Endicott at gunpoint, the boys are willing to concede that Tolar probably was the killer. And that should be the end of it, except Tolar is too dead to talk. Now they're wondering who knifed him in that alley. And why. After Roderick left, they had a different theory. They think that someone sent Tolar to rob Endicott and then come after Julia, which means we have bigger fish to fry. And these big-city boys like that angle, since they've been trying to make a connection between the Gardonez family and some illegal activities filtering up from Mexico."

"Drugs or illegal human beings?"

"Neither. They think someone was cooking the books for the family and sending some unclaimed profits to Mexico for safekeeping."

"And Alfonso Endicott just happened to be the CFO."

"Bingo."

Eric rubbed the bridge of his nose. "So you think this all goes back to the family, after all?"

"It sure looks that way. But I don't think it's Luke Roderick. I think it's someone very close to the family, maybe using the company as a front."

"A front for what?" Eric asked, his mind whirling.

"That's the burning question. But the boys here are willing to bring in the feds to help us figure it out. And they're also willing to move Julia and Moria to a safe house until we can prove something."

Eric leaned back against the kitchen counter, a sudden relief washing over him. "I'm thinking that might be our best bet for now." He explained about the attic break-in. "It's just another piece of the puzzle. Obviously, they think Julia has something they need—something that would expose whoever is behind this. And I'm thinking Alfonso Endicott was up to his eyeballs in it and that's why he's dead now."

"I hear that," Adam said. "I'm going to work out the details here, and then I'll be home. You might want to warn Julia that she needs to start packing."

"I will. And, Adam, I'm not letting her leave here without me. You might want to warn the San Antonio Police Department and the feds about that."

"I don't think—"

"Just do it, Adam."

"Uh…I'll try my best."

Eric was about to stress that he didn't intend to let Julia out of his sight when he heard her screaming his name from the top of the stairs.

"Got to go!" he shouted, dropping his phone as he rushed up the stairs.

Julia stood there, sobbing and wringing her hands. "She's gone, Eric. I've looked everywhere, but Moria's gone. And so is Regina. They've both just… disappeared."

She couldn't stop shaking. Julia tugged at the chenille blanket Cat had wrapped around her shoulders, but still she couldn't seem to find a shred of warmth.

So she rocked back and forth on the couch in the den, her eyes glued to the Amber Alert that was flashing across the television screen, her mind shouting the words that no mother should ever have to hear.

My child is gone. My child is gone. Dear God, help me. My child is gone.

Eric came to sit down beside her, his hand reaching for hers as all around them officers and officials swarmed like bees, setting up lines and making calls.

Dear God, my child is gone. Please help me.

"Here's what we know," Eric said, his voice husky, his head down, his hand holding hers steady. "Regina's rental car is gone. We're searching for it right now. We have every reason to believe Moria is with her and this is in no way connected to the Tolar case. Julia, we think your mother-in-law kidnapped Moria, maybe thinking it was for her own good, maybe because she wanted to have her granddaughter with her for a while. You have to believe Moria is safe—"

Julia pulled her hand away. "I won't believe that until she's back here with me, Eric." Rocking even harder, she said, "You promised me. I trusted you and you promised—"

She stopped, put her hand to her mouth. The look in his eyes tore through her with a whipping, blistering rawness. She saw the tears misting in his dark eyes, saw the hurt her words had inflicted. "Oh, Eric." She tried to reach for him again, but he shot up off the couch, away from her, away from the truth that stood between them.

Silent and straight backed, he walked away.

Julia tried to get up, but her legs were too weak. Cat came and fell beside her, taking her into her arms. "It's all right, honey. We're all at our wits' end right now. Things will be better when we have her back." She rocked with Julia, back and forth, as they both cried. "And we will have her back. Adam is on his way here right now to help. And Eric will see to it that she comes back to us."

Julia's gaze slammed into Eric's as he watched them from the kitchen. She'd never felt so alone, so numb. She'd not only lost her daughter; now she'd lost the man she loved, too. It was more than she could bear. Turning away from Cat, she fell against the cushion on the sofa and sobbed into her hands, the nightmares playing over and over in her mind like a silent horror movie.

Eric listened to the radio for any sign that they'd located the rental car. How could an old woman slip right through their fingers like this? How could he have let this happen? He wanted to shout to the heavens in anger, but instead he fell to his knees right there in the middle of the sunporch. And he prayed to God to help him, to find this innocent child and bring her safely back to her mother.

When he felt a hand on his arm, he looked up to find Harlan standing there, his own eyes watery. "Son, are you all right?"

Eric shook his head. "No, Pop, I'm not. I failed—"

"You did everything you could possibly do," Harlan replied, his fingers digging into Eric's shoulder. "Say your prayers, then get up and get back to your job. That's the best way to help them."

Eric knew his daddy was right. He couldn't lose it now. He had to find a way to bring Moria back to her mother. He loved them both so much. And although he felt certain that he'd lost Julia forever, the least he could do was make sure he found the daughter she loved. He owed her that.

So he got up, wiped his eyes and found the strength to put one foot in front of the other so he could get on with his work. "I'm going out to look for them," he told Harlan. "I have to do something, so I'm going out."

Harlan nodded, his eyes full of understanding. "I'll stay here with Julia and Cat. The Ulmers are making sandwiches for all of us. Want something?"

"No." Eric didn't look back as he left the sunporch and headed out to his truck.

If he had looked back, however, he would have seen Julia watching him from her bedroom window. Watching him, and sending a prayer out with him on the wings of her one last hope.

He took the back roads, figuring Regina was smart enough to stay off the interstate. He had no idea why he felt the need to roam the countryside just west of town, but he felt sure the woman was heading for Mexico. And again, something wasn't sitting right with this situation. It just didn't add up. He'd tried so hard to protect Moria from some unseen force when maybe the danger had been right there in front of his eyes all along. Right there in front of him.

Looking in his rearview mirror, Eric recognized Mickey Jameson's Mustang coming up on his bumper. Mickey started flashing his lights.

Eric pulled over, impatient and ready to tear Mickey's head off, until the other man got in Eric's truck.

"Listen," Mickey said on a quick breath. "I want to help— "

"Then get out of my truck and let me get on with my job."

"Eric, it's the grandmother," Mickey said, his fist hitting a pocket-size notepad. "The grandmother is the one who's after Moria. And I have the proof."

Eric's heartbeat hit hard against his ribs. "I'm listening."

"I had a contact in San Antonio who knows how to hack into records—bank records. Regina wrote a check to Tolar two days before he robbed the café. A very big check." He let out a sigh. "And there are a lot more where that one came from, even one written about a week after her son died."

Eric looked over at the reporter. "You'd better be sure."

"As sure as the sun is shining," Mickey replied. "I want to help you find that little girl. Because my gut is telling me her grandmother didn't take her out of love and concern."

Eric nodded. "So is mine."

And then it all came together like a ray of brilliant sunshine hitting across the lake waters.

Regina Endicott.

Regina had known Mingo Tolar. Had hired him to work in her yard. Could she have possibly sent him to find Alfonso that night? Could she have sent him here to find Julia?

And had all of this been an elaborate plan, so that Regina could take her own granddaughter?

He thought about the broken dishes in the attic. Regina could have easily set that up. She'd been alone in the house earlier. Did she go up there searching for something, breaking dishes and throwing things as she went? Had she purposely lied about an intruder?

The window.

Eric remembered how the lock had been open. From the inside. The lock wasn't broken. Or at least it hadn't been, until someone had tampered with it *from the inside*.

Regina had faked the intrusion, because she'd already broken the dishes earlier. Another smoke-screen, another piece to this puzzle. But what had the old woman been searching for? Maybe there wasn't anything to find. Maybe she'd just set all of this up to scare Julia, to distract her until the perfect moment. Until she could take Moria.

Eric punched numbers on his cell. He had to talk to Adam one more time.

* * *

Julia heard the call coming over the radio. They'd found the car. She listened, intent on hearing the location. Then before anyone noticed, she slipped down the stairs and hurried to her own car. She had to see with her own eyes if her daughter was safe. She had to know. And she had to confront Regina and ask her why she'd do something so cruel to a mother and her child.

Dressed in jeans and a T-shirt, she started her car and sped off, the sound of Cat calling after her the last thing she heard before she hurried out of town, away from the laughter and the happiness of the festival that was taking place in the square.

Soon, she was on the old two lane that led west toward Dallas. She knew the crossroads where the car had been located. It wasn't that far out of town.

But when she pulled up, Julia saw Eric standing there, staring at the car, his hands on his hips. He was surrounded by sheriff's deputies and other officials.

She didn't see Moria or Regina anywhere.

Eric heard the car stopping, turned to hear brakes screeching to a halt. "Julia!"

He hurried to her, grabbing her before she could glimpse inside the car. "Julia, you shouldn't be here."

"I have to be here," she said, fighting at him to let her go. "Where's Moria? Where's my daughter? Eric, please."

Eric guided her back, away from the scene of the wrecked car. Holding her tightly by the shoulders, he looked into her eyes. "Listen to me. Listen. Regina is in the car. She's hurt, but she's alive."

She peered around him, her eyes wild with fear. "And Moria? What about Moria, Eric?"

He pulled her into his arms, holding her head against his chest. "Honey, she's not in there. She's not in the car. We can't find her. We're looking in the woods and along the road, but…we haven't found her yet."

"Hey, Deputy Butler?"

Eric and Julia both looked up as one of the searchers came toward them, holding something in his hand. "Recognize this?"

Eric felt Julia stiffen. It was Rosa, Moria's favorite doll.

He held on, even when Julia collapsed against him, a keening wail shattering her fragile body as the early-morning sun shimmered golden and hot in the eastern sky.

SIXTEEN

Eric pulled Harlan to the side. "We've searched the woods and the road, Pop. We can't find Moria anywhere."

Harlan's wizened face looked haggard and aged. "Do you think she was thrown out of the car?"

"We thought that," Eric said, making sure Julia wasn't nearby. After he'd forced her to come back to the house, Cat had tried to get her to rest. But Julia had been pacing all afternoon, lost in the shock of hearing that her daughter was out there somewhere, either alone or with someone else. So she held Rosa and she paced, and she refused to give the doll over to anyone to analyze or test.

Eric turned back to Harlan. "The passenger-side door was flung open. We don't know what happened, but Regina somehow lost control of the vehicle and it plunged into the ditch. My gut is telling me someone took Moria—maybe it was a planned swap—or maybe not. We won't know until Regina regains consciousness. Adam is at the hospital, waiting for the word to question her." He lowered his voice. "We've called in the search dogs."

He hadn't voiced the possibility of a swap to Julia, but the authorities were certainly looking at that angle. If Regina had help, maybe Moria was safe… for now at least. Unless her own grandmother had thrown her to the wolves. Or worse, unless someone had deliberately taken the child from the unsuspecting grandmother.

His father summed up both scenarios.

"So either Mrs. Endicott passed the child to someone, or possibly someone was following Mrs. Endicott, and maybe forced her off the road and took the child?"

Eric let out a breath. "Yes, and if that's the case, then it's worse than even I imagined. I don't like this. We've got a town full of strangers at this festival and the rest of us are in pure panic mode. I have to go talk to the task force."

Julia saw Eric stalking toward the command center in the kitchen, then watched as he had a long discussion with the other investigators. When Adam walked in, Eric went with him to a corner.

Julia wanted to find out what they were all talking about, but she couldn't seem to move. Eric wasn't keeping her posted right now. He hadn't talked to her on the way home. Instead, he'd just held her hand, as if the strength of his touch could keep her from sinking into the despair that refused to let her go.

Did he already know where her daughter was? Was he trying to spare her the very worst?

Eric had been her rock, her link to sanity. And now that she'd lashed out at him, she might lose that link. Wishing she could take back her earlier words to him, wishing she could turn back time and have Moria here in her arms, she thought about what might have prompted Regina to take her child.

She knew Regina loved Moria. But Regina's love could sometimes be smothering and claustrophobic. Hadn't Alfonso expressed that enough when he was alive? And it had gotten worse once Regina had lost her husband. Much worse.

Julia clung to Rosa, the doll's presence a sharp-edged reminder that her daughter was missing. Why had Regina come here? Trying to remember any clue, any tidbit of information, Julia suddenly halted in her pacing, her gaze locking with Eric's across the room. Time seemed to stop as she remembered that other desperate day when she had searched for him and found him looking at her across the café. Julia tried to relay her need, her panic, to Eric now. And she saw his eyes go wide, saw him step away from Adam.

"Eric?" She heard her own measured whisper, waited as he hurried toward her.

"What is it?"

"I…I remembered something."

Eric guided her to a chair. "Take a breath and tell me what you remembered."

She sank down, her hands shaking as she clutched

Rosa to her stomach. "Regina said something the first time she called me—you know—she just called one night, right after the fire."

He nodded. "Go on."

"She mentioned this house. She said something about Moria being able to run around in this big, rambling house."

Grabbing Eric's arm, Julia leaned close. "Only, I never told Regina about Cat's house. I never once mentioned to her that Cat had a big, rambling house. She...she'd never seen this house before. So how could she know about it? How, Eric?"

He looked down at her, his eyes devoid of hurt or anger. "Because I'm afraid Regina is behind this, honey. All of it. She didn't take Moria to protect her."

"What?" Julia blinked, thinking she'd misunderstood. "What do you mean?"

"Julia, your in-laws knew Mingo Tolar. He worked for them, around their house. Luke Roderick confirmed that, after Adam showed him a picture of Tolar. And Luke told Adam that Alfonso had helped Tolar get a job at De La Noche, but Luke never met the man there. He only saw him once, at your in-laws' house. The police think Tolar killed your husband, but we still don't know why."

"But...what about Regina? Why would she be behind all of this? How?"

He looked down, but Julia shook his shoulder. "Eric, tell me the truth!"

Motioning to Adam, Eric waited until Adam came

across to them. "We need to tell her everything. Even what Mickey found out."

Julia's pulse raced at a dizzying speed. She could feel the blood rushing through her temples. "Tell me what?"

Adam bent down, then touched a hand to Julia's arm. "Mickey Jameson was trying to get a break on the story, so he got in touch with a source down in San Antonio." He told her about Mickey's discovery. "Regina has been paying Tolar for months now, even though he no longer works for De La Noche nor does any yard work."

Julia couldn't fathom what she was hearing. "Why would she stay in contact with Tolar? She lives in Mexico now. Have you asked her about this?"

Adam shook his head. "She's awake now, but she's not talking."

"I need to see her," Julia said, trying to stand.

"Hold on," Eric said. "There's more."

Adam waited for her to sit back down, then continued. "The authorities in San Antonio think someone at De La Noche was cooking the books. But they could never prove it. Luke got suspicious, then hired an investigator after Alfonso died. They did an internal audit and found some discrepancies. Mr. Roderick thinks that might be why Alfonso was killed. They think your husband either had a part in it or he knew who did. And they believe the evidence is still out there somewhere."

Julia put a hand to her mouth. "Alfonso wouldn't have done that. He was honest. He was—"

"But what if he didn't have a choice?" Eric asked. "What if he was being coerced by someone very close?"

Julia's head shot up. "His mother?" She stood up, pushing at them. "You think Regina had her own son working to commit accounting fraud?"

Eric nodded. "Not only that, Julia. We think she might have had her own son murdered."

Julia stood in the hallway of the hospital, the numbness that wouldn't go away causing her to hold her breath. Earlier at the house, she'd told Eric and Cat she wanted to be alone, then she'd gone upstairs. After about an hour, she'd managed to come back down and sneak out a side door.

She'd driven to the hospital without anyone even noticing she was gone. She had to see Regina, had to ask the woman what she had done with Moria. And why she might have killed Alfonso.

Now Julia needed to get past the police officer guarding Regina's room. Thinking she'd just tell him the truth, Julia slowly walked toward the private room. "I need to see my mother-in-law."

The young officer looked confused. "Uh, I'm not sure that's such a good idea. I have my orders."

"I know you do, but we're family. I'm worried about her. I need to talk to her."

He glanced away, then Julia heard footsteps coming up the hallway. The young officer looked relieved. "Deputy Butler, this woman wants to see—"

Eric gave Julia a concerned look. "It's okay, Joe. I'll take her in."

Julia let out a breath as Eric pulled her with him to the room. "This is against regulations, Julia."

"I have to talk to her."

"Yeah, well, so do I. Let's just hope I don't lose my badge because I'm letting you go in there with me."

Julia was beyond reason. When Eric opened the big door, she rushed past him to find Regina awake, her eyes full of confusion and fright.

"Where is my daughter?" Julia said, the words coming out through gritted teeth as a cold rage clutched at her heart. She felt Eric's arm on hers, restraining her.

Regina seemed to shrink back, the wires and tubes connected to her body swaying and rattling. "What do you mean? Isn't she back with you?"

"You know she's not," Julia said, shouting the words. "What did you do with my baby?"

Regina began to sob, big tears rolling down her face. "I don't know. We were on that strange road and I got confused. I missed the turn and went into the ditch. She opened the door and ran away."

"What? Moria got away? Are you sure?" For the first time in twenty-four hours, Julia felt a shard of hope piercing her soul. "Where did she go?"

Regina's sobs increased. "I don't know. I…I hit

my head. I must have passed out. I don't know. Where is she, Julia? Where is my baby?"

Julia tugged away from Eric's grip. "She is not *your* baby and you will not see her again, ever, do you hear me?"

Eric held her away from the sobbing woman, but she heard him speaking into his radio, issuing an alert. "I repeat, Moria Daniels Endicott left the vehicle on her own. We need to proceed with a search of the entire area surrounding the accident scene."

Julia heard him describing her daughter in official terms. Age, weight, height, hair color, last seen in a pink floral jumper and matching pink tennis shoes. She looked back down at Regina, rage turning her world red. "You'd better hope they find her, Regina. And while they're looking, you're going to tell me why you had my husband murdered."

It was very late when Julia and Eric returned to Cat's house. Eric knew Adam and the others had gone out on the search, but he couldn't leave Julia. He was afraid she was going to crumble into tiny little bits any minute now, and he wanted to be the one to pick up the pieces when she did so. He had to be here with her. He had to prove to her that he wouldn't leave her, ever. That he loved her, wanted to help her. He wouldn't fail her, even if she thought he already had.

Cat greeted them at the back door, pulling Julia

into her arms. "C'mon, honey. Let's get you something to eat."

Julia moaned, pushed at Cat. "I can't eat."

Harlan stood between the kitchen and the den. "I thought I'd stay here and keep Cat company. The Ulmers are in the den."

Eric nodded. "Thanks, Dad. No word yet?"

"Nothing. They've got the search dogs out there." Harlan looked at Julia. "They're doing everything humanly possible to find her."

Cat guided them into the den where the Ulmers sat watching the television with blank expressions. When Nina saw Julia, she rushed to her, cradling her in her arms. "Poor, poor baby. We love you. We love both of you. We're praying for her. We've got the prayer chain in action, everyone calling around. C'mon and sit here, honey."

Eric watched as Julia allowed Nina to guide her to the sofa. Then he turned to Harlan. "We got a confession out of Regina Endicott."

Cat heard him. "What did she say?"

Eric sank against a leather recliner, exhaustion washing over him. "It's almost impossible to believe." He looked over at Julia, wondering if she could stomach hearing this again. Maybe he needed to hear it himself, just to believe it. "When Regina's husband, Bill Endicott, worked for De La Noche, he made a good living. But Regina wanted more. So in order to please her, Bill started smuggling things in from Mexico. Exotic plants, animals, even humans at one time, according to Regina.

"Then Alfonso joined the company and Regina started in on him. We're not sure how, but he started slowly skimming money off the top and squirreling it away down in a bank in Mexico. But apparently, after his father died, Alfonso wanted to stop. Regina said Alfonso told her there was plenty of money for her to live comfortably on, but from now on he was going to control it. But she didn't believe him, and she didn't like not having access to the money. She kept badgering him to keep it up. Then she threatened to tell the Gardonez family and have him fired."

Julia spoke up at last. "She forced her own son to continue the embezzlement. But Alfonso couldn't live with that. He told her he was going to confess to Luke Roderick. Only before he could do that, Regina had him killed."

She started crying, her tears silent and steady.

Eric watched as Nina wrapped an arm around Julia's shoulder, then he finished the story. "Regina claims she sent Mingo Tolar to the office that night just to find a disc. Apparently, Alfonso had some sort of flash disc that he kept with him at all times. Tolar was supposed to get the disc for Regina, so she could find out where the money was located. But he panicked and stabbed Alfonso. He never found the disc."

Julia wiped at her eyes. "And she was there that night, too. That's why Moria kept seeing her grandmother in her dreams. The voices—one of them was

Regina. She was there, but thankfully, she didn't know Moria was there. Not until later."

Eric finished. "We think Tolar was blackmailing Regina, but she held him off with the promise of a lot of money."

Julia sat up, grabbing a pillow to hold it tightly to her stomach. "So Regina sent Tolar here to…to take me. I was supposed to tell him where the disc was. Regina thinks because Moria was in the building that night, Alfonso gave her the disc. That's why Tolar came here and that's why my house was broken into and burned down by another thug she hired. And that's why my daughter is missing right now."

Eric hushed her with a hand on her arm. "Regina paid the second man to kill Tolar and set the house on fire. It was just a distraction to get Julia and Moria out of the house. But the man panicked and can't be found. So she came here herself, hoping to find the flash disc. She broke the dishes in the attic, hoping to scare Julia into coming to Mexico with her—or at least letting her take Moria."

"So she could harass Moria until…until she remembered," Julia said, gulping back a breath. She pushed away from the couch. "I…I need to…to find my daughter. Eric, I have to find her."

Eric pulled Julia into his arms, his heart breaking with each sob he felt shuddering through her shoulders. "We'll find her. I promise."

But he was fast running out of promises.

Then he heard the back door open, and Adam

came bursting into the room. "The dogs, Eric. The dogs tracked Moria's scent back to this house. We think Moria might be hiding somewhere in here."

Cat jumped up and ran into Adam's arms. "Oh, bless you."

Then Eric started bobbing his head. "You're right. She plays hide-and-seek. That's her game. And she hides things all over the house, right?" He looked over at Julia. "Think about it. If Alfonso coached Moria to hide the disc and to hide herself, then she's probably been right under our noses since she left that car. Julia, she might be right here, playing hide-and-seek, waiting for us to find her."

Julia sank against Eric's chest, tears of joy washing over her. "We have to look for her." Then she turned to Adam. "We can't bring the dogs in here. They'll scare her. Just…give me a few minutes by myself to try and find her, okay?"

"C'mon," Eric said, "we'll look together." Then he stared down at Julia. "But where do you think we should start?"

Julia sent up a prayer, afraid to hope. "She loves the turret room."

Julia looked in Moria's room, trying to imagine where her daughter might try to hide, her prayers as steady as the beat of her heart coursing through her body. Glancing around, she immediately stopped when her gaze moved over the old vanity. "Eric, her yellow rose is missing."

"What rose?" Eric asked, right behind her.

"The one Alfonso gave her. It was a huge, silk thing on a heavy stem in a pot with fake grass. She loved that flower. She brought it over here when we left the cottage."

"You think she has it with her?"

Julia nodded. "She dropped Rosa in the grass by the car for some reason. And she never lets go of Rosa. Next to the doll, that silk flower was her favorite possession."

"Maybe she has it with her now," he said. "Let's keep looking."

Julia softly called Moria's name. "Moria, honey, are you here? Please answer Mommy."

As they made their way through all the second-floor bedrooms, Julia shuddered when they neared the one Regina had stayed in. "This one is right near the turret room," she whispered. "But I don't think Moria would go in there, especially if Regina threatened her or scared her."

"Okay. We'll have to send the team in here anyway to see if Regina left anything for us," Eric said. "Let's try the turret room first."

Julia started up the narrow spiral stairs to the octagon-shaped turret room at the top of the old house. "Moria, it's Mommy. Please answer me. This isn't a game, honey. We need you to come out."

At first they heard nothing. Then there was a slight shifting sound coming from inside the tiny room.

"Moria, it's Mr. Eric. You're safe now. You don't

have to hide anymore. And you don't have to hide anything that your daddy gave you, either. The bad men won't be coming back."

Julia pushed at the tiny door, then slowly opened it, willing herself to stay calm, no matter what they found. And inside, sitting by the window box with her yellow silk rose clutched in her hands, was her daughter.

Later that night, after the officials had taken statements and after the neighbors and well-wishers had left, Julia stood out on the back porch, breathing in the sweet scents of honeysuckle and clover. Off in the distance, she could hear the celebrations at the Wildflower Festival.

Now the town had a real reason to celebrate. Moria was safe, at last. The sheriff had announced it on the loudspeaker immediately after they'd rushed downstairs with Moria clinging to Eric's neck. And all the people who'd been holding vigils now were laughing and rejoicing.

Moria was safe. Julia let those words echo in her mind over and over. A doctor had checked her out and proclaimed her to be physically fit. Her trek back up the road to town had brought her a few scrapes and bug bites, but she was fine. She had somehow known to run—run toward her family, run toward home.

Emotionally, though, Julia knew her daughter was still suffering. How did you explain to a little girl that her grandmother had gone off the deep end because of greed and grief and money? It would take months of therapy to make sure Moria had no more nightmares in her life.

And Regina would be spending a lot of time behind bars, thinking about what her greed had done to her family. Moria had shown them the tiny little flash disc, hidden safely in the bottom of the florist moss covering her beloved yellow rose. The rose her father had given her, telling her to keep it with her always. Moria hadn't even known the disc was there until she'd sat hidden and afraid in the tiny room, waiting for someone to come and find her.

Julia understood it all now. Alfonso had been afraid Regina would try to take Moria in order to blackmail him into cooperating. He was trying to protect his child by bringing her to work with him, by keeping her close. Just as Julia had tried to protect her since his death. How he must have suffered, all alone and afraid, too ashamed and embarrassed to tell even his wife.

I didn't love him enough, Julia thought now. I didn't help him enough. She silently asked God to give her a second chance to really, truly love. To love God and to love Eric.

Then she heard the screen door creaking open and turned to find Eric walking toward her, his dark eyes glinting in the muted yard light.

"Hi," he said.

"Hi." She closed her eyes, hoping she could tell him everything inside her heart. "Eric, I'm sorry—"

He pulled her close, wrapping his arms around her waist as he leaned his head on top of hers. "It's over. All of it. Time for a fresh start. Time for that date I wanted to take you on."

She smiled, her eyes still closed. "I'm having a moment."

"Are you? And what's happening in your moment?"

Snuggling back against his strong body, she said, "It's spring and the wildflowers are blooming out by the lake. You and I are walking along, holding hands. Moria is running in front of us, chasing a butterfly. We're safe, we're happy—"

He turned her in his arms. "And I'm kissing you, right?"

She opened her eyes. "Right."

His lips touched hers, warm and solid and endearingly sweet. Then he lifted his head and looked down at her. "You know, I'm having a moment of my own."

"Really?"

"Uh-huh. I can see you dressed in something frilly and pretty, walking up the church aisle toward me. You're smiling. And Moria is your flower girl. She's carrying a basket of bluebonnets and black-eyed Susans. The church is packed and I'm waiting to take my wedding vows. I'm waiting to make you my wife."

Julia sighed, touched a hand to his face. "I like that moment."

"How 'bout we make it a lifetime, instead of just a moment?"

"I like that even better."

"You're safe here with me, Julia."

"I know that now."

He held her there in the moonlight, and as she looked over his shoulder and out into the night, she could see the wildflowers dancing in the grass, dancing as part of God's celebration. And as part of His promise of a love so strong, nothing could break it.

* * * * *

Dear Reader,

We all have secret places where we hide things. Maybe it's our jewelry or money, or we might keep a secret for someone close. That is what little Moria was trying to do in this story. She loved her father and tried to do as he'd asked by hiding something very important. That strong love and her need to remember her father caused this child to have nightmares. It also put her in danger. Eric and Julia both wanted to protect Moria, but the answers were hard for them to accept. It's always hard when someone we love and trust betrays us. Julia couldn't trust Eric because she felt betrayed by her husband's secrets, and that betrayal endangered her child. We sometimes might feel this way about trusting God, but if we give our secrets and our fears over to Him, we will find peace.

I'd love to hear from you. Visit my website at www.lenoraworth.com!

Until next time, may the angels watch over you, always.

Lenora Worth

Questions for Discussion

1. Why did Julia insist on keeping her past a secret?

2. What did Eric do to gain Julia's trust? Why do you think it's hard to trust others at times?

3. Why did Moria keep what her daddy had given her a secret? Do you think Alfonso was wrong to ask this of his young daughter?

4. What motivated Julia's mother-in-law to do what she did? What would you have done in her situation?

5. How does greed cause us to lose sight of our faith? Has this ever happened to you or someone you know?

6. Eric was an honorable man, but he had a soft spot for Julia and Moria. Do you think this clouded his judgment?

7. How did Eric help Julia find her faith again? Do you think small-town living is better than the big city? Why or why not?

8. What kind of relationship did Eric have with

his father? Do you wish you could be closer to those you love?

9. Did Julia do the right thing in moving away from San Antonio? Do you think she was safe in Wildflower? Why or why not?

10. How can we reveal the secret things we're hiding? Should we turn to God and tell Him first? What secrets would you like to let go of in your own life?

Love Inspired
CLASSICS

Enjoy these four heartwarming stories from
your favorite Love Inspired authors!

NO PLACE LIKE HOME and
DREAM A LITTLE DREAM
by Debra Clopton

NO PLACE LIKE HOME

Dottie Hart made a promise and has to get to California. But when the
candy maker gets stranded in Mule Hollow, Texas, handsome sheriff
Brady Cannon—her polar opposite—has her dreaming of staying
forever. With the help of town matchmakers, she may find a way to call
Mule Hollow home for good.

DREAM A LITTLE DREAM

After writing about the lonely ranchers in Mule Hollow, reporter
Molly Popp is responsible for all the would-be wives who travel to the
Texas town. One confirmed bachelor cowboy isn't too pleased—especially
when he can't seem to get the pretty city slicker off his mind.

A TREASURE WORTH KEEPING and
HIDDEN TREASURES
by Kathryn Springer

A TREASURE WORTH KEEPING

Teacher Evie McBride plans to spend a quiet summer on Cooper's
Landing. Yet when handsome Sam Cutter asks her to tutor his troubled
teenage niece, she can't turn them away. Soon enough, it's Evie and Sam
who are learning more about love and faith than they ever expected.

HIDDEN TREASURES

All Cade Halloway wants is to sell the family vacation home that
reminds him of bad memories. But now his sister insists on marrying
there. Wedding photographer Meghan McBride and her camera just
may help him discover the treasures of family and love.

Available in October 2013
wherever Love Inspired Books are sold.

www.LoveInspiredBooks.com

LIC1013

REQUEST YOUR FREE BOOKS!

2 FREE RIVETING INSPIRATIONAL NOVELS
PLUS 2 FREE MYSTERY GIFTS

Love Inspired®
SUSPENSE

YES! Please send me 2 FREE Love Inspired® Suspense novels and my 2 FREE mystery gifts (gifts are worth about $10). After receiving them, if I don't wish to receive any more books, I can return the shipping statement marked "cancel." If I don't cancel, I will receive 4 brand-new novels every month and be billed just $4.74 per book in the U.S. or $5.24 per book in Canada. That's a savings of at least 21% off the cover price. It's quite a bargain! Shipping and handling is just 50¢ per book in the U.S. and 75¢ per book in Canada.* I understand that accepting the 2 free books and gifts places me under no obligation to buy anything. I can always return a shipment and cancel at any time. Even if I never buy another book, the two free books and gifts are mine to keep forever.

123/323 IDN F5AC

Name	(PLEASE PRINT)	
Address		Apt. #
City	State/Prov.	Zip/Postal Code

Signature (if under 18, a parent or guardian must sign)

Mail to the **Harlequin**® **Reader Service:**
IN U.S.A.: P.O. Box 1867, Buffalo, NY 14240-1867
IN CANADA: P.O. Box 609, Fort Erie, Ontario L2A 5X3

Are you a current subscriber to Love Inspired Suspense books
and want to receive the larger-print edition?
Call 1-800-873-8635 or visit www.ReaderService.com.

* Terms and prices subject to change without notice. Prices do not include applicable taxes. Sales tax applicable in N.Y. Canadian residents will be charged applicable taxes. Offer not valid in Quebec. This offer is limited to one order per household. Not valid for current subscribers to Love Inspired Suspense books. All orders subject to credit approval. Credit or debit balances in a customer's account(s) may be offset by any other outstanding balance owed by or to the customer. Please allow 4 to 6 weeks for delivery. Offer available while quantities last.

Your Privacy—The Harlequin® Reader Service is committed to protecting your privacy. Our Privacy Policy is available online at www.ReaderService.com or upon request from the Harlequin Reader Service.
We make a portion of our mailing list available to reputable third parties that offer products we believe may interest you. If you prefer that we not exchange your name with third parties, or if you wish to clarify or modify your communication preferences, please visit us at www.ReaderService.com/consumerschoice or write to us at Harlequin Reader Service Preference Service, P.O. Box 9062, Buffalo, NY 14269. Include your complete name and address.

LIS13R

SPECIAL EXCERPT FROM

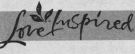

*Brian Montclair is about to go from
factory worker to baker.*

*Read on for a sneak preview of
THE BACHELOR BAKER
by Carolyne Aarsen, the second book in
THE HEART OF MAIN STREET series from
Love Inspired. Available August 2013!*

He took up her whole office.

At least that's how it felt to Melissa Sweeney.

Brian Montclair sat in the chair across from her, his arms folded over his chest, his entire demeanor screaming "get me out of here."

Tall with broad shoulders and arms filling out his button-down shirt rolled up at the sleeves, he looked more like a linebacker than a potential baker's assistant.

Which is what he might become if he took the job Melissa had to offer him.

Melissa held up the worn and dog-eared paper she had been given. It held a short list of potential candidates for the job at her bakery.

The rest of the names had been crossed off with comments written beside them. Unsuitable. Too old. Unable to be on their feet all day. Just had a baby. Nut allergy. Moved away.

This last comment appeared beside two of the eight names on her list, a sad commentary on the state of the town of Bygones.

When Melissa had received word of a mysterious

benefactor offering potential business owners incentive money to start up a business in the small town of Bygones, Kansas, she had immediately applied. All her life she had dreamed of starting up her own bakery. She had taken courses in baking, decorating, business management, all with an eye to someday living out the faint dream of owning her own business.

When she had been approved, she'd quit her job in St. Louis, packed up her few belongings and had come here. She felt as if her life had finally taken a good turn. However, in the past couple of weeks it had become apparent that she needed extra help.

She had received the list of potential hires from the Bygones Save Our Street Committee and was told to try each of them. Brian Montclair was on the list. At the bottom, but still on the list.

"The reason I called you here was to offer you a job," she said, trying to inject a note of enthusiasm into her voice. This had better work.

To find out if Melissa and Brian can help save the town of Bygones one cupcake at a time, pick up
THE BACHELOR BAKER
wherever Love Inspired books are sold.

Copyright © 2013 by Harlequin Books S.A.

LIEXP0713

Love Inspired

CARING Canines

Both Abbey Harris and Dominic Winters long for a second chance at love, and it'll take two adorable dogs and a sweet little girl to bring them together.

Healing Hearts
by Margaret Daley

Available August 2013
wherever Love Inspired books are sold.

www.LoveInspiredBooks.com

LI87830

The Master Matchmakers

Emma Pyrmont hopes to convince single father
Sir Nicholas Rotherford that there's more to life than calculations
and chemistry. As she draws him closer to his young daughter,
Nicholas sees his daughter—and her nanny—with new eyes.

The Courting Campaign

by

REGINA SCOTT

*Available August 2013 wherever
Love Inspired Historical books are sold.*